DEFYING ETERNITY

DEFYING ETERNITY

MELANIE MARTINS

BLOSSOM IN WINTER

BOOK FOUR

Melanie Martins, LLC
www.blossominwinter.com

First published in the United States by Melanie Martins, LLC in 2021.

ISBSN ebook 978-1-7333564-9-7

ISBN Paperback 978-1-7333564-3-5

Printed and bound in Great Britain by Clays Ltd, Elcograf S.p.A

This is a 1st Edition.

DISCLAIMER

This novel is a work of fiction written in American-English and is intended for mature audiences. Names, characters, places, and incidents are either the product of the author's imagination or used fictitiously. Any resemblance to actual persons, living or dead, is entirely coincidental. This novel contains strong and explicit language, graphic sexuality, and other sensitive content that may be disturbing for some readers.

To all of you, my dear readers.
Thank you.

"Death may indeed be final
But the love we share while living is
Eternal."

— Donald E Williams Jr.

PROLOGUE

Rotterdam, December 5, 2020
Tess Hagen

A small squeak catches my attention. I don't typically sleep well at night, especially not on a night like tonight, and any little noise can easily wake me up. I crack my eyes open for the hundredth time, and turn to the nightstand to check the time. My room is as dark as it gets, with only the red light from the alarm clock flashing the digital numbers acting as a source of light. Oh gosh, it's already 4 a.m. but the creaking sound is still present and it's giving me goosebumps. I then recall Carice's insistence on keeping a gun by my bedside—at the time I found the idea totally ridiculous—but now, it doesn't seem that far-fetched. I feel antsy as I swear that I keep hearing footsteps somewhere, but they are too low to be from inside the room. Maybe it's just the wind blowing against the windows that is causing such strange noises. No, I should know better. It sounds more like someone tiptoeing across the tiles. They are barely audible, but I have good ears and they must be coming from somewhere else in the house—maybe the entryway? The living room? Yet there are no other sounds, nothing that would indicate that there is, in fact, a stranger in the house, just the wooden-floor creaking from time to time. *There it goes again!* My skin prickles with a shiver and I look around for my iPhone to call the police. But I draw out a breath in annoyance just as fast as I remember I left it in the living room to avoid texting Petra again to try dissuading her from marrying that monster. As Carice had told me, if Petra wants to go ahead after everything I'd told her, then I should also go ahead and expose her lovely groom to Jan and let him know what he did to his daughter. I'm sure the wedding at the cathedral will be very entertaining once Jan knows the truth.

Anyway, enough of that, I need to gain some courage and go get my iPhone. As I come to think of it, good grief, it's most likely just the dogs that managed to get out of the kitchen. They are smart boys and I'm more than sure that they know how to twist the handle with their mouths. I leap off of my bed, put on a warm robe, and head outside the room rather slowly. I turn the lights of the hallway on immediately, and see nothing—just an empty hallway. Heaving a sigh of relief, I start walking, perfectly aware it's most likely all in my head. Strange noises that we can't identify usually fuel our wildest fears. Though my eyes suddenly fix themselves on the semi-open door of the living room, I see it's just as dark in there as it had been in the hallway before flicking on the light. I roll my eyes at my own paranoia. I open the door a bit further, my gaze landing on the fireplace and the paneled-walls that stand on my left. Stepping in, I turn on the lights, and as I look to my right, I am startled immediately.

"Oh God!" I shout in shock, gasping for air, as my eyes alight on Margaret, who's sitting on an armchair as if she was waiting for me there.

"Finally," she says. "I wondered if I had to send someone to go and wake you up."

I blink twice, then rub my fingers on my eyelids to make sure this is not a dream. "How did you get in here?" I bark immediately, my nerves boiling under my skin.

"Your security is non-existent, Tess…"

Her snickering is even more irritating than her voice. I squeeze my eyes tight, wishing I could throw bullets at her, and then, pointing my index finger at her, I shout, "Get out of my house!"

Despite the loud-pitched sound of my voice, Margaret doesn't even bat an eye. "Or else what?" she asks, just as serenely as she remains calmly in the armchair.

I'm about to step back, but my foot touches a shoe and I nearly scream as I turn to look at the tall, bulky man that stands behind me in his long, greenish coat and black boots. His stern eyes make me swallow the lump in my throat and I instinctively glance around the room, trying to find a sharp object that I could throw at him. Yet his hands are now holding my wrists and despite me trying to pull them away, he isn't letting me go. I don't even know how he grabbed me so quickly.

"Don't touch me!" I bark at him as I try to release myself from him. Then I look back at Margaret, who remains quietly sitting on the armchair, her face revealing nothing. No emotions, no fears, no rage. Nothing. How could someone be as monstrous as her? How?

She eyes her security, giving him a nod, and the man ushers me forward as he drags me toward her. Then he forces me to sit on the sofa beside Margaret. Even as I am sitting, he keeps within an arm's reach—I suppose it is in case I try to make any sort of moves.

As I refocus my attention, my eyes narrow at the note that is resting on the low table in front of us.

"A very kind message from you, isn't it?" Margaret takes the note and opens it for me to see. "If you thought I'd let you threaten me without facing any consequences, then you are very mistaken, my dear."

"There's nothing you can do to prevent Jan from knowing the truth," I snap just as fast. "You can kill me, but he'll find out soon, regardless." My lips twist into a smirk as her anger grows. "His end is near." And to my greatest shock, my throat gets squeezed right away by the stranger. My mouth remains wide open as I try to drag some precious huffs of air into my lungs, but I find myself gasping and failing to do so. My heart brisks, pumping faster at every second he keeps tightening around my neck.

"You're testing my limits, Tess…" I hear Margaret's mumbling despite feeling my face turning red at the lack of oxygen. Margaret eventually gives another nod at the man and he finally releases me. I gasp for air, tears starting to form in the crevices of my eyes. She then leans forward, her eyes cold and stern, remaining focused on me. "I'm not going to kill you yet. But your time will come soon." She raises up from her seat and leaves. The man gestures for me to do the same, so I stand up, wondering what she is up to. Margaret goes in front and leaves the living room, and her security pushes me forward to keep walking. I follow because I'm pretty sure he must be armed, and as I step in the entryway, I see two more agents guarding the front door where Margaret is heading. I stop for a second, realizing they are taking me away with them. I try to run back inside, but the security that stands behind me, holds me again. So I punch him as much as I can, kicking him from right and left, my anger consuming me. "Stop it! Release me!" I bark. "Help! Help!"

Then I feel another man walking from behind me while I'm battling with the first one and screaming as much as I can. Yet I can see from over my shoulder that he's carrying something. Oh gosh! No! "Don't touch me! Help!" I keep screaming as loud as I can. But in a quick move, he slams a handkerchief over my nose and mouth, and despite battling as much as I can, my mind starts feeling dizzy and my body goes numb.

CHAPTER 1

Manhattan, February 8, 2021
Petra Van Gatt

I still can't believe I just sat and watched Eric take Alex to the police station. The pain I felt while hearing my husband pleading with me and being unable to answer him makes my heart reel.

"You did the right thing," Carice says as she remains sitting beside me with Matthew. "It's hard to see the man we love for what he truly is. But you did the right thing, I mean it."

I heave a long sigh, exhausted after such a mentally and emotionally draining day. I have to remind myself that Alex is a murderer, a kidnapper, and at the end of the day, a criminal. But my heart is too stubborn, and despite all these things, I still manage to love him and it hurts like hell seeing him being taken away. *Oh, stop it!* I slap myself mentally just as fast, bringing back some rationality to tame those stupid feelings. *He killed your mother, for fuck's sake!* I remind myself. *And even lied to you over and over again about so many things!*

Matthew steps in, draping an arm around my shoulder—small goosebumps appear on my skin at the sentiment, though I don't really notice. "Hey," his voice, low and warm, soothes me. "It's gonna be okay. We are here for you."

Yet I can't stop thinking about the arrest that just happened a few minutes ago. "Do you think he will get out today?"

"Well, I'd guess so," Carice is the first to answer. "He's gonna call his lawyer and will, most likely, be released on bail."

Despite the annoyance thick in her tone, a small smile settles on my lips, knowing he should be back home before I go to sleep.

I hear the creaking sound of the main door opening, so I stand up from my seat to check who's coming. I watch as Maria enters, carrying a plethora of grocery bags. I go and talk to her so that she knows Alex might not come back home in time for dinner. Then, Maria gives a quick glance at the living room where Matthew and Carice are seated before asking me discreetly, "Are they staying for dinner?"

"Um," that's a question I wasn't expecting, but today I'd rather have some company in case Alex doesn't come back. "Yes, they are staying here for dinner."

"Alright, then," she nods knowingly and leaves to continue with her task.

As I'm about to return to the living room, my iPhone starts ringing inside my pocket. *Maybe it's Alex!* I can't help but think to myself with a wistful smile.

As I take it out to check, though, my smile fades away just as fast seeing Emma's name pop up on the screen.

"Hi, Emma," I greet once I pick up the call, my voice slightly monotone.

"Hey, how are you?" Emma asks, her tone hurried. "Oh my gosh, I just read the news! Why didn't you call me?"

"Wait—you *read* the news?" I ask, quite surprised.

"I mean, my maids did. And according to them, it's like everywhere that Alex killed your mom. Is it true?"

Well, I see Eric's office didn't waste time to do a press release. "Um, they have strong evidence against him, yeah, but Alex told me he had nothing to do with it before being arrested, so who knows…"

"Shit!" Emma exhales loudly in return, without saying much more. "This is insane! And, um, do you know what she died from?"

"We don't know yet. We are still waiting for the results from the lab," I tell her.

"Damn," Emma utters, still in shock. "When is the funeral? Are you gonna have it here?"

"Yes." I press my lips tight, remembering the video Mom left for me. "Mom's last wish was to be buried somewhere close to me. So I'm thinking of doing the funeral in Bedford Hills."

"What?" she snaps in disbelief. "Are you serious right now?"

"Of course I'm serious!" I answer. "Honoring her last wish is the least I can do."

"And have you spoken to Alex about that?" she keeps enquiring.

"When he gets back home, I will." Then I pause, thinking something through. "Tomorrow I'll call Father Thomas. Mom liked him a lot. It'd be great if he could come here and do the Mass."

"Alright, if you need help with prepping the funeral, you can count me in." Before I can thank her, though, she adds, "Can I invite Yara?"

My jaw nearly drops at her question. And I'm not sure what I'm supposed to make out of it. "You want to invite my in-laws to the funeral?" I repeat, making sure that's what I heard her saying. "Because you know if you invite Yara, she's gonna bring her sisters, her mom, and basically everyone else…"

"I mean, they are your family, too. No?"

I blow out a breath, remembering what that lovely family did to Hendrik and what they also did to my own mother. "Yeah, but they might have something to do with her murder," I tell her bluntly.

"One more reason to invite them, then." I raise my brows, taken aback by her answer. "At least Eric can interview them and gather more info for the case."

To be fair, that's not an entirely bad idea; if they come to the funeral, Eric can have a word with them, and maybe even have them arrested too. One thing is for sure: Julia is just as guilty as Alex. She was involved in Mom's abduction and Eric has the proof on tape. Inviting them to the funeral would be a good way to bring them to New York without raising any suspicion.

"You know what?" I say. "I think it's a great idea. Do you mind helping me with the funeral preparation?"

"Of course not! Tell me what you need and I've got you."

My lips raise up at her enthusiasm. "I will give you Carice's contact info, my mom's attorney, so that you can both work on a guest list, and, um, we have to contact the mortician to get everything ready for Sunday. What do you think?"

"Alright, sounds doable. Meanwhile, I'll reach out to a few event planners that work around the clock."

"Thank you for everything, Emma." My tone is lower, but it's warmer and filled with gratitude for having her in my life. And if there's one thing I know, it's that whatever happens between Alex and me, Emma will always be there for me.

"Do you want me to come over? Are you doing okay?" As she asks, I notice that her tone has also switched, now matching mine.

"I'm good. Matt and Carice are here too, and we're gonna have dinner soon." As I say those words, I see Maria from afar walking into the living room carrying two lemonades, which she hands to Matt and Carice while they patiently wait for me to finish up with my phone call. I find it rather noble seeing Alex's housekeeper treat his enemies with such courtesy and respect. Though I'm not entirely sure if she knows who they are, but regardless of that, it reminds me that even at war, respect goes a long way.

After dinner, and while Matt and Carice have become new besties, I check my phone discreetly, hoping to find a new text message from my husband.

Yet, there's nothing.

Dammit! It's already ten p.m. though.

Amid the giggles emanating from a joke Carice is telling, I type in while pretending to be paying attention: *Did you get out of jail yet? Are you coming home tonight?*

Regardless of the arrest, I just hope he'll come back soon so that we can talk about everything that has happened. I'm not sure how he'll justify lying yet another time, though. And worse: I don't even know what we'll become even if he does come up with a believable excuse.

"Is everything okay, Petra?" I hear Matt asking.

I slip my iPhone back inside my pocket, and turning to him, I smile innocently. "Yeah, of course. I'm just getting sleepy."

Carice glances at her watch before standing up from her seat, looking a bit embarrassed. "Oh my goodness, it's already ten. We should really get going. I'm sorry for staying so long."

"Don't worry about it," I tell her immediately as Matthew and I also stand up. "I really appreciate that you both took the time to stay with me." It's actually true, they were a great distraction and I needed just that. Plus, we spoke at length about the funeral that would be happening on Sunday in Bedford Hills.

"Thank you for the lovely dinner," Carice says as she gathers her coat and purse. "Tomorrow I will get in touch with Emma and we will finalize the arrangements for the funeral."

"Thank you," I tell her, putting on a pleasant smile. "I really appreciate it."

I escort them to the front door, and to my greatest surprise, Carice plunges me into a tight hug as if she's known me for years. Since she's around the age of my mom and they look quite similar, her hug feels a bit maternal, yet oddly foreign at the same time. "If you need anything, call me," she whispers into my ear. "No matter the hour of the day or night."

As she releases me, I give her a nod in acknowledgment and then turn to Matt, who's standing beside the door.

"Thank you for coming," I say before opening my arms to give him a friendly hug.

"Always," he mumbles as we embrace each other. Then he leans in and gives me a quick peck on the cheek. The touch was unexpected, but a small smile pulls on my lips in response.

Once they head out, Matt mimics my smile, right before they get into the elevator.

Closing the door, I heave a long sigh, mixed with both relief to be finally alone and exhaustion. Then I can't help but take my iPhone out again and check if Alex has replied to my text.

Nothing, still...

My heart drops to my knees, seeing my message has been left unread. I consider calling Ryan, his attorney, but it's already so late, so instead, for the better or worse, I call Alex directly. The ringtone goes on and on until it ends on his voicemail. Well, either he's in a cell without his phone, or he's purposely avoiding me. I just hope it's the former.

I go and say goodnight to Maria before heading back to our bedroom.

My eyes grace the bed—the ironed sheets still perfectly stretched over the mattress. Then I undress and put on my pajamas. I don't usually sleep with them anymore as I end up too warm because of Alex's body heat, but I don't really think he'll be spending the night here. And as I come to think of it, if he's found guilty, I might have to spend the next fifteen years or more without him sleeping beside me. The idea petrifies me. I can't accept a reality where I might live here alone and raise our baby all by myself. What a freaking nightmare this is!

I fold over the comforter and climb inside—I'm happy I decided to wear my pajamas because despite the heater, it's pretty chilly between the sheets. Turning off the light, I look at my right side and I can't help but despise him for lying to me, for breaking his promises, and for putting our relationship in jeopardy.

The more I think of Alex's behavior, the more I know that I lured myself to him, glossing over his flaws, despite knowing perfectly well that his habit of lying would lead to our downfall.

* * *

Manhattan, February 9, 2021
Petra Van Gatt

I wake up, and instinctively turn to check the right side of the bed, which, as expected, is still empty. Given the amount of sunlight casting through the room, I'd say it's already way past nine o'clock. And yet, Maria hasn't come in to wake me up. I know she never has to do that with Alex, but if no one wakes me up, I'll end up sleeping in far too late. And today, I've got a lot to do when it comes to the funeral. As I leap off of the bed,

I take my iPhone from the nightstand and immediately check my text messages. Despite being nine-thirty, Alex still hasn't replied to anything. I do have a new text message though, but from Matthew: *Good morning! Thank you for yesterday's dinner. It was lovely. I hope you spent a great night and managed to sleep well. If you need anything, just let me know. X*

His message manages to warm my heart, and it feels good to read something like this when I'm feeling pretty alone. I write back: *Hey, thanks for your kind words. It was great having dinner with you both. I slept okay, yes. I was really exhausted. I'm getting started with the funeral arrangements. I'm thinking of inviting my in-laws too.* And I press *send*. Then I leave the room and head to the terrace. I'm not sure why though, but I think it's the habit of going there and finding Alex sitting at the table while drinking his usual espresso. But as I reach the outdoors, my eyes alight on the breakfast table with only one place setting—mine.

There is no one there that is sipping an espresso, or reading on an iPad, and no one to make me smile either.

I take a seat as per usual, but my heart aches, feeling so incredibly empty—just like the chair in front of me.

"Good morning, ma'am," Maria greets as she walks in, carrying a matcha latte and a plate with scrambled vegan eggs. Damn, even the freaking eggs remind me of him. "Did you sleep well?"

"Good morning, Maria," I tell her, though I am unable to match with her melodic voice. "Yes, thank you."

I take a first sip on my matcha and as I look again in front of me to the empty chair, I can't help but heave a sigh filled with sorrow. Despite hating him for what he did, I wish he could be here, eating his breakfast with me. Heck, this reminds me of what Yara had said a few days before our marriage, *"Petra, I know you are furious at him, but can't you be furious and married to him?"* I'm definitely furious at him, yet I'd rather be furious at him while taking my breakfast with him.

My phone starts beeping and my heart nearly jumps out of my chest. I look at the new text message immediately, only to be smashed with disappointment.

Alex told me yesterday about your mom. Are you doing okay? Shall we meet for lunch and have a talk? I tried to contact Alex, but he hasn't answered. Call me back when you can. X

Now that's new… How come Alex told my dad about it? Well, in any case, I call my dad just as fast. In the middle of everything, I'd totally forgotten to tell him about her death. In a way, I'm glad Alex actually called him to deliver the news. It's still better than reading it in the *New York Post* or God knows where else.

"Hi, Dad," I greet once I hear his breathing from the other side of the line. "How are you?"

"Petra," his tone sounds more joyful than usual. Well, in a way, Mom was his bully and his blackmailer, so I'm pretty sure Dad won't miss her looming around. "I'm alright. Ryan told me Alex got arrested."

"Oh, Ryan called you?" I repeat, a bit surprised that he called my dad but not me. "That's very kind of him… Um, do you know if Alex has been released yet?"

"He hasn't answered my calls, so I think he's still in there." His answer eases me a bit. At least that would mean Alex isn't mad at me because of what I did. "What if I pass by and have lunch with you? We could discuss your mom's funeral and where it should be held."

I can't help but find it amusing that Dad is very much looking forward to his ex-wife's burial. "I'm thinking of doing it in Bedford Hills, actually. I'm gonna call Father Thomas after breakfast and—"

"In Bedford Hills?" There's an ounce of astonishment in his tone. "You mean you want to bury her there?"

"Dad, we have land that stretches for miles. I don't see what the problem is."

"The irony," Dad snaps. "When your mom was alive, you never wanted to be near her and now that she's gone, you want to bury her in the backyard. I don't get it."

"It's her last wish. I'm just honoring it," I tell him. "Don't worry—if she starts bothering me, I will send her back to the Netherlands."

A quick laughter erupts from the other side of the line, and I'm glad I managed to light up his mood. "That's a viable option. Well, shall I pass by around one-thirty?"

"Yes, that would be great."

Before I can finish the call, though, Dad asks, "You aren't gonna miss her, are you?"

"Um," his question leaves me a bit speechless and I wonder if it's truly a question he's asking to me or to himself. Regardless, I press my lips tight, pondering it. "I don't know. I, um, it's a weird feeling for sure," I venture. "In a way, I'm not gonna miss her, but in another, I had hopes we could get to a better place and that she'd finally turn the page...you know?"

"Ah, yes, hope never dies."

"And you?" I ask him.

"Well…" I can sense the uneasiness in his voice as he searches for the best words to put on. "Despite everything we went through, she *was* my ex-wife and your mother, so I guess I also hoped she'd have turned the page after seeing how you and Alex were living happily together."

"Yeah, but alas, she didn't. I think she's by far more stubborn than both of us combined," I tell him.

Dad exhales loudly in return. "It's a pity she was so obstinate. A bit of flexibility would've gone a long way. But her sense of moral righteousness has always gotten in the way." As he says those words, I can't help but remember when Mom reported him and Alex to the police twenty years back. Dad had only told her the truth about Janette, but Mom didn't waste any time betraying him. Maybe that's why he never considered dating again afterward.

* * *

A few hours later, I finally received some good news: I managed to persuade Father Thomas to fly in on Saturday to do the Mass. A pity I'll see him again under such circumstances, but I'm sure Mom would've appreciated the gesture.

I check my iPhone once more and since Alex hasn't texted me back, I decide to call his attorney directly. After all, I'm pretty sure Ryan knows what's happening. I press the call button and put the phone against my cheek. The ringtone starts radiating through my ear and I wait and wait…

"Yes?" I hear a male voice asking from the other side at long last.

"Hi, Ryan, um, it's Petra…" My voice sounds way too soft, so I steady it a bit. "How is Alex doing? Um, do you know where he is? I've tried calling him many times, but he isn't answering me."

"Hi, Petra," he greets, his tone polite as always. "Yes, he just got released an hour ago or so and is spending the rest of the day in his private residence."

"His private residence?" I ask immediately. "I'm here at our condo, and he isn't here."

"I meant, he's staying in a hotel which provides private residences."

"Oh," I utter, the news troubling me even more than I'd like to admit. "And, um, is there any reason why he isn't coming back home?"

"Your husband is taking a few days off." *What?* His unexpected answer crushes me to the core. "He needs some time alone. Don't take it personally, but he needs time to process everything that happened over the last twenty-four hours. I'll keep you updated."

Despite the best of his intentions, his answer doesn't satisfy me. "But why? Why doesn't he want to talk to me? Where's he staying?"

"Petra…" He takes a deep breath, trying to find the best words to put on, yet nothing seems to come out. "Give him some time, alright?"

That's all he has got to say? Wow. It's clear Ryan wants to keep me in the dark, but I can't figure why he can't just tell me what's really going on.

"Alright, thanks." And I hang-up, still barely believing my husband isn't coming back home after everything that has happened. Despite wanting to call him one more time, I refrain myself from doing so. The last thing I need is for him to believe I'm desperate. Hell, no! If he wants to play and torment me with his stupid game by all means, he can do as he wishes. I do, however, send him one last text: "*Just spoke to Ryan who told me you aren't coming back home for the next few days. Wow. What a responsible adult you are. Btw, I'm doing the funeral in Bedford Hills this Sunday. You are welcome to join. Father Thomas will be flying in to do the Mass. Enjoy your private residence.*" I want to call him a few names, but I refrain myself from doing so.

A minute or so after sending the text, my iPhone starts ringing again, and for a split second, I thought it was my husband who had just read my message and decided to explain himself to me. But alas, it isn't, and despite the disappointment, I draw out a breath, and pick up the call.

"Good morning." Matt sounds like a ray of sunshine casting light on my gloomy mind. "How are you feeling today?"

"Hey!" I try to match his tone, but fail miserably. "Um, I'm okay more or less…"

Despite my answer, Matt keeps his voice just as joyful. "Guess who's having her first prenatal check-up Friday at four p.m.?"

"Matt!" I snap back. "I can't believe you booked it for me."

"Of course I did, and I'm pretty sure if I hadn't done it, you wouldn't do it yourself until maybe next week or even the week after that."

He isn't wrong, though. We still have to finalize the funeral arrangements and there are another gazillion things to do following the death of my mother.

"I'm not even sure if that test is accurate or not," I insist. "Like, I don't even have any symptoms…"

"One more reason to go, then," he says just as fast. "At least you'll be a hundred percent sure."

Heaving a sigh, I ponder his words. "Alright, I should be free around that time. But please, no more appointments without checking with me first."

"Yes, ma'am," he teases, and his sense of humor brings a much-needed smile to my lips. "By the way, um, did you manage to talk to him? My dad told me Alex just got released an hour or so ago."

His question takes my smile away, and I drop my gaze as I think of an answer to give him. "No, he isn't answering me right now. I guess he's just doing it as some sort of revenge because I did the same to him yesterday."

"Damn," he utters, before falling silent for a moment, most likely not knowing what else to say. "I'm sorry for his behavior."

"It's not your fault," I tell him. "I guess it's what we call payback."

"Do you want to come over and we spend the day studying here or at the library?" he asks, most likely in an attempt to change the subject.

"Um, I have a few things to do today, but we'll see each other on Friday for the check-up."

"Alright, if you need anything, don't hesitate to call me."

"Thanks for everything, Matt." My voice is lower than usual, but it's mainly because I don't want Maria to hear me. "I really appreciate your support."

"Always, girl," he answers just as low.

As soon as we hang-up, I hear the doorbell echoing across the condo and footsteps walking through the hallway to open the door. That's odd, it's not even one-thirty. Why would Dad arrive half an hour earlier? There's a glimmer of hope, thinking maybe it's Alex who decided to come back. I leave the terrace and hurry up to check. Unfortunately, and to my greatest displeasure, I see Carice, who steps in, carrying a few files with her. *Oh shit!* I had totally forgotten I had agreed to meet her for lunch.

Despite wearing her usual black suit, with a black turtle neck underneath and matching glasses, she looks a lot less stern than yesterday, maybe a bit more relaxed too. I imagine the death of her best friend must have left her in a state of near-depression, but she seems to be coping with it relatively okay. As her eyes set on me, she gives me a bright smile and paces in my direction.

"You didn't forget about our meet-up at one, right?" she asks, visibly amused.

"Of course not," I answer, walking forward to give her three cheek-kisses. Then I invite her to the terrace where we take a seat at the table.

After making some small talk, Carice takes a document from her files and says, "As you probably know, your mom had life insurance so that if something happened to her, you could receive the fund to pay for the expenses of the funeral, and keep the rest for you." I nod at her, and she glances once more at the document before proceeding. "The insurance company received all the paperwork this morning, so you should receive around two million and four hundred euros in your account in the next two weeks." My jaw drops at her announcement. *Wow.* I never thought Mom had such a high coverage, which leads me to believe she knew sooner or later that she'd die at their hands. She was most likely planning her death a long time ago.

Then Carice takes another file and says, "Regarding the nonprofit, your mom was the managing director and main owner of the organization. Since you're now the new titular, I was wondering if you'd like to appoint a new director?"

My brows raise at her question. I find it touching that despite Carice being my mom's best friend, she still decided to leave her nonprofit to me—which I barely know anything about. "Oh, um, would you be interested in taking over in my place?" I ask her. Carice immediately stares at me with astonishment, so I try my best to convince her, before she can make up her mind. "I know you work there as an attorney, but you were also my mom's best friend, and she trusted you a lot. I'm pretty sure she'd have wanted for you to take over the organization."

Her lips curve up in appreciation, and she remains silent for a while, considering my proposal. "I think you are right. We can expend the legal team, get some new lawyers on board, and I'll take over the management."

"I could also donate a million euros from my Mom's insurance to the nonprofit," I say. "With such a capital injection, it should give you some room to operate, right?"

Now she stares at me with her mouth agape. "Oh, wow. That's…" She pauses, searching for the best words to put on. "Well, that's very kind of you, but this is a lot."

"How many months can you last with it?" I ask.

"I haven't checked the finances of the company, but I'd say around eighteen months."

"Well, then, that's plenty of time to keep the firm afloat and to expand it. My mom loved her nonprofit and I'm sure she'd have wanted to grow it further." I notice some glitz in her gaze as she listens to me talking. "Do you have a team that takes care of fundraising?"

"We do, but we raise money mostly through charity events where we invite family offices, NHW individuals, and so on. Your mom used to host them." There's the faint of a smile settling on her lips as she recalls those memories. "She was such a great host. They used to write us big checks thanks to her charisma."

I smile tenderly at her words; despite knowing Mom used to attend many charity events, I never thought those events were to fundraise for her nonprofit. "I'm sure you'll manage to do the same, regardless of her being here or not," I say, keeping my voice warm.

A few instants of silence ensues while Carice takes some notes before proceeding. "About the funeral, did you decide on the location?"

"Yes, we'll do it in Bedford Hills this Sunday and Father Thomas already confirmed he'll fly over on Saturday. Emma is getting a mortician and an event planner so that we can have a beautiful setting in her honor."

"Oh, that's great. Good job," she praises, as she ticks off some of the things on her list. "As you might know, Eric's office did a press release yesterday and your mom's death has been communicated to the Dutch media too. A few reporters would like to attend the funeral and cover it. I know them personally, would that be okay with you?"

"Yes, of course. Just let me know how many people from your side will attend so that we can arrange everything properly," I tell her.

"From my side, I can confirm at least twenty people—from friends and coworkers—can attend. Then maybe five reporters and their cameramen will go on top of that."

As I do the math, it seems like we will have around fifty people in total, which is perfect, since I didn't want to do something too big.

"Good afternoon…"

I turn immediately, recognizing the male voice behind me and my eyes fall upon my dad, who looks more tired than usual, but just as elegant and formal.

"Hi, Dad," I greet as we stand up. "Carice, this is my dad, Roy…"

"I know." Carice stiffens up as she shakes his hand, a forced smile on her lips. All of a sudden though, someone's phone starts ringing, but I know it's not mine as it's a different ringtone. Carice takes her phone and after checking who's calling, leaves the table. "Excuse me," she says as she walks past me and goes to a quieter area of the terrace.

Once we are left alone, Dad gives me a cheek-kiss and leans forward as if he's about to whisper something.

"What is she doing here?" His tone is barely audible.

"Um, we are just taking care of the funeral and some details about Mom's nonprofit," I say.

Dad gives a quick glance over my shoulder, before proceeding, "Do you know what are they up to?"

I frown at his question. "What do you mean?"

"The Bradfords and Carice," Dad says. "I imagine Alex is their suspect number one, no?"

"Yeah…" I let my words trail off as I consider him. "I think they're gathering as much evidence as possible before the trial."

"Do you know if they have anything good?"

"I suppose," I tell him. "They know about Janette's death."

Dad's eyes widen in surprise as my words sink in to him. "They do?"

"Mom gave Eric the police report," I explain. "But I don't think they are after you."

"Are they gonna tell Jan?" he keeps pushing, the reality hitting him hard. I watch as he adjusts his shirt collar uncomfortably.

"I don't know," I answer as sincerely as I can.

"Petra?" I hear Carice calling. Then I turn, my eyes alighting on her. "Eric wants to talk to you."

Oh, that's Eric on the phone? Now that's interesting…

I walk over to where she's standing, and she gives me her phone.

"Yes?" I take a few steps away from Carice, so that I can be left alone to talk with him.

"Petra, how are you?"

"Hi, Eric. I'm doing well, thank you," I say, impatient to know what he's up to.

"Look, we just got the results from the lab, and um, it seems like your mom was, in fact, poisoned."

"Oh my gosh," the words roll off my tongue. "But how?"

"That's the problem—the lab found some traces of nanotechnology in her bloodstream. We don't know yet how she got it, but it's inside her body and those nano-particles had the opportunity to attack her organs at any moment. They essentially just needed to be activated."

"Can they be activated from the outside?" I ask.

"Yes, which makes me believe your mom didn't escape as she told us, but was freed instead. This is definitely not just some random plant you can buy and use to poison someone, it's a highly illegal bioweapon." My heart freezes at his words —this was premeditated. Mom was destined to die if she ever tried to talk to me. "Do you know anyone who could have access to it?"

I ponder his question for a moment. "Well, Maud is a scientist, and she works at a lab. I'm not sure what kind of projects she works on, so I don't know if she'd have access to this kind of technology or not."

"Who's Maud?" Eric asks immediately.

"Oh, um, one of Alex's sisters. She's very reserved and quiet, so I don't know too much about her."

"Is she coming to the funeral?" he keeps enquiring.

"Emma's trying to persuade my in-laws to come, so we'll see."

"It'd be great if I could talk to her. Either way, it's the first time in my career that anyone has been killed with nanotech. What a year to be alive."

"Are you gonna do another press release about it?" I ask him, already worried he's gonna do a new one. "I don't think the public needs to know those details."

"Well, Tess was quite well known in her country. I'm sure the public wants to know of what it is that she died from."

"They already know it was from a cardiac arrest, they don't need to know the gritty details," I argue. "If the news gets out, Maud might not come over."

Eric remains quiet for a few moments as he considers. "True, I won't do any press release until after her funeral. I have to go for now." And to my great surprise, he just hangs up without even saying goodbye.

CHAPTER 2

The Netherlands, December 5, 2021
Tess Hagen

The creaking sound of a door opening quietly wakes me up. My head is still as dizzy as when they had initially knocked me out, meaning I must have slept a lot since then. My eyes can barely cope with the brightness of the room, so I squeeze them tight again, before slowly reopening them. I find myself lying on a twin bed that is leaning against a wall. I want to spread my legs wide to stretch but I learn quickly that my ankles are tied together, which is clearly meant to prevent me from running. I silently chuckle at the whole thing—while Eric prosecuted Alex for kidnapping my daughter, I should've known sooner or later he and his family would truly kidnap someone for good. I just didn't realize this someone would be me. Petra didn't need to be kidnapped. The girl is so deluded that she'd let him carry her away without protesting. They can only kidnap those they can't control. And those include me and Carice. Oh gosh, I hope they didn't do anything to her. Well, if she advised me to get a gun, she most likely has a better security team than me. A gush of air leaves my lungs as I realize how naïve I was to have not invested in full-time security agents. I thought two big dogs sleeping in the kitchen would be enough. I do have cameras outside and an alarm though. How weird that neither went off. They must have turned it off somehow. As I hear footsteps approaching I gain some courage and look at the man who stands in front of me.

"Where am I?" I ask, my voice laced with anger but still pretty feeble. I notice the man is dressed all in blue like in a hospital, carrying a tray with food, plastic cutlery, and a small goblet with a few pills inside. Oh, if they think they can drug me, they're very mistaken. I'll pretend to swallow the pills and put them under my tongue.

Since he doesn't answer, I take in my surroundings—it looks like I'm in a bedroom, yet it's as minimalist as it gets with only a bed, a nightstand, and a desk and a chair. I look for a window and find one but very small and way too high for me to reach and to check outside. As he puts the tray on my nightstand, I ask, "What's your name?"

"Winter," he answers with a pleasant smile.

"Winter?" I repeat, barely able to believe it. Of course he won't give away his real name. Winter has to be some kind of nickname.

Winter nods, not telling me anything else, so I try a more sympathetic tone. "Do you know how long I will stay here, Winter?"

"I don't know, miss." He sounds very polite but I'm not sure if he's lying or not. "I'm just here to bring your food and medicine."

I give a quick glance at the food, and notice it's vegetarian. At least there's that. Since he looks friendly and approachable, I extend a hand to shake his. "Tess Hagen," I say as we give a quick handshake.

Suddenly, another squeaky sound startles me and I see another man entering the bedroom, followed by two others, who are armed. The one in front I recognize instantly—it's the guy who was in my living room with Margaret.

"Did you sleep well?" he says after striding closer to us. There's some sarcasm in his tone, despite his stern expression.

"What do you want from me?" I ask instead. "Where am I?"

"You aren't asking the questions here, I am," he snaps just as fast. "Now," he pulls the chair from the desk to sit in front of me and I narrow my eyes at the iPhone and piece of paper in his hands. "You will repeat this script as a voice message to your daughter."

As he gives me the paper, I read the message and my heart instantly falls on my knees. "What time is it? She's already married?"

"No questions!" he growls.

"I can't do that." And I hand him the paper back, avoiding his dark eyes.

Yet he leans forward, getting way too close to me. I try to back up, but the bed is tiny and I don't have much space left to go. He grabs my jaw, forcing me to look at him. "If you want to stay alive, you follow the rules, *snap je?*"

What a disgusting monster! I don't want to play by their rules, but if I want to stand a chance and live yet another day, I will have to comply. If Winter keeps giving me food every day, maybe I can gain his sympathy in time and he can help me to get me out of here.

"Now, read this out loud and we are going to record it. Don't try to deviate from the script, because we won't send anything but a perfect voice message that rings true." I swallow the lump in my throat, despising him and this moment more than anything in life. "You ready?"

I read the first lines in my mind again and nod at him. Once he gestures me to get started, I put on my best voice and read the note. "Petra, it's me… Your mom… I, um, I suppose by now you must be married and partying with your friends and new family…" I take a deep breath, taming the anger I have inside me before I can proceed and read the rest. "I'm gonna take a break, um, I'm leaving the country for a few days, maybe weeks, who knows…" I pause once more so not to break down at this whole charade. "I need some peace and quiet to think about my life, about me… Anyway, I wish you all the best and, um, I love you."

The agent taps the phone before pressing play to hear the whole voice message. As we listen to it, I sound tired and sad. Not sure if that's what they want.

"It's perfect," he says, a smile on his lips. "If you keep cooperating, you'll stay alive."

He then stands up, and right before he can start walking away, I ask, "When do I get out?"

"Get out?" he repeats in astonishment before erupting in laughter. "You are imprisoned now. For as long as you shall live."

CHAPTER 3

Manhattan, February 9, 2021
Alexander Van Dieren

I stand in front of the window, taking in the breathtaking sunset view with the Hudson River right in front of me. I have been to countless private residences in Manhattan, but this one offers hands down the best view. After spending the night in a disgusting cell, what a contrast this place is. And I'm glad I'll spend the next few days here. As I come to think of it, I had never in my entire life spent a night behind bars before yesterday. And I hope to never, ever repeat that experience again.

"Still thinking about yesterday, huh?" I hear Ryan asking as he remains sitting on the couch of the living area.

I turn, my face softening with a smile as I see the worry in his gaze. Poor Ryan, this new case has given him some serious headaches. After winning all the cases against Eric last year, he's definitely less confident about this new one. Besides, I can't blame him—the headlines aren't pretty. After pressing charges against me for kidnapping, then sexual assault, of course murder was the next in line. The problem this time is that I had plenty of motives to kill. After all, Tess was the one who tried to destroy my reputation, was firmly against my relationship with her daughter, and if Eric knows anything about Janette's death, then he can also use it as an extra motive.

"She didn't even look at me," I tell him, ruminating on yesterday's events—the way Petra ignored my calls all day long only to tell me at the end of the day that she's at the condo so that I could get arrested. Needless to say, her attitude left quite a sour taste in my mouth. And I feel... well, I feel fucking betrayed to be honest.

"Don't worry, I'm working on your defense and in a few days we'll know what evidence Eric holds against you."

The ringing of the doorbell starts echoing across the apartment, and a few moments later, my eyes alight on Roy as the butler opens the door for him. A quick smile settles on my lips catching him taking in his surroundings.

"Beautiful design," he points out as he gets into the living area which is adjacent to the entryway and dining room. Ryan stands up and goes to shake his hand, then Roy walks in my direction, stands beside me, and checks the view more closely. "And one hell of a view."

"It is," I mumble, my eyes taking in the last rays of sunshine as the sun goes down on the horizon.

Roy leans in and discreetly asks, "Can I have a word with you?"

"Ryan knows everything so you don't have to worry." Then I take a few steps in Ryan's direction because I want him to be involved in whatever conversation Roy is about to start.

"Alright." Roy then looks at both of us and says, "Eric knows about Janette's death—Tess gave him the police report."

While Ryan curses in shock, I can't help but have only one single question in mind. "Was it Petra who told you that?"

"Yes," he says. "And, um, it seems like the lab found some nano-particles in Tess's bloodstream that might have attacked her heart and killed her."

Now that's something I wasn't aware of. But as I come to think of it, I'm not surprised that Mom or Julia took such a preventive measure.

Ryan keeps taking notes and then asks, "Do you know what Eric intends to do with the report?"

"I have no idea. Petra didn't tell me much. I managed to get that info over lunch, but she's been very secretive."

While Ryan seems surprised at Roy's news, I just shrug in return, agreeing with him. "She's been very secretive, yeah."

Then Roy looks at me, curiosity laced all over his face. "By the way, what happened yesterday?" Roy inquires. "Petra told me you haven't spoken to her since you got arrested."

I pace around, pondering how to tell him what's going on between his daughter and I in the most tactful way possible. "Well, Petra said she was waiting for me at the condo, when in fact it was a set up. Two cops, along with Eric, were there waiting for me."

His eyes widen in shock as he processes my words. "And did you speak to her about it?"

"Not yet," I admit, and despite knowing it's gonna sound stupid, I tell him the rest. "Something tells me I should be careful with her."

Roy squeezes his eyes in total confusion. "What do you mean?"

"Eric and I have a meeting on Friday," I disclose. "Until I know exactly what evidence they have against me, I want to keep minimal contact with her. Ryan already told her I will spend a few days here."

"But why? That doesn't make any sense. She's your wife, you owe her the truth." His emotional reaction wasn't really what I expected from a man who got betrayed by his own wife.

"She spent the whole afternoon at Eric's office before heading to our condo with him and the cops. I'm not sure what they did in there, but I'll soon find out," I reply calmly. "Until then, I'm gonna keep my distance and be careful."

"You're being psychotic here," Roy responds just as fast, flailing his arms in conjunction with his words. "My daughter loves you a lot. Her allegiance is to you, not to her mom or to the Bradfords."

"That's not what I saw yesterday," I riposte.

"You guys need to talk." He shakes his head, displeased by my reaction. "Being apart is not the solution."

"And we will…once I know what it is that they are up to."

CHAPTER 4

The Netherlands, December 31, 2020
Tess Hagen

I'm becoming more and more desperate as the days go by. Every single day is the same doleful routine; I wake up, shower, then Winter comes in with my breakfast. I eat, read a book, then Winter comes in with my lunch. I eat, keep reading, then Winter comes in with my dinner. I eat, and read until I fall asleep. And worse, I haven't seen anyone except for him. I'm starting to believe the pills he's giving me are to prevent me from falling into a deep state of depression or from going crazy. Yet, since I haven't swallowed any of them, I'm feeling anxious all the time for being locked up here. I haven't step outside since I arrived and the only rays of sunshine coming in are the ones from the window that stands too high for me to reach. They are testing me—I'm sure they are. They want to drive me to the edge until I have a breakdown and give them what they want. The day I tell them I'll no longer share the report with Jan is the day they will set me free. At least that's what I think. Fortunately, Winter brought me some books upon my request, which has helped me stay sane. Make no mistake—this is even worse than a prison; in prison, those who are incarcerated can go out and walk. Here, I have barely walked and my body is starting to feel it. And they can talk to other incarcerated too. Meanwhile, here I have no one but my books to talk to. Despite everything, I can't lose hope, I'm sure the police and Carice are searching for me. Plus, Winter and I have been speaking and getting closer. Maybe one day he'll call the police and they will come here to rescue me.

The creaking sound of the door opening no longer startles me—I have come to expect Winter every day. Yet as I look at the door, I'm a bit put off by the fact that it's not Winter that is walking in, but rather the security agent that forced me to do a voice message to my daughter on her wedding day. Despite sitting against the headboard of the bed, I straighten myself, my brows furrowing as I watch him marching in my direction.

"What do you want?" I snap while he grabs a chair to sit at my bedside.

He's carrying a recorder with him and I know at this point he wants me to do a new voice message.

"Good morning, Tess." His tone might sound agreeable but I don't bother to reply. "You know what day is it today?"

I shake my head because I have no idea; all I know is that it feels like I have been here for an eternity.

"The thirty-first of December," he answers happily. "So why not leave a cute Happy New Year to your friend Carice?"

"Carice?" I ask, my heart already on my knees at the idea they have been tracking her. "What do you know about her?"

"All I know is that she misses you."

I take a deep breath in and out, trying to tame my growing pain; the fact Carice is still looking after me and risking her life at the same time makes me want to cry.

"Please, don't hurt her," I plead, sounding weak and exhausted. "She knows nothing."

The security agent doesn't say a word. Instead he just takes a sheet from his inner pocket and hands it to me. As I start reading the letter, my heart squeezes at the lies I will have to tell my best friend. But I'll do whatever it takes to make sure she isn't a target. And if I have to read a script and lie about my well-being so be it.

"We need you to read this," he instructs, his tone demanding. "There's no point going off the script because we won't send anything until it's exactly as we want."

My stomach is in knots as he stands the recorder in front of me. I clear my throat a few times, making sure I didn't lose my voice. I close my eyes for a brief moment as I try to find some strength to get through this. He then nods, giving me the okay to go ahead. "Hi, Carice, it's me, Tess. Um, I wanted to wish you a Happy New Year and let you know I'll be spending the rest of the winter away, reflecting on my life." I pause for a beat as I struggle to steady my emotions. "Don't worry about me, I just need some time alone." I focus on breathing in and out despite wanting to cry at everything I'm going through. "I'm not telling you where I am because I simply don't want to be found, but I'll be fine…" I look upwards, tears resting on my eyelids. Fortunately as I look again at the letter, I see I'm nearly done. "I wanted to wish you a Happy New Year and I hope you're enjoying your evening. I love you. Bye."

And he presses stop. "Good. That's all we needed."

Without saying anything further he just stands up and before he can start walking, I ask, "I'm not going to do a new one for my daughter?"

"No," he snaps. "The less you talk to her, the better."

I can't help but shake my head at his disgusting answer. What a bunch of monsters! If I ever get out of here, I swear I'll call her straight away and tell her everything. Heck, I'll even take a plane and go see her in New York to tell her the whole truth.

While the security agent opens the door and leaves, someone else comes in.

My brows raise up in surprise and I blink twice, barely believing it. "Van Dieren?"

"Good morning, Tess."

The sound of his voice makes my blood boil and my throat clog with rage. If I'm here, it's because of him, it's because of this despicable and disgusting man. One day or another, he's gonna regret everything he has done. "You have no shame, do you?"

Alex saunters in my direction, wearing a long black coat and gray tweed suit. He looks tanner than usual, which I assume is because they likely spent their honeymoon in a tropical place. "Well, if I can't kill you, then I'm left with no other choice but keeping you here." He pauses, standing in front of me, his hands casually hanging in his pockets. "At least, here you aren't a threat to anyone."

"How are you gonna explain to Petra after a year that I haven't returned to the Netherlands, huh?" I snap, my tone filled with anger and hate.

"You will simply disappear," he answers flatly.

I snicker at his pathetic plan. "Carice is looking for me as we speak!" I retort. "You're done! Sooner or later, you are done!"

"Carice can search as much as she wants, she won't find anything."

Then my heart freezes at the eventuality she might go through the same fate if she *does* find something. "Please, don't kill her. She knows nothing."

"I don't intend to do anything to her. She isn't a threat." He pulls the chair and sits at my bedside, blowing out a breath in exasperation. "What a pity you have so much hate in you, Tess." He then leans in, getting closer to me, his forearms resting on his knees, and my stomach bottoms out with repugnance as I see the wedding band on his finger. "Do you realize just because of your behavior, you'll spend the rest of your life here, alone and miserable, instead of alongside your daughter?" Despite his tone being laced with disappointment, I don't let myself be fooled into his trap. "If you were reasonable, you could even spend New Year Eve's with us all. Your daughter would've been delighted."

I chuckle at his failed attempt to try to manipulate me. "You'd never allow that."

"I'm not interested in wars," he says, keeping his tone just as calm and serene. "I know Petra wants you to change. I know she'd like to have you back in her life. But your heart isn't there, is it?"

"You are lying," I riposte, keeping my temper in check. "My daughter doesn't give a damn about me."

"She does. Actually, she doesn't stop asking about you."

He's lying, that's all he does.

"Tess, all I want is for us to move on. I'm giving you a chance here."

"Giving me a chance?" This man is totally delusional! Yet, I can't stop laughing at this nonsense. "You are a murderer, a liar, and a man who should be behind bars," I spit, pointing a finger at him in disgust. "I don't negotiate with people of your kind."

Despite my aggressive tone, his facial expression tells me nothing. "So you'd rather stay here for the rest of your life?" He sounds surprised I'm not going along with his lies.

"You aren't giving me much of a choice, are you?"

"Of course I am," he answers back. "If you decide to leave the past behind and embrace the future with us, let Winter know." In other words: they'll most likely ask me to burn the original police report and any copy left, and I'll never do that. Oh no… Since I've got nothing else to say, Alex rises from his chair and my gaze travels up with him. I remain always on my guard as he stands tall before me. His eyes are devoid of any hate or anger, and to my surprise, I only see pity in them. "Goodbye, Tess." Then I watch him turn his back on me and walk away.

CHAPTER 5

Manhattan, February 12, 2021
Petra Van Gatt

It has been three days since my husband has been released, and it has been three days since I sent him my last text. He hasn't bothered to reply, and I haven't bothered to be upset with his childish behavior either. Yet, I can't for the life of me understand why he's ignoring me like that. Does he know about my deal with Eric? No, that's impossible. I'm sure we'll talk on Sunday at the funeral, anyway. As I reach downstairs, I am happy to see Matt is already waiting for me with the biggest smile on his face as he leans against his car.

"Hey!" he greets me, genuinely excited—which is surprising considering this checkup is about a potential pregnancy with a man he despises. "You ready?"

"Why are you so happy?" I ask, furrowing my brows.

In a quick move, he opens the door for me and steps aside for me to get in. "Why wouldn't I be?"

I just shake my head, suppressing a laugh and climb inside.

Once we are both in the car, he runs the motor again and starts driving. "So, I went to check with Columbia Doctors if they knew a good OB, and they recommended the lady we are going to see. I checked her out online, and she's like the best in the entire city," he says. Then he reaches for the storage compartment, opens it, and takes a document out, which he hands to me. "Look at her CV. It's insane! Obstetrician, doula, pro humanized-birth, member of a nonprofit advocating against obstetric violence, and she's even an influencer on Instagram—teaching about the whole labor process and stuff."

What? He printed her CV out? As I look at the sheet between my hands, I can't help but laugh. "Matt, we are not recruiting, it's just a prenatal check."

"I know but it's super dope, right? Like I stalked her feed, and she does a lot of livestreams and interviews about humanized childbirth."

I squint my eyes at his last two words. "*Humanized* childbirth?" I repeat, trying to keep a straight face, but Matt is just too funny. He's taking this prenatal check like if it was another study or something. "What does that even mean?"

"Well, I don't know much about it, but it's like a movement against non-consensual medical interventions, the disregard of woman's choice, negligence and so on. Like did you know a lot of women get stitches without consent after labor?" My brows raise, astonished at the amount of research he has done. "And most of them don't even need it. That's so fucked up. I was reading a report about it, and there's a lot of medical interventions done to them that they are not even aware of. It's insane."

I can't contain the growing smirk on my face as he speaks. "You're such a nerd, Mr. Bradford," I tease. "You know I'm not giving you a grade for your studying, right?"

Matt erupts in laughter. "I know, but I can't help it, this stuff drives me nuts. It's just insane the horrors she was sharing," he says, some sadness in his tone. "I think I'm gonna interview her for my Youtube channel."

And I'm even more astonished now. "Isn't your channel about economics?"

"*Socio*economics," he corrects. "But it's also about social issues and human rights, so that fits perfectly well. Everything is tied up."

As I come to think of it, I ask, "Is my dad still one of your sponsors?"

Matt doesn't answer immediately. Instead he looks at me, a corner smile settling on his lips. "Yep, every month I get ten thousand from him. But I mean, thanks to that capital, our channel just reached one million subscribers."

"Wow," I utter in surprise. "That's insane!"

"Yeah, it's a lot of work, but I enjoy it thoroughly." Matt turns left and keeps himself focused on the traffic jam that stands ahead of us.

Meanwhile, I start having tons of questions about him. "Are you gonna be a YouTuber full time after college? Or would you rather stay more traditional with your path?"

His eyes widen and he presses his lips tight, considering me. "I'm just in the second year, so who knows. But yeah, I like to teach things to people… so I wouldn't complain."

With a smirk on my face, I say, "I think you'd be a fine professor."

"Me?" He sounds surprised, and it's really funny seeing him like that. "Being a prof?"

"Yeah, Prof. Reich also has a YouTube channel where he teaches economics. I could totally see you being his younger version."

"I don't know, we'll see… After my bachelor's, I still have the master's to do, maybe a PhD later on to top it all off…but yeah, that's a viable option."

"Do you do sponsored content on your channel at all?" I ask.

Matt cracks in laughter again, shaking his head. "Why do you want to know that?"

"What? You have to eat, no? How are you gonna buy food and pay the rent? Or do you receive enough through donations for that?"

"I live with my pops, Petra." He says that like I didn't know.

"Okay, but you don't intend to have your own place?"

"I don't know, I like living there."

Wow. What a big contrast from the tensions they had last year. I remember Matt always complaining about his dad and how he needed to start saving to move out.

"Lately we have had a better relationship, and he doesn't bother as much."

"Trust me on this, it's always wise to have some savings if things go south."

"Yes, ma'am, I know," he keeps teasing. "Don't worry, my YouTube channel is giving me some assets to keep me afloat." Then he looks on his right and says, "Ah, here we are."

I look at the building on my right and it definitely doesn't look like a typical clinic or a hospital. On the contrary, it's a very beautiful Italianate limestone townhouse—which is quite rare to find in Manhattan.

After we park, Matt and I get into the townhouse, and instantly, we are welcomed by a receptionist. The entryway is classical, with a beautiful chess marble floor, and white walls. While I keep taking in my surroundings, Matt is already talking to the lady at the reception. He then asks me to hand her my ID and once the check-in is complete, the lady escorts us to the waiting room. There's only two other women in there, both of whom are definitely in a later stage than I. We smile at each other and I say a quick "Hi" under my breath.

As we patiently wait, Matt takes the first magazine from the low table and starts flicking through it. As I check the cover, it's a copy of *Pregnancy Magazine*, which is appropriately featuring a pregnant woman. I force myself to suppress a laugh—I've got the feeling if my pregnancy test was a false positive, Matt will be even more bothered than me.

"Oh, look," he says, pointing at the page he's reading.

As I do so, I realize it's an interview with Dr. Mariana Torres—the obstetrician I'm about to see, discussing childbirth at home versus at the hospital.

"Petra Van Gatt?" I hear someone calling.

We both look in front of us to the woman that stands in the doorway. She must be the OB healthcare assistant or something.

"Good luck," Matt whispers as I raise from my seat.

Then she escorts me to Dr. Torres' office and as I get in, I notice a desk with a woman standing behind it, a big smile on her lips. "Hi, Petra, how are you?" she says, extending a hand. I give a quick look over her shoulder and notice the wall behind her with the framed diplomas and the training programs she has attended.

I return the smile and shake her hand wholeheartedly. "Hi, Dr. Torres, I'm great. Thank you." She then gestures me to sit and we both do so.

"Please, going forward just call me Mariana," she asks. I nod in agreement, and she proceeds. "So, this is your first prenatal checkup, right?"

"Yes, um, I did one pregnancy test a few days ago, and it was positive, but apart from not having my period for the past two months, I have no other symptoms."

Mariana nods, taking some notes of what I'm saying, then she leaves her desk and asks me to go and sit on the checkup bed. There, she does a full physical exam—checking my temperature, blood pressure, and heart rate, followed by my eyes, ears, nose, and throat.

"Everything seems okay here. Let's do an ultrasound and clear this all up. Shall we?"

I take off my shirt, then unbutton my jeans, and she brings the ultrasound machine closer to her while I lie again on the bed. After putting the gel on my abdomen, Mariana sits and starts moving the transducer around the lower part of my belly. The screen starts showing everything black except for a few white shapes.

"Is everything alright?" I ask her given how quiet she has become. Then I look at her face more meticulously, and notice concern in her gaze. She keeps looking at the screen where there are two rounded white shapes inside of a darker circle.

"Why are there two white spots?" I further question, since last time I had an ultrasound there was only one. Mariana doesn't answer immediately as she keeps herself focused on the screen, but my heart is already racing anxiously fast in apprehension.

"Well, this is very interesting…" she mumbles, her hand still rubbing the transducer around my abdomen. Her face remains just as serious though. She keeps pressing here and there while taking screenshots of the ultrasounds. She finally looks at me and says, "It seems that you are having twins."

"Twins?" I squeak.

"Yep," she says with a smile. Then she points her finger to the first shape. "That's baby A here, and that's baby B right there."

That's Matthew pulling a prank for sure! Where's the camera?

I'm still pretty convinced there's something going on. It can't be true—it can't be the ultrasound of my own uterus. "Are you sure it's mine?"

Mariana blinks twice, looking at me with a straight face. "Yes, I'm sure it's yours."

Fuck… Despite her seriousness, it feels impossible to be real. I need more answers than that. "And, um, how many weeks am I?"

"Around fourteen-weeks," she answers casually while taking a few more angles for the pictures and measuring each fetus.

My jaw falls instantly—it can only be a joke. "Fourteen weeks already? But I have no symptoms."

"Each pregnancy is different. Many women can go up to twenty-weeks without symptoms."

"But my belly hasn't grown at all," I keep insisting.

She raises an eyebrow, giving me a weird look. "Have you looked at yourself? You are so underweight that if you gain a bit of volume, you would barely see it." She pauses for a breath and then adds, "I've had skinny patients who didn't have any bump at twelve weeks. And I have had others who looked like they were in their final trimester."

Then some silence ensues as we keep observing the images displayed on the screen. "Baby B is very small though compared to Baby A." I can sense the concern in her voice as she points that out.

"Why is that?" I ask her.

"By what I can see, you have monochorionic diamniotic twins, which means they share the same placenta but each have their own sac. As you know, the placenta is what provides oxygen and nutrients to them. Sometimes the vessel connections within the placenta are not evenly dispensed and there's an imbalance in the blood exchange between the twins. Baby B is what we call the donor twin, giving away more blood than it receives in return and runs the risk of malnourishment and organ failure." I'm trying to process everything Mariana is explaining, but she's talking at light speed, making it hard to understand her. "Baby A is the recipient twin and receives too much blood and is susceptible to overwork of the heart and other cardiac complications."

Despite her great explanation, I'm not really getting her point. "So what does that mean at the end?"

She ponders for a while, thinking something through. Her face deepens and I know in that moment this isn't gonna be a pleasant answer. "It means Baby A *might* grow just fine, but…" she lets her words trail off as she considers me. "I'm not sure if Baby B will make it until the end."

My heart takes such a reel at her last words that I have to close my eyes and focus on my breathing to prevent the tears from falling. I take a deep breath in and out, and try to remain positive. "Is there something we can do so that both receive a more balanced exchange?"

"We're gonna run a few prenatal tests and then I'm gonna recommend you to a colleague of mine who is a fetal surgeon to see what we can do."

A fetal surgeon? Oh gosh… I'm getting even more anxious at the idea I may have to undergo a surgery.

At the end of our discussion, I realize she didn't give me a delivery date, which the other doctor had done at my first checkup. "And, um, do you know my delivery date?"

Mariana puts a hand on my shoulder and says, "We'll check it after we get the results of the tests."

The idea that she doesn't even believe the babies stand a chance squeezes my heart so tight that I can barely breathe.

Amid a heavy silence, she cleans the gel off of my skin and I get dressed again before she sends me to another room to draw blood, which I truly hate doing. Yet this time my mind is so busy ruminating on everything that Mariana has just told me that I don't even feel the needle. One thing is sure—this is definitely not the prenatal checkup I had expected.

* * *

One hour and a half later and after doing countless exams, I'm finally free to go. The lady at the reception gives me my ultrasound pictures, but I don't bother to check them out, so I only take the white envelope with me and head to the waiting room, where Matt has since dozed off. I sit on the chair beside him, the envelope in my hands, and poke his arm a few times. "Matt?" I whisper.

He opens his eyes slowly, before stretching himself out. "Did you finish?"

"Yep," I say, thinking we will just leave the place now.

But Matt feels chatty. "And?"

I take a deep breath, searching for the best words to put on. "And, um, I'm pregnant with twins."

His face literally falls, and it's quite fun to watch him trying to keep his composure. "Are you serious right now?"

"Yeah, but one of the babies is taking too much oxygen and nutrients while the other not enough."

He creases in confusion, before staring down for a few seconds. "So what's the solution?"

"Um, I don't know yet," I tell him, unable to verbalize the rest. "I mean, she said she'll put me in touch with a fetal surgeon, so I'm sure there is a way out of this. There must be one but I guess we'll have to wait and see…" I don't tell him she didn't bother to give me a delivery date. It's clear she didn't do that because she doesn't have much hope they will make it until the end. And, truthfully, after my last loss, I'd rather not get too attached to this pregnancy either.

A few instants of silence ensue as Matthew gathers his thoughts about everything I told him. "Are you gonna tell him?"

I chuckle because how am I supposed to talk to someone who is ignoring me? "He isn't even answering my calls, how am I supposed to tell him?" And I can't help but shake my head at my husband's childish behavior.

"Well, text him then," he suggests.

"This isn't the kind of thing you say over a text message. When I see him again, I will tell him." Despite my rational answer, I can't help but take my iPhone while Matt and I are heading out and discreetly text him again: *Why aren't you answering me? We really need to talk. Please call me back.*

After pressing *send,* I heave a long sigh as my mind keeps ruminating on what Mariana told me. "*Baby A might grow just fine, but I'm not sure if Baby B will make it until the end…*"

What terrible timing to be pregnant, I think to myself.

Well, Louise told me my relationship with Alex would be filled with death and misery. And this pregnancy only attests to how right she was. Jeez, what a pity I didn't believe her back then.

CHAPTER 6

Manhattan, February 12, 2021
Alexander Van Dieren

Why aren't you answering me? We really need to talk. Please call me back.

I look once more at her text message as I wait for Ryan to walk into the living room. Despite my intuition telling me something is off, and me feeling tempted to call her right away, I know it's better to do so after the meeting. As Ryan steps in, I tuck my phone back into my pocket, go shake his hand, and invite him to sit on the couch while I take a seat on the armchair. He looks more tired than usual, with dark circles under his eyes, and I wonder if it's because of the case.

"Do you have any updates for me?" I ask, impatient to hear the progression of the case.

"I do," he says, concern thick in his tone. "So yesterday, after your indictment, Eric sent me two files and told me he was open to a sentence bargaining before we do your second arraignment." I keep listening as Ryan continues, "You need to know two things though—One, you have been under investigation most likely since the day Tess left the country, which means your phone has been tapped since then. And Two—"

"Wait—What?" I cut him off, barely believing it. Then I wonder if Petra knows about it and if it's the reason why she wants to talk to me via phone. "How do you know that?"

"Eric is legally obligated to show us all the evidence before trial and this was one of them." He takes his iPhone out, puts it on the table and presses play.

"*Hey, how are you?*" My heart stops for a moment, recognizing Julia's voice.

"*Hi, Julia. Look, I just spoke to Petra, and it seems like Carice, Tess's attorney, just reached out to her.*" Fuck! Fuck! And fuck! I run a hand through my hair, pressing my lips tight to contain the rage from consuming me. Yet I can't help but wonder which other conversation they listened to. One thing is sure though—Petra obviously knows I knew about the abduction of her mom. Jeez, she must be hating me to the core now, which means she's most likely planning some sort of revenge against me.

"*I'm not sure what they talked about, but Petra is certainly having some suspicions, so be careful.*"

"*Should I ask Tess to talk to Petra?*" Julia asks.

"*No, she could tell her the truth and even if it's the last words she says, we can't risk it.*" I chuckle, head shaking at how stupid I was for saying that over the phone. What an idiot...

"*You're right. I will ask her to do a direct voice message to Carice to appease her, then.*"

"*That would be great, yeah... Be careful with the GPS tracking. Make sure your agents take care of it.*"

"*I know. Well, talk later.*" And Julia hangs up.

"Fuck," I can't help but say. Then some silence ensues as I take a deep breath to calm myself down. Yet, I can't help but think how this tape is gonna make our defense so much weaker. "And two?"

"You were right about your wife."

I crease my brows at his words, expecting the worst. "What do you mean?"

"She's cooperating with them."

Well, here we are. "What kind of cooperation?"

"I think you should watch this." Ryan does something on his iPhone, before turning it to me and pressing *play*. This time though it's a video. In it, I can see my wife standing in a meeting room which seems to be in Eric's office, and holding a white sheet between her hands. She seems stressed and rather uncomfortable with what she's about to do. She looks down at the document, heaves a sigh, and starts reading from it.

"*I, Petra Van Gatt, agree to cooperate with the office of the State Attorney General and the Department of Justice in the prosecution of Alexander Van Dieren for the alleged homicide of my mother, Tess Hagen.*" She pauses, taking a breath. "*In exchange for immunity, I accept that I will be a witness in the upcoming trial and provide taped conversations that can help the case. I shall only assist the prosecution and not the defense and keep my cooperation totally confidential.*"

There are no words to describe the pain that is watching my wife betraying me as she sides with the man who eagerly wants to ruin my life and send me to jail.

I felt angry when Roy and Sebastian betrayed me, but when it comes to her? I can't find the right words. None of them would be suitable. Why? Because of all the people who I thought would betray me, Petra never made the list. And yet, I was wrong. I swallow the lump in my throat, looking away as I gather my thoughts. Despite her betrayal hurting more than anything, I can't say I was caught off guard. Yet the bruises I have inside me are bleeding and I don't know how to make them stop. It's hard, so fucking hard to keep my composure in front of Ryan while her words replay in my mind.

"Are you okay, Alex?" I hear him asking as I look to the void.

"How did you get that video?" I manage to pull out of myself.

"Eric gave it to me."

I chuckle at Eric's brilliant move. If he wanted to destroy me by showing me my wife's true nature, then it's working pretty well. As I come to think of it, my intuition was right. Deep inside, I knew since the moment Petra was ignoring my phone calls and only replied back in order to get me arrested that something was off. At the time though, I just couldn't pinpoint what it was.

"Look, when it comes to the abduction, the act was committed in the Netherlands, so you don't have to worry about it here." I think Ryan is talking to me, but I can't help thinking about my wife and all the amazing moments we spent together. Seeing her betraying me like that has left me totally numb. She could've contacted me, she could've asked Eric for some time to think about the deal before jumping right into it. But she didn't. She simply sided with them, throwing her loyalty for me under the bus. "Alex?" I blink twice, my gaze drifting back to him. "Are you okay?"

It takes everything in me to say, "I wasn't expecting such a statement from her. I'm just shocked, that's all." Blowing out a breath, I look away for a moment, yet my mind can't stop thinking about that video. "I'm so… disappointed."

Ryan keeps quiet while considering me. "Look, I'm sure there's a good reason for her to have done that. In a way, she has immunity. He's leaving her out of this mess. So, it's not really a bad thing."

Despite his reassuring words, I don't buy it. After all, Petra could've talked to me about this whole ordeal first, but she didn't. Plus, if she is innocent, she doesn't need that immunity for anything. It sounds more like she's really doing it for revenge because I lied to her and now she thinks I'm the one who killed her mom. But to be fair, she made herself very clear when she said, "*Next time I might not be as forgiving…*"

"Alex?" I look again at Ryan. There's something in his gaze that switched; it's now more empathetic and friendlier. "I know it's gonna be hard with the trial, the media portraying you in a bad light, and your wife testifying against you, but you can't shut yourself down."

I stand up and stroll toward the floor-to-ceiling windows at the end of the living room, still ruminating about what Ryan showed me. Then I stand in front and contemplate the magnificent view to the Hudson River. "You have to warn Julia," I tell him. "Make sure it's not a tracked line, but contact her and see if she's attending the funeral or not. If she is, then make sure she's carrying her judicial immunity with her. And kindly ask her to check with the rest of my family."

"Okay, I will talk to her." While I remain standing in front of the window, I hear Ryan rising from his seat and walking toward me. Then he stands beside me and asks, "Do you want me to say something to your wife?"

I ponder his question for a moment. "No." Then I stare back at the horizon ahead of me and take a deep breath. "I'll do it myself."

"Alright," Ryan mumbles before proceeding. "I'm sure there's a reason why she did what she did. Maybe Eric coerced her, you know how they are."

I look at him, a small smile playing on my lips. It's touching to see him worrying so much about us. Most lawyers wouldn't give a fuck. On the contrary, they'd maybe encourage a divorce procedure or so at this point.

"I'll also need a new line and phone," I tell him.

"That has already been taken care of."

I nod, and for the sake of trying to think about something other than my wife's betrayal, I ask, "Do we know when the trial is?"

"Only after your second arraignment we will," Ryan replies.

"Mr. Van Dieren?"

I turn to look at the butler who stands at the entrance of the living room.

"Eric Bradford is here," he announces.

I glance at my watch and realize it's time for our meeting with that son of a bitch. "Sure, let him in."

Ryan tenses, so I put my hand on his shoulder to ease him a bit. "Let's say hi to our friend," I whisper to him.

My eyes alight on Eric who walks in and I'm even more surprised he came alone. I can only come to the conclusion his department is not aware of this meeting.

I observe him as he takes in his surroundings—from the ample entryway, the minimalist sculpture that stands in the corner, the high ceilings, the abstract paintings... "You're gonna have a hard time adapting to a federal cell," he says with a smirk on his lips.

"I won't have to adapt to anything," I riposte just as fast, returning the smile.

The living and dining room being in an open space, Ryan and I start walking toward the glass table and we take a seat, waiting for him. Then Eric does the same and pulls a chair in front of us.

Once we are all seated, Eric skips the civility and goes straight to the point. "I'm gonna make it very clear for you, Alex. As you probably know, we've got some strong evidence against you." The fact he's calling me "Alex" which is only for friends and acquaintances makes me want to punch him in the face. "This isn't a case you can win." His tone is irritating, but I take a deep breath, and let my attorney do the talking.

"Do you have anything new for us?" Ryan asks, keeping a professional posture.

Since Eric is legally obligated to show us everything that will be presented to the court, he opens his briefcase and takes from there a document that he hands to us. "This report here clearly shows us that Tess knew about the death of your friend's daughter. She knew you and Roy were involved. I'm pretty sure Jan isn't gonna be happy about it once he knows."

I can't help but chuckle, already anticipating his next move. "Let me guess, you want me to plead guilty at the arraignment or else you tell him?"

His face softens with a smirk and he leans back on his chair. "I'm a simple guy."

I huff at his arrogance. "You're delusional."

"Am I?" He brings himself forward, his gaze never leaving mine. "I see only two options here: either you plead guilty and spend fifteen years behind bars and Jan will never know about this report. Or you don't, and in a few days, it'll be all over the Dutch news and God knows what's gonna happen to you, your father-in-law, and the rest of your lovely family after that."

Despite his threats, I'm not impressed.

"Either way, I win."

Before I can tell him to fuck off, Ryan steps in. "My client will plead not-guilty at the arraignment. It's in a few hours so we don't have time to assess everything properly."

Exactly!

"However, can we give you a final answer before the trial so that we can check the rest of the evidence?"

What the fuck? I look at Ryan, my jaw clenching.

"You have ten days, not more," Eric demands, and Ryan like an idiot just nods at him. Then they raise from their seats, sealing their agreement with a handshake. Eric looks at me and says, "See you at the funeral." I fist my hands, containing the urge to punch him on the face. Given the fact he's attending, I'm not even sure I will go.

Once that asshole leaves my residence, I press my lips tight, barely believing what they just agreed on.

"I don't need ten days to tell him to fuck off with his deal," I snap.

"Alex, calm down," Ryan answers. "Let's look at it rationally, shall we?" I take a deep breath as Ryan ponders his next words. "If Jan knows about that incident, he can hurt your mom, your dad, your sisters, your wife…" he then pauses, letting this eventual reality sink into me. "Is that what you want?"

"I'm not gonna spend fifteen years in jail for a crime I didn't commit," I tell him. "And I wasn't expecting you'd even think twice about that deal." I shake my head, feeling quite deceived by his defeatist mindset—of all the lawyers in the city, the last one I thought would be impressed with a deal like this is him. "My family has got the best security possible. I'm sure they'll be able to take care of themselves if Jan wants to go ahead and take revenge against me."

Ryan heaves a sigh, rubs his eyelids tiredly, and silence ensues for the next few seconds. "Alex," he begins, sounding more poised than before. "Let's be honest, you want to spend the rest of your life with security wherever you go? Going to restaurants and wondering every time you do if the waiter is going to poison your food or not?" Since I don't react at his fear mongering, he keeps going. "That's the kind of life you want?" Ryan takes a sip of his water and I can't believe he's seriously considering making a deal with Eric. "And Petra? Does she want a life where she can't have any freedom because Jan might try to kill her? I don't think this is an option you want to go with."

"We have to take care of Eric," I tell him. "He needs to drop the case before Jan knows anything."

Ryan chuckles in return. "You can't be serious…" But as he knows I'm not joking, he says, "This case is like his own child, he's *never* gonna drop it."

"We have to find a way," I insist, pondering the best way to do so.

Ryan shakes his head in disapproval. "Look, even if you threaten him with his own life, he won't do it. And if you kill him, you'll be charged for homicide *again*. You'll be suspect number one, believe me on this. Killing him isn't gonna solve your problem."

Despite his alarming tone, I keep ruminating about another option. "We need to find something about him that we can have leverage on."

His brows lift in surprise, and I can't prevent the smile on my lips as he does so. "You want to blackmail him?"

"We need to find something so shameful that if the public knows, it'd end his career in politics."

But Ryan doesn't seem to like the idea. "Alex, we don't have time for this; we need to give him an answer in ten days." He sounds worried and even anxious. "Finding his skeletons not only takes time but you don't even know if he has any."

"Every politician does. And I will find his."

"As you wish…" Ryan stands up, goes back to the living room, pacing with annoyance, and takes his briefcase. Then I go to where he's standing and we shake hands. "You have ten days to come up with something," he reminds me, his tone quite serious. "Remember that report is a very strong piece of evidence and it can create a myriad of legal issues for Roy and everyone else."

I nod at him, knowing perfectly well what's at stake.

* * *

While I have kept my distance with Petra, I haven't minded Roy's company and help. After all, he at least has been clearly on my side. It feels awkward to step in his home office in Park Avenue though. The last time I recall coming over was to announce Petra and I were leaving for Singapore. Instinctively, the corner of my lips curve up as I remember how she didn't hesitate wanting to go with me. I wonder if nowadays she'd have done the same.

"Do you want to drink something?" I hear Roy asking as he pours himself some Macallan.

"Are you sure she isn't coming?" I ask instead.

"Why on earth would she come here? I'm pretty sure she prefers to stay over at the condo as much as she can." Then he shows me the bottle of Macallan and says, "One glass? You look like someone who needs it."

To my surprise I hesitate a bit, but after everything that happened today, I agree to it.

Then Roy walks to where I'm standing, carrying the two drinks. He gives me mine and we clink each other's glasses. "Cheers," he says, before we quietly take our first sip. Afterward, he gestures for me to sit and we do so without saying a word.

A few beats of silence go by until an unexpected question breaks through the room. "Have you spoken to her yet?" His voice is laced with genuine concern and I can tell he's worried about us.

I take another sip, trying to conceal my uneasiness. "I texted her saying we will talk on Sunday."

Roy nods, studying me. I feel him hesitating whether to ask something else or not. "Well, at least there's that." Then he leans back on the Chesterfield sofa, observing me attentively. "What's going on, then?"

He knows me well. I feel tempted to let him know his daughter is cooperating with Eric, but it's better to keep it to myself as Roy could go and repeat it to her and I want to have the pleasure to do it myself. So instead I say, "Eric made me an offer."

His eyes widen in surprise. "Which kind?"

"Either I plead guilty and get fifteen years, or else Jan will know the truth."

He keeps staring at me without blinking even once. "That's a very bad offer." And I'm glad he thinks so too, because it truly is.

After taking another sip, I ponder my next words, look him in the eye, and say, "We need to gain leverage on him."

Roy nods, considering my answer. "Well, you're gonna have to dig pretty deep to find something," he says, before finishing his drink. "What if Margaret takes care of him instead?"

"I'll be the number one suspect, so forget it," I tell him. "It's too risky."

"Suspect yes, but if they have zero evidence that you were involved..."

I cock my head to the side, slightly drawn to his advice, but I know the Department of Justice will do anything to avenge him. And Petra will believe them just as fast and go against me again. The trust we have for each other is already so low and fragile that another murder will probably lead to our end—if this one doesn't. "All I want is for him to drop the case," I say. "I have until next Friday to find something. Otherwise he'll share the report in court and subsequently to the media."

"What if we contact Jan and tell him it's all bullshit?"

"He won't believe us," I say. "The report matches with the location they found his daughter's cadaver. He'll know Tess was telling the truth."

Roy blows out a breath as his anguish takes over him, but he keeps quiet, considering other options. "What if we take care of Jan instead?"

But I find the flaw in his new suggestion once more. "Eric will be convinced it was me and contact his family, anyway." And to make myself clear, I add, "It's Eric we need to take care of. He needs to drop the case."

"And what if he doesn't?" he asks, forcing me to face this eventuality. "What if we don't find anything in time for him to drop it and he goes to court with the report?"

"Then, I'll let my sisters know that Jan might come after us."

* * *

Despite Roy's insistence, I don't go back to my condo where my wife is. After all, Roy doesn't know that Petra is cooperating with Eric, which makes her unreliable and untrustworthy. *"I accept to be a witness in the upcoming trial, and will provide taped conversations that can help the case."* Those words… fuck… I can't take them out of my head. It hurts seeing her like some sort of enemy, but it's the truth and I have to remind myself she voluntarily sided with them. I go to my private residence instead where no one is there to deceive me.

Reaching the apartment, I walk into the empty hallway and head to the bedroom. Turning on the lights, I notice the housekeeper already slightly opened the sheets of the bed, which she does every evening, but my attention goes to the nightstand and my eyes narrow at the envelope leaning against the base of the lamp with *To Mr. Van Dieren* hand-written on it. Jeez, I can recognize that handwriting anywhere. Curious enough, I take the envelope, open it and find inside a photograph of Petra and I taken during our wedding at De Haar. We are smiling at each other without noticing the camera. It's a candid moment that makes my heart reel and my lips pull up at the same time. I turn it and read, "*Don't forget us*" written on the back. I shut my eyes tight because this is torture. She must have given the envelope to Ryan, and he gave it to the concierge. That's why Ryan was so forgiving toward her actions. They must have been in touch a few times. Why is she doing this though? To make me go back home so that she can start helping Eric convict me? I could go home so easily, but what for? She made a statement in front of the state's Attorney General on what her real intentions are. Unlike Ryan, I know she's just doing it for revenge. And the way to do so is through my heart.

CHAPTER 7

The Netherlands, February 6, 2021
Tess Hagen

I have been locked up here for so many weeks and without seeing anyone but Winter and the security agents that I'm starting to believe I'll never see my daughter ever again. As always, Winter walks into my room, carrying my breakfast to start yet another day, but I barely find the will to wake up.

"Good morning, Tess," he greets softly, his voice always so welcoming. Winter is such a nice person that it's hard to believe he's cooperating in such a criminal activity.

I open my eyes timidly, the room already bright from the sun. Then I sit up on my bed while Winter puts the tray down onto my office table.

"When can I go out?" I ask him for the very first time since I have been here.

Winter looks at me a bit surprised. "You mean outside?"

"Yes, please, let me just breathe some fresh air and feel the sun beaming on my face." It sounds like I'm begging him, but in reality, I am—I'm in desperate need of soaking up the sun. I feel sick to my core for being locked up here for months. Even my dogs would always get me to go outside every single day.

"Fine," Winter says. "I'm sure I can escort you for a walk after breakfast."

Wow. My eyes widen in surprise at how easy it was to convince him.

"Thank you," I manage to pull from my excitement. I never thought Winter would agree to that so easily. And I remain staring at him, totally baffled, until he leaves my room again.

I hurry up to eat breakfast, my heart racing at the idea I will finally step outside. It must be freezing, but that's the last of my issues. Afterwards, I jump into the shower and get myself ready.

A few minutes later, Winter walks again into the room, holding a coat for me. He's already wearing his, plus gloves and a wool scarf. He helps me out with the coat and then asks, "Ready?"

"Oh, yes!" My smile is up to my ears and I even clap my hands with joy.

Winter opens the door for me, but as I reach the hallway, I find two security agents, holding automatic rifles over their shoulders. I tense immediately, and wait for Winter before taking one more step. Well, I imagine they will escort us to make sure I won't try to run away. Needless to say, I don't think they will hesitate to shoot if I try to do so.

Winter and I cross the hallway until we reach the main door of the house. He twists the doorknob, pushing the door wide open. The freezing air from outside hits my bones and I shiver instantly. Jesus! It's so damn cold!

Yet, there the bright blue sky and sun are, and to me, that's all that matters. We reach outside and Winter gestures for me to take the stairs that go down to the gardens and to follow the pathway in between the fields of snow. As I take in my surroundings, I realize we are in the middle of nowhere surrounded by nothing but snow and woodland.

My attention then goes to the house itself—it looks old and rustic, which leads me to believe we are most likely in a rural area, far from any city. I spin around, searching for any other sign of life, but all I can see is the woods stretching for miles on the horizon.

Yet, I open my arms wide, tilting my head back, and close my eyes, reveling in the rays of sunshine that are beaming on my face. "Why didn't you take me out before?" I ask Winter upon looking at him.

He just shrugs. "You never asked."

We start walking the pathway between the fields, and out of curiosity, I look behind my shoulder, noticing the security agents walking behind us but keeping a pretty big distance from us. Enough to give us privacy.

After a few minutes of silence, savoring the freezing air of the countryside, I quietly say, "If I decide to cooperate with Mr. Van Dieren, would he set me free?"

"If you decide to turn the page, yes," he answers, his tone matching mine. "I work directly for him, actually."

"Oh," I utter, slightly surprised. "I didn't know that."

"Mr. Van Dieren wanted to make sure you would be taken care of," he explains, his voice very low and discreet, always looking in front. "The other agents work for the Van Den Bosch family though."

I lower my voice even more, and whisper, close enough to his ear, "They are a horrible bunch."

Winter snorts with laughter, but tries to stop himself just as fast. "They aren't very empathetic, I must say."

"What are his terms?" I ask out of curiosity.

We keep walking always ahead, but we have slowed our pace. "His only request is that you burn the original and any copy left of the police report."

I knew it was something along those lines. "And if I do so, will he set me free?"

"Yes, I will drop you off at your house, and everything will belong to the past." Winter makes it seem like cooperating with his criminal boss is a walk in the park. Yet, for me, this isn't that easy, no.

"And I will be able to get my phone back?"

"Of course, but remember—you can't talk about your stay here to *anyone*. Otherwise," he glances behind his shoulder and then leans closer to me to say, "*they* will kill you." I swallow the lump in my throat, knowing those guys wouldn't hesitate to do so. "On all accounts, you have been traveling through Asia, between Thailand and Bali, visiting a few meditation retreats."

Cooperating with Van Dieren feels all too easy to me. After everything that I did to him, would he really set me free if I just comply? Impossible! It must be a trap. Or is he testing my trust? For better or worse, I decide to test the waters. "Fine, tell him you can come with me to my house, and I will burn the police report in front of you."

"This is excellent news," Winter states, his expression always so gentle. "I will call him right after we get back inside, then."

After our walk, we go back inside the house and Winter escorts me to my room. He asks me to wait inside while he goes out to talk to Alex. Though it feels gloomy to be back in the tiny cell of a room, I feel some relief in knowing I'll be free soon enough. I sit on my bed and start reading a book in a failed attempt to keep my nerves under control, but I'm just too anxious to know the outcome of his conversation with that monster.

Thirty minutes later, the door cracks open and I see Winter emerging back inside, a phone in his hand. He walks toward me, then leans down, and says, "Mr. Van Dieren wants to talk to you."

Oh gosh, here I am, having to speak to this criminal again. I heave a long sigh in displeasure before taking the phone and putting it against my ear. "Hello?"

"Tess, how are you doing?" He sounds overly excited and happy to have me on the phone. "Winter told me you have finally accepted our terms and would like to move on?"

"Yes," I lie, just wanting to get the hell out of here.

"You know, you are doing the right thing. Petra will be so happy to know that."

"What do I have to do?" I ask.

"Winter will drive you home so that you can delete the police reports," he tells me. "Just don't say a word about our agreement to the agents. They aren't on our side."

"I see," I mumble.

"Do you want to come to New York and visit us?" he asks, his friendly tone getting on my nerves.

I ponder his question for a moment; if I get on a plane he booked for me, I won't be able to escape him from the moment I leave this place to the moment I arrive in New York. Do I want to go to New York and see my daughter? Oh, yes! But I don't want him to be tracking me down.

"I will when I feel better," I answer, making up an excuse. "Right now I need to go back to my NGO. I have a lot of work to do."

"I understand," he says, sounding polite. "So, do we have a deal, Tess?"

"We do," I answer dryly.

"Do you swear on your own daughter's life you won't break it?"

"Oh gosh," the words roll out of my mouth. "What do you mean?"

"You don't want to bring her any misfortune because you lied to me, right?"

"Of course not," I snap. "What are you gonna do to her?"

"Me? I'd never do anything to hurt my wife," he says right away, sounding nearly offended for me thinking so. The simple word *wife* makes me want to puke. *What a disgraceful jerk!* "But I hope you won't break your oath and bring misfortune upon her." Given the fact I'm not answering, he repeats the question once more. "So? Do you swear on Petra's life you won't break it?"

A gush of air burst from my lungs, the idea to swear on my daughter's life terrifies me, and I consider his question for longer than I thought. "I do."

* * *

After lunch, Winter comes in to take my empty plates, but then he walks closer to me, and quietly says, "I'll leave the door unlocked, the security agents should fall asleep in a few minutes. I put a little something in their lunches," he says, giving me a quick wink. "Meanwhile, I will get the car ready."

I nod at him, and at this point, I realize Van Dieren is most likely going against his own family to set me free. He seems to be genuinely interested in building a bridge between us and turning the page.

Once Winter leaves, I notice he doesn't lock the door, and I stand there, patiently waiting for him to come back.

After two minutes though, I'm just too impatient to wait any further, so I walk toward the door, twist the doorknob, and quietly crack the door open just enough to get a view of the hallway. There's no one outside, so I open it even more until I can finally go out. The hallway is dark, but I hear voices, laughter and applause coming from a room somewhere not too far, but as I pay closer attention, it sounds like it's coming from the TV. Nevertheless, I follow the sound and find myself standing in front of the kitchen, where the two security agents were having lunch and had fallen totally asleep in their chairs. My eyes zoom in on the semi-automatic laying on the table between plates and glasses, and for better or worse, I decide to quietly approach them and take the gun with me. I secure it under the waistband of my jeans and I promptly walk out of the kitchen, speeding up my pace to reach the front door of the house.

As I step outside, I find a small Fiat waiting for me, the engine up and running. *Finally!* I run down the stairs and hurry myself to slide into the passenger seat.

Winter greets me with a bright smile, like I'm his newest best friend. "Here we go," he says, looking excited. We exit the property and after a few more seconds, we finally reach a national road. "Happy to get out?"

What a stupid question! How can he manage to be such a happy and bubbly human when he's literally working for a criminal? At least the agents weren't pretending to be nice. Why is he faking so much?

The road is in the middle of nowhere, surrounded by nothing but fields of snow and woods.

"We are going home, right?" I ask, always on my guard.

"Correct," he answers. "Do you want me to put some music on?"

"Yes, please."

Winter turns the radio on and starts singing along, following the lyrics of a pop song. While he's totally thrilled to be driving me home, my heart is racing at a thousand miles an hour, thinking about a plan to get rid of him.

I look out of the window and behind us; we are far but not far enough from the farmhouse. In order to execute the plan I have in mind we need to be really far from it. A few more minutes and we should be good. Winter keeps singing and dancing in his seat under the lyrics of a pop singer. He looks pathetic and I can't help but roll my eyes at him.

I glance at my watch and take a deep breath in and out as I try to calm myself down. In a sudden move, I take the gun out of my waistband and firmly point it to him.

"Pull the car over!" I snap with all the strength I have.

Winter startles at my order and nearly begins to cry from it.

"Please don't hurt me," he whines between sobs.

Wow. I never thought he would break down like that, but I keep myself just as focused. Once he pulls over, I give him my second order. "Get out of the car."

He hesitates a bit so I hold the gun with two hands and shout, "Now!"

Winter unfastens his belt and opens the door, stepping outside.

"Give me my your phone and mine too."

He runs a hand inside his coat and takes a smartphone from there. He tosses it onto the driver's seat before doing the same with my iPhone. "What's your code?"

"Three, four, three, four."

I don't dare to try it now because he could do any stupid move and I don't want to have to shoot.

"Now go to the other side of the road."

Winter keeps his hands in the air and after turning his back on me to safely cross the road, I leave the passenger seat and slide onto the driver's seat. I close the door and press down on the pedal, the motor roars, and I'm finally alone. My gaze is as focused as an eagle on the road. I decide to go to Amsterdam rather than home, because home is the first place they will go to look for me. Time is not in my favor, but I have an idea.

With my iPhone in hand, I dial Eric's number and call him immediately. The ringtone goes on, and on…

"Hello?"

I gasp, finally hearing his voice. "Eric, it's me—Tess."

"Gosh, Tess! How are you? It has been such a long time."

"I don't know if this line is safe, but I managed to escape them and now I'm on the road, heading to Amsterdam," I tell him getting straight to the point. My tone is urgent, matching with my current situation.

"Escape? You mean, you were really abducted?" Sounds like he knew a thing or two about it.

"Yes, I need to go somewhere safe where they can't find me."

"Come to New York, you will have full protection," Eric suggests straight away.

"But I don't have my passport with me, I don't have anything."

"Don't worry," he says, his voice steady and radiating confidence. "I'll call the immigration office in Teterboro and get you on a plane to New York. Head to the International airport of Amsterdam and then go to the private terminal. There will be a plane waiting for you there."

"Eric, thank you so much for this," I breathe, trying to contain my emotions. I can't break in tears now. I'm close, so damn close to leave this whole nightmare behind.

"How did you manage to escape?"

"I pretended to make a deal with Van Dieren," I explain.

Eric sounds impressed. "So he knows you are out?"

"Yes, but he doesn't know that I have zero intentions of following through though, until Winter, his minion, inevitably tells him."

"Don't worry," he replies. "I'm gonna make a few phone calls and I'll let my son know about your arrival."

"Thank you," I tell him once more. "Eric? Can I take my lawyer with me? Carice has been searching for me non-stop and I think she might also be in danger."

"Yes, sure," he says. "Well, I'm gonna make a few phone calls, alright? We'll speak soon. Good luck!"

After we hang up, I type Carice's number and call her right away.

"Hello?"

As soon as I hear her voice, I can't hold my tears back any longer and let them fall down my cheeks. Oh gosh, it just feels so good to finally be able to talk to her. But I have to stay focused, so I wipe my tears away and say, "Carice, you have to come with me to New York."

"Tess! Oh my God! Where are you?" she asks, sounding alarmed. "Are you in the Netherlands? I have been searching for you since December!"

"Yes, I managed to escape, but they'll be looking for me very soon, and maybe you too. It's not safe to stay here," I tell her, pausing to regain my breath. "Eric is getting a plane ready for me to leave to New York. You should come with me. It's safer."

"Now?" she asks, like she isn't aware of the gravity of the situation.

"Yes, now, Carice," I snap. "Take your passport if you have one, go to the airport in Amsterdam and head to the private terminal. A plane will be leaving shortly."

"Okay, um, I'm leaving the office now." I can hear by the sound of her accelerated breathing that she is speeding up her pace. Good, at least she has taken me seriously. "Have you spoken to your daughter yet?"

"I'm gonna call her right after," I say, not leaving my eyes from the road. "Carice, I'm driving, I can't speak much longer."

"Of course, well, we'll see each other at the terminal. Bye."

After hanging up, I need to take a few deep breaths and tame my emotions first. I don't want to break down in tears again as soon as I hear my daughter's voice. Once I get a hold of myself, I type in her number and put the phone against my ear, my heart thundering as I wait for her to answer.

The ringtone stops and I hear someone breathing on the other side of the line. "Petra? Can you hear me?"

"Mom?" Recognizing my daughter's voice, I want to sob at how happy I am, but I focus on inhaling and exhaling and keep my composure. "Gosh, everyone thought you were dead! Where are you?"

"It's a long story. Are you in New York?" I prompt myself to ask.

"Um, yes, we came back last month," she says, my mind still barely believing that my little angel is talking to me on the other side of the line. "What happened to you?"

"Great," I say, pulling myself back from my thoughts. "Can I talk to you in person?"

"Um, yes, sure. But, wait—are you coming to New York?" She sounds surprised. "Is everything alright?"

"Radars, ahead, please slow now," I hear from Winter's smartphone. Jeez!

"I don't have much time to talk right now. Shall we meet in Park Avenue at around one tomorrow afternoon?"

"Tomorrow? Um, okay, but what happened?" she insists.

"Petra, it's not safe to talk over the phone," I tell her, stumbling over my words. "I'll explain everything once I'm there. Please don't tell anyone we've been in contact. *No one*," I repeat, fearing she'd tell Van Dieren the truth. "Do you hear me?"

"Mom, you're scaring me. Please, call Eric, he'll arrange security once you land."

"Eric is already informed I'm traveling. He and Matt were the first ones I reached out to," I tell her, making a left toward Amsterdam. Only twenty minutes to go and I will reach the airport.

"What about Carice? Did you call her?" Petra keeps asking, her tone laced with concern. "She was so worried about you."

"Yes, I did," I say as I keep my eyes on the road. I just hope there are no cops around given the fact I'm driving and being on the phone at the same time. The last thing I need is for the police to ask me to stop. "Well, I have to go. I love you so much. See you soon." And I hang up, tears stinging my eyes. It hurts having to end a phone call with my daughter so abruptly but I can't risk being pulled over. If everything goes according to plan, tomorrow I will finally be with her.

CHAPTER 8

Bedford Hills, February 14, 2021
Petra Van Gatt

It's raining again. *Crap.* I hope the guests brought umbrellas. Standing by the window of Alex's office in Bedford Hills, I remain motionless observing the rain as it pours heavily on the gardens, drenching the pathway that will lead us to the burial. I hope Father Thomas won't mind such bad weather. The sound of thunder shattering not too far away makes the day even more sinister and gloomy. Truthfully, I wouldn't have expected anything less for a funeral—especially for *her* funeral. Jeez, I still can't believe Mom is no longer here. Death is such a strange thing. On one hand, I hated her for everything she did to Alex and me. Yet, on the other, knowing that she's dead doesn't bring me any sort of happiness or relief. Especially with the circumstances—God maybe she was right for hating Alex so much. Death, in her case, was... well, *unnecessary.*

Yes, her death was unnecessary.

Killing her was unnecessary.

To me, killing someone is an irreparable mistake. Once done, it's done. *Forever.*

I give a long sigh, knowing Mom will never meet her grandchildren. And they'll never meet her—the fierce and stubborn woman who kept her head high no matter the adversity, no matter how much hatred she had toward her. Now that she is dead, we'll never reach an understanding—an understanding I'm sure time could've brought us. Yes, time could've brought us much-needed healing and peace. But she's no longer here so why am I even thinking about it?

Knock. Knock. Knock.

Three knocks on the wooden door are not enough to make me blink. There comes three more. But I don't answer.

"Petra, it's Emma."

Petra—when was the last time Emma called me by my first name? I can't even remember. She always called me baby girl, baby, babe, or girl, but Petra? It feels like an eternity since I've heard her saying my actual name.

"Are you alright?" Her voice now sounds louder, so I turn around to find her standing in the doorway. As I look at her, Emma closes the door behind her and walks toward me, with a face unusually grave and serious. Approaching with caution, she stops in front of the desk and asks again, "Are you okay?"

I follow her with my gaze, but I don't find the will to talk, so I just nod in return and make an effort to compose a smile —a small one that goes just as fast as it came.

"Guests are here," she informs, her tone unusually low. "Father Thomas too."

"Oh," I utter, giving a quick glance at my watch. No wonder they are—it's already ten o'clock. "It's still raining though. I don't know how we'll manage to do the ceremony in the gardens."

Emma creases her brows in confusion. "We are doing the ceremony on the terrace," she says, before cocking her head to the side. "I told you yesterday I'll transform it into an indoor place."

"Ah yes, you did." The corners of my mouth softly lift at my lie. The truth is I don't remember much since the day Alex was arrested. I barely remember the meetings and calls with Carice and Emma about the funeral. What I do remember is the prenatal checkup and how I haven't seen my husband for days. I wonder if he received my envelope with the photograph. At least Ryan told me that he gave it to his butler and he said he'd place it on his nightstand, so he *should* have seen it. I just hope it helped him somehow to not forget to be here today as I bury the woman he or his family killed. Fuck… I should forget this asshole once and for all and move on, but we need to clarify a few things first.

"Petra?"

Hearing Emma's voice again pulls me back from my thoughts and I blink twice, looking back at her.

"Carice would like to have a word with you," she informs me. "Do you want me to let her in?"

"Sure." As Emma goes to open the door, I smooth out my black dress and straighten my posture.

I smile, seeing Carice stepping in and, without thinking twice, I give her a hug. She accepts it and her arms go up to embrace me.

"Are you okay?" she asks in a whisper, looking me in the eye.

I nod, concealing my emotions the best I can. The truth is I'm not sad because Mom's gone, I'm sad because of everything that happened as a consequence of her death.

"The dutch reporters are asking if you can give them an interview after the funeral."

"What?" My lips part at her request. "That's not what we agreed on."

"I know, but you are her daughter. If they could get a few words from you they'd be so grateful." Since I remain quiet, considering her request, Carice proceeds, "They came all the way from the Netherlands to be here. Give them just a few words." What a big contrast compared to Alex who always advised me not to give a single word to journalists.

"I don't know, it's such a private matter, Carice."

"Just answer a few questions," she insists, seeing me visibly undecided. "Kenneth from RTN is here. He used to interview your mother before. He knows her well. Just give him a quick interview and the other channels will share it."

I heave a sigh, thinking something through. "I want to know the questions beforehand," I tell her assertively. "And I won't answer any question that I don't agree with upfront."

"Okay, I will let him know."

Emma opens the door, inviting Carice to leave. "Oh, Mr. Van Gatt," she says upon seeing my dad standing outside in the corridor.

I turn just as fast to welcome him. "Hey," I greet as Dad walks in, sporting a black suit with a long, black overcoat. Dad has always dressed quite formally, and today, not surprisingly, he isn't making any exception. I look at Emma, giving her a nod of acknowledgement and she goes outside with Carice, closing the door behind them. Alone with my dad, I plunge myself into his arms, and shutting my eyes tight, I keep quiet, reveling in the moment. It feels good to have him here. After everything he went through because of Mom, I'm glad he came to give me some support. "Thanks for being here," I whisper.

"Always," he answers, matching my low tone. "I wouldn't let you do it alone."

This office has witnessed so many hard moments but I never thought one day it would witness my dad and I getting ready for the burial of my mom.

After a few beats of silence, I release him from my hug, a smile of appreciation hanging on my lips and then ask shyly, "Did he arrive already?"

"Who?"

I cock my head to the side, raising an eyebrow. "You know who."

His expression gives nothing away though, and he takes a morbid second to answer me. "I haven't seen him, no, but he told me he'd come." His words freeze me on the spot and I can't help but draw out a breath in disappointment. "Give him some time. I'm sure the fact it's all over the news is not helping."

"And the Bradfords?"

"They are at the terrace, talking to some guests." Oh, somehow I kinda knew they would be the first to arrive.

"And my in-laws?" I ask him. After all, they haven't said a word since they landed in Teterboro.

"They should be here any time," Dad says. "Look, whatever is going on between you and Alex, just be polite with them.

95

They don't need to know the ins-and-outs of your relationship."

"Of course." I wonder if Alex told him the reason why he hasn't been talking to me. Even though they are friends, he's still my dad, so I'm pretty sure he'd tell me the truth. "Did Alex tell you why he's been so distant lately?"

"No, he didn't," Dad answers and he seems rather honest. "I asked him about it, but he didn't tell me anything. But I think it's because you helped Eric get him arrested."

I nod, looking away for a moment. My mind starts wandering to a place where I don't have to bury my mom, where I don't have to cooperate with the Bradfords, and where my husband isn't trying to avoid me.

"Well, it's time. Shall we?" Dad asks, halting me from my alternative reality. I nod, draping an arm around his as we make our way out of Alex's office. He gives me a squeeze of encouragement and I sigh.

As we arrive at the terrace, which is now covered with glass walls and a roof, I realize what an amazing job Emma did in transforming this place from an outdoor space to a classic and minimalist memorial setup. At the entrance, we find a beautiful framed board with a photograph of Mom saying, *Celebrating the Life of Tess Hagen, 1967-2021*. Stepping inside, I notice a fairy garland of lights hanging from the ceiling. The room is decorated in beige and white tones, with matching candles, tablecloths, and flowers. A podium with a microphone stands in front of two rows of white chairs which stretch the length of the terrace. Behind the podium, and against one of the glass walls, lies a long memorial table filled with framed photos of Mom. It's intimate, simple, yet elegant, and I wonder if this small memorial service will disappoint the reporters that are standing behind the last row of chairs with their cameramen as they take some footage of the place. Looking at my right, I notice her coffin has been left semi-open, allowing only her face to be seen. I gather some strength and walk forward to see her closed eyes one last time. Dad escorts me, which surprises me since he has never had the stomach to see dead corpses in movies, yet in real life it doesn't seem to bother him. We stand still in front of Mom's coffin, and a small smile plays on my lips seeing her expression just as serene and peaceful as the last time I'd seen her at the morgue. Despite the makeup, her face is pale, but her hair is impeccable just as she likes. My eyes travel up to my dad's face, and not surprisingly, he's stoic and emotionless. I wonder if seeing his ex-wife lying in a coffin has any impact on him, but with such a poker-face, it's hard to tell.

"It's weird, huh?" I say quietly as we stand beside each other. "One day she's making our lives miserable and the next she's peacefully asleep."

Dad takes a deep breath in and out, nodding pensively at me. "Indeed…"

Then I give a quick glance around, making sure Matt and Eric aren't listening, and lowering my voice, I ask, "Do you think it was him?"

His lips twitch to one side as he considers my question. "I don't know. Your mom had many enemies."

"You weren't aware of anything at all?" I keep inquiring, slightly surprised. "Not even that she was abducted and kept captive for three months?"

His expression finally switches and I can see the astonishment in his gaze as I share such details. "No, I didn't know about it." He pauses, looking downwards for a while, before his attention goes back to Mom's face. "I have always been firmly against doing anything to her."

His eyes remain pinned on her as he says those words and it seems Dad truly means it, which might explain why Alex and his family kept him in the dark about any of it.

I feel someone poking me on the back and after turning to check who's doing it, I'm a bit taken aback to see Matt, and to my surprise, dressed in a suit.

"Hey," he greets with his usual bright smile. His hair however remains as messy as usual.

"Oh, wow, Matt in a suit," I tease, checking him out from top to bottom. "You look great." Then I plunge him in a quick hug as we always do.

"You look great too in this black dress." His face gets slightly more serious and lowering his voice, he asks, "How are you doing?"

"I'm okay, and you?" I answer for the sake of politeness. After all, what am I gonna tell him? That Alex hasn't talked to me since he got arrested? That he hasn't come back home either? What for? Matt doesn't like him and he'd be the first one to remind me how wrong I was for marrying him.

"Do you know when your in-laws are coming?" His question makes me frown, but then I recall his dad wants to talk to them about the nanoparticles found in Mom's bloodstream.

Right before I can answer him, my gaze goes over Matt's shoulder, to the group that enters the terrace. And as they do so, all eyes set on them; it's not hard for Margaret, Julia, and Yara to draw attention to themselves. After all, they carry such an enigmatic energy that one always wonder what they are up to. All three are dressed in long black overcoats, their posture just as straight as usual, and their faces grave and serious. I lean over to Matt and say, "Speaking of the devils." Sebastian and Elliot enter afterward, but I don't see Maud with them.

Matt discreetly turns to check them out for a second. Then he simply stands beside me, so he can have a direct view. "Who is who?" he asks, his voice barely audible.

"The older lady is Margaret, Alex's mom," I tell him, while Dad is already on his way to greet them. "The one dressed with equestrian boots is Yara, his youngest sister." At least, she had the decency to bring black breeches. "And the blond one is Julia, the oldest sister."

"Where's the scientist one?" Matt asks just as fast.

"I don't know," I say, finding it quite strange because Maud told me she'd come. Then I see Eric heading inside alongside a man I don't recognize. "Who's the man with your dad?" The stranger is in business attire, carrying a briefcase with him.

Matt shakes his head, his face just as curious as mine. "I have no idea."

Then I see my dad introducing Father Thomas to Margaret and her family. To my surprise, the man who was with Eric leaves him and walks toward them. He reaches Margaret, leans in, and whispers something in her ear. Margaret nods in return, giving him a quick pat on the back. Something tells me he works for her, but I don't know what kind of work.

"Hey, good morning," Eric greets me as he stands before us.

I exchange a few words with him, before Matthew finally asks, "Who is that man you were talking to?"

"Oh, it's their attorney," he says simply.

"Their attorney?" we repeat at the same time.

Eric gives a quick chuckle seeing our synchronized astonishment. "Yes, and not surprisingly, they all have a diplomatic immunity and five bodyguards at the entrance."

"What?" Matt remains just as shocked, but them having security doesn't impress me. "You mean they came here with security of their own?"

"Yep," Eric answers. "I can't do anything with a diplomatic immunity. And those agents look like they are military-trained or something." He pauses, giving a quick glance around. "Needless to say, they were expecting me."

"I didn't tell them anything," I say just as fast in case he thinks I helped them out.

His lips twist into a smile. "I'm glad you didn't." Then he takes one step closer to me and leaning toward my ear, he adds, "After the memorial service, I have an audio recorder for you to put on."

My heart squeezes tight at his words. Damn it! He was really serious about taping conversations. What a pity Alex isn't here. I can't even warn him. Not that I can, but the last thing I want is for him to be caught off guard about my taping conversations between us.

I try to find some sort of excuse in order to ditch the audio recorder, but I can't find any. After all, I had agreed to it and even read a statement out loud.

I see my dad walking over to us alongside Father Thomas, so I try to brush those thoughts away and focus on them.

"Petra," he begins, a hand resting on Father Thomas's shoulder. "I know last time you saw him you were a few months old, but this is Father Thomas, the man who married me and who baptized you."

Father Thomas is of short stature, but of empathetic face, with transparent glasses on, bald on top of his head, and by the wrinkles around his eyes, I'd say he's in his seventies. His hand comes toward me, and I shake it wholeheartedly.

"I'm so sorry to meet you again in such circumstances," he says with such a friendly voice that it warms my heart. "Your mom was such a wonderful woman. But I can assure you she's in a better place now."

Father Thomas knows what to say to bring comfort to those mourning. Alas, I don't think he knows Mom and I didn't really have the best relationship.

"Thank you so much for coming," I tell him. "I know Mom would have wanted you to do her memorial service." Despite my smile, I can't mirror the warmth in his voice.

Then I glance across the terrace and see that everyone is already here—some are already seated on their chairs, while others are standing and waiting for us like Emma and my in-laws.

As I come to think of it, I should go and greet them. After all, it's the least I should do given the fact they have come from so far away. "If you'll excuse me," I say with a small smile, before leaving the group and walking toward Margaret. I put on my most polite smile and do my best to conceal the hate I have for those criminals. Yet, it's hard to swallow the fact that Julia abducted my mom and had no issues toasting with me on New Year's Eve like nothing happened.

As I approach their group, I can't help but wonder what I am supposed to say to those who planned my Mom's abduction and then her death.

Standing in front of them, I notice they all stop talking and Margaret turns to greet me with a smile like she knows nothing. "Petra." She is the first to speak. Her voice is sweet like honey and she brings me into her arms, giving me a hug that feels everything but sincere. "How are you coping with all of this?"

Oh, what an interesting question. No *sorry for your loss*, or *my condolences*? I'm glad she didn't say any of those things—coming from her it'd have been ridiculous.

"I'm okay, Emma and Carice have been helping me a lot." It's the first thing I can think of.

"Good," she says simply. "And your husband? How is he doing?"

Interesting how for once she referred to him as *my husband* rather than *her son*.

"We haven't spoken since he was arrested," I tell Margaret. Her brows rise in astonishment at my sincerity. "And you? Have you spoken to him already?"

"I did, yes," she answers. Then a small pause ensues, before she leans slightly closer to me and says, "Petra, I can assure you he's innocent."

"If he is, then you certainly are not," I grit between teeth as I try to remain calm despite facing the woman who most likely killed Mom.

Margaret doesn't avert her gaze from mine. Instead she keeps staring right through me and says, "Every choice we make has consequences." She then pauses, gauging my reaction, but I remain just as stoic. After everything she has done, nothing surprises me or outrages me anymore. "Every. Single. One."

"That's right," I answer calmly, my eyes never leaving hers. "Just make sure yours don't come back to haunt you."

All of a sudden though, Emma steps in, draping an arm around mine, ready to drag me away. "Petra, shall we start?"

"Sure," I reply, before my attention returns to Margaret, who seems to have lost her tongue. "Have a seat, Father Thomas will start soon." And I politely turn my back on her, walking with Emma to the first row of chairs.

As we take a seat beside each other, I'm glad that for once she isn't spending her time with Yara. I notice her arm is still draped around mine and a smile settles on my lips, my heart filled with gratitude for having her here during such a horrible time in my life. While most couples are out celebrating Valentine's Day, here I am burying my mother without my husband even bothering to attend. No matter how bad my relationship with her was, I'd have rather spent the day with Alex with Mom still alive, than here watching Father Thomas as he starts his speech.

After twenty minutes in, Father Thomas turns his gaze to me and asks, "Petra? Do you want to say a few words?"

Oh, crap.

Time really flies when your mind is half here, half somewhere else. I didn't even notice that it's now my turn to do a eulogy. I take a deep breath, trying to tame my growing nerves, stand up, and smooth my dress as I walk in the direction of the podium. Standing behind the lectern, I adjust the microphone to my height, and take from the inner pocket of my blazer the sheet of paper where I wrote my speech, putting it in front of me.

"Good morning," I greet, looking around the room, especially at my dad, Emma, and Matt. Familiar and friendly faces make it easier to speak and helps me calm down. "Thank you everyone for joining me as we say goodbye to my mother, Tess Hagen." Everyone smiles at me, and I briefly check my notes, before proceeding. "I am very grateful that this room is filled with so many people that knew and cared for her."

Well, except my in-laws, but I digress.

"Seeing the tremendous love and support here for her is humbling and inspiring." I pause and take a breath. "Truthfully, Mom and I didn't have the best relationship. In fact, we had many disagreements, yet, despite all our ups and downs, she was the most determined person I have ever known. She fought tooth and nail to protect the most vulnerable ones in society, which is why she dedicated her life to her nonprofit."

I look at Carice who is seated in the second row with a few other women—most likely colleagues of hers from the nonprofit—but I didn't have time to talk to them, so I can't be a hundred percent sure. However they all look pretty emotional, and I can only conclude they were quite close to Mom.

"Although we had our differences, I learned some incredible lessons from her about love, strength, determination, and sacrifice." My attention suddenly goes to the entrance where I see Maud quietly walking in with her husband. We exchange a quick smile and they sit at the last row. I can't stop wondering why on earth she arrived so late though, but I have to focus on finishing my speech, so I look back at the crowd, take a deep breath to steady myself, and continue.

"Admittedly, this is a very emotional and challenging time for me. I've struggled to understand and accept this situation. Losing your mom is a deeply painful experience, especially at such a young age. It comes with a hurricane of emotions, along with never-ending trials of processing and reflection."

And especially when she gets abducted and killed by those seated in this very room.

"My mind wants to reject it all. But this is the reality. My mom is no longer with us in this world." I turn the page on my notes, my heart growing heavier as the words I said sink in. "I don't know how you can summarize or speak of an entire person's life. There are so many intricacies. People are dynamic and their relationship with the world is infinitely complex. My mom was a unique human who was more than any of us can fully comprehend or speak to."

* * *

Once the memorial service is over, the staff members close the coffin and start carrying it out of the terrace and down the pathway that leads to her grave. As we step outside, fortunately the rain has stopped—at least momentarily. The sky is of a dark gray that looks just as sad and gloomy as I am. For the sake of precaution, Dad takes his umbrella with him and we follow closely behind Mom, slowly crossing the gardens that stretch for quite a distance.

"What a great speech," Emma praises in a low voice. "Honestly it was wonderful."

"Thanks," I say, matching her discretion. Once we are all walking on the pathway, I glance around and ask in a whisper, "Have you seen him yet?"

Emma heaves a sigh, looking to her right and left. "No, I haven't."

Wow. There are no words to describe the disappointment and pain I feel for Alex not showing up. Even his mom and sisters are here. What's wrong with him?

Emma puts a hand on my back and starts rubbing it to give me some strength. "I'm sure there's a reason why he didn't come."

Oh yes, I know the reason—he hates me for what I did on the day of his arrest. But Emma doesn't need to know that.

A few minutes later, we finally surround the grave where the staff members put the coffin on the casket-lowering device and press a button which makes the casket descend into the ground. As I watch Mom disappearing from my sight, Dad wraps his arm around my shoulders, pulling me closer to him, and presses a kiss on my head.

"Thanks for being here," I tell him as I nestle against him.

"Always," he whispers. The warmth in his voice helps to heal the wounds in my heart. Yet, I wish it'd been Alex doing it instead.

While Father Thomas says a prayer, we start scattering some white petals on her coffin, and my attention goes up to the other side of the grave where a line of people are doing the same. A gasp suddenly rolls off my lips as I catch Alex standing in between them, staring right at me. I blink twice to make sure it's not my mind playing games, but he's still here, wearing a black suit and matching overcoat, his blue eyes piercing right through my heart. Oh gosh, I had missed them so damn much. The seriousness on his face is perfectly adequate for the circumstance; his lips remain in a straight line, concealing all emotions. And despite wanting more than anything to call him aside and talk, I switch my attention to Father Thomas as he finishes blessing the grave and we all say *amen* in sync. Dad and I go and shake his hand, thanking him once more for having come here to host the funeral. Meanwhile guests start talking between themselves since the ceremony is officially over. And before I can start looking for Alex, Carice walks in and gives me a hug, congratulating me for the amazing eulogy I gave. Then she introduces me to the man standing beside her. "Petra, this is Kenneth, the reporter I told you about."

Kenneth bows his head slightly upon hearing his name and extends a hand to shake mine.

"Kenneth, this is Petra—Tess's daughter."

"It's a pleasure meeting you, I'm so sorry for your loss," he says politely as we shake hands. After exchanging a few words, Kenneth slides a hand out of his pocket and takes out his iPhone. "Here is the list of questions I would like to ask you."

After taking his iPhone, I read the seven questions he typed in on his notes app. "Yes, I'm okay with answering them all except numbers four and five." Those were related to Alex and my in-laws and there was no way in hell I was going to talk about them. The rest were perfectly acceptable given the fact they were just about the nonprofit, and Tess Hagen as a mom and a person.

"Oh, okay." Kenneth can't hide his disappointment. "Is there any question I can ask you regarding your relationship with the Van Dierens?"

My brows raise at his blunt move. "Um, I don't have any interest in talking about them at the moment," I tell him, keeping my tone polite. "I can talk about Mom and the future of her nonprofit, but not about them." I look around us, making sure they aren't listening.

Kenneth knows he has no option but to accept my terms if he still wants to land an interview with me. He ponders for an instant, his lips pressing together before he finally accepts. "Okay, that's fine." Yet his tone is filled with frustration. "Shall we go back to the lounge that connects to the terrace? Carice told us we could do it there."

"Yes, sure."

Before we go back inside though, I can't help but scan around the grave to check if Alex is still here. Yet, I only see Dad and Father Thomas, Carice and her colleagues, along with Matt and Eric, and a few other people. I notice my in-laws have also disappeared and I can only come to the conclusion that are all back inside given how cold and unstable the weather is. Hopefully Alex is there with them and it wasn't my imagination fooling me.

*　*　*

The interview has been progressing well and I must say I'm quite proud of my perfectly crafted answers. Some moments were sadder than others, but Kenneth has been an incredible interviewer for the duration of the experience.

"Was your mom's activism an inspiration for you? Did she motivate you in any particular way?"

Oh gosh, I saw that question in his notes, and didn't think much of it, but now... Now I have no idea what to tell him. "Of course. Mom always taught me to fight for what I believe in," I say, knowing the answer is pretty vague, but that's intentional. "I truly admire everything she has accomplished, which is why we'll keep expanding the nonprofit. Her legacy will continue even after her death."

Kenneth nods at me, a small smile playing on his lips. He then looks down at his notes, before proceeding to the next question. "Your husband is currently suspect number one of your mom's homicide. Do you think he or his family have anything to do with it?"

My jaw drops, unable to hide my shock over his move. That question was precisely one of the two I didn't want him to ask! Yet he made all the others before to ensure he had the rest of his interview done. What the fuck? Everything was going so smoothly, why did he have to do that?

"I'm not going to discuss the legal circumstances regarding my husband," I answer him with a tone proper and courteous for the sake of the cameras.

"How is he doing?" he keeps asking, and he sounds genuine and caring but I guess that's bullshit. "Did he come to the funeral like your in-laws did?"

I can't believe he's still insisting! I'm torn between telling him to fuck off or at least telling him that Alex is doing well. No, I can't give him that. I have to put an end to this or it will get worse. So I take a deep breath and say, "I'm sorry, Kenneth, but this interview is over." My tone is not rude, but rather disappointed with his lack of ethics and professionalism. Then I just stand up, smoothing my dress and nod at Carice who walks in to tell him to pack his stuff and go.

CHAPTER 9

Petra Van Gatt

After the disastrous interview with Kenneth, Eric and Matt call me aside and request a meeting with me, but somewhere a bit more private than in the lounge—which is understandable since it connects directly to the terrace where everyone remaining is gathered. Thinking for a moment, I decide to invite them into Alex's office, I mean, our office. After all, it's the perfect place to talk and also an opportunity to go and check if Alex is in there with his family. We cross the hallway, and I notice the door of the study has been left semi-open, which can only mean it's empty. "Here we should be safe," I tell them, seeing the uneasiness in Eric's gaze as he steps inside.

While Matt looks pretty chill, his dad on the other hand, starts checking around the study, his eyes going up to the ceiling and then to the walls. "Are there any cameras around?"

"I don't think so, no," I tell him, slightly amused at how he's roaming across the room, and making sure the sculptures, paintings and books don't have some hidden camera in them.

"Did you manage to talk to my in-laws despite the immunity?" I ask in order to bring Eric back to focus.

"No," Eric answers, looking pretty displeased. "Their lawyer won't let me approach them without a warrant."

While I'd have expected Julia as a judge and her family having an immunity, I didn't know the rest of the Van Dierens would also have access to one. "Maud and Yara too?"

"Yes," he answers. "I did a background check on them and it's incredible how little I could find."

While I'm not sure how he did it, I remember when I tried to Google Alex's family and I, too, found very little info about them.

"They protect themselves way better than your husband does." Then he adds, "But I did found that Maud works for a lab specializing in nano-tech in Germany."

Oh wow! This info could actually help Alex's case and prove he's not guilty, but rather Maud and his family is! Despite my excitement, I try to appear just as stoic, concealing the glimmer of hope that my husband could win this case.

"Yet it's gonna be impossible to have her speak with her immunity."

"So how are you supposed to interview her about those nano-particles found in my mom's body?"

"That's why we need you to do it for us."

"Me?" I ask, my jaw dropping. And as I come to think of it, I add, "Now?"

"Yes," Eric replies, taking something from his pocket. "We don't have time to waste. It's not every day that your in-laws are here."

My eyes narrow at the small rectangular device between his fingers. "What is this?"

"It's a micro voice recorder," Eric explains as he puts it inside the pocket of my blazer. "It can record up to twelve hours of audio non-stop. The audio is automatically stored in the cloud, so you don't have to do anything else."

What? The fact I'm gonna have to wear this audio recorder all day long doesn't sit well with me. "But I thought we'd start taping conversations only *after* the funeral…"

"We'll start now," he says promptly. "Don't forget to charge it every evening."

"And, um, what if I wear something without pockets?"

"You can pin it under your blouse, but be mindful to hide it well," he answers.

"Can you also listen live to it?" I keep asking, given the fact I know nothing about this device.

"Yes, if I connect directly to the app linked to this audio recorder, I can listen to it live."

I share a quick look with Matt, before he says, "Don't worry, if you aren't talking to your husband or his family, you can switch it off. Right?"

"Yes," Eric replies. "We need to have a confession about those nano-particles and also how she escaped—that would be great too."

Before they can start pacing toward the door, I suddenly remember something. "By the way, you never told me about it…" I stare at them, waiting for one of the Bradfords to tell me the truth. Yet, they don't look very excited to do so. "How did she manage to escape?" I ask again as they look at each other. "Mom told you about it, no?"

Eric heaves a sigh as he ponders my question. "According to her, a so called 'Winter' freed her."

I frown at the name; it doesn't ring me a bell. "Who is he?"

"The guy who would bring her food," Matt replies back. "He left the door unlocked, and she left during the day."

"And there were no guards? No one else to stop her?" I ask.

"They felt asleep after Winter placed something in their lunch."

Despite Eric's explanation, I remain just as confused. "But why would the guy who brought her food help her?" I keep asking. "That doesn't make sense."

"That's what we are trying to find out," Eric tells me. "Either Winter freed her because your mom was persuasive and gained his trust, which is what she told us, or he received orders from above to let her go."

From above? I don't see why Margaret, Julia, or anyone else would free her and then kill her a few days later.

A few knocks on the closed door startles me, but I hear Emma's voice on the other side announcing herself, so I tell her to come in. She cracks the door wide and I notice how she tries not to look surprised to find me with Matt and Eric. "Can you come over here for a minute, please?"

"Sure." I step outside the office and Emma closes the door behind us.

Then she leans in and says in a low voice, "He's here. And he wants to talk to you."

My heart jumps from excitement at her words. "Where is he?" I ask immediately.

"In the atelier."

I take Emma in my arms and embrace her tightly. "Thank you for letting me know."

"Good luck," she whispers as she rubs her hand on my back, giving me some much-needed strength.

Then I go back inside the office and start shaking Eric's hand a bit too hurriedly. "Thank you for coming," I tell him, before giving a quick hug to his son. "It was really nice of you both to have come here. I have a few other meetings to attend now."

"Of course." Matt gives me one of his charming smiles. "The pleasure was ours."

Once the Bradfords leave, I instruct Emma to show them the way out, while I go upstairs to my atelier. My heart is hammering inside my chest at the idea we will finally talk after all these days. Plus, this is such a meaningful place for me. After all, that's where I placed the painting he bought me from Pierre Soulages. Damn, and that was nearly two years ago. Incredible how it still feels like yesterday.

As I stand in front of the door, I knock for the sake of courtesy before twisting the handle and cracking the door open. I look instantly to my right side where the painting is hanging and my eyes alight on his back—a white shirt perfectly stretching his wide shoulders, his hands in his pockets as he admires the masterpiece he gave me.

Oh gosh, I can't believe Alex is here. And I have this freaking audio recorder in my pocket. Damn it! He turns around, giving me one of his irresistible smiles. Those that make me melt on the spot. Jeez, I want to be mad at him for everything he did to me, to us, to my mom. I want to hate him, slap him, and tell him to go God knows where… But as my eyes linger on him, standing here in my atelier, all I can do is run in his direction, jump into his arms and let myself cry from exhaustion and pain from everything that happened since Mom died. His embrace is home, and despite everything, it still feels like the right place to be after such a gloomy day.

Familiar to the gesture, Alex doesn't decline me. On the contrary, he wraps his arms around me, holding me tight and I just let my head rest on his chest like I have always done. "Hey," he whispers warmly.

"Hey," I reply, my voice matching his. Amid the silence, I keep my arms clasped around his waist while I take a deep breath in and out, trying to tame my loud beats. Then I look him in the eye, but he keeps an expression so formal and contained, that I don't kiss him. "Thanks for coming. Um, Ryan said you needed some time off, so I didn't call."

"You did well," he says politely. "How are you feeling? Are you managing to cope with everything?"

I nod, and as Alex releases his arms from me, I do the same. "Emma is giving me a hand and, um, Matthew too."

"Good, I'm glad you're doing okay." He sounds so robotic, jeez, I'm not used to talking with him like this, but I play along and adopt the same tone.

"And you?"

"I'm good, waiting for the trial which should start in March."

I close my eyes for a moment, letting his words sink in. Then the day where he got arrested starts replaying in my mind and I know he expects an explanation for what happened there.

"Alex," I say in a whisper, looking him deeply in his blue eyes. "I didn't have a choice, they found her dead body in her hotel room and you were the first suspect they thought of…" I know this conversation is being taped but he needed to know the truth. "When are you coming back home? I miss you so much."

His lips remain in a straight line, revealing nothing. "I'm staying elsewhere for now."

"Why?" My heart takes such a reel at his answer that my lips part as I try to drag some precious air into my lungs. "That doesn't make any sense."

Despite my question, Alex keeps his expression just as contained. "It does for me."

"Why are you doing this?" I ask, my tone coming out more outraged than I expected. "You're my husband, you have to come back."

His eyes drift down for a moment as he considers my question. "Because I can't trust you anymore."

I gasp, his words crashing me to the core. "What do you mean?"

"You know what I mean." And there's no need to ask anything further, because I read the answer in his gaze.

I don't know how he found out, but I knew sooner or later he would, so I just tell him the rest. "I didn't have a choice."

"We all do, Petra," he ripostes flatly.

"I didn't!" I snap back. And before we get into a useless argument that would bring further division between us, I focus on what truly matters to me. "Please, come back home," I plead softly, reaching for his collar. "I don't care if you don't talk to me, but at least come back."

"Are you gonna testify against me?"

His question is enough to paralyze my entire body, I drop my gaze to the floor, searching for the best words to put on, but there are none. "I…"

Alex removes my hands from him like I have the plague and takes a step back. "If you need anything, you may contact my attorney."

I can't blink, I can't move, I'm totally numb at his formal and harsh attitude toward me. He's behaving like we aren't even married anymore, like we are some sort of strangers.

"See you in court, Ms. Van Gatt."

My lips part, unable to hide my disappointment. The tears are resting on my eyelids as I watch Alex walking past me, ready to leave this conversation behind.

"So are we done?" My question hangs in the air, making him stop mid way. And I'm glad it did. "After everything we went through, you want to break up now?" My mind is blank, my heart barely beating, my ears barely wanting to hear his answer.

Alex turns around, rubbing his eyelids tiredly, before looking me in the eye from where he is, and sounding defeated, he says, "I don't think I can forgive such a betrayal."

"You killed my mom!" I remind him.

"I didn't," he ripostes. Then he starts marching back toward me and says, "They have nothing to prove that I did. Did I have motives? Yes, I had, just like you did, but I didn't kill her." He pauses to calm himself down while he stands right in front of me. "I didn't even know about the nano-particles in her body until your dad told me about them."

I smile internally, knowing this is also being taped. Well, if they expected a confession, the only one they will get is that he is innocent.

Looking him straight in the eye, I ask, "So who did it?"

"I don't know." I'm sure he knows that it's his family—his mom, his sisters, maybe Sebastian—but Alex will never denounce them, and that might be a problem in court. Since he has already spoken enough about the case, I focus the conversation on us, because to me, that's what I'm here for. "Can't we forgive each other and move forward?"

My eyes never leave his, yet Alex starts looking in the void as he considers me. Finally his eyes meet mine, yet his face is just as emotionless as before. "Once the case is over, I'll reassess our situation."

"Our *situation*?" I don't hide the astonishment in my tone, and then I just huff at him. "Well, when it comes to *our situation* I have something to tell you first." Alex frowns, cocking his head to the side, and waits patiently for me to do so. Oh boy… I wanted to play tough but now I have to go through it until the end. I've got no idea how he'll react, but I can only hope he won't react like last time. I take a deep breath in and out, before making him one single question. "Do you mind coming with me to the next prenatal appointment?"

Alex creases his brows, looking at me with narrowed eyes. "What?"

His confusion was expected, so I explain further. "I had a prenatal checkup two days ago…" Then I swallow the lump in my throat, my eyes meeting his again, and I tell him the rest. "I'm expecting twins."

His eyes widen in shock while his lips part. "Twins?"

"But there are some complications and, um, one might not survive…" I heave a sigh, knowing I finally told him the most important and hardest part. "I'm not telling you this for you to stay with me if you don't want to. I just want you to be present as a father. That's it."

Alex stares away in the void for a moment, processing everything I just told him. Then he looks back at me but his expression is just as lost as before. "You are pregnant?"

Now I'm the one frowning at him in confusion. Did he listen to anything I said or what? "Yes…"

"With twins?" he repeats.

"Yes," I answer again in a chuckle.

"Are you serious?" Alex seems to be under a wave of shock as he remains gaping and looking at me like he's barely here.

A laugh escapes me because I wish I could record his face right now. "I am."

"How many weeks are you in?" he finally asks, his expression softening.

"Um, fourteen," I reply. And since he looks so weird and lost, I add, "I have the ultrasounds in case you want—"

"You are *really* pregnant?"

Oh gosh! Is he okay? I nod, unsure what else to do if not confirming once more the reality. "Yes, I am." I can't contain the amusement in my tone at how funny his expression is becoming though.

There's something in his gaze that switches. "Oh my God…" To my surprise, he pulls me to him, embracing me tightly. "I still can't believe it," I hear him saying in a whisper.

"Are you happy?"

"So much so."

My pulse is bouncing hard at his words. This wasn't really planned but I'm glad I told him, anyway. I'm not sure if it's because of our past loss or not, but I can hear him sniffling, which I rarely do.

"After such a shitty week, finally some good news."

I can't help but chuckle as I remain in his embrace which is definitely longer than the first one.

Then as he releases me, I notice he is way more relaxed than before, so I take the plunge and ask, "And, um, can you move back home, please? Without you there, it won't be the same."

"I'll be a father," he says, meeting my eyes. "I want to be present at all the checkups, meetings, and I can't wait to meet our kids…" His gaze goes briefly to my belly before meeting mine again. "But that doesn't mean I'm moving back in."

"What?" The word barely escapes my throat as my heart stops for a moment. And I gasp for air, oxygen, love, anything. I need to breathe but I can't bring myself to. "But why?" I finally say.

"You have chosen your side." His tone is just as severe as before, but it's also unbothered and nonchalant. "It wasn't my decision. It was yours."

"I didn't have any choice!" I bark at him. "They would've made me a suspect if I didn't cooperate."

"We always have a choice," he scoffs. "Always."

I shake my head because it's not how I felt in that moment.

"You should've called me. You should've trusted me. Me— your husband. Not them!" He starts to walk again back to the door so I grab his wrist to make him stop. He turns, looking me in the eye. "Maria will take care of everything you need—"

"The only thing I need is you," I interpose, before stepping closer to him. My eyes are on the verge of tears and I have no idea what I can say or do to change his mind. If the pregnancy didn't, then I don't know what else will.

"I can't come back," he says once more, his voice as low as a whisper. I close my eyes tight, but a tear starts coursing down my cheek, and to my surprise, I feel his lips pinning soft kisses on my head trying to soothe me. "Not until the case is over or until you stop cooperating with them."

I wipe my tears away, my heart smashed into a thousand pieces, but I remain just as silent; Alex knows I can't withdraw my cooperation. God knows what they'd use against me if I did.

"I love you," he whispers. "And I want to believe we'll get through this." He then pauses and takes a long breath. "But for the sake of keeping my sanity, I need to be away."

Despite wanting to persuade him once more, I don't argue —Alex knows I will testify in court against him, he knows I'm siding with Eric and he knows I'm recording our conversation. I just hope he truly believes we can get through this as he says. I too want to believe we can. Or at least my stupid heart does.

Nevertheless, I try to get one last concession from him. "Did you know today is Valentine's Day?"

As I look up at him, Alex remains just as unimpressed. "And?"

"And can't you at least stay here and have dinner with me?" I ask with pleading eyes and pouting lips.

His face softens with a smile and my heart parts in fury at the sight of it. "I'll see what I can do."

CHAPTER 10

Bedford Hills, February 14, 2021
Alexander Van Dieren

Pregnant. With twins.

I still can't believe it. She told me over and over again and yet here I am still not used to this new reality; my wife is pregnant with twins. It might not be the best time for a pregnancy, but damn, I'm floating on cloud nine at the eventuality we could welcome our first kids in six months time. By then, the case should be closed and no—there's no way in hell that I'll end up in jail. I'm innocent and Eric knows it. That's why he's trying to tear me and Petra apart. He knows I had motives to kill Tess, but that's all he's got. So far he has no concrete evidence that prove I was the one who killed her, which leads me to believe that's the reason why he asked Petra to cooperate with him and why he offered me that deal using the police report as a threat. He knows there's no evidence and no witnesses.

"How are you and Petra?" my mother asks as she sips her drink, comfortably seated in front of me on the sofa. For a split second, I had forgotten I was in the trophy room with her, Yara, and Julia, to discuss some pressing subjects. I know Petra hates this place and with a security agent guarding the door, I'm pretty sure we should be left alone for the next hour.

"Like you and Dad," I say with an ounce of sarcasm.

"Oh, that didn't take long," I hear Yara sniggering just as fast as she remains standing tall by the fireplace.

And as I keep playing along, I add, "The only difference is that she isn't trying to kill me, just putting me in jail, so I guess I'm considered lucky."

"She is?" Julia asks, furrowing her brows as she remains sitting beside Mom. "What do you mean?"

With the exception of Maud who stayed upstairs, I didn't tell the rest of my sisters that Petra is cooperating with the prosecution, but I guess they should know what she is up to. "Petra is taping our conversations in order to find and use evidence against me."

"She is?" Julia looks at me in total disbelief. "How do you know that?"

"Eric told me," I say simply.

Yet Julia keeps creasing her brows in confusion. "But why would he tell you that exactly?"

"I guess to destroy us," I say. "His son, Matthew, is completely in love with her," I disclose. "So the more division Eric creates between us, the closer she'd get to him." And despite knowing this is all a brilliant game for Eric, Petra fell for it instead of staying loyal to me. "Now that I know she's on their side, I have no option but to limit my interactions with her."

"But why has Petra sided with them so easily?" Mom asks, ruminating about everything I told her. "I don't get it."

"Because she knows I lied, she knows her mom was abducted, and she knows one of us killed her."

Mom heaves a long sigh, before taking a sip of her tea. My answer seems to have rendered her speechless.

"That would explain why she doesn't speak to us, then," Julia points out. "She was so distant and cold at the funeral."

"They have no evidence about the latter though," Mom replies, still thinking about what I had just said.

"Correct," I reply. "And Eric knows that."

"Have you found something against him yet?" Julia asks, ruminating about our next move. "You were right—he didn't waste time trying to talk to us once we arrived."

"No, but I've got a few people searching…"

"You know what's at stake," Yara reminds me. "Jan knowing the truth is not an option."

"And neither is me going to jail," I snap back.

"Why don't we simply take care of Eric?" Yara continues.

"Because I'll be suspect number one," I riposte. "This case is all over the news, Yara. If Eric dies, they will think it's me." I pause to take a breath. "And then Matt or Carice can just hand the report to Jan, anyway." As I come to think of it, I say, "Maybe Jan knowing is inevitable at this point…"

"What?" Yara squeaks. "May I remind you that my name is in there?" She turns, facing me as I remain sitting on the armchair. "Jan knows his daughter and I used to hang out together. If he reads that report, he'll know I was the one who took her to that party."

"Well, maybe it's time for everyone to take responsibility for their past mistakes, what do you think of that?"

"Alex," Mom chides. "After everything we have done to protect you, this is how you thank us?"

"You were the one choking her," Yara ripostes, having none of it. "Not me."

But I reply just as fast, "And who was it that introduced her to MDMA, cocaine, and everything else?"

"Enough you two," Mom steps in. Then turning to me she says, "At the end of the day, we have to admit Tess played well. She anticipated her death and made sure someone would continue to blackmail us afterwards."

"Which means her death was totally unnecessary," I tell them. "And who let her go in the first place?"

"Winter," Mom mumbles. "At least our guards told us it was him. He drugged them, and while they were asleep, freed her." She takes a deep breath before finishing her drink. The slight tap of her foot gives away that she's on the edge. "I'm just glad Maud got me that nano-chip to put under her skin before she escaped, or else Tess would've told everything to Jan—and then Eric."

Jeez! It's the first time I hear Mom talking about the nano-particles directly. With concern laced all throughout my features, I add, "And these nano-particles, is there anyway they can link them to you or Maud?"

"Not that I'm aware of," Mom replies, her lips twisting into a smile as she continues observing me.

I feel tempted to look away, but I don't want to give her the benefit of the doubt.

"Don't worry, we have already taken all of the necessary precautions at home. No one is going to bother us there."

Then we all keep quiet as we observe Mom entirely engrossed in her thoughts—as if she's plotting something within that mischievous skull. She rubs her fingertips together for a moment before continuing her spiel.

"We need leverage on that Eric—something strong enough that will make him drop the report once and for all." *Well yeah, duh, that I know.* "Yara, when is the initiation ceremony in Venice?"

"Next Saturday," she answers. "Why?"

"Do you think we can get a list of all the members attending?" Mom asks, her expression just as thoughtful. "If we manage to find anyone on that list who is linked to Eric we can have leverage on him."

"I should be able to get that," Yara tells Mom, before her eyes drift back to me. "Fortunately one of us is still part of the club and can save us all."

Instead of going along with my sister's remarks, I simply say, "I'll put you in touch with my team. They should be able to help and identify which member can give us the most leverage."

"Yara," Mom says, her tone steady. "Be fast, okay? Time isn't in our favor."

"Don't worry, I'll have a copy of the guest list very soon."

"When is your trial?" Mom asks.

"March sixteenth," I tell her. "But Eric wants to give the report to Jan before that."

"When?"

I give a glance at my watch. "In precisely eight days."

"Fuck," Yara utters, before taking out her iPhone and typing something on it.

Mom, on the other hand, does her best to conceal her astonishment at how short our time to convince Eric to drop the report is. "Well, let's just hope one of his close friends is attending the ceremony." Then she stands up from the sofa and Julia does the same.

"By Tuesday I should have the list," Yara replies as we all start heading out.

I open the door, and my sisters are the first to step outside, then Mom stops in front of me and nods at my sisters, so they keep going.

Once we are left alone, Mom says, "It's Valentine's Day today." I'm quite surprised that she knows that, but I keep my face just as unreadable. "Whatever is happening between you and your wife, you should put it aside for tonight."

"I don't know if it's prudent."

"Alex..." She reaches my cheek, stroking it with the back of her fingers. "Even in times of war, enemies can dine together."

I wonder if Mom spoke to Petra about it, but I refrain myself from asking. Instead, I just smile politely and say, "I'll think about it."

* * *

To my surprise, as Mom and I reach the terrace, I find Petra surrounded by Carice and her horde of minions, while the rest of my family and Roy are on the other side of the terrace as far as they can get from them. The funeral has been over for two hours now and it's already early afternoon, so why on earth are Carice and her friends still here? Even Father Thomas and the Bradfords already left.

"Are they having lunch with us?" Maria discreetly asks as we both remain staring at them.

"They're not supposed to." I ponder for a moment if I should invite the living version of Tess Hagen to have lunch with us or not. With a smile on my lips, I decide to go and talk to them. As I approach Carice and her group, I notice how their expressions switch from joyful to annoyed in a split second. "Carice," I greet, standing in front of her. "It's great having you here with us." I can't prevent the sarcasm in my tone though. "Do you and your friends want to stay and have lunch with us?"

"Thank you for the invitation," she replies with a fake smile. "But we were just saying goodbye."

"Oh, what a pity…" By the look on her face, Carice is expecting me to go away and leave them alone so they can spend the next hour doing some more tittle-tattle, but I don't. I remain standing here, waiting patiently for her and her crew to leave. Knowing there is no escape, each one of them gives a hug to my wife and one of the security agents escorts them back to their cars so they can leave the property once and for all.

Standing finally alone with Petra, I want to be playful and make some kind of joke about Carice, but I recall that she might have a recorder taping our conversation, so I bite my tongue and say instead, "Are you hungry? Maria made slow-roasted aubergine with tamarind."

"I'm starving," she corrects, before she holds my arm and we head together to the dining room where everyone is already sitting.

It reminds me of the dinner we had on Christmas Day, the first time she met my family. From her side, there was only her dad in attendance and today, with the exception of Emma, is quite similar. Jeez, time flies so fast.

As we sit beside each other, I try to catch what the current subject is that's being discussed at the table. Not surprisingly, they are discussing just mundane stuff—at this point, they all know Petra is a mole, so the conversation is as superficial as it gets. Yara is entertaining everyone talking about her last polo game in St. Moritz, as well as her new cover and interview in *Polo&Lifestyle,* and while everyone seems pretty excited, I can't help but wonder if Petra is going to switch the subject and talk about either her mom's death, abduction, the funeral, or even make an announcement about her pregnancy. But no—Petra doesn't do any of that. Instead, she starts talking to Emma, who's sitting beside her, avoiding Julia like the plague, even though she is sitting right in front of us. Well, I can't really blame her—after everything my sisters did, I'm sure Petra sees them in a very different light than back when she met them originally.

***

As the luncheon comes to an end, Petra hasn't mentioned anything about her mom, nor about her pregnancy. She spent most of her time speaking to Emma, like she was the only person worthy of her attention. I shouldn't have minded the fact she has been ignoring us as if we weren't here, yet, as I look at her hand resting on the table and so close to mine, I can't help but feel tempted to be affectionate and take it onto my palm. *Jeez, so pathetic…* I can't forget what she did for fuck's sake! If I let my heart have its way, I will lose sight of reality and embrace only illusion, pain, and deception.

My wife is gonna testily against me, I remind myself. *She's gonna screw me over and destroy my reputation.*

And that is the sad truth. Sooner or later, when the day of my trial comes, Petra is gonna sit in the witness chair, and portray me like a monster to the delights of Eric and the media. Suddenly, as a new voice echoes around the room, my attention goes back to Mom who is saying something I'm working to piece together. As she speaks though, I remember what she told me during our meeting before lunch, *"Even in times of war, enemies can dine together."* Should I really dine with Petra despite everything she did? I mean, she did bury her own mother today, so maybe I can make an exception and have dinner with her… But why does she want to have dinner with me in the first place? Is it because she loves me or because she wants to tape our conversation and pry info out of me? That's the problem when there's no longer trust in a marriage. I don't even know if my own wife has an ulterior motive for asking me to dine with her.

Roy, who's sitting beside me, discreetly leans in and asks in a low voice, "Can we have a word in your office?"

My brows crease at the nervousness in his tone, but I just nod, already wondering what he's up to. Since we have already finished our coffees and the lunch is officially over, we excuse ourselves as we stand up. I look at Mom especially, avoiding turning my head to the other side as I leave the table—I want my wife to feel just as ignored as I felt during the whole lunch. A small payback but still something.

Roy and I might be crossing the corridor in total silence, yet I can sense how troubled he is, especially with his accelerated breathing. After inviting him into my office and closing the door behind us, I wait patiently for him to start the conversation, but Roy seems far away—totally engrossed in his own thoughts.

I notice how he roams around the office, like he's lost for words or an old, lost pair of glasses. Then he finally looks at me and all of a sudden asks, "Do I have any reason to be worried?"

"You?" I can't prevent the astonishment in my voice.

"Well, yes, Eric barely spoke to me today." He pauses, heaving a sigh. "He's been talking a lot to my daughter but not me."

"Oh, what a lovely friend he is," I say before taking a seat on the armchair—I've got the feeling this is gonna be a long talk.

"He can't give that report to Jan or to the court," Roy presses, his tone anxious. "We need to do something." My lips suddenly twist at his words. "You have a plan, right?"

"Relax," I tell him despite knowing it will be in vain. "I do have one, yes."

He narrows his eyes, looking at me intently. Since I don't press any further, he asks, "And what is it?"

A quick chuckle escapes me seeing him so nervous. "Let me worry about it, alright?"

As I expected, my answer doesn't satisfy him. "Are you sure?" He steps closer to me before sitting on the edge of the leather sofa, looking as if he's going to teeter off the edge. "You don't want my help to ensure Eric won't share that report to anyone?"

My lips curve downwards, truly impressed at how willing he is to go against Eric. What a big contrast from last year when they seemed so close. "What if he learns you are helping me out though? I don't want to bring you any trouble."

"He wants to give that report to Jan and the court," Roy reminds me promptly. "He's my enemy as much as he is yours now."

I nod in agreement, but that's not a reason for me to tell him the plan Yara and I have in mind—the less other people know, the better.

Aiming for a steadier tone to reassure him, I say, "I'm working on that. Eric won't give that report to anyone."

"Good," he utters simply, his eyes drifting down as he ponders my words. "By the way," he looks back at me, his voice sounding rather uncomfortable. "I know this is none of my business but…" He presses his lips tight as he considers whether or not he should go ahead with his question. "Have you spoken to Petra yet?"

For some reason, I was expecting that one. "I did."

"And?"

Since I'm not interested in giving him the gritty details of my marriage, I simply play along. "And what?"

"Are you still mad at her?"

"I'm not mad," I say as I search for a better set of words. "I'm just keeping my distance."

Roy, on the other hand, can't keep his astonishment out of his face and I knew I should've closed this subject as soon he got started with it. After all, my relationship with his daughter is a private matter and it should be kept that way. "But why? I don't get it."

I heave a long sigh, annoyed at his persistence. But for better or worse, I tell him the truth. "Because she's not only taping our conversations, but she's also gonna testify against me in court." His jaw drops slightly, but he closes it just as fast, and not wanting me to see the shock in his eyes, he looks down at his lap for a moment. "So as you may understand, she's the last person I want to be around."

After a while, his attention goes back to me. "But why is she doing that?" he asks, looking visibly confused.

"For immunity," I answer. "Otherwise she would've been arrested just like me."

"What?" Roy breathes out, now totally perplexed. "You mean, what you are going through could have happened to her too?"

"Yep," I say, reveling at his realization of how twisted Eric can be. "By what she told me, it was either being with them or against them."

Roy starts shaking his head. "I can't believe it…"

"She made a pledge in front of a camera so believe me—it's true."

"Jeez," he fesses out. "Eric is just doing it to destroy your marriage. You can't let him win."

"I know, yet Petra made her choice, and she chose betrayal instead of loyalty."

"You think being coerced is having a choice?" he asks straight away, annoyance thick in his tone.

I knew Roy would side with her, he just can't help himself. I mean, as I think of it, I'd probably do the same if I was talking to the husband of my own daughter. So after measuring carefully my next set of words, I say, "Roy, I love her and you know that, but I have to safeguard myself—I don't know how dirty she's gonna play against me." And I hope we can close this subject once and for all and move on.

"When is your trial?" he asks, most likely thinking something through.

"The first session in court is March sixteenth." I look at him as he considers me, and then adds, "Eric is gonna do everything he can to push her to portray me as a monster to the jury and media." I cut eye contact, my mind already picturing that dreadful moment. "At the end of the day, it's up to her to go ahead with his plan or not."

Roy doesn't say anything more; after all, I think I made myself quite clear. He heaves a long sigh, understanding better my situation—of course I love my wife, but right now she has decided to be a prawn in Eric's game to save herself, and only after her testimony I can fully assess how willing she is in putting me behind bars. "Do you know who did it?"

"I don't," I say instantly. "And I'm not interested in finding out. All I know is that I have nothing to do with the death of her mother."

Roy nods as he processes my answers while I stand up, thinking the meeting is about to end. He does the same, yet he seems to be ruminating about something else. "Are you gonna keep living in that private residence?"

My lips twitch into a smile at his curiosity. Why on earth is he so concerned about that? "I will."

He shakes his head in disapproval. "You can live under the same roof and simply not talk about your trial and her mom's death you know."

"Roy," my tone is now more assertive. I put a hand on his shoulder and say, "I appreciate your concern over my marriage, but I know what's best for me."

"That's not how marriage works."

Oh, the divorced man thinks he is an expert on the subject now? The irony...

"It's not about what is best for *you*, it's what is best for *you both*." His words sink into me in a way I wasn't expecting. "Is it the best for you both, or just for you?"

I take a deep breath in and out, thinking about an answer to his question. Truthfully though, that's a question for which I don't find an answer.

* * *

Despite knowing perfectly well that Petra betrayed my trust and stated out loud that she is siding with the Bradfords, my stomach still manages to flip in thrill as I see her emerging onto the terrace for our dinner. Jeez, she is so mesmerizing with her dark-red dress; it reminds me of the one she wore in Rome for our first date, even though technically it wasn't one. My eyes slowly linger from her chest down to her waist and then her legs and a smile settles on my lips at how it molds her body so perfectly.

"Wow!" she utters as she takes in her surroundings. Her eyes share the same glitter as the garland of string-lights hanging from one side of the ceiling to the other, and like an idiot I can't stop staring at her glowing face, then at the natural swing in her hips as she walks closer to the table to observe the romantic dining set. She turns around, her gaze finally landing on me and she asks, "Where's everybody else?"

"I kicked them out," I answer without an ounce of guilt. As I start slowly pacing in her direction, my eyes fall at her lips and I realize I haven't kissed them since the arrest. But I blink, my eyes returning up to meet hers.

"But I thought your family would be having dinner with us?"

Given the fact I had told her we'd be having dinner with my family after the meeting with her dad, I understand her astonishment. "I changed my mind," I lie. I never intended to have them over for dinner; I just wanted to surprise her. "Are you that disappointed to have dinner only with me?"

Her lips twist into a smile I haven't seen in a long time. "No, on the contrary," and her smile keeps growing beautifully across her face. "I just didn't expect you'd be okay with having a private dinner with me."

Not wanting to show her how excited I am to have her here alone, I go and take the bottle from the ice bucket and start opening it. "I wanted us to celebrate your pregnancy," I tell her for the sake of having a reason to accept her invitation. As I start filling our flutes, I notice she narrows her eyes on the bottle, so I add, "Don't worry it's Champomy."

"Oh, that's what I used to drink when I was a kid."

"Well, that's also the ideal fizzy beverage to keep myself sober." And to make sure I won't start flirting with her because to me this is a civil and cordial celebration, that's it. I give her a glass, yet her expression is filled with concern.

"We still have so many months ahead though," she tells me, sounding worried. "I'm scared to be happy and then…"

"Hey," I cup her face with my right hand, softly stroking my thumb on her cheek. "The two are alive now, no?"

"Despite one being smaller than it should be, yeah, they are."

"So let's take it day by day," I suggest. "And today we have a good reason to celebrate."

"You are right."

Oh, am I? It's not very often she says that. I should write that down.

"It's much better to fill my head with positive thoughts."

Undecided whether to make a toast to the babies or to her, I ponder for a few instants, and a smirk plays on my lips as I predict her reaction. "A toast," I say, raising my glass. "To my dear wife, the woman I love and hate at the same time."

Petra shakes her head, huffing at my words exactly like I thought she would. Teasing her is just too priceless. "How funny," she replies sarcastically. "To my husband, the man I can neither live with, nor without."

"What a cliché," I comment, before we clink our glasses.

Then we quietly give our first sip to what tastes like fizzy apple juice.

"I brought something for you."

Petra rests her glass on the table and takes something from her clutch. Then she hands me a few small photographs and as my eyes land on the images, I can't help but say, "Oh my…" Jeez, it's something to know your wife is pregnant, but it's definitely something else looking at the ultrasound pictures. "They are so tiny." Truthfully, they look like white peanuts in the picture.

"I told you." Her voice is sweet and melodic, warming up my heart at the simple sound of it. She then points to the bigger one. "That's Baby A, and that's Baby B, the smaller one."

"Did the OB tell you the delivery date yet?"

"No." She pauses for a beat, heaving a sigh. "She wants me first to check with the fetal surgeon before giving me a date."

Seeing the distress on her face, I bring her into my arms, giving her a kiss on the head. "I'm sure everything will go fine." While I'm saying that to reassure her, I genuinely hope that this pregnancy won't end up like the last one.

Suddenly, Maria walks in, carrying two plates. We then go and sit, while she places the dishes in front of each of us. Petra wets her lips, her eyes already widening at the food. "Oh, mushroom risotto, it looks delicious."

"I figured you'd like it." I thank Maria who then returns inside.

"I missed this," she says, her voice low and soft.

"You mean the risotto?" I ask, humoring her.

"No," she answers with a chuckle as she takes her first bite. "I missed having dinner with you." She then presses her lips tight, thinking something through. "We used to have dinner every night at six-thirty sharp, and then breakfast every morning on the terrace…" Her lips curve up as she recalls those memories, and mine too. "Home without you is not the same."

She then lets out a sigh and sips her drink. There's something in her expression that makes my heart ache; it's like I can feel the pain she is feeling.

Her nostalgia has rendered me speechless. I'm not even sure if she is taping this conversation or not. That's the problem with my wife; I simply cannot trust her. I have to remind myself that right now Petra is the enemy—she is cooperating with Eric and will testify in court against me. That is the reality. Yes, she is divine in this dress, and yes she is telling me sweet words that make my heart flutter, but right now, I can't lose focus of what this is all about. "You know why I'm doing this," I tell her, eye on eye. "Choices have consequences."

She cuts eye contact, taking a deep breath in. Then she stands from her chair, paces slowly around the table, her hips deliciously swinging as she does so, and to my surprise, she deliberately sits on my lap, her arms wrapping around my neck, while her jasmine perfume hits my nose, reminding me of so many good memories.

"If we have a girl, we have to call her Jasmine," I find myself telling her.

Her eyebrows raise in surprise at my unexpected comment. "You were thinking about baby names?"

"Not really, but each time I see or smell jasmine, it reminds me of you," I confess, containing the urge to kiss her bare neck. "So if we have a daughter I'd love to give her a name that reminds me of her mother."

There's a twinkle in her eye as I say those words. "Jasmine is a beautiful name," she says, her full lips smiling at me. "But please, no baby showers, no nurseries, nothing until they are born."

I can't keep the astonishment out of my face at her request. "Are you that scared something will happen?"

"Yes," she mutters. "I just don't want us to get too attached until they are here." She pauses for a beat, before adding, "And, um, don't tell anyone I'm pregnant, there's no need for that."

"No one knows but me?" I ask, surprised. "You didn't even tell Emma?"

"No one except Matt knows."

A laugh rolls off my mouth and I say, "The boy who has a crush on you knows? Poor guy…"

"I'm sure he's already moved on," she replies just as fast, but she doesn't really sound convincing. "He's quite happy for me."

"He doesn't seem like a bad person," I tell her and I truly mean it. "A pity his dad is who he is."

"And if we have a boy, do you have any name in mind?"

I twitch my lips, thinking about it. Suddenly though, Petra quietly starts unbuttoning my shirt, before sliding her hand on my bare chest. I haven't felt her touch for days and the simple sensation of having her here is making me grow hard. I know why she is doing it… But I ignore her and remain just as focused on searching a name I'd like if we have a son, yet none is coming to mind. Meanwhile her lips start lingering slowly on my neck, before she traces wet kisses all the way up to my cheek. *Jeez, this is getting out of hand.*

"Petra," I say, making her stop.

"Mm?" she murmurs, already pulling my lower lip with her teeth.

Looking her eye in the eye, a smirk arises as I ask, "Are you trying to seduce me so that I sleep with you tonight?"

Her face grows red at my blunt question, and her lips twist into one hell of a sexy line. "Well, you aren't going back to Manhattan, are you? It's too late for that."

A chuckle escapes me at her answer. "There are six bedrooms in this house though."

She heaves a sigh in displeasure looking downwards for a second, before meeting my eyes again. "Why are you playing so hard to get?"

I shake my head, quite amused at her sweet little voice; I just love seeing her so annoyed and desperate. "Because you played me a few days ago. Remember?"

"Are you gonna hold a grudge against me forever?" she asks, her face inches away from mine. "You hid so many things from me, yet I forgave you."

"The things I hid from you were to protect us." Including the abduction of her mom—if Petra knew about it she would've been considered an accomplice, and it'd have put her in trouble. Yet, I don't know if we are being taped or not, so I refrain from telling her that.

"What is done is done," she says softly, her lips brushing against my cheek. I wonder if she can feel my boner against her ass or not. Before I can worry about it any further, she leans down to my ear and whispers, "Can't you just forget what happened for tonight?"

I scoff, half-tempted by her invitation. Being this close to her and having this type of conversation causes my heart to patter against my ribs. My hand goes to cup the back of her head, and as I look deeply into the infinite blue of her eyes, all I can see is my downfall and the pain that lies ahead of me. *She is your enemy*, I remind myself. *She's gonna destroy you.* Yet, before I can cool down, Petra closes the small gap between us, pressing her delicious lips on mine. Fuck… Her kiss dispels any rational thought out of me, and all I can do is shut my eyes and think about how in her arms, I'm home. Maybe for tonight I can forget what she has done, maybe for tonight I can let myself go. She deepens our kiss, her arms tightening around my neck and her tongue slips inside my mouth, sensually fondling mine, leaving my body to prickle with heat. She moans at the connection, making my boner harder than granite. I was not ready for the passion in her kiss, the heady sensations of her touch, and the way her love can make me forget everything but us. Her tongue twirls around mine with pleasure and need, mounting the desire between us. A grunt rolls off my throat as I finish our kiss. Her lips are swollen and wet, but my mouth goes down to her neck and without thinking twice, I tug on her flesh, sucking and blowing on it. I have missed it, I have missed every bit of it. The way she tilts her head back, giving me free access to her bare skin fills me with rapture and I deepen the suction until her flesh gets a beautiful purple mark.

"Ahh," I hear her whimpering, before she presses her fingers directly on the hickey. "You missed me that much?"

Amid our loud beats, her question is barely audible, but her sweet little voice resonates though me and my heart nearly suffocates as I picture everything else I want to do to her.

My thumb goes to her full, kissable lips where I pull her lower one, making her gasp with pleasure at the touch.

"Yes," I breathe as I watch her lips parting for me. Then I squeeze them between my fingers, before slamming her mouth on mine in a hungry despair to devour her. *I can have her for tonight, just tonight…* and tomorrow I will go back to my private residence.

After breaking our kiss, she wets her lips, stands up from my lap, and takes me by the hand. I raise from my seat, and she starts leading me back inside the house and then upstairs. And I know exactly where she is taking me…

As we climb the stairs, I watch her hips swinging and tempting me hard. I lick my lower lip picturing undressing her and roaming my hands all over her smooth skin. Jeez, I wanted to play hard, but I failed miserably. Tomorrow she'll go back to the condo and we won't see each other for a while, so tonight it will be like we're saying goodbye.

Then, we walk through the hallway, until we reach the door of our bedroom. Without thinking twice, she twists the handle and cracks the door open. She turns and looks at me before reaching for my ear and whispering, "Just tonight."

CHAPTER 11

Bedford Hills, February 15, 2021
Petra Van Gatt

I shouldn't be surprised to wake up in an empty bed. After all, I know Alex loves to get up early. Yet, after seven days living in separate places and sleeping apart, I thought this time he'd make an exception. But rather than spend the morning with me, spooning or cuddling in bed, he thought it would be better to leave me alone—most likely to serve as a reminder of what my future is gonna look like. I shouldn't care about it. He betrayed my trust so many times that he doesn't deserve any of my sympathy. And yet… I'm not sure if it's because of the pregnancy, the hormones, or the fact we made love until the early hours of the morning, but I can't find the will to keep my distance from him. My heart wants us to be together, turn the page, and start all over. *Oh for fuck's sake! Stop being stupid!*

I heave a long sigh, before stretching my arms and legs and focus on reality—he participated in the abduction of my mom, hid it from me, lied, and now she's dead because of him. That's what I have to remind myself of. Then my mind goes to the audio recorder that I left inside my blazer yesterday before putting on my dress and I wonder if I should take it with me for breakfast or not. I feel conflicted; on one hand, Eric asked me to provide taped conversations, but on the other, he didn't really give me any specifics. He didn't say how many conversations I should provide or how many hours of audio, and he didn't mention if I should be recording all the time or not. He doesn't have to know I spent the evening and the morning with my husband entirely off record…

All of a sudden, the ringtone of my iPhone echoes across the bedroom, startling me. I take it from the nightstand and check who's calling so early in the morning.

What? Eric Bradford? Damn it! A gush of air rolls off my lips as I glance around the room to make sure that I'm totally alone. Then I answer the call and bring the phone to my ear. "Hello?"

"Hi Petra." He sounds in a rush and knowing him as I do, I've got the sensation he'll get straight to the point, without wasting any second. "Look, I managed to hear the first conversation you had with him. The sound quality is pretty good."

Holy shit! He already did? Damn, he's really obsessed with this case. And I can't help but wonder if he's really doing it because of Mom or because of the hatred he has for Alex.

"However there's nothing we can use in court."

Oh, because my husband said he was innocent? We technically have a confession but of course it's not the *right one.*

"Why didn't you bring the voice-recorder with you during your dinner with him?"

My eyes widen in surprise at his question, and I wonder how he knows I had dinner with him in the first place. But instead of interrogating him, I quietly say, "I was wearing a dress, and it'd have shown."

"You need to talk to him or to your in-laws about the nanoparticles," he instructs. "If we find who injected them into your mom, it can give us enough evidence that they would be held responsible for her homicide."

I can't stop looking at the door, mortified at the idea of Maria or Alex walking in and seeing me talking to Eric. In order to lower my voice even more, I put my palm in front of my mouth and proceed. "How am I supposed to talk to him about it if he doesn't trust me?" I ask him in a whisper. "It's on the tape he wants to stay away from me."

"I'm sure he'll let down his guard," Eric answers, his tone overly confidant. "The heart can be our worst enemy."

His insinuation doesn't ease me. Unfortunately, I know he's right. Yesterday Alex was already letting his guard down and acting more comfortable around me than he has since this all started. Yet, I don't want to toy with him, I don't want to betray him, despite knowing he deserves it. "I'm not sure if I will see him again." I close my eyes tight, knowing it wasn't my mind talking, but my heart in order to protect him. And I'm pretty sure Eric knows it.

"Of course, you will. I'm sure he'll go with you to all the prenatal appointments. As the pregnancy progresses, he'll be totally smitten."

"I'm sorry?" I can't contain the shock in my voice. "What does that mean?" I ask immediately, hoping it's not what I'm thinking.

"Well, everything regarding your pregnancy will bring him closer to you." It seems like Eric is trying to avoid the subject.

"Yes, but that doesn't mean I'm going to record my private, medical checkups," I tell him, making sure it's not what he had in mind.

Eric draws out a loud breath, most likely displeased. "Fine, but next time you are with him, kindly record it." And just like he usually does, he hangs up without saying goodbye like it's the most natural thing to do.

A gush of air leaves my lungs as I ponder the phone call I just had. Not only can Eric be a fucking asshole because of our agreement, but what will happen if Alex is truly innocent? What if it's his family who killed Mom without him even knowing it? After all, Alex admitted he didn't know about those nanoparticles until my dad told him—and I could tell he was being sincere. If I can get Alex on tape denouncing his family, then Eric might leave him in peace and go after them instead. Decided, I leap off of bed, go take a shower, and put on one of those dresses I know Alex likes, then I spray some jasmine perfume and place the voice-recorder in my bra. I'm not too sure if the sound quality will be good, but this dress doesn't have any pockets, so I don't really have any other choice. After leaving the bedroom, I stumble in on Maria who informs me Alex is on the terrace finishing his breakfast. Oh, it seems like he's enjoying the fact the terrace is now winter-friendly. As I cross the lounge room, I can hear my heart hammering against my ribs. The fact I'm recording our conversations doesn't sit well with me, but if it means finding the truth and getting him out of this mess, then so be it. My eyes fall on him as he's completely engrossed in his iPad, glasses on, and drinking his usual espresso. Despite my best attempt, a quick sigh escapes me as my heart recognizes its owner. I wonder how I will find him today; cold and distant or warm and approachable like last night?

I slowly walk onto the terrace, heading toward the chair in front of him. "Good morning," I say, loud enough for him to hear. "May I have breakfast with you?" I never thought in my entire life I'd be asking my husband for permission to do such a mundane act, and yet here we are. Is it because I feel gullible for recording us? Most likely… Alex looks up at me, his lips in a straight line. Not a good sign.

"Of course," he answers politely. "Have a seat." As I do so, he puts his iPad down, switching his attention to me. "Did you sleep well?"

My eyebrows raise at his question. He doesn't sound angry or mad at me. "I did," I answer while his expression softens with a smile. "And you?"

"I did too, thanks." He brushes that off, like he wants to change the subject to something else. "Petra…" he lets my name trail off as he keeps staring at me.

I wait a bit for him to develop, but Alex seems to be lost for words. "Is everything okay?"

After finishing his espresso, he looks back at me and announces coldly, "What happened last night was a mistake."

Well, that felt like a knife to my chest, but I do my best to conceal my agony and remain just as stoic as he is.

"I don't want to give you the false idea that I'm moving back home or that everything is forgotten because we spent the night together."

While his statement was kinda expected, deep down my heart hoped he'd have changed his mind. My mouth goes dry and yet I don't have the confidence in me to drink from his water, so I just wet my lips and try to find the will to say something. "You're talking like we are just a fling," I point out, my tone laced with annoyance. "May I remind you, we are married."

"I'm not the one who forgot," he says flatly.

I snigger at his ridiculous answer. "It's because of your lies that we are where we are today."

He shakes his head, looking at the void as he thinks something through. "Everything that I did was to protect you."

I can't help but chuckle as I hear him repeating the same thing he said yesterday. "There's always some kind of excuse, huh?"

"You are siding with them and that means I can't trust you."

His words are delivered with the same emotion of a robot. I wonder what changed between last night and today, but I keep quiet. I'm just too sad and disappointed to even talk.

"Whenever you have a prenatal appointment, let me know and I'll go with you, but our interactions will be strictly limited to things related to your pregnancy."

I huff, shaking my head at his formality. My mind starts going to a dark place and then my biggest fear hits me. "And what if something goes wrong while we're apart? You won't even be there for me."

My concern leaves him speechless. And Alex looks away, before heaving a long sigh as he considers me. "If you want, we can hire a midwife to live with you."

Before I can tell him a word or two about having a full-time midwife but not a full-time husband, he asks, "Do you know when your next appointment is?"

"On the twenty-sixth," I grit between my teeth. "Mariana told me I should have a growth scan done every two to three weeks." I look down at my lap as I remember I don't even have a delivery date yet. "We did a few tests the last time I saw her and she'll go through the results that day."

"Petra?" His voice is way more gentle than before. I look up and see how his expression has softened becoming much more empathetic.

"I'll be here for whatever you need." He sounds genuinely concerned. "We aren't living in separate places because I don't care about you."

"The condo has plenty of rooms for you to sleep in," I press, my heart stuck on my throat. "You don't have to live elsewhere."

"I already told you; I can't live under the same roof as you."

Shaking my head, I mutter, "That makes zero sense."

"It does to me," he ripostes just as fast. Then he takes his iPad from the table, leans back on his chair, and starts reading again signaling that he's done talking to me. "Zach will take you back to Manhattan at the end of the day."

His arrogance makes my blood boil and I can't prevent the gap between my lips at his disgusting attitude. "You must be out of your mind," I blurt out.

"Am I?" He rises from his chair and my gaze travels up with him. After crossing the table to stand beside me, he sits slightly on the edge of the table and looking me straight in the eye, he asks, "Aren't you the one recording this conversation?"

Jeez! My heart drops to my knees at his question. Unable to hide the shock out of my face, my eyes drift down to my place setting while I swallow the lump in my throat, not wanting to admit it.

He lets out a breath filled with disappointment. "That's what I thought." And Alex simply leaves, walking back inside the house.

I remain totally paralyzed as I let everything sink in. I feel horrible for what I'm doing to him, and ultimately to us. I'm not sure I'll have the stomach to look him in the eye again after that. What we did yesterday was a mistake and Alex is right—It mixed reasoning and lust, blurring everything for us. I inhale and exhale slowly, trying to accept the fact that until the case is closed, we should keep our distance. I might hate the idea of Alex and I living separated, but at least it's a more honest relationship than being here taping him. I too leave the terrace, heading back to our bedroom in order to gather my things. Eric knows Alex won't talk to me. It's literally on tape, so why would I waste my time here? I remove the device from my bra, feeling pathetic to have accepted this deal in the first place. Jeez, I should've negotiated a better arrangement; one that wouldn't include taping conversations—despite it being legal. I hear a few knocks on the door and as I turn, my eyes meet Maria who seems slightly perplexed as to why I'm packing.

"Um, your breakfast is on the table."

"Oh, thanks, Maria. I'll go down soon," I tell her for the sake of leaving me alone. Once my luggage is ready, I text Zach to come and pick me up, and go downstairs to at least have something in my stomach before returning to Manhattan.

Alone in the backseat, I'm reading a book for one of my on-line courses, and trying to focus deeply on the content and its meaning. All I want is nothing more than to forget what happened between Alex and I since his arrest. Maybe I should just forget that we are together, that would help tremendously. Yet as I look at my left hand and more precisely at the golden band, it feels quite impossible to do so. I heave a sigh, turn the page and keep reading. Amid the quietness of the car, my iPhone starts ringing and I wince, wondering who is calling me. One thing is sure: it's definitely not the man who placed that ring on my finger. Taking my iPhone out, I narrow my eyes as I read the name of my caller. *Why is Carice calling me out of the blue?*

"Yes?" I say as I put the phone against my cheek.

"Petra, I swear I didn't know Kenneth would do that."

My brows crease in confusion at her nervousness. "Huh? What do you mean?"

"Oh," she blurts out. "You haven't seen the article yet?"

"Which article?" My heart starts thundering anxiously knowing Kenneth published something about me and it seems like it isn't a good thing.

"Just forget what I said," Carice presses on. "I thought you knew about the article."

"I insist. Tell me." I hear her heaving a sigh on the other side of the line as she considers my request for a moment. "If you don't, I will Google it and find out, anyway."

"Okay, fine… I just sent it to you."

I go and check on my SMS app and find the link to the article. I click on it and the page loads with the following headline:

"*Exclusive Interview: Petra Van Gatt Buries Mother Amidst Husband Being Suspect Number One.*"

"Why is this in the *New York Post*?" I ask immediately, even more troubled that the interview itself was published via an American news outlet. "I thought Kenneth was a *Dutch* reporter?"

"I think he sold the story to the highest bidder." She sounds sincere and her assumption makes sense, meaning I can't assume she's lying. After all, the whole interview was in English and he didn't even bother to ask me if we could do it in Dutch. "Petra… I truly didn't know he would do that."

While I know Carice is talking to me, I can't help scroll down the article, which has plenty of headshots of Alex, myself, and the funeral. Then there's the video with my interview and I feel tempted to watch it. I might regret it afterwards, but I have to check what she is so upset about. I press play and start watching the video. After a few minutes in, Kenneth asks the first question I didn't want him to.

"*Your husband is currently suspect number one of your mom's homicide. Do you think he or his family have anything to do with it?*"

Holy shit! And to my biggest shock, it's not even my own answer that follows up, but an edited one! "*Of course, but I'm not going to discuss the legal circumstances regarding my husband.*"

I can't believe it! They cut the part where I said *of course* from my previous answer and put it right before I tell them I won't answer it! What a fucking joke this guy is! I can't believe it! I don't even have the original interview with me to show Alex the truth! I know I'd have never said *of course* to this question, that I'm sure. This is fake and edited! My mind is no longer focused on the interview, but on Alex and I wonder if he already saw it or not. "Does Alex know about it?"

"Um, well…" Carice mumbles, quite undecided whether to say the rest or not. "He's the one who told me about the article."

"Fuck," I blurt out, already picturing him hating me right now. With the entire PR team he has at Gatt-Dieren, no wonder they are scanning everything about him. He must have been so disappointed in seeing this.

"Petra, I swear I didn't know Kenneth would do that. I remember perfectly how you insisted about not wanting to talk about the case or your in-laws, and I said that to your husband, by the way."

"Alright, thank you," I say. "I will talk to him now." And without further ado, I hang up.

I don't know if Alex will pick up his phone or not, but it's worth trying. The ringtone goes on and on…

"Hello?" I say as I hear someone breathing on the other side of the line. "Alex?"

"It's about the interview, isn't it?"

The disappointment in his voice petrifies me. Yet, all I can do is swallow the lump in my throat, and tell him the truth. "Look, I understand I gave you plenty of reasons to not trust me. But when it comes to this interview, I swear on everything you want, I never said a word against you or your family. Especially not to the public. My answers have been edited." And I make sure to insist on the latter.

"I trust you on this."

My jaw drops at his answer. He said only four little words, yet they are enough to warm my heart and make me smile.

"I know the media very well, that's why we have a team monitoring the content they publish about us on a daily basis." I heave a sigh, released at his rational attitude. "I called Carice because I know she was the one who arranged the interview. Kenneth is known for hating my family and has spent a big part of his career trashing on us."

"Wow," I utter at the revelation. "I'm sorry, I didn't know about that, otherwise he'd have never set foot at the funeral." As I come to think about Kenneth and his hate to the Van Dierens, I ask, "But why is he so against you all?"

"I don't know. I guess some people just hate us for being who we are."

His words resonate through me so perfectly that I'm left slightly nostalgic about how much I like talking to him. I chew my bottom lip, undecided whether to tell him how much I love him, miss him, but instead of all these ridiculous feelings, I simply say, "I understand. Thank you for siding with me on this." My tone is polite and contained, and that's how it should be. "I, um, I don't want to bother you any further. So have a great day."

"No problem," he answers, matching my courteous tone. "If you need anything else, just let me know."

I need you and I need us to be like we used to be, my heart thinks, but my mouth says, "Sure, thank you. Well, have a good one."

"You too. Bye."

And we hang up, like two rational adults, as if we weren't even married. I take a deep breath, looking out of the window. After everything we are going through, are we ever gonna be the couple we used to be? I want to believe so, even if I shouldn't want to. If Alex is found not guilty, then maybe our relationship still has a shot.

But what if he is found guilty though? What if he is sentenced to imprisonment? Oh gosh, I chase those thoughts away just as fast and bring myself to focus again on my book.

Despite Louise's premonition that our relationship will lead to nothing more than death and misery, I still want to believe in the precise opposite.

CHAPTER 12

Manhattan, February 17, 2021
Petra Van Gatt

"And what did Prof. Reich told you exactly?" I ask Matt, anticipating his answer like my next breath.

Sitting beside me at a table in the library, a smile plays on his lips, most likely because of my curious nature. "Well, he said I should start working on my Master's degree right after graduation and while I'm doing so that I could be a teacher's assistant—which will give me the experience I need if I want to become a prof later on."

"See?" I say joyfully, given the fact I was the one who advised him to talk to Professor Reich. "I told you he'd help you out. Plus with your Youtube channel, it'll be very easy for you to land a job here."

"Yeah, he also said I should submit a senior thesis during my last year and the more I write about subjects I want to teach, the better."

"I can perfectly see you as a prof in fifteen years," I tell him to cheer him up. "You have always been so passionate about research, academia, and teaching. It's gonna suit you perfectly."

"You think?" he asks like it isn't obvious. "It's such a competitive field though. Everyone I know wants to be a prof."

"I'm sure you'll be fine," I reply promptly. "And, um, what subject is it that you'd like to focus on?"

"There are so many; I like Public Economics, but right now I'm having a big crush on Ethics." I nod, sharing the same excitement as him. We might only be in our second year of college, but it's great that Matt is already getting some advice on what to do after graduation. "So I might keep researching on both and we will see." He pauses for a beat and then adds, "The group and I have also launched a blog to write about several subjects in those areas."

"That's impressive," I praise, putting a hand on his arm. "Congrats, I'm glad the talk with Prof. Reich was helpful."

Before my attention can return to my books though, Matt changes the subject to something completely off topic. "By the way, I'm planning a little dinner this Saturday with Sarah, David, and Katrina. There're also a few new friends from my philosophy major who are coming." I can hear the pride in his voice as he speaks. "It's at seven p.m. at my place. You're gonna love it."

I find it amusing that he's already assuming I'm attending his dinner. Maybe I should go. After all, I have nothing booked for the weekend, and Alex made it clear that until the trial is over, he isn't coming back home.

"Okay, sure." I give him a quick smile and my eyes drop to my book in order to keep reading.

"Petra?" But Matt seems to be particularly chatty today, which might explain why we have barely studied anything so far.

"Yeah?" I say, looking up at him again.

"I just wanted to tell you I'm very proud of how you are coping with everything."

Now that was unexpected. My brows furrow in confusion at his compliment. "What do you mean?"

"Well, you know, about the trial, your mom, everything."

His kind words make my lips twist into a smile filled with appreciation. "Thanks," I say, my voice warmer than usual. "It's not easy, but I'm living it day by day."

My eyes are about to dive back into my book, but Matt continues, "Is it true you and Alex are living in separate houses?"

I narrow my eyes at him, slightly surprised at his question. I feel tempted to ask him who told him that, but I recall his dad has been religiously listening to the taped conversations between Alex and I so he must've been the one who shared such info. "Yeah, Alex doesn't want to see me until the case is closed." My gaze travels down as memories from our Valentine's night start filling my head. Jeez, that night was so amazing. He was just as intimate and romantic as he used to be before the arrest. What a big contrast with breakfast the next morning.

"Maybe that's a good thing," Matt ventures.

I shrug, not wanting to engage in further discussion that involves Alex and I. Suddenly, my ringtone starts breaking across the library, making everyone turn in my direction with censoring eyes.

I take my iPhone, turning off the ringtone abruptly. To my surprise, it's Maria calling. Well, that's odd. She rarely calls me. I mean, she *never* calls me. I didn't even know she had my phone number. Since answering the phone in the library is viciously frown upon, I stand up, ready to head outside. "I'll be right back."

Once I reach the outdoors, I call Maria back. "Hi," I say, after hearing her voice from the other side of the line. "Is everything okay?"

"Yara is here," she announces softly. "She'd like to talk to you."

"Yara?" I repeat, barely believing it. "Talk to me?"

"Yes, ma'am," Maria says. "Should I tell her to leave or to wait for you?"

Why on earth would Yara want to talk to me in the first place? Jeez, plus knowing her as I do, she can get physical when displeased. After that face-to-face talk at the Breitner House, meeting her alone isn't really something I look forward to, but I'm just too curious to send her away. Maybe she wants to tell me something about her brother or my mom's death, who knows? "Kindly let her know I'm on my way."

"Very well," she answers before we finish the phone call. Then I message Zach to pick me up and go back inside to pack my stuff.

"I'm gonna have to go," I say to Matt as I shoulder my backpack.

"Every time we meet in the library you run away," he points out in amusement. "It's becoming a ritual by now."

A quick chuckle escapes me. "I know, I'm sorry." I lean in and give him a quick kiss on the cheek. "See ya later."

"See ya Saturday," I hear him correcting me as I walk away.

Arriving at the condo, Maria opens the door for me and before I can even ask her about Yara, she leans in and says, "She's in the pool."

In the pool? I raise my eyebrows in surprise at her answer. Wow. Insane how Yara thinks she can just walk in and behave like she's at home. Okay, granted, she *is* my sister-in-law, but still, I wouldn't dare go to her house for a swim without her permission. For an instant, I wonder if I should go and take the audio recorder to tape our conversation. But, for better or worse, I decide not to; maybe she'll share compromising info about my husband—info that can land him in jail. And despite everything we are going through, I don't want to add more oil to the fire.

I take off my coat and sneakers, and head upstairs, trying to conceal my annoyance at Yara's behavior.

Reaching the pool area, the heat and humidity smack my face, and I'm remembered that I should have put on a bikini before coming here. I stand by the entrance and watch Yara's tall and slim body swimming from one end to the other while she waits for me. The more I observe her, the more it seems like she's inside the water totally naked. No, it can't be. She wouldn't do that...

"You could've texted me first, you know," I shout loud enough for her to hear me.

Yara finally stops swimming, pulls her wet hair out of her face and turns to look in my direction, a smile forming across her lips. In silence, she reaches the stairs and as she climbs them to get out of the water, I avert my gaze just as fast at the sight of her nudity.

"Maria told me my brother hasn't been living here since he got arrested. Is it true?"

What the heck? Why on earth is she asking me that? Despite her audacity, I swallow my frustration and reply politely, "He needs some time alone."

While I don't dare to look at her directly, it seems like she stopped by the sun loungers where her clothes are. Is she grabbing a towel or something?

"Does he?" Now I feel her presence approaching toward me, which might explain why her voice is sounding clearer than before. "Or is it because he doesn't trust you anymore?"

I try to keep my eyes off of her, but it's hard now that she is standing right in front of me. So I force myself to focus on her gaze and ask just as bluntly as her, "What are you doing here, Yara?"

One of the corners of her mouth softly lifts upon hearing her name. "I came here to give you some answers."

I can't hide the shock from my face. "Answers?" I repeat, making sure that's what I heard. "To what?"

"Venice."

A gasp of air expels from my lungs, and I stiffen immediately, unable to hide my astonishment. "How do you know about that?"

"I'm good at knowing things," she says, reveling in my nervousness. "And I know this year is going to be particularly interesting."

"Why?" I ask straight away.

"Maybe you should go and check for yourself." To my greatest surprise, she hands me a papyrus scroll, closed with two wooden rods, and a ribbon in the center. As I remove the ribbon and spread the paper wide, I start reading what seems to be like an invitation:

Il signore e la signora Van Dieren,

Siete cordialmente invitati al Ballo della Luce che si terrà a Palazzo Pisani Moretta, Venezia, il 20 febbraio 2021, alle 21:00.

Codice di abbigliamento: obbligatoria maschera veneziana e abiti da cerimonia per donna e uomo.

Il consiglio

My heart nearly jumps out of my chest as I finish to read the invitation to the ball. There's no signature or name of the host though, except "Il consiglio" which means the council. There's also two crossed keys printed at the header of the invitation. They must represent something but I don't know what. As I pay closer attention, I notice how the keys are beautifully ornamented and quite unique. Each one has a crown and birds with wings at the bow and an "X" at the tip. Then looking up at her dark-brown eyes, I ask, "Is this the party he used to attend with Amanda?"

She observes me with delight, her lips curving up at my curiosity. "It is," she answers.

And for some reason, my intuition tells me this is also the same type of party Janette used to attend. One thing is sure though; this trip could bring Alex and I together and bond us over a part of his past he has tried hard to hide from me. "Are you the host?"

"Nope," she snaps, sounding rather honest. "But since my brother used to attend every year with his ex, I thought you would want to go and check it out for yourself."

"Why are you doing this?" I ask, narrowing my eyes at hers. "I'm sure your brother won't be pleased at knowing you exposed him."

The corners of her mouth twitch into a grin at my words. "He won't be pleased, no," she says, letting out a quick chuckle. "But it's up to you if you tell him it was me or not."

A few moments of silence go by before I say, "What if I do?"

Yara just shrugs, unbothered. "It's all good with me."

I look away, thinking something through, before my eyes meet hers again. "What do you want in exchange? Surely this invitation isn't free."

To my surprise, she bursts out in laughter, and I'm not even sure what to make of her reaction. She seems to genuinely find it funny. "I want you to paint me." My eyes widen at her blunt request. "Naked."

And my jaw drops right after. "Me?"

"Yes, you," she presses on in a suppressed laugh. "My brother told me you are a fine painter."

He did? Now that's even more surprising. "I can paint, but I'm no Ralph Heimans." A slight frown creases her brow, not understanding my joke. So I translate, "I mean, I'm not a master at hyperrealism."

"I'm not interested in hyperrealism," she says. "I want a more..." she looks away, searching for the best words to put on, "romantic version of myself."

Regardless of what she wants, I'm not gonna paint Yara's naked body. That's out of the question. "There are countless nude painters here in New York, why me?"

"Because I don't want anyone else seeing me naked." Instinctively, my eyes dart down at her breasts still wet from her swim. *Petra!* I slap myself mentally for doing so. The unconscious and inappropriate act must have turned my cheeks a sharp shade of red, because I literally feel them heating. "We are sisters, after all." Her voice is sweeter than usual bringing my attention right back to her face. "And you deserve to know what your husband used to do in Venice, no?"

"Even if I go, I'm not sure if Alex will," I disclose.

"I'm sure if he knows you are attending, he'll go too." She sounds quite sure of herself.

I heave a long sigh, considering her offer. "I need around a month and a half to have the painting ready."

"That's okay," she says, her eyes never leaving mine. Her piercing gaze is making me quite uncomfortable, so I move away and go to the lounge chair where her clothes are gathered. "Do you have any idea what kind of position you want?" Since she seems to find the question amusing, I correct myself just as fast. "I mean, for the portrait."

"I do, yes." She walks in my direction and I do my best not to look her way. "Should we go to your atelier so you can take a few pictures?"

How does she even know I have an atelier here? Jeez, it's frightening how much she knows about me. But for the sake of leaving this hot and humid room, I nod and lead the way. "Sure, it's downstairs."

I thought she'd at least put some clothes on before we leave, but nope. Among the clothes that are on the lounger, Yara only grabs a black leather briefcase. Wow. I didn't even notice one was there in the first place.

As we go down the stairs, I can't help wondering if this portrait is a gift for her husband. Maybe it's for his birthday or their wedding anniversary, who knows. As I come to think of it, it's actually a pretty cool idea. Maybe I should do a pregnant portrait of myself and gift it to Alex.

No, forget it—he'd find it pathetic and childish, I think to myself.

Reaching my studio, I turn on the lights, and start organizing the space to make it a bit more presentable. Then I take a clean canvas and put it vertically on the painting board. "Is this size good?"

"It's perfect," she says, before her attention returns to the canvas drying against the wall. Painting has been a great way to destress and forget about my problems, and I must say, I'm particularly proud of my last two pieces. "He's right; you are really talented."

My eyes follow her voice and I find her still scanning through the multiple canvases. "Thanks." Then I check the space available in front of me and say, "For the portrait, do you want to sit, lie on a couch, or remain standing?"

Yara puts her briefcase on a chair that stands at the end of the atelier and takes from there a few accessories before she starts placing one around her neck. Since she has her back to me while putting them on, I can't really see what they are. Against my better judgement, my attention goes to a bright mark right above her butt-cheeks. Wait—this isn't a mark; those are initials.

"You are branded?" The question rolls off my lips, unable to keep the outrage out of my tone.

As she turns to face me, I have pretty much given up on the idea of not looking at her naked. Holy shit! Now Yara is wearing a leather choker collar with a large rose gold "O" ring and matching handcuffs on each wrist. The view is shocking and disturbing to stay the least. How can she be so comfortable with presenting herself like that to me? I do my best to keep an emotionless expression, but it's a failed attempt.

"Yes." She lets out a quick chuckle, reveling in my nervousness. With a smile hanging on her lips, she walks in my direction and, after standing close enough, she turns her back, showing me the initials "E.V.L" branded on her skin.

My stomach literally flips in disgust and I feel like vomiting. I can't believe she burned her skin permanently to imprint those initials. This woman is a fucking psycho, I knew it.

"It stands for Elliot Van Lawick, in case you were wondering. This painting is for him."

Oh my goodness! Breathe, Petra, breathe…

I can't believe I'm gonna paint Yara naked and with that stuff around her neck and wrists. Jeez… Trying to push the imagery of her branded skin out of my head, I switch to a lighter subject. "So, um, you want to put yourself in position so that I can take a few pictures?"

CHAPTER 13

Manhattan, February 18, 2021
Alexander Van Dieren

"Mr. Van Dieren?" Cate says as she enters my office. "Your sister Yara is here."

"Ah, yes, let her come in." Finally! I can't wait to know the outcome of her research about who's attending the ceremony.

I stand up for the sake of politeness and watch Yara walking in, wearing her usual white polo breeches and black equestrian boots, but paired with a long, black overcoat that hangs on her shoulders. "Do you have any info for me?" I ask, my curiosity dismissing all civility.

The corners of her mouth lift reveling in my impatience. Once Cate leaves us alone and we hear the door cracking closed, Yara takes off her coat, putting it on one of the chairs, and tosses the file she's holding on my desk. As she steps closer to me, I sit back, open the file, and my eyes land on a photograph taken by one of my security agents—which has been cooperating with her—featuring a man that seems to be in his seventies with salt-and-pepper hair, wearing a suit, and leaving a restaurant downtown.

"Who's he?" I ask immediately.

"Senator Julian Schumer—one of Eric's mentors and best friends," Yara explains, sitting slightly on my desk. "He's the one who brought him to where he is today."

I nod, enjoying her findings so far. "And why is he relevant?"

"He's one of the attendees in Venice this weekend," she answers back.

My heart jumps in excitement at her answer and I can't contain a chuckle. "That's a hell of a lot of luck."

"Not really," she says. "The initiation ceremony happens only once a year, so all the members are attending. You should know that by now."

I ignore her bitter comment and proceed, "So what's the plan?"

She stands up and goes to check the view behind me. "The plan is to catch him with one of the underage girls," she says, looking at the skyscrapers standing tall in front of her. She then turns slowly, a smirk playing on her lips. "Then, once we've got leverage, we ask him to step in and talk Eric into dropping the case."

"He'll be wearing a Venetian mask though."

"And?" she says, not impressed. "We can easily take a video, hold him in hostage, and unmask him."

I consider her plan thoughtfully; if this senator is truly Eric's best friend and mentor, then surely Eric will drop the case to save him from a possible scandal. "Make sure he goes to a private room with the girls, and that there's a camera recording them."

"Will do," she answers back. Then a quick silence settles in while Yara keeps observing me with that twisted smile on her lips. "I have one condition though."

"Why didn't I expect otherwise?" I reply, knowing she wasn't into saving my ass for free. "Which one?"

"You have to attend too."

"Are you serious?" I can't hide the astonishment from my face. She knows perfectly well that I'd stopped attending after Amanda and I broke up and that I have zero intentions going back there ever again. "I'm not attending. Forget it."

"Your wife is going though," Yara announces just like that, without an ounce of bother.

I blink twice, barely able to process those four words. She must be joking! It must one of those pranks she likes to do. "She is what?"

"I invited her." There's no trace of humor in her tone as she tells me that. "It's time to test her loyalty once and for all— either she is with us or she is against us."

I huff, shaking my head at her move. I was so happy with the plan she had in mind, only for it to be smashed down with her stupid condition. "She fucking stated in front of a camera that she is with them, Yara," I remind her, and the simple memory of it leaves a sore taste in my mouth.

"Yes, but her heart isn't." I close my eyes, her answer squeezing mine tight. "Trust me on this. Take your wife to Venice and enjoy a romantic weekend there with her."

I shake my head, unable to comply with this. Yara's so delusional. "There's nothing romantic about going to that depraved ceremony with her."

"Funny how you used to love them," she snaps.

"Now it's different," I retort, trying to find a way to dissuade Petra from attending. "Is Emma going?"

Despite Yara taking her time to answer me, I can read the truth in her gaze. "I can't tell you that."

I chuckle, looking away for a moment. "That means she is." My tone is tired and I heave a long sigh. "Petra is gonna hate me if I don't prevent her from getting into that shit."

"You aren't supposed to know about Emma in the first place." My sister pauses for a beat, before saying, "Just pretend you know nothing."

"Does Petra know Emma is going to be one of the initiated?"

"Of course not," she replies promptly. "Why would she?" I cock my head to the side at her naivety. "Unless Emma broke her oath and spoke about it, but I don't think she would."

"I can't attend," I tell her once more. "I promised myself I will never step foot there again." Yara folds her arms over her chest, annoyance laced all over her face. "To me, all of this belongs to the past now."

"As you wish," she says simply, like she already turned the page. Then she straightens herself and gives me a quick pat on the shoulder. "In case you change your mind, you know where it is."

I'm slightly surprised at how easily she stopped insisting on me going. "Thanks for everything." I stand and give her a hug. "If your plan works, you are saving us all."

"I know." She gives me a brief smile in return, and walks away to take her coat, putting it back on her shoulders. "Well, see you later," she says as she opens the door. "Don't forget we have dinner before my flight."

To my surprise, as my sister leaves, Cate comes in at the same moment. "Mr. Van Dieren, I'm sorry for interrupting, but are you going somewhere this weekend?"

I frown at her question. "I'm not, why?"

"Well, the jet is booked for tomorrow night and Mr. Van Gatt isn't flying either."

Holy shit! "Thank you for letting me know."

As soon as Cate closes the door behind her, I pick up my iPhone and call Petra immediately.

"Hey," I say as she answers.

"Oh, look who's calling me…" Her sarcastic voice might be sweet and cute, but I don't lose focus.

"May I know why my wife booked the company's jet to go to Venice tomorrow night?" I ask her like I know nothing about her plans.

"I'm going there to attend a masquerade," she replies like it's no big deal. "You're also invited by the way."

"You aren't going," I snap, throwing my courteous and polite tone out of the window. "Forget about it."

"Too late for that," she ripostes. "I already made up my mind and you aren't going to change it."

"Petra, this is not the type of event you want to go to, trust me on this."

"Thank you for your concern, but I'm perfectly capable of leaving a place if I don't like it."

What a fucking stubborn woman! I draw out a breath in displeasure, containing myself from cursing. And to check if she will be honest with me or not, I ask, "Who gave you an invitation?"

"I found it in the mailbox."

Bullshit. It's insane how she would even protect my own sister instead of telling me the truth. "Are you home?"

"Why?"

"I just want to talk to you."

"If it's to dissuade me, don't bother." I shake my head at how well she knows me. "The jet leaves tomorrow at nine p.m. from Teterboro. Goodbye." And just like that, she hangs up on me.

What. The. Heck? How rude is she?! I can't believe she is forcing my hand to go. Yep, that's exactly what she is trying to do, which is most likely why Yara didn't insist harder. She knows I'm incapable of letting my wife go alone so she's playing with it.

No, no, and no! There's no way in hell I'll fly to Venice just because my wife has decided to attend that ceremony. Suddenly though, I've got an idea! I grab my land-phone and call my assistant. "Cate, can you cancel the jet for tomorrow, please?"

"Okay, sure. I'm gonna check if I can do so."

"Perfect, thanks."

After a few minutes, the landline starts ringing again.

"Yes?" I say, picking up the call.

"Hi, Mr. Van Dieren," Cate starts. "So I tried to cancel it but given the fact the booking has been made under your wife's details, only she can cancel the booking. A code needs to be sent to her mobile number so that she can cancel it."

Fuck! Obviously she won't be canceling shit. "I see…" I rub my eyelids, trying to find another way to cancel the plane. Yet, I don't see how. "Thank you, Cate."

As I finish the call, I feel tempted to send security to our condo to prevent her from flying tomorrow. But knowing her as I do, she will just call Eric or Matt and report me, which will create even more problems.

Fuck, and fuck! The last thing I want is to go to Venice and attend that ceremony with my wife. But with only one day from the flight, I don't see how I can prevent it. If I have to go, one thing is sure; I'll be so distant and cold to her, that she is gonna regret it for the rest of her days to have decided against my will.

CHAPTER 14

Teterboro, February 19, 2021
Petra Van Gatt

As I arrive at the airport I'm buzzing with nervous excitement—Yara had tipped me off that Alex wasn't going to let me travel alone, and that he should be here waiting for me. After nearly a week being separated, I just can't wait to see him again. The simple idea we are gonna spend the weekend in Venice makes my heart part in a fury.

Going through the immigration process, I crane my neck this way and that, looking for Alex around the tarmac. My heart starts to sink with each passing minute that I fail to see him or his car.

I approach one of the airport employees as they take my bags to load into the plane.

"Is there someone else coming?" I ask.

The young man checks his clipboard and shakes his head.

"No ma'am. We are ready for takeoff once you board."

Well, crap. I feel deflated. Maybe he is already waiting for me in Venice. Dejectedly, I hitch my purse onto my shoulder and climb aboard the plane. My eyes are glued to the floor when I hear a familiar voice, sounding sarcastic as always.

"About time," Alex says, checking his watch.

"You changed your mind?" I ask, concealing my excitement as much as I can while I keep walking in his direction. Despite Yara telling me Alex would be coming, it's always reassuring to see him in flesh and bones.

He looks like he wants to roll his eyes, but he rubs a hand down his face instead, groaning. "Let's make it very clear; I'm coming with you because you have no idea what you are getting yourself into, but I won't touch you and don't you dare try anything with me."

He seems pretty confident of himself, especially since we last slept together less than a week ago.

"Why not?" I tease, biting my bottom lip in a failed attempt to contain my growing smile. I just love seeing him so serious and playing hard to get. "You didn't like our last night together?"

Alex heaves a long sigh in displeasure before saying, "You don't deserve any pleasure from me. You are the enemy."

"I'm also your wife," I remind him. "It's kind of your duty to give me pleasure." I draw out the second word into a purr, earning me a scowl from him.

"It's kind of your duty to be loyal to me and yet this isn't happening, is it?" he bites out.

"I have to cooperate with them," I say stoically, before giving my purse to the hostess so that she can store it on the back. Then I take a seat in front of him and add, "If you are not guilty as you claim, then you have nothing to worry about."

Before Alex can growl something back, the hostess steps in to welcome us onboard. "May I serve you a drink?" she asks with a bright smile.

"I'll have a cold-pressed juice, thank you."

"I'll have a glass of Macallan," he answers, his tone slightly more annoyed than usual. Then, as the hostess leaves our side, his gaze returns to me. "I'm gonna need a few drinks to forget I'm here with you."

"Oh relax," I say, chuckling. He might look angry to be here with me, but I'm on cloud nine. As I think something through, I rise from my seat and go to where he is. "I'm sure you can survive a weekend with me in Venice." I motion for him to lean back, but he doesn't budge.

"You aren't sitting on my lap," he snaps, annoyance dripping from his voice.

His attitude is getting really tiresome. "I always do," I protest.

"Not anymore," he insists. "I told you that night was a mistake." I frown at his behavior, yet Alex doesn't seem to mind. "You have the whole plane to sit." And his gaze dips down to his iPad where he starts reading something in it.

I sulk, walking back to my seat and plopping down in it. Crossing my arms and leaning back in the seat, I stare out the window, my jaw clenching. I had almost jumped for joy when I saw Alex sitting in his usual seat as I boarded, but his grumpy attitude is souring any excitement I had felt. After a few minutes of silence, I give a quick glance at him, as he remains busy on his iPad and totally indifferent to me. Is he gonna ignore me the whole trip? Jeez! Shaking my head, a long sigh of displeasure escapes me.

"Can you stop pouting like a petulant child?" he sneers. "I can't concentrate with you acting like that."

Why is he such an arrogant asshole today? Is it some sort of payback to have decided to go to Venice against his will? I fight the urge to stick my tongue out at him, trying to instead focus on the world passing me by outside. The hostess brings me my juice and explains where she stored my bag. I give her a smile in appreciation before taking a sip. It's pineapple and mint—I used to drink a lot of them in Seychelles during our honeymoon, which reminds me how happy we were back then. As I come to think of it, I wonder if Alex told them what to stock for the flight.

Resigning myself to sitting alone with zero attention, I get up to grab my purse, intending to get my own iPad to ignore my husband the same way he is ignoring me. I dressed in something I knew he would like, just in case he'd show up, so I was at least going to strut my stuff a little. I'm wearing a white fit-and-flare dress that falls below my knees; simple, innocent, and pretty similar to the one I wore in Aspen, paired with a pair of nude heels. I put a little extra sway in my hips as I pass by Alex, the dress swirling around me, and I'm rewarded with his swift grasp on my wrist, stopping me.

"Can you go sit somewhere that I won't have to look at you for the rest of the flight?"

I jerk my hand away, offended. "Oh, so now even the sight of me is abhorrent to you?"

Alex exhales sharply. "No; it's just that spending hours in your presence is distracting."

His answer brings a smirk to my lips, and I perch myself on the arm of his seat, leaning in. "Is it because you are thinking about some of the things we've done in these seats? Wishing we could do them now?" I trail my hand down the front of his shirt, and I can feel the warmth of his skin through it.

But Alex grabs my wrist again, stopping its descent down his chest. "You are trying my patience, woman."

"And you're trying my patience, Alex!" I pull my hand back to release it from his grip and continue. "It can't be sex one day, and then you treating me like I'm your enemy the next."

"It can be," he hisses, finally meeting my gaze. "Especially because it's true."

"I don't get why you're trying to force this narrative that we shouldn't want or desire each other. We are going to Venice," I remind him, my voice dripping with excitement. "If I know you at all, we'll share a room so you can monitor me, and also be my personal escort around the city." I pause, gauging his expression. "You're trying to tell me that even though we won't be leaving each other's sides, you still won't touch me?" I try to keep my voice level, but a little quaver sneaks in at the end, betraying my emotions. I can't help but feel near tears at the thought of days spent in beautiful Venice, bereft of his touch.

Alex sighs heavily, turning his body slightly and refocusing on his iPad. He doesn't push me off the arm of his chair, but he makes it clear enough that he is no longer bothering himself with me.

"Petra," he begins since I'm not leaving. "This is not some romantic vacation for us to reconnect." His voice is low and discreet, but I can taste the irritation in it. "This is something you forced my hand on, and now I have no choice but to escort you."

"You didn't have to come," I huff.

"Yes, I did," he snaps, matching my tone. "You have no idea the mess you're getting yourself into." He rubs the bridge of his nose between his fingers, obviously stressed. "You can't even let me be alone to deal with your betrayal." He lets out a breath, letting his words sink in. "This whole escapade is just you using my annoyingly persistent concern for you and your ever-present naivety to force me into babysitting you for a weekend." His voice is curt and clipped.

What? I've had enough! *Babysitting? Really?* I think angrily. I shoot up, stomping to the back of the plane to get my bag. If anyone is being a child, it's him. I settle back into my seat, pulling up the book I was reading on my iPad and try to shut out the world. I don't want to think about Alex, Venice, or anything else besides the text I have right in front of me, yet I can feel tears sneaking into the corners of my eyes as I remind myself of the poor state of our marriage, but I dash them away, hoping he doesn't notice. While I thought this trip would help us reconnect, the precise opposite is happening.

Leaning my chair back, I'm finally able to engage with my book, enjoying a snack of hummus when the hostess comes by next and succeeding in not looking in Alex's direction. The plane is quiet, almost silent, and my iPad is getting heavy in my hand. I put it down on the table in front and roll onto my side, pillowing my head on my hands and thinking about the two little lives growing inside me, sad that even that permanent connection isn't enough to persuade my husband to give me the time of day.

My eyelids are getting droopy, and I resign myself to a nap. I cross my arms over my chest. It's a bit cold on the plane, but my ricocheting emotions, early pregnancy, and lightning-fast packing for Venice have exhausted me, so I drift off slowly to sleep.

Just a few minutes later, I'm roused minutely by a blanket being smoothed over me. The plane's interior is dark now, and I'm grateful for the blanket, snuggling into its warmth. I'm still mostly asleep, so I tell myself to thank the hostess in the morning when I hear, "Sleep well, little Petra."

CHAPTER 15

Venice, February 20, 2021
Petra Van Gatt

The silent stalemate between Alex and me still remains after I wake up and get served breakfast by the hostess. Alex, of course, looks perfectly unrumpled after a night spent on the plane. I know he must have slept some of the time, but it's just like Alex to look perfect upon waking.

I'm patting my mouth with a linen napkin after breakfast when my husband finally looks up from his tablet at me.

"You're going to want to put on something a little more substantial," he politely suggests. "It might get really cold outside."

I look down at the white dress that I had hoped would impress him, now wrinkled from sleep, and frowned. *So much for an in-flight seduction...* With a quiet sigh of resignation, I get up from my seat and stretch my arms over my head to relieve my tensed muscles. Alex pretends to ignore me, but I see his quick glance as my stretch hikes my dress up over my thighs. I grin to myself as I go to change for the landing. Right before I can enter the bathroom, I hear him tell me quietly, "It was a nice dress, Petra."

I don't respond, but I hold the compliment close to my heart. At least he had noticed. For my arrival in Venice, I've chosen a pair of brown leather calf-length boots with no heel, just in case the whole gondola ordeal is difficult for me, a pair of my most comfortable jeans, and a knitted sweater. After showering, I apply my face cream, brush my teeth, and loosely braid my hair away from my face, leaving it artfully messy.

Just as I exit the bathroom and head back to my seat, the inflight announcement informs the two of us we are landing shortly. Despite Alex stubbornly ignoring me for most of the flight, I'm brimming with excitement. We're finally here! Not even grumpy Alex can ruin my enthusiasm.

The plane lands without a hitch, and to my shock, as we descend the stairs, Alex offers me his arm. I take it gingerly, not wanting him to change his mind, and offer him a warm smile. When we hit the open air outside of the plane, we're buffeted by the cold wind coming off the water. It takes me off guard, and I try to snuggle closer to Alex. I would have never expected it to be so chilly since the sun is shining like a warm summer's day—but instead of balmy sunshine, it's freezing!

I try to slip my icy hands under Alex's jacket to warm them on his skin, but he shrugs me off with a glare.

"Don't push it," he tells me, but he doesn't protest when I continue to lean into him slightly.

I can see the long bridge entering the city and the green-blue waters surrounding the island that is Venice. Since the airport is on the mainland, we still have a bit of distance to travel before we arrive to the old city. We take our time departing, in no rush. The air smells salty and sharp, and I'm antsy to get out of the modern airport and see the ancient town.

When we finally make it outside to the docks, I watch as airport employees load our luggage onto one of the smaller boats.

The boats are so different looking than the ones I've ridden on in the states! They sit low in the water, and the whole boat is beautifully polished wood grain. Ours has a glass cabin and a few open-air seats in the back. Alex helps me board, taking his hand in mine as I step down, and I'm infinitely glad I went with the no heels option.

As the crew finishes loading our luggage, Alex speaks to the driver in Italian, sounding much livelier than he had on the plane. I know he used to come here every year with Amanda, and I wonder if it was only because of that masquerade ball or also because he has a special bond to this city.

I'm sitting in one of the cream leather seats, enjoying the breeze and the sunshine when Alex sits down next to me. To my delight, he slips his arm around my shoulders as the boat launches.

"It's about a twenty-minute or so ride in. Are you comfortable?" he asks, his expression open and sincere. I'm touched by his concern.

"Yes, thanks for asking." I examine his expression. "You like it here, huh?"

He nods. "It's just nice to get away for a minute, and despite how annoyed I still am with you, it's like seeing a place for the first time when I get to see you experience it."

"I knew you wanted to come here!" I lean my head on his shoulder, gripping his arm. Alex rumbles in his chest but says nothing, yet he doesn't disengage himself from me either. I would accept the tenuous truce for now.

"I have to apologize," Alex starts after a few minutes. "Cate had them chill some champagne and orange juice for mimosas, but, well…" he looks down pointedly at my belly. "I guess it slipped my mind to tell her."

I giggle. "Orange juice alone is fine if you're offering."

Alex gets up and returns shortly with two glasses of orange juice in champagne flutes. It's so relaxing to be cruising over the open water after being cooped up for so long on the plane. He is quiet next to me, but not the cold, harsh silence of before; it's a companionable quiet as we sit, thighs touching and me leaning into him.

I can see the city coming into focus, the round roofs and brick and white stone buildings almost glowing in the bright sun. Each of the regal buildings has a dock of its own attached, some looking nearly as old as the buildings themselves while others seem to be brand new. Boats ranging from the luxury taxi boats like ours all the way to simple gondolas pass us in the canal, and our driver gives a cheery "Ciao!" each time one passes. The passing driver replies in the same manner, sometimes with a tip of the hat. The effect is charming.

As we get farther into the city, I can see the gilded domed roofs of some of the buildings and wonder if one of those grand structures is our hotel.

"Which hotel are we staying in?" I ask him curiously. "I scheduled a booking but—"

"None," he interposes, still looking ahead. "We're staying in my family palazzo."

I turn to him in surprise, and blink a few times, destabilized by his answer. "What! Really?" I look around more intently now, trying to catch sight of the different palazzos we pass. Light filters sporadically through the gaps in the structures, making it difficult for me to see the minute details.

Alex's own family palazzo, I think to myself giddily. *So freaking insane...* It's another glimpse into his past that I'm excited to see.

"Which one is yours?" I ask, straining to see more of the city as we approach.

"You'll see soon enough."

The boat driver approaches a white dock and parks the boat expertly. At the end of the immaculate dock is a butler, who must have known we were coming. He bows his balding head quickly to us, speaking in quick Italian that I don't catch, before taking our bags and ushering us inside.

This must be it! I crane my head back to take in the palazzo. It's large, but not overly so, made from stone slabs with evergreen shutters on the window. The building wears the patina of age gracefully. I recognize the architecture as Venetian Gothic, with its pointed windows and sweeping arches. I tilt my head back to take it all in, noticing a balcony on the second floor with plush outdoor seating facing the canal. It would be a beautiful place to enjoy morning coffee. It's opulent, stunning, and exactly what I would expect from him.

He helps me out of the boat and links our arms again, walking us down the long dock as it sways with the motion of the sea.

"This palazzo has been in my family for generations. I've always found it to be one of our more beautiful properties."

I squeeze his arm in response, still taking in the sights. The door he opens for me is made of a dense, pale gray limestone —most likely Istrian stone. I run my hand over the cool surface of it as we step into the lobby area. The stone is smooth with age, and I'm distracted by thinking about the age of the building when I'm suddenly struck mute by the interior.

I walk in slowly, trailing behind Alex, trying to look in every direction at once. Everywhere I look is decorated in beautiful Renaissance era art, some paintings and tapestries reaching floor to ceiling. Rich red carpets are strewn over the floors, and the decorations dotting the tables and shelves aren't even trying to be subtle. Every little piece of art looks like a priceless museum display. Even the ceiling is covered in beautiful, exquisitely detailed frescos. I feel like I have walked into the home of a Venetian Duchess.

"Wow..." I breathe, unable to focus on any one thing at once. Alex chuckles, grabbing my hand and pulling me through the hallways.

"Alex," I tell him, "this place is incredible."

Alex shrugs. "It's beautiful, I'll give you that. It has always just felt a little *gaudy* to me."

He stops in front of an ornately carved wooden door, opening it and gesturing for me to go inside. The bedroom, like the rest of the house, is decorated impeccably, if a bit busily. The centerpiece of the room, an enormous four post bed, is covered in heavy down blankets and fluffy pillows, partially concealed by velvet privacy curtains. I bet that if I was to climb into the bed and pull the curtains closed, that it'd be like its own little private world for sleeping…and other activities.

I look over at him speculatively. He's opening dresser drawers and checking the entire room over when I walk behind him and slip my arms around his waist. I feel him stiffen, and he stands straight, slowly turning around in my arms. When he looks down at me, his eyes are hooded, and my insides feel tingly. I recognize that look. His expression softens as I move my arms to loop around his neck, standing on my tiptoes and leaning into him. My lips are mere inches from his, and I whisper his name. He cups the back of my head, and I'm sure he's about to give in and kiss me here in this fairytale bedroom when suddenly he sweeps my feet out from underneath me, holding me in his arms, and walks toward the bed. Mentally, I'm celebrating my victory over Alex and his insistence on celibacy when he tosses me on the sheets…

And pulls the curtains shut, closing me in alone.

"Hey!" I yell, and Alex snorts.

"Douse the fire in your loins, Petra, and get ready, we've got some shopping to do."

I sputter, untangling myself from the blankets and yanking the curtains open.

Alex is still standing at the foot of the bed, the palm of his hand pressed to his mouth to hold in his laughter. I try to kick him, but he simply steps back, still grinning behind his hand as he does so.

"What's your problem!" I screech.

He removes his hand from his face and shrugs. "I'm not sure what you mean. You came onto me when I was trying to make you comfortable in your bedroom," Alex replies innocently.

I pause. "Wait. You mean *our* bedroom, right?"

He shakes his head. "No, I mean *your* bedroom. I will not be sharing your bed in any capacity."

"This is ridiculous!" I rebuke, stomping after him as he leaves the room. I grab my coat on the way out, and we pass the house employees emptying the first taxi boat of our belongings as Alex leads me to a second, smaller taxi boat. I'm still ready to give him a piece of my mind when he holds out his hand for me to step into the boat, but before I can start, my stomach rumbles audibly. Alex's eyes widen and I can tell he's fighting a smile. He says a few short words to the boat driver as we get settled down for the trip to go God knows where.

Now that my indignation is starting to fade, I realize how hungry I really am. I hold my stomach and Alex pats me on the shoulder.

"I told the driver to make a pit stop since apparently I have allowed you to starve," he teases.

I want to snap at him, but I don't want to ruin any chance of a yummy side trip. Alex allows me to snuggle close to him as the boat launches into the canals. Warm against his body, I take in the sights of the glorious city, which is so different from anywhere I had ever been before. Everything looks classic and centuries-old, and I imagine how it would look to float slowly down the water with the city fully lit up at night. All the buildings are brick, stone, or marble, and the entire city seems like it could have materialized from the pages of a book.

I feel Alex watching my expression, and I glance up at him with big eyes. He blows out a breath and turns away from me, but he points out certain sights of interest, giving me a private tour in his deep, quiet voice. I hang on his every word, enraptured.

"This is the Rialto Bridge, built in the twelfth century. It's the oldest bridge that spans the Grand Canal, and…"

I nod as he narrates, paying less attention to his words and more to the timbre of his voice vibrating through his chest where I am pressed close to him. He can tell me the chemical composition of the water for all I cared, as long as he was speaking to me because truthfully, I've missed my husband deeply.

The driver slides the sleek wooden boat into a small docking area, and we depart. I see people dining outside of restaurants and try to guess which one Alex will take us to, but he passes them all. I turn around, looking forlornly at the pasta and pizzas on other patrons' plates.

"Hey, Alex," I begin, but he shushes me.

"I know what you're thinking, hungry girl, but I'm taking you to a well-kept secret place to get you something special." He waggles his eyebrows at me, and I roll my eyes with a knowing grin. After passing all the amazing-looking bistros, Alex stops at a mundane-looking street food cart. My grin turns into a frown.

"Stop pouting," Alex says, but there is laughter in his voice. He speaks to the purveyor, and after a few minutes, he's handed two large paper cones, overflowing with something that smells heavenly. I can see fried tempura vegetables on top of something creamy and bright yellow with a spoon sticking up out of the cup. The scent makes my mouth water. I reach out and snatch a cone from his grip, and he laughs harder. Inspecting the cone, I see tempura broccolini, peppers, and asparagus pieces. They are all crispy, brown, and covered in seasoning. Underneath the veggies is the creamy yellow substance that I'm pleasantly surprised to find is polenta with wilted spinach, garlic, and sun-dried tomatoes.

Alex looks at me expectantly as I pop a ring of fried pepper in my mouth. I nearly go cross-eyed from pleasure as it melts in my mouth, an explosion of spices and crunchy breading. I must have made an audible noise because Alex nods his head in satisfaction and starts on his own snacks as we walk back to the boat.

I'm craning my head at the surrounding buildings, about to put a piece of asparagus in my mouth, when I hear the click of Alex's phone camera. I whip around at him and try to grab his iPhone from his hand, but he holds it above me.

"Knock it off, Petra. Let me pretend for a moment like everything is normal between us and take some pictures of my favorite woman enjoying my favorite food."

"Fine," I say, heart softening. He may try to act like a hardass, but I can tell that he's struggling to not throw himself into fully enjoying the weekend as a married couple. If he wanted some goofy pictures, so be it.

I finish my polenta, licking the spoon, and after an internal argument with myself to not lick the paper as well, I toss the container away. My belly is full and I'm feeling nostalgic for the happier times with Alex, so I lean on the wrought-iron railing around the dock, positioning myself so the sunset behind Alex is lovingly lighting my face. The light is slipping through the spaces between the beautiful old buildings, glinting on the gold and bronze accents and the water of the canal.

"Can you take a picture of me?" I ask Alex. He takes a few steps back and raises his phone to snap the photo, but before he does, he looks up from the screen and freezes, a look of hunger that has nothing to do with food on his face before he shakes himself out of his reverie and takes the picture.

"You look lovely," he tells me as he shows me the shot. Then we continue walking and head to a Venetian mask shop that Alex tells me is called "Ca' Macana." I purse my lips and send myself the picture from his phone. Brief memories, just in case.

After a short walk through the narrow, cobblestone streets of the city center we make it to the iconic store. According to him, it's the oldest mask shop in Venice, and I can see why. In the glass front display, dozens of masks are beautifully showcased. There are feathered bird masks, theatre ones on hand-held sticks, and a huge variety of Venetian masks, both half and full-face. Inside, Ca' Macana is a sprawling building, filled with masks hanging from the ceiling to the walls and spread over several tables. The place is brimming with jewels, sequins, and lace.

We are perusing the masks when I see Alex come up behind me in the mirror reflection. His expression is amused, and he has something hidden behind his back.

"Close your eyes. I want to put this mask on you. I think you're gonna love it."

Biting my lip, I close my eyes and feel his rough fingers sliding the mask onto my face, hooking it behind my ears. He squeezes my shoulders lightly and turns me to face the mirror.

"You can open them now," he whispers, much closer to my ear than I thought he was. I jump, but then open my eyes, expecting something sexy and regal.

It's a clown mask, red nose and all.

"Alex!" I screech, turning to smack him on the chest, much to the disgust of the other shop patrons who scowl at us. Alex cackles, shielding himself from me before he grips my shoulders again, holding me at arm's length.

"Okay, okay… I'm sorry. I have a real one. I just couldn't resist. Close your eyes again."

I huff and cross my arms but close my eyes for him. He takes off the clown mask and settles something lighter on my face.

"Open."

When I open my eyes this time, the mask is much more in line with what I expected. Around my eyes the mask is a delicate black lace, allowing my ivory skin to peek through the whorls of the lace, but as it sweeps up past my temples, the lace becomes solid silver wings that extend nearly four inches past the sides of my face. The wings are an almost weightless metal. The mask is not gaudily adorned, rather, it's simple but striking beauty stands alone.

I gasp quietly, trailing my fingers up the wings on the sides of the mask.

"Alex, it's incredible…"

"I thought so too." He smooths my hair back, tucking it behind my ears. "You're very striking in it, little Petra."

His praise has me glowing, and my choice of mask is decided. Alex picks a full bronze metal mask that frames his full lips in a "U" shape as it ends in points on his cheeks. His mask is decorated in raised, subtle swirls. It's masculine without being plain, and the bronze sets off his tawny skin and dark hair perfectly. He looks like a sun god, cocky and almost too handsome to behold.

The cashier carefully bags up our purchases, wrapping them delicately in tissue paper to protect them. To my surprise, Alex threads his fingers through mine as we exit the shop. The sun is dipping below the horizon, and the sky is painted in warm pinks and oranges.

"Now, wife, let's prepare for this enormous mess you've gotten us into."

* * *

I step back from the gilded mirror hanging over the vanity in my room and inspect my reflection with approval. I was a little concerned about getting ready on my own, since I'm so unfamiliar with the masquerade we are going to, but I had shaken off my insecurities and set to work making myself as delectable as possible. If I can't seduce Alex tonight, I might as well just throw in the towel.

My gown is form fitting, flaring gently at the base, with a plunging sweetheart neckline. It's not what I'm used to, but I followed Yara's advice, and got a more daring dress than I'd usually go for. This one creates a see-through illusion, and when I first put it on, I was almost embarrassed at how convincing the illusion was. The inner slip of the dress is a flesh color that matches my skin perfectly, and the upper layer is swirling with intricate black lace and sheer. The effect had taken my breath away. It really looked like I was naked under the dress!

Not wanting to distract from the effect of the gown, I opted for a simple, silk, black choker, and large, natural-looking ringlets in my hair. I left it to hang loose besides two French braids at my temples that meet on the back of my head and are secured with a tie. This will allow me to wear my mask and not worry about my hair getting caught, and I have a feeling I will not want any distractions tonight. I finish the outfit off with a pair of black stilettos with a shining silver heel.

Taking a deep breath, I slowly unwrap my mask, turning it back and forth in my hands, making the silver portions catch the yellow light of the room. It looks too beautiful to wear, like something that should be hidden behind glass at a museum. I've never been to a masquerade before, and it's a little intimidating while also sending a secret chill through me. After all, with this mask on, I can act however I desire, and no one would ever know it's me! Well, everyone but Alex.

Speaking of which, a quiet knock sounds at my door. I look over myself one final time.

"Come in!" I call, sitting the mask down on the vanity.

The door cracks open and Alex walks in, dressed in an impeccable tux, black on black and tailored to fit perfectly. It nips close to his waist, accentuating his fit body even under the layers of his formal wear. I feel tingly all over, raking him from head to toe with my eyes. Alex is equally invested in what I'm wearing, but not as shocked. He's always been so much better than me at hiding his emotions.

I give him a quick spin, the bottom of the skirt twisting in the air. "How do I look?"

"You look stunning, as I'm sure you know." His compliment sounds polite and contained, like he's just saying that for the sake of civility. To my surprise though, he walks forward to take my hand in his and brush his lips over my knuckles. I shiver, the touch of his lips barely there but enough to affect me.

"Thanks," I tell him softly. "You look pretty handsome, too."

"All I can say is don't get too attached to the dress."

I pull at the fabric. "This dress? Why? I bought it, not rented it."

He snorts, tapping me on the tip of my nose. "I'm not saying anything else. You wanted to go to this masquerade so badly, so let's go."

I narrow my eyes. "Alex, that's really ominous."

"Hush," he says, leaning down to pick up my mask. "Come here and let me put this on you."

I want to ask more questions, but I know it's pointless. When Alex decides he's going to keep a secret, there is no amount of complaining that I can do to get an answer out of him. He's a steel trap. I go and turn my back on him, closing my eyes as he places the mask on my face. The metal on the sides is cold, but his fingers are warm as he loops the silk ties behind my head and ties them, drifting his fingers over the skin of my neck and jawline when he finishes. I turn to face him and my eyes flutter open to meet his pupils, dilated and dark.

"Alex," I murmur. His lips are so close to mine that I can feel his breath, and I can't stop myself from canting my head sideways and leaning in, intent on kissing him. At first, he seems to mirror my movements, moving closer to me, but at the last second he pulls away and my lips land on his cheek and he steps away.

"I said no kissing, and I mean it," he tells me, jaw clenched.

I feel like screaming. I was so close! Alex seems determined to make me miserable, holding me at arm's length constantly. I'd skip the damned masquerade if he would just take me to bed.

He must see the frustration on my face, and for once he seems to take no joy in it. I get the feeling he'd like to take me to bed, too. We could pull the heavy curtains closed and take our time reacquainting each other with each other's bodies... but no. Stubborn Alex and his ironclad self-control had won again.

Resigned, I take Alex's arm as he offers it, and we depart. My heels make no noise on the carpeted hallway, but as soon as we make it to the marble foyer that leads to the docks, the clicking of the metal stiletto fills the awkward silence between us. Alex reaches into the coat closet, pulling out two lengths of dark fabric. One of them, I notice, is the darkest midnight blue I've ever seen, and the other is pitch black.

"Which do you want?" he asks.

"What are they?" I thought they were blankets at first, but Alex unfurls one and I get a good look at it. It's an honest to God cloak—with hood and all! I'd seen no one wear one in real life.

"Blue," I say quickly, and he throws it over my shoulders like a matador's muleta. The arch of fabric settles on my shoulders, and I'm instantly warmer than I had been seconds before. The cloak, made of wool, is thick and soft, and when I close it in the front it overlaps itself significantly, hiding my coquettish gown completely. I feel mysterious and seductive, a masked vixen that no one recognizes, but everyone desires.

Alex dons his own black cloak and his bronze mask, fitting it to his face expertly—He's clearly done this before. I feel like we are two phantoms, walking down the dock to our boat waiting in the darkness. A light fog hangs over the water, and instead of the loud taxi boat from earlier there is a silent gondola, gondolier just as silent as we board, and Alex tells him the destination.

My heart is racing. It's finally time! I'm itching to discover Alex's secrets and get a glimpse of his life before we got together. I wasn't nervous before, but Alex's warning about not getting attached to my dress and the sly looks he keeps shooting me have me on edge. He's hiding something.

Well, I'll know all the intricacies of the masquerade shortly. For right now, I focus on how brilliant the city looks at night. Lights hang like stars around Venice, twice as beautiful as the water reflects their image back. The fog and the ethereal lighting give the canal a dream-like vibe that I'm totally in love with.

Alex must have noticed my wandering eyes because he drapes his arm over my shoulders and pulls me close. I don't fail to notice that he's let me be close to him on every ride through the city, and it warms my heart a little. It's such a mundane, domestic action that lets me know that, even if he insists differently, he still cherishes me as his wife in his mind.

"Are you excited?" he asks, voice deep and hushed.

"Yes. Mostly curious. I've never been to a masquerade before. How are they different from other balls besides the masks?"

Alex chuckles, squeezing me closer. "You're about to find out. Though…it might just be *this* masquerade that is so…off beat."

I purse my lips but remain quiet. I will not take his bait and beg him for answers.

"Do you know the history of the masquerade, wife?"

His question takes me totally off guard. "No, except from what I've seen in the Phantom of the Opera number."

He's running his knuckles up and down my bare arm under my cloak as he speaks. "It's actually from ancient Egypt. Most people assume it's from Victorian Europe, but they're mistaken."

"Really?" My interest is piqued.

"Mmhm," he pauses, gathering the story before he continues. "It was originally a festival to celebrate the Egyptian goddess of the moon, Isis. Her worshippers would dress as animals and other gods and goddesses, parading down to the river to wish the departing sailors good luck."

"Wow. That's amazing. I never would have guessed."

"It's true. Isis was both a queen and," he lowers his hand down to rest over my belly, "the patron goddess of motherhood."

A goddess, queen, and mother. Why don't we revere figures like that anymore? I place my hand over his hand on my belly, too eager to fully relax. There is a chill in the night air, and I wrap my cloak tightly around my body.

Alex stands, sighting something in the distance. It's a building. Enormous, domed, with tall spires and made from brick like many of the others. The windows are in recessed arches, but instead of the white and yellow lights that lit the surrounding buildings, the lights illuminating this building are blood red.

Great. More ominous signs.

"This place is a little freaky," I comment.

He laughs sardonically. "Just you wait."

"*Eccoci qui,*" the boat driver announces as we stop in front of a deck.

Alex puts a hand on mine, turning my attention to him. "Remember—whatever happens inside, it belongs to the past," he tells me, his tone more serious than before. "I'm no longer associated with any of this."

I nod, ogling at everything as he helps me from the boat. Most of the other palazzos have shorter docks that butt up against the stone street, but this one is different. It's long and winding, lit by flame torches in even intervals. What's even stranger are the guards posted between the torches, wearing the same long cloaks as us and featureless white masks. It gives me the serious heebie-jeebies to look at them as Alex leads me down the dock, so I try to do my best to ignore them. We finally reach silver double doors that are twice my height and carved with mysterious scrawling and symbols that flow into the intricate decorative swirls. There are two guards posted on either side of the door, and as we grow near they pull the doors open with a creaky sound.

Alex looks down at me. "Last chance."

I consider taking him up on the offer to leave, but I've come this far. It'd be foolish to turn away now. I straighten my posture and nod. Alex sighs heavily and leads me inside.

I had an image in my mind of what the masquerade would look like, and the inside of the palazzo certainly matches my vision, only on a much grander scale. It isn't just a home decorated for a party; it's a whole different world once we walk through the doors. I can hear music and the murmurs of people talking through the walls, but the room we enter is eerily empty aside from a single woman in a full Venetian mask that is painted with a huge golden crescent covering her face. She looks like a magician in this attire. Instead of the plain cloak that Alex, myself, and the silent guards are wearing, the woman's cloak is a brilliant pearl color, interspersed with gorgeously detailed moons, stars, and suns. She stands behind a table, flanked by more featureless masked guards.

The room itself isn't too different from the ones I've seen at Alex's palazzo. The floors are chess marble, and the walls are covered in velvet flocked damask wallpaper and gold-framed paintings, lit only by candlelight. It isn't until I inspect the paintings that I realize the subjects are all some level of nude, some even engaging in…

Uh, wow. Engaging in a *lot* of different things.

I turn my attention back to the woman who stands tall to welcome us. In front of her is a low wooden table holding a myriad of unique items: a leather tome, a delicate blade with a gold handle, a chalice, and a deck of tarot cards. It's a strange collection, but I think it's going to be a weird night all around.

"Welcome, welcome," she purrs, straightening up. "Do you have an invitation?"

Alex hands the roll of parchment paper to her and she opens it wide before checking it thoroughly. "Very well. If you're a member, state your full name. If not, come forward to pay your entrance." She looks down at the leather bound, gold leafed book on the low table in front of her, ready to search for our names.

"Alexander Van Dieren," he says. "And she is not yet a member."

The woman quits reading just as fast, her mask traveling up to look at him. "Welcome back, we have missed you." Her attention then goes to me. "Please come forward to pay your dues." She crooks her fingers toward me, and for some reason it terrifies me.

"What's the payment?" I ask Alex nervously. He glances down at me, looking frustrated.

"Well, my dear, it's your blood," the woman replies. "If you are to join us tonight, we must know you fully, right down to the blood in your veins."

My *blood?* No way! It's time to break out my very first pregnancy excuse. "I can't donate any blood. I'm sorry. I'm–"

Alex steps in front of me, cutting me off. "She's terribly afraid of blood. I will pay the price for her."

"Alex, no!" I hiss.

"Relax. It's only three drops," he says, trying to reassure me. That is a little bit of a relief, but still. I have no interest in making Alex bleed for me.

The woman however shakes her head. "It isn't that easy. We must see if luck is on your side tonight. If it is, you can go ahead and pay on her behalf. It if isn't, then she will have to pay with her own blood, or you both shall leave."

Alex shrugs, unbothered.

With a flourish, the woman pulls out a huge gold coin from her cloak and flips in. Alex calls out "Heads." And sure enough, the coin lands with a clatter and spins a few times before landing definitively on heads.

"Very well. Pay the price."

Alex strides to her, standing his hand from his cloak and holding it palm up to the woman. She grasps his hand with one of her own almost reverently, before picking up the small, gold-handled knife from the table. With surprising speed, she slices a tiny slash over the pad of his pointer finger. Alex is still as a statue; she might as well have blown on the finger for all the reaction he had.

The woman flips Alex's hand over and holds it above the chalice, squeezing his finger until three crimson drops audibly plop into the cup.

Once done, she takes five cards off the top of her deck and approaches me. I can see that her legs are bare where her cloak parts, and it makes me curious about what else could be bare. "As a non-member, you'll have to pick a card to decide your fate for the rest of the evening. Whatever role you are to assume, you will wear it for the remainder of the night." She then fans the cards out, showing me nothing but their backs.

I look at Alex, bewildered. "What is this?"

"Since you are not a member, your status inside the ceremony, including what you'll be wearing, will be decided by the card you choose."

What? I'm caught completely off guard by his explanation. "So I won't be getting inside dressed like this?"

"Do you mind showing her?"

The Magician—if I can call her like that—uncovers the five different cards she is holding, and I notice all but one illustrates a different woman. "There are five statuses inside the ceremony; queen, duchess, courtesan, slave, and nun."

"Queen," I choose immediately.

Alex chuckles inwardly for some reason. "You don't get to decide, you pick one card from the whole pack and luck decides for you."

What! My heart starts racing at the idea I have to let fate decide what I'm gonna wear inside among the crowd. "Oh gosh..." As I pay closer attention at the different cards I notice the queen is fully dressed with a gown, Venetian mask, and tiara, and there is even a man bowing and kissing her hand; then the duchess card is also a woman fully dressed in a gown but only with a Venetian mask on; the courtesan card, on the other hand, is dressed only in lingerie with a Venetian mask on and a choker collar; but the worst is the slave which is fully naked just with a Venetian mask and a choker collar; and lastly, the last card is just a golden cage and a bird inside.

I narrow my eyes and squeeze his arm lightly. "What happens if I get the bird in a cage?"

"It's the perfect card for you." There's an ounce of sarcasm in his tone and I wonder why.

"Tell me…"

"It means your pussy gets locked up for the whole night."

I gasp instantly. "So it means no sex?"

"Exactly. That should be your card because that's exactly what you are getting anyways." His lips twist into a devilish smile as he says so and then he leans in and adds, "I'd love to lock it up and keep the key in my pocket."

"What a monster you are," I snap, pinching his arm tightly. Then the magician starts shuffling the cards and puts them face down on the table. My heart is hammering against my chest as I hope I will get neither the nun nor the slave.

Please give me the queen…

"This one," I say, touching one of the cards and praying for it to be a decent one. The magician turns it face up and…

"The courtesan?" I blink twice, making sure it's the one I have chosen. I'm petrified for a moment at the idea I'm gonna be only in lingerie until I realize one thing. Putting on a slutty tone, I run a hand on Alex's chest, leaning in and say, "You're gonna have to watch me in lingerie all night long…" I can't contain my growing smirk as he doesn't even smile. "Have you imagined? Me as your courtesan?"

"What a nightmare," he replies flatly. And I wonder if he's being sarcastic or not because he doesn't even laugh. "You might be my courtesan for the night, but I'm not touching you."

"We'll see…"

I can't help but whip my cloak around dramatically as I leave Alex's side, and I hear him snort at my theatrics. I expect the Magician will provide me with the clothes… or lack thereof… but instead, two of the guards peel off and come to gather me. As they walk, I notice something that I had missed before; the guards are women! Their shapely legs reveal themselves behind the swishes of their cloak, and I feel much more comfortable knowing that my fellow women would help with my costume.

I try to see past the empty black holes of their eyes, but I still can't see anything besides the flat white of their masks. It's very unsettling, but I shake off my uneasiness as they usher me from the entrance room, through a door, and into a large bedroom. The bedroom is decorated in blacks, whites, and silvers, and interspersed on the brilliant white comforter are several slinky outfits, all very boudoir, and insanely revealing. A thrill runs through me, knowing I'll be wearing one of these with Alex all night. There is no way he can resist me now.

One of the silent women finally speaks. "Choose," she says, motioning toward the different outfit choices. I walk around the bed, tapping my lips with a finger as I consider them. They're all scandalous in their own way. I guess the queen and duchess outfits must be in another room.

One outfit catches my eye. It's a bra and panty set like most of the others but made of black lace with three velvet straps attaching the bra to a choker collar. What sets it apart for me is that the cups behind the black lace are solid silver, like the wings of my mask, and silver filigree runs along the waistband of the panties. The silver stiletto of my shoes, the silver waistband of the panties, the silver cups of the bra, and the silver wings of the mask all interspersed with deep, dark black. I love when things come together like this.

"This one," I tell the women, who only stare back at me silently. Um, okay. I guess I have to change in front of them.

My face burns, but something tells me I am far from the first person to do this tonight. I change quickly, covering myself with my cloak as I do. I button the choker collar on, and I'm ready. I wonder where I should leave my dress, but they just extend a hand indicating for me to give it to them.

Alex is waiting for me back in the foyer, no longer wearing his cloak, with a snifter of whiskey in his hand when I enter. He watches as I walk in, and I know he's waiting for me to show him my outfit. For a second I consider not showing him, only letting him catch glimpses of me as the night goes on, but I'm impatient. I want his reaction now. I drag the cloak away from me, so it is just my body framed in a sea of silver-black fabric.

Alex sucks in a breath before he laughs sarcastically. "And here I thought nothing at these masquerades could surprise me anymore."

"Do you like it?" I ask quietly.

He raises a single eyebrow at the question, coming to my side and putting his arm around my waist to usher me into the principal part of the party. I guess he will not bless me with an answer. Too bad for him. I already know how much he must like it. He can play hard to get if he wants, but I'm his wife, and he can't fool me.

One of the guards helps me to take off my cloak and I stand beside my husband with nothing but my three piece lingerie. I feel totally self-conscious given the fact he's in a tuxedo and I'm barely wearing anything. I feel weird, truly like a courtesan accompanied by her client or something.

Two of the guards open an enormous set of double doors for us, and I gasp as we enter the main part of the palazzo.

It's part carnival, part formal ball, and part sex club. We are on a circular walkway, and down a short staircase is a sunken ballroom. I can see an orchestra playing. The music is upbeat and seductive, wrapping around me like smoke. All the musicians are dressed in black with full black Venetian masks, but they are the most modest in the sunken ballroom by far. I lean over the railing of the walkway, hardly believing my eyes.

The dance floor is black marble, shot through with red veins. Behind me, red velvet curtains conceal the walls, like at a theater, and everything is lit by candlelight. The sparse illumination causes everything, us included, to cast long shadows. The effect is sensual, and a little eerie.

There is a duchess or two dancing, but the nude women totally overshadow them. The "slaves" and "courtesans" are wearing either lingerie or only collars and are pressed close to their men of choice as they dance. Some of the men are shirtless as well, but from what I can see, only the women are completely nude. The atmosphere is dark, and some couples are clearly doing more than just dancing.

"Want to join them?" Alex asks.

"Shush, you," I mumble, causing Alex to laugh. I watch the dancers for a moment more. "Are we going to have to do that?"

"Even if I was going to touch you, I don't think I'd have you naked on the dance floor. There are so many other…" He runs his hand down my back, grazing my ass. "More interesting things to enjoy here. Especially with a novice like you."

"What more interesting things?"

"Let's go find out, why don't we?" Alex says, taking my arm in his again.

We walk the huge perimeter of the walkway. Every few feet a hallway or room breaks off from the circular room, each one full of something new. Alex leads me into the first room, and we have to push a curtain out of the way to see the entertainment. It's a woman in a tightly wound corset and the skeleton of a ballet skirt blooming around her hips, only bits of ragged tulle hanging on. Her mask is equally strange. It looks like it was meant to be a doll with rosy cheeks and red lips, but one side is peeling away. She dances on pointe, twirling and sweeping her arms on top of a tattered platform while tinny music plays. A broken music box ballerina.

We watch for a moment. She makes me feel sad for some reason, and I tug on Alex's sleeve, showing I want to move on. The next attraction is up a set of stairs off the main walkway. There is tiered seating, like a circus, and in the middle of the floor is a man dressed as a ringmaster. At his feet sit three women, the first holding a single torch, the second holding three, and the third a hoop. They are scantily dressed in thongs, corsets, and thigh-high fishnets.

The ringmaster motions the women to stand, and they make their way to three different places around the ring. Suddenly, he grabs the first woman and pulls her to him, kissing her deeply. The make-out session is uncomfortably long, but when he releases her, she staggers back as if in pain. Her body heaves before she throws her head back, and to my absolute shock, spits a gout of flame into the air six feet above her.

I yelp, covering my own mouth as if fire could come out of me too. The fire-breather holds her single torch into her fire stream, lighting it, and throwing it to the second woman as her flame dies down. The second woman immediately begins to juggle her now four torches. On the first rotation, she touches the flaming torch to her tongue, and on the next pass, she touches an unlit one to her tongue. It ignites like the first. She continues until they are all lit before throwing one to the third woman.

The third woman catches the flaming torch and holds it to her hoop, and it ignites. She spins it around her waist in a hula-hooping belly dance, and as she does, flames lick up her clothes, burning them away bit by bit, until she stands nude, spinning the flaming hoop around her naked figure until at last the flame dies down and the hoop falls to the floor.

"Oh my God!" I say, shaking Alex's arm. "That was insane!"

"Very entertaining. Now come on."

I want to stay and watch more of the circus performance, but Alex is leading me back onto the main walkway and then up a set of stairs. We exit onto another walkway, but this one isn't empty. Harlequins are dotted about. Some are doing card tricks, others distributing champagne, and still others reading palms. The first one to approach us is wearing red and black checkers, and she grabs my hand.

The harlequin runs her gloved finger down the lines of my palm before looking back up at me.

"Your love line is long but broken. You will know grand passion and great heartache. Will you be able to put your line back together, little mother?" the harlequin says, her voice high and breathy.

I jerk my hand away, putting the other on my flat stomach, spooked.

"H-how did you—"

"There are no secrets at the masquerade," the harlequin says ominously before disappearing into the crowd. I look at Alex for an explanation.

"Pay it no mind," he tells me, but I can tell he's a bit unsettled too. "Come on, let's move on."

* * *

Alex grabs me a glass of sparkling grape juice and himself a glass of champagne as we continue perusing the area. I notice some patrons gathering around the railing that looks over the dance floor, murmuring amongst themselves. Suddenly, an organ starts playing, the new melody echos around the palazzo, and the sound of a deep baritone voice emerges from downstairs doing guttural sounds like he's chanting with words I can't discern. I pull Alex in that direction, wanting to see what all the fuss is about. Once we reach the edge of the balcony, I grip the railing and look down. The orchestra has departed, as have all the dancers.

In their place is a man dressed in red with a solid gold Venetian mask that covers all of his face completely. He's wearing a blood-red cloak with the hood cinched at his chin and black leather gloves, making sure that no single inch of skin or hair is visible. The cloak falls straight to the floor and pools there. He is an enigma, completely covered and unknowable.

He's holding a chain, and on the end of the chain is a golden censer, decorated in complex filigree and spilling smoke that hangs over the floor like a fog. I can smell the incense that is making the smoke from here; it smells like night-blooming jasmine. He swings the censer back and forth, spreading the smoke in a slow circle.

The man isn't alone, though. There are nine people spread around him in a circle, all of them wearing some form of a full-face mask. The masks are their only distinctive feature, because they also wear cinched black hoods that are attached to floor-length black cloaks. Since they are kneeling, the cloaks puddle around them on the floor, obscuring their shapes. The smoke curls around them, dissipating as it rises higher into the room.

While the nine people and the…uh…master of ceremonies are the only ones on the floor, a small crowd rings around the edges, all of them masked and watching silently. The man in red slowly paces around the circle of black cloaks figures, and as he stops in front of each one he draws a strange symbol in the air with his hands, the censer still billowing smoke. When he finishes the symbol, the person stands and sheds the cloak. It flutters to the ground, and the woman stands completely nude except for her mask and leather collar. The man in red seems to observe her nudity for a moment before moving on to the next. This process repeats until each woman is completely naked, and the red man moves back to the center of the floor. His cloak is so long that he seems to float instead of walk.

The man waves his free hand in the air, and all the women join hands. They begin to chant in a language I don't recognize. It must be humiliating to stand there, naked, with everyone watching you intently. I shiver, glad that I'm not one of the women on the floor. I turn to Alex, who seems to watch the ceremony bored.

"What is this all about?"

"It's an initiation ritual," he explains, his voice low.

"For what?" I keep asking.

He heaves a sigh in displeasure at my usual curiosity, but proceeds, nevertheless. "To be a part of this fraternity."

"Are they becoming members or just their toys?"

We look in each other's eyes and I can see a smirk rising across his mouth. "For now, toys," he answers back. "The more they show their allegiance to their masters, the higher they can rank."

"Why would they accept that?"

He blows out a breath, considering my question for a moment. "I think it's the idea of belonging to something or someone that lures them into it."

I narrow my eyes at one of the women standing there. She's the most tattooed and as I pay closer attention to her tattoos, my heart sinks to my knees, recognizing her.

"Alex," I whisper, gripping his arm even more. "Emma is downstairs." I can't look any further at the ceremony, knowing my best friend is down there, participating in a degrading rite entirely naked. Holy shit! And when I thought being paraded in lingerie would be the worst thing that could happen tonight, somehow this managed to get worse. What on earth is Emma doing here? And who brought her here in the first place? Oh gosh! Was it Yara? After all, they have always been so close. But why would she participate in this initiation ritual and not just watch it from here? Does she want to be part of this thing? It breaks my heart seeing her naked with only a Venetian mask on and a choker collar. Why does she need to be part of this perversion? Is Yara who persuaded her to do it?

Is she her master? Or is she gonna be handed to a stranger she knows nothing about for the night? Nothing makes sense to me, but the fact she is willing to go through this type of degrading act has rendered me totally speechless and sad. I heave a sigh laced with disappointment knowing my supposed bestie never disclosed her desire to be part of something like that. After all, she knows everything about me. There's nothing I haven't told her, and yet, it seems like it isn't mutual. My heart is bleeding at the realization that my best friend might have a double life I know nothing about.

"You want to leave?" Alex asks quietly.

But I know perfectly well that's exactly what he wants, so I take a deep breath and say, "Just let me know when it's over."

To my surprise, I feel his hand giving mine a quick squeeze. And this gesture, although so simple and fast, means the whole world to me.

I keep hearing the sound of a bong and curiosity taking the best of me, I give a quick look downstairs and see an initiated leaving the dance floor and walking back to her, um, master? Members are standing tall surrounding the dance floor, all wearing full Venetian masks so it's hard to know if Yara is among them. The sound of the bong hits the palazzo again, and a new woman leaves the dance floor and goes to meet with someone in the crowd. What a weird ritual… At each new bong, a new woman leaves the dance floor and goes to be with someone amid the crowd.

"Where are they going now?" I ask Alex as I see Emma going away with someone.

"To fuck," he says bluntly. "They're beginning their new role as toys for the more senior members." I swallow the lump in my throat, but I still feel sick to my core at his explanation. "The members they left with will own them tonight and to a certain extent afterwards."

"They fuck here, at the party?" I ask, shocked.

"Are you surprised? I thought you realized that there's a lot of sex going on around us, even if we can't exactly see it."

I chew my lip for a moment. "Yeah, I mean I figured that out, but having to sleep with a stranger at a party surrounded by everyone else? It seems so...demeaning."

Alex shrugs. "That's sort of the point. With their bodies, they pay the dues to join the fraternity. Here they don't want your money, or your status, they want your body and whatever comes with it." He looks me up and down pointedly, and I resist the urge to try to hide my flushed face.

"I'm really glad it isn't me," I breathe.

Alex snorts. "If we weren't just pretending here tonight, you'd be paying your dues to *me*. No ceremony or initiation bullshit. Just you serving me..." His voice is sultry and my lips part. His words give me vivid imagery and my heart starts racing at the need to fulfill them.

I perk up at the lust in his tone. "I'd be okay with that."

"Of course you would." Alex rolls his eyes, crossing his arms.

I make a sexier pose, putting myself on display. Alex tries not to look, but he can't help it and I smirk, leaning into him. "Maybe we can go somewhere quieter now that the ritual is over."

"Not a chance," Alex snaps back. "We're taking a quick look around and then going home."

"Why? It's not every day we are here in this type of…" I glance around, trying to find a proper name to describe this place, "masked orgy party."

"I said no," he hisses.

"But—"

"There is no *but*…even if I would love to."

"We are in Venice," I keep insisting, my tone sweet and low, "in a palazzo filled with people fucking around us." I pause, observing attentively his flexed jaw. "Isn't there a place we can go and do the same?"

Alex chuckles, unimpressed. Then his gaze leaves the empty dance floor and goes to meet mine. "You wanna fuck, huh?"

His question is intimidating to say the least. Why does he have to be so blunt like that? Is it to make me feel self-conscious and ashamed about my desire? But before I can avert my gaze and look elsewhere, he grabs my neck, forcing me to face him.

"Look me in the eye and tell me what you want." His hands are cupping my jawline, and his thumbs start stroking my cheeks. His touch makes me shiver, leaving me even more desperate.

"You know what I want," I tell him, my tone slightly annoyed at his need to make me feel embarrassed.

"No, I don't," he ripostes just as fast. "I want to hear it from you. Or else you're gonna run dry tonight."

I can't prevent my mouth from gaping at his horrendous threat. "You wouldn't dare."

Alex gives nothing away, except a smirk. "You wanna bet?"

"Fine," I hiss, disarmed by his piercing blue eyes. "I wanna be with you."

"To do what?" he insists, keeping his eyes locked on mine. Holy moly, him being dressed in a tux, half his face covered with this mask, and me here dressed in a three-piece lingerie makes me really feel like his courtesan.

"To fuck," I finally pull the word out of my mouth. "I wanna go somewhere to be with you and fuck."

There's something in his eyes that switches after saying the word *fuck*. "Was it that hard?"

"A bit."

"It's gonna be on my terms, you understand?"

Oh gosh! My heart starts racing in excitement. "Yes," I breathe, already wondering what he is up to.

Alex grips my hand firmly and walks me across the palazzo until we take the majestic stairs to go to the second floor. There we cross the corridor, the lights just as red and the vibe just as sensual and Alex takes a golden key—that looks exactly like the one from the invitation—from his inner pocket and opens a wooden-door. I wonder where he got the key, but at this point I'm just too excited to go into a private room with him.

Where the seductive red lighting of the rest of the palazzo is cut through with the warm yellow candlelight, our private room is just red. Red lighting, red everything. It seems otherworldly, and it sets me on edge for some reason as we walk in. Maybe because it feels like somewhere the devil would take his concubine to steal her soul. I look at Alex, fully dressed and half his beautiful face hidden from me. If anyone is an irresistible devil, it's him.

The floor, which I can only assume is red from the lights, shines to the point of being reflective, and the entire room can only be described as "sensual and lush." Every surface seems suited for sex, with pillows piled everywhere. There is a wall with whips, handcuffs, paddles, and other more traditional sex toys hanging up that grabs my attention until I notice the bed.

I had never wanted to fall into a bed with Alex more than I had with this one. It's enormous and opulent, with silk sheets and dozens of soft pillows, and directly above it hung a mirror so anyone getting down and dirty in the bed can watch their antics.

I'm still considering the bed when Alex comes up behind me, putting his hands on my shoulders.

"Remember, tonight you are a courtesan, *my* courtesan, and I'm the client."

"What does it mean?"

"It means, my dear, that tonight your job is to please me."

"And what," I say as I turn to him and rest my hands on his chest, "will please you tonight?"

Alex motions toward the enormous bed. "Take a seat."

I follow directions, perching on the edge of the bed. Alex walks over to one cabinet that I now notice is a bar, and pulls out a bottle of Macallan, pouring himself two fingers. He takes a sip, sitting down on the loveseat that faces the bed.

"Since I've already clarified that I won't touch you, I'd like to watch you touch yourself."

I frown. "Alex, that's not—" I start before he cuts me off.

"I don't care what you have to say about it. You're my courtesan, and this is what I want. If you don't like it, we can go home," he tells me firmly.

Going home is the last thing I want to do. So fine. If he wants to watch me touch myself, I'm going to make it so hot for him that he can't keep his hands off me. He will not get me to quit that easily. I cross my legs and lean forward, my boobs pressing together and spilling over the lacy cups of the bra.

"Okay, master," I purr, playing along. "Tell me what I can do to please you."

He raises his eyebrows at my acceptance but doesn't miss a beat. "Start with your tits."

I lower my eyes, dragging my hands up my torso until I can cup my breasts. The bra snaps in the front, so while fondling myself over the bra, I undo the clasp, letting it fall completely open. I palm my tits, squeezing and plumping them before moving to my nipples.

Alex is watching me like a hawk, occasionally taking drinks of his whiskey while he does so. A big part of me wants to be embarrassed, but I can't give him that satisfaction. I keep my eyes locked on his as I run small circles around my nipples, making them harden before pinching the tips between my fingers. I moan, throwing my head back. It isn't Alex, like I want it to be, but my own touch is still enough to turn me on, especially if Alex is watching me.

"Lick your fingers," he says from across the room.

Like a good courtesan, I do as he likes, licking my fingers and wetting my nipples with them as I continue to fondle myself. The wetness makes my nipples cold in the room's air, and they harden even more. I can feel my pussy getting wet, and I'm becoming more and more aroused as I put on my sexy show.

Alex isn't one for waiting, so soon enough he commands me to remove my panties. I throw them behind me and spread my legs wide. "And now?"

Alex throws his whiskey back and sits the glass down forcefully, leaning forward to watch me more closely.

"Now touch yourself for me."

I follow his directions, sliding my hand down my stomach and between my legs. Wow, I am way wetter than I had expected. I work my hand up and down my slit while the other continues touching my nipples. I rub my clit the same way I do when I'm alone, and I can feel my hips moving with the motion of my fingers.

"Lick your fingers again. I want to see you taste yourself." His voice grows rougher with each command.

The air is heavy with lust as I lick my fingers that are still covered in my own juices, and the taste is almost sweet. I return to fingering myself, this time holding my pussy open with my other hand so Alex can see everything. I keep rubbing my clit with one hand and after a few minutes, I sink two of my fingers from the other hand into my well. The fresh sensation of having something inside of me has me closing in on my orgasm fast.

"I'm going to come," I breathe. My legs are shaking hard now, and something feral flashes in Alex's eyes at my admission.

"Do it. Come for me Petra."

I'm breathing hard as I keep working myself. I force myself to look into Alex's eyes as I come, and when my gaze locks with his it explodes inside of me, wracking my body with waves of pleasure. I moan, small desperate sounds as I come on my own hands. Alex is so intently focused on me that he doesn't move a muscle.

My climax winds down, and I'm left panting as I remove my hands from between my legs and try my best to resist falling back on the bed for a nap. My mission is still to get Alex to fuck me, and if the wild expression on his face is anything to go by, I shouldn't have to wait too much longer.

He stands, walking over to me with purpose. "You're my own personal hell. I've never wanted anything more, but every time I give in and take you like I want, I suffer for it." When he reaches me, he unhooks my bra from my collar and gently pulls me to my feet with two fingers under the collar. I rise, legs still a little shaky, and lean my body weight into him. He actually wraps his arms around me before tracing my bottom lip with his thumb.

I take the chance, looping my arms around his shoulders and going for the kiss. If he kisses me, it's over. I have him. But of course, right before our lips meet, he turns his head and my kiss lands on his stubbly cheek.

"Why won't you kiss me?" I ask, sounding desperate. "Even a client kisses his courtesan on the mouth."

"You know why."

"No, I don't."

"Kissing you makes me forget what you did," he confesses. "And I don't want to forget your betrayal."

"Is there a way we can negotiate that?" I ask, my lips brushing his.

But Alex pushes me slightly back. "I don't think so."

While he might say so, I know him well enough, so I keep thinking something through and then ask, "What if you punish me?" His body tenses at my question and I know he wasn't expecting me to ask him that. "Would you kiss me afterwards?"

Alex doesn't hide his astonishment at my question and considers me for a moment. "If I punish you the way I want, and if you accept it, then…" His gaze goes down for a moment as he assesses our deal. "Yes."

My heart explodes like fireworks at the idea he would kiss me again. I feel triumphant, but I push it down. I don't even know what kind of crazy scheme he's going to propose, so I shouldn't celebrate too quickly. My mind goes back to the naked women during the initiation, and I shudder.

"Just promise me, no crazy stuff in front of other people."

Alex laughs. "I have a much better idea than that, and I want to be the only one here to see you punished."

He slides his hands down my back until he reaches my ass. He cups a cheek in each hand and squeezes them hard, causing me to jump. What nefarious things could he have in mind? Alex kisses my neck and collarbone, continuing to knead my ass as he does so. I'm melting in his arms when he whispers my punishment to me.

"I'm gonna spank you with the whip that's hanging on the wall over there."

I stiffen and pull back to look him in the eye. "Alex! You promised me no whips."

The idea of the whip actually frightens me—it reminds me of Amanda and so many other things I'd rather not think about. I know he'd never hurt me, but I also know how angry at me he still is. Alex searches my gaze for a minute before kissing me on the nose.

"You are right. I'll spank you with my belt, then." I gasp, sucking in the dense air as he says so. "How does that sound?" His voice is wicked in my ear.

"Oh...okay. I think that will be alright." Not really, but it's an upgrade. "How many lashes?"

Alex considers it, before saying, "Twenty."

"No way! I'll be too sore to walk!"

"I can't believe we are negotiating this." He leans his face even closer to mine, his lips only a whisper away from kissing me. "Ten hard ones and the subject is closed."

"Deal," I whisper back, and as soon as I agree, his mouth is on mine.

He's kissing me! Finally! I would have cried in relief if I wasn't so busy trying to keep up with his kiss. Despite what he told me, it's clear from his passion that he wants this too. He kisses each corner of my mouth before laying his lips fully on mine, and I feel the press of his tongue. I open for him, tilting my head for a better angle, and his tongue darts into my mouth, our tongues tangling sensually. This kiss is beyond intense, and our teeth clack together as we taste each other for the first time in days.

Alex pulls away too soon for my taste, and I try to pull him back to me, but he resists and steps out of my embrace.

"It's time for your punishment, courtesan." He walks to the bed, undoing his belt and folding it in two, then he slaps it loudly against his hand and the sound of it makes me squeak. "Come here and bend over the bed."

Oh, gosh. I'm so nervous that I wring my hands together. Alex raises his eyebrows, and I know he expects me to back down, so I stop the handwringing, forcing myself to be confident and sexy as I saunter over to him. It isn't until I have to bend over the bed that my heart starts to race. I feel ridiculous with my chest on the sheets, my butt lifted up, and I'm scared. Not the best combination for someone wanting to seem sexy.

Alex runs his care hand up and down my back soothingly. "Don't tell me you are regretting our deal? I can feel your heart pounding."

"I'm not!" I huff. "Just get on with it!" My voice nearly squeaks at the end, causing Alex to chuckle.

"If you say so."

I have a few more seconds to panic, and so I do—but only internally. Is it going to hurt? Will he take it easy on me? What happens next? But before any more frantic thoughts make it into my mind, Alex raises his arm and strikes my bare ass. The "slap" of the belt on my skin rings out in the room, and I jerk, yelping. It did hurt! The sting is much worse than his hand, but also like his hand, the sting fades into hot pleasure, spreading over my warm flesh almost immediately.

"Ow," I whimper.

"You don't count?"

"One," I say loud enough for him to hear it.

He raises his arm and smacks me again, and I squirm.

"Two," I say, deadpan.

His other hand roams up and down my butt, reveling in the hot sting emanating from the skin.

"Alex, wait—" I try to ask for a second to breathe, but the next three strikes come in rapid succession. The sting is so intense that my mind has a hard time keeping up. My ass is on fire, and I'm questioning how much more I can take. We're only halfway through!

"Five," I cry out again, and humiliatingly, I feel tears stinging my eyes.

Alex rubs my burning butt-cheeks with his hand for a moment, and I swipe the tears from my face before he can notice.

"Last push," he tells me. I tense my body, breathing in and out slowly to stay calm, but the next five lashes take my breath away. I can hear myself whimpering at them, but Alex doesn't stop. Finally, mercifully, it's done. I can feel my pulse in the stinging on my backside. I gasp for air as Alex helps me to lie face down on the bed. There's no way I can lie on my back right now.

"I'm impressed. You took your punishment with grace and dignity, all things considered." He kisses my cheek, and I groan, turning to look at him.

"I hated it," I whine.

"You're supposed to hate it," he quips back. "Hence the word 'punishment.'"

I groan again into the mattress. I feel Alex getting off the bed, and by the time I turn to see what he's doing, he's taken off his shirt and is working on his pants. My mouth goes dry, and my heart is jumping inside my chest.

"I'm going to give you your reward now, but since your ass seems to be so sore I'm trying to think of the best way to fuck you without it hurting." His pants hit the floor, and he steps out of them. He's erect already, and sore ass or not, I will not pass up this opportunity.

"Cowgirl," I blurt. I know it's his favorite.

Alex considers it, and then he nods. "What a good courtesan you are."

He climbs up on the bed next to me. I gingerly sit up, moving to straddle him. I'm a little embarrassed to realize that, now that the pain of the spanking has faded mostly, the warm soreness is actually quite pleasurable.

Alex, for the first time in days, welcomes me with open arms. Seeing him laying here, spread out for me with his arms folded behind his head, has me wet and ready. I can barely contain myself as he guides me, with his hands on my hips, to hover my pussy over his cock and slowly slide down. We both exhale sharply at the contact, and I take my time, letting my inner walls stretch around him.

Finally, my husband is in me fully. I look down to see where we connect and watch as I slowly rise off of him and back down. He reaches up to stroke my breasts, pinching my nipples lightly.

"Are you gonna fuck me now, Petra?" he asks, voice thick with lust.

Oh jeez, no matter how many times I have heard him, I'll never get used to such language. The simple question takes my breath away, and I barely manage to say, "Yes."

I try to put all my feelings, all the days I had spent missing him, into that one word before I start to tell him with my body. I set a steady pace, riding Alex with my hands balanced on his chest, grinding into him hard when I come down. After a few minutes, we are both sweating, and I sit completely up, circling my hips as I fuck him, so he hits me in all the right places.

Alex puts his hands back behind his head, content to let me lead for once. I fall back a little and grab his thick thighs in my hands as I move. An orgasm is building within me, just out of reach, and no matter how I move, I can't grasp it. It's maddening, and I bite my lip in frustration.

Alex must see what's wrong with me, even in the dim red light, because he reaches up and grasps my hips in a firm grip, guiding me as I ride him. It's more of a forward and backwards motion, and I can feel the change instantly. The new rhythm forces his cock against my g-spot continuously, and it renders me nearly speechless.

"Right there!" I gasp.

Alex growls deep in his chest, his grip on my hips tightening. "Touch yourself," he commands between clenched teeth.

For what must be the millionth time tonight, I follow his orders without question, snaking my hand to where we are joined and rubbing my clit. It's like gasoline on a slowly burning flame. The slow building of my orgasm suddenly becomes frantic, and I can feel myself getting ready to finish, my inner walls clamping down on Alex.

I can barely gasp out his name before it's pouring over me, and I'm drowning in sensation.

"I'm coming," I sob.

Wave after wave overtakes me, but before I can ride out my orgasm, Alex flips me over onto my back with a grunt. I'm coming too hard to even feel my bruised ass cheeks. Alex grabs one of my legs and hitches it over his shoulder, and before I can take another breath, he's fucking me roughly, chasing his own climax. His relentless movements drag my orgasm out, and I'm still feeling the aftershocks when he finishes, pressing himself against me hard with the last thrust. I feel the rush of warmth pouring from him into me.

The seconds pass with us locked together. Alex pulls out slowly, falling beside me as he tries to catch his breath. I do the same but roll over onto my stomach as I feel some of the soreness on my butt coming back.

"You are such a terrible temptation," he tells me, still breathing hard.

I smirk, feeling like I had won. I roll over to his chest and lean down to pull his bottom lip. "Doesn't it feel good though?"

"Physically? Yes. Mentally? Hmmm." Alex pulls me into his arms, and I nuzzle my face into his neck, giggling.

"I knew you couldn't resist your wife," I tease playfully.

"I knew it too." He lets out a laugh, head shaking at himself. "I just sort of hoped that I had a little more self-control, but I never do when it comes to you." Alex sighs, kissing the top of my head.

CHAPTER 16

Venice, February 21, 2021
Petra Van Gatt

I don't remember how I ended up in my bed in Alex's palazzo instead of his without complaint. Or did he share the bed with me and leave before I could wake up? My head is fuzzy, and I wasn't even drinking.

Heading to the bathroom, I see that I'm still in the black lace bra and panties and I groan. How the hell did I get back here wearing only this? I cover up with a floor length silk robe, tying it at my waist before brushing my hair and teeth. I splash some water on my face and realize I'm parched, so I slide a pair of slippers on and head to the living room.

I can hear Alex as I approach the front of the palazzo, and smile to myself. We certainly had an interesting night, that's for sure. Maybe he can answer my questions about how I'd gotten into my bed last night, and if we slept together.

I stop dead in my tracks as I turn the corner. Perched on the arm of the gold and red velvet couch is Yara, looking like she has just walked out of a magazine instead of coming from the same party I was at last night. She's wearing her usual breeches and black boots. Her legs are crossed, and she is bouncing one of her feet while she drinks what appears to be an espresso as she chats with Alex.

"Yara?" I ask, barely believing it. "What are you doing here?"

"Did you have a good night?" she asks in return, completely ignoring my question.

"It was okay," I say distractedly, looking around. "Where's Emma?"

"Sleeping," she answers, before standing up and getting ready to leave. She looks at Alex once more and says, "Well, have a great day in beautiful Venice." And she walks past me and exits the living room. I blink at her abrupt departure, and turn to Alex, who is also sipping espresso and looking bored.

"What was she doing here?" I ask him, planting my hands on my hips.

"She came just to say hello," he replies, before he also rises from the couch and makes to leave the room.

Not so fast! You've got some questions to answer, I think to myself.

I know he's lying about Yara, and I'm going to get to the bottom of it.

"Tell me the truth." I stand in his way to make sure he answers me. "What was Yara doing here? What happened?"

Alex tries to brush me away and walk past me as he answers, "I told you, she just came here to say hi."

"Alex, please," I trail behind him, not ready to give up my interrogation. "Is it something to do with Emma?"

"It has nothing to do with her!" he snaps, whipping around to face me. "Can you stop now?"

"Is it because of your trial?" I take a step back now that he's facing me, trying to look innocently curious. The trial is a major sore spot between us, but I just have to know.

Alex heaves a sigh, displeased by my usual insistence. "Are you recording this?"

I shake my head rapidly. "No, I can only tape conversations in New York."

"Oh, that's good to know," Alex responds, raising his eyebrows in genuine surprise.

"Can we talk once and for all about this?" I ask, my eyes on his.

He doesn't reply immediately, but his gaze drifts down as he considers me. "If you're going to insist on talking, let's at least go out onto the terrace and I'll have the butler bring you some tea."

We head outside to a heated terrace, me still in my robe and Alex fully dressed in a crisp suit. The butler brings him another espresso and a cup of hot green tea for me, as well as two brioche rolls with custard, a slice of Italian frittata, and a plate of mixed red fruits. I take a bite of the frittata and sigh in pleasure. This is really delicious. I gaze at Alex, preparing for the conversation.

"I'm sorry for siding with Eric," I tell him sincerely. If this is about having an honest conversation, then I suppose it's fair to start with an apology. "He wanted to press charges against me and—"

"And you freaked out," he interposes, yet his tone is not rude. "That's what they do. It's their job to scare you. The more scared you are, the more they can control you." He snickers, looking away for a moment before standing and digging his hands in his pockets. "I still can't believe you're going to testify against me though."

I look down at my lap, fiddling with the tie of my robe. "When the pregnancy test was positive I simply didn't want to risk going on trial and getting convicted for something I hadn't done." Then I stand up and try to walk over to him and put a hand on his arm, but Alex just paces around the terrace, trying to get away from me. "Why don't you try to understand my side of things?"

"Because you betrayed me," he snaps, his tone laced with a sadness I wasn't ready for. "You are going to testify against me in a trial open to the public." He goes to the railing of the terrace and leans on it, staring blankly out into the city. "Do you realize the negative impact this is going to have on my reputation?"

"It's not like last time—no one's going to vote you out," I insist.

"You don't get it, do you?" he asks, irritated. "After everything I went through because of us, my wife herself is gonna talk shit about me in court." His voice is nearly a growl. "This is gonna be way worse than what I went through last year." He finally turns back to me, hurt plastered all over his face. "If you were on my side, we could face this together, we could show strength and unity, but you aren't…" Alex draws out a breath, running a hand through his hair.

"Don't make it sound like it's all my fault," I tell him promptly. "You abducted my mom and lied to me about it."

"No, I didn't," he retorts. "I knew they'd take care of your mom since she wanted to give Jan the police report on our wedding day, but I had nothing to do with her abduction." His voice is stubborn, trying to conceal the pain he is so clearly feeling.

"So why didn't you tell me the truth back then?" I ask, flabbergasted. "Why?"

"Because you were against it," he snaps bluntly. "You asked me to promise you that nothing would happen to your mom —no matter what she tried to do against us." The truth smashes me in the face, and I gasp, not knowing what to say. "Once she was detained, she wasn't a threat anymore. She was like in jail, except with a proper bed and healthy food, no one was hurting her."

"And for how long were you thinking you'd keep this secret from me?" I'm shaking my head in disbelief, and sit down on my chair again, my legs feeling weak.

"Until the day you had me arrested," he says with finality. "I had reached an agreement with your mom and Winter freed her. Yet she betrayed my trust and didn't have any intention to follow through."

I swallow the lump in my throat at the revelation. Oh my gosh… Well, at least he's being honest for once.

"Despite everything else, I had no idea that they injected her with the nano-particles." His tone is sincere, and I feel a pang of regret as I realize it. "Now, if you want to use what I just told you against me in court…" he lets his words trail off, searching for my intentions in my gaze. "Do whatever you think is right." And he stomps past me, walking back inside the house. I want to stand and follow him, but I don't—Alex is opening up to me for the first time in a while, so maybe I should give him some space to decompress.

I'm so tired of these wars that I don't feel the need to share what he told me with anyone else. No matter what I do, nothing will bring Mom back. But there is one thing I'm sure of: I will never, ever trust my in-laws again. They are the most horrible criminals one can be. Why? Because they've mastered the art of deception like no one else, pretending to be a bunch of civilized people, while at the same time killing anyone who stands in their way. Margaret and her daughters might have killed my mom and gotten away with it, but I will never forget what they did. *Never*.

I relax into the chair as much as I can, putting my feet up on another chair across from me and enjoying my tea and avocado toast while I watch the city awaken. There is a little bit of a chill in the air, and the butler brings out a chunky cable knit blanket for me to wrap myself in upon request. The entire scene is very domestic and cozy, and it's only missing one thing: my husband. It's such a unique place. Even if Alex won't enjoy it with me, I want to soak up my time in Venice. Who knows when I'll get to return next?

After breakfast, I go to change, planning on visiting the city a little more before we leave. The cold rolling off the water has persuaded me to dress warmly, so I pass up the sexy dresses I had packed hoping to catch Alex's eyes and instead choose a pair of jeans, knee high riding boots, a plaid flannel, and a huge warm scarf. I top the ensemble with a faux fur lined poncho that I throw over my shoulders.

Once ready, I check around the palazzo, but I don't find Alex anywhere. Did he leave without telling me a word? Very well… I'll visit Venice without him then. I descend the stairs outside my room, finding Severino the butler cleaning up breakfast back on the terrace.

"Yes, ma'am?" he asks in his thick Italian accent. "How can I help you?"

"I'd like to do a little bit of sightseeing. Ah, alone, actually, so could you call me a taxi boat with a driver that knows where the best sights are? Alex isn't here to escort me."

"Of course, right away," Severino says, bustling away to call the boat. I tuck my poncho around me and lean over the railing, watching the sun sparkle on the water as the curling fog dissipates. The butler returns to let me know the taxi boat has arrived, and he escorts me down to the dock, even assisting me in stepping down into the taxi.

"Thank you Severino," I tell him, and he nods, heading back to the palazzo to finish cleaning the massive home.

The boat driver asks how much time I have and what I've seen already, and after some brief discussion we decide I should head to Saint Mark's Basilica, one of the most extravagant and important places in Venice. It sounds perfect to me, and I imagine that there will be plenty of other sightseers around, so I won't feel totally alone.

I used to love being alone, but for some reason, I'd have preferred to have finished this visit to Venice with Alex. After all, I thought this trip would be the perfect time to reconnect and get closer. There's some nostalgia taking over me, and I would almost rather stay home than venture out alone into an unknown city all by myself.

Oh, for fuck's sake! Enjoy Venice, I tell myself.

After all, if I had stayed in the palazzo and read by the fire all afternoon, I'd be kicking myself later for not taking full advantage of being here.

Speaking of reading, I pull the novel I'm currently on out of my bag and do a little reading while the taxi boat glides nearly silently through the water, interrupted only by the charming "Ciao!" exchanged as the boats passed one another. It's idyllic, to say the least.

The driver pulls up at the dock outside of St. Mark's Square, a sizable gap in all the similar red and white brick buildings surrounding it. I thank him, grabbing my bag and stepping out. A quick shiver of stress runs through me at being completely alone now, but I shake it off and make my way into the square. The stone floor of the square is a worn, vaguely shiny, gray stone that varies from pewter to nearly ivory, some stones plain and others decorated with looping scrollwork as part of a huge decorative rectangle. The surrounding buildings shadow the square, but there's no missing the crowning jewel of the area on the opposite side: St. Mark's Basilica.

You'd think that after all the fabulous places I have visited during my life, that architecture wouldn't surprise me anymore. This place, though… wow. I knew the cathedral was beautiful, but seeing it in person is an unbelievable experience.

It had been built on a floor plan resembling a Greek cross, with one enormous main dome and four small domes spreading out around it. The architects topped each dome with an elaborate cross, and several spires sprung from the front of the Basilica, directly above gilded mosaics that takes my breath away.

Holding a hand to my heart, I approach slowly, cutting through the crowds to get a better look at the paintings nestled below sweeping stone arches that are supported by towering stone columns.

Each mosaic tells a different story, unique and splendid in its own way. They speak of the Old Testament, and the story of the church's namesake, St. Mark, all of them painted on a background of blindingly bright gold. I had read somewhere that the gold was not just to represent the wealth of Venice at the time of the mosaic creations, but also to stand in as the glowing light of God himself.

Several statues also guard the entryway, some of them men, others angels. For some reason, the winged seraphim makes me think of Emma and the butterfly wings stretching across her chest. With a jolt, I remember seeing her kneeling on the floor of the dance floor at the masquerade, and Yara's cryptic answer about her whereabouts this morning. Could Yara and Emma be together? The idea is almost bizarre, but then again, Yara is stunning and cold, almost harshly attractive when her hair is pulled back from her face, putting her high cheekbones on display. I can see why Emma might hold a candle for her. I make a mental note to text Emma before leaving Venice.

I take a few photos with my phone while I wait to be allowed inside. Eventually I make it in, gawking at the equally stunning interior of the Basilica. In the main walkway, I look down, and beneath my feet, the marble floor is decorated in intricate geometric designs and shapes. Rising from the ground are huge columns, also marble, with round arches between each one. The inside of the arches are also decorated geometrically, but instead of a marble backdrop, these shapes are painted on more gold.

In fact, as my eyes crawl up the walls, I notice that the red brick stops about halfway up, and the entire ceiling appears to be golden. *Certainly this all can't be genuine gold, can it?* I muse to myself.

The entryway ends in the impossibly high-ceiling main dome of the cathedral, this time painted with artwork depicting the New Testament. Everywhere I gaze is a priceless work of art, created directly on the walls and ceilings so everyone could see them for centuries to come. It's almost like stepping into a time machine.

Buttery yellow light illuminates the main dome, giving it a heavenly, otherworldly aura. I think that there is no way for me to take all of this place in during one visit, but I will give it my best shot.

After gazing at one mosaic for a few moments, I go to turn around, but there is suddenly a pair of hands resting on my shoulders. I freeze, terrified, until the stranger speaks.

"It seems I can never escape you," the man says.

A smile tugs at my mouth, and I turn around to see the amused face of my husband.

"I could say the same about you. I came here to be alone, and yet here you are," I tell him, planting my hands on my hips.

Alex chuckles, making a show of looking around us. "You come to the most crowded place in Venice to be alone?"

"You know what I mean," I reply, poking him in the chest.

I'm glad to see Alex, but I'm not sure if he still holds any animosity from this morning. His face is open and welcoming, so I'll just go along with it unless otherwise noted. He brushes my poking hand away and slips his arm around my waist to turn us around, pointing up at the raised front portion of the room.

"Do you see the gemstones in the decorations there? The Basilica used to have hundreds more of them, but Napoleon himself stole them away."

I consider the scene, and shrug. "It already looks like there's a tremendous amount. I couldn't imagine there being much more."

"It's rather an incredible sight, but St. Mark's Basilica has been changed and improved upon for hundreds of years. I like to think about how it looked in the very beginning," Alex tells me, his arm still around my waist.

I take in all the ancient statues and architecture and try to see it through Alex's eyes. It's all so busy and crammed full of amazing art that I can't comprehend it looking even more grand in the past.

"You should just quit your job and be a tour guide," I tell Alex teasingly. He doesn't look at me, still focused on the Basilica.

"I'm just fascinated by the history here. It's such a small place yet it's so full of stories and important events," he says absentmindedly.

I hum in agreement and let Alex lead me around the place. He shows me the real Horses of St. Mark, placed safely inside away from the elements while their identical replicas had graced me when outside of the cathedral. Afterward we view the Pala d'Oro, an altarpiece bedecked in gems and gold.

I listen, asking questions when he talks too fast, but mostly remaining quiet so I can listen to his deep voice and enjoy being in company as husband and wife again. I wonder if he has followed me here, or if it really was a chance encounter. Either way, it's a blessing.

We leave the cathedral into the bright light of afternoon, and it's warm enough for me to shrug off my poncho and hold it over my arm as we walk around the square. Alex is still explaining the important points of the area to me with excitement in his voice.

He stops for a moment, and I take my chance, interjecting, "Alex, are Yara and Emma together? She seemed weird when I asked her about Emma this morning."

Alex purses his mouth, slightly shocked at my question. He remains quiet for a moment, before he finally says, "I think you should ask Emma if you really want to know. I could tell you, but I think the truth will be more meaningful coming from your friend."

Oh my God! So does it mean they are really a thing? Of course it is! "You're probably right," I respond, leaving him at that. It's just the idea of asking my best friend if she's sleeping with my husband's sister kinda creeps me out. Yet, finding out from Alex and never knowing if Emma would be honest with me isn't the right way to go. I guess I'll just have to meet her once she's back in New York instead of sending a text.

"Will you show me more of Venice?" I ask with my most innocent voice. "When I go alone, everything is still incredible to see, but it's like seeing a totally different side of it when you're with me."

Alex looks down at me, surprised, but his expression softens. I see the love and adoration on his features before he turns away, and it pulls at my heartstrings. He makes a show of checking his watch before he answers.

"We have a few hours left before the flight, so yes. I think I can show you around a little more."

"Good," I tell him, giving him my brightest grin. "It's going to be so much fun."

* * *

After boarding the plane, I head straight for the bedroom in the back, tired all the way down to my bones. I let myself fall on the mattress, heaving a sigh of exhaustion. Alex had really taken his job of showing me around Venice seriously, and it was a fight to not take a nap in the taxi boat on the way to the airport. After walking around the city non-stop with just a few hours of sleep from last night, I'm totally exhausted. It's an early afternoon flight, definitely not my favorite, but Alex wants to land by 6 p.m. New York time. I imagine he must have had his fair share of getting his days and nights mixed up from flying so much, so I understand his worries.

I thought that after our romantic morning tour across Venice that my husband would be feeling a little softer toward me, but alas, as soon as we exited the taxi boat Alex seemed to get colder and colder toward me with each passing second. Then when we started to climb the stairs into the plane, he barely even acknowledged me, which isn't usual for him—at least before everything happened.

Whatever. I can only assume he's back to his usual jerkish behavior, and I'm too tired to care. Plus there is only one bed on this plane, and unless he wants to take a nap in a seat like I stupidly did on our way to Venice, he will crawl under the covers with me in no time.

Before going to sleep though, I eat the packed to-go lunch Severino had prepared for me. We were supposed to have lunch at the palazzo, but with the city tour Alex gave me, we didn't have any time left. The sweet old butler had almost looked misty eyed as he patted me on the shoulder to say goodbye, but I guess a hug would have been out of line.

"*Made especially for you, ma'am. No meat,*" I recall him telling me. What a sweetheart he had been!

I'm in just an oversized sweatshirt, leggings, and sneakers for the plane ride home, and now that I'm within sight of the king-sized bed in the plane's bedroom, I can't get undressed fast enough. I strip down to my underwear and tank top, throwing all my other clothes into the adjacent chair, and shimmy under the huge down comforter as fast as I can.

I think about all the crazy things that happened while I was in Venice, but most of all, I think of the sensual, seductive masquerade. Drawing the courtesan card had made me nervous at first, but it had filled me with a sense of power as I donned my costume under my cloak. Then there was the red room. The memory of performing for Alex, the punishment he had given me, and the subsequent fucking, has me blushing under the covers. I touch one of my butt-cheeks gently and wince. *Yep, still sensitive.*

I snuggle down into the pillow and consider what I will do when Alex joins me. I don't want to come on too strong and make him leave, but I also want him to know that I'm willing to do more than just take a nap…

My dirty thoughts can only keep me awake for so long, and before I know it, I'm drifting off to sleep. The quiet buzzing of the plane's engine is soothing, and I'm almost completely knocked out when I see the light of the bedroom door being opened.

Alex seems to think I'm sleeping, because he goes to gather extra pillows and blankets from the linen closet on the other side of the room as quietly as he can. To my annoyance, after he gets the linens, he begins to go back out into the plane's cabin. I sit up and he stops in his tracks.

"You don't want to sleep with me?" I ask blearily, only seeing his silhouette standing in the doorway.

"Don't worry, I'm just gonna take a quick nap over there," he tells me, waving his hand toward the cabin.

"Please stay…" I say softly, pushing the covers away so I can get out of bed. "There's enough space for us two."

He sighs heavily and runs a hand through his hair. "Fine… don't get out of bed."

Happily, I pull the covers back over myself while Alex goes to the restroom to prepare for bed. When he returns, he slides into the bed next to me, but stays as separated as possible. That won't do. I scoot over to him, and he has his back to me, so I wrap around him in the big spoon position. He stiffens for a moment, as if to pull away, but with a resigned huff he relaxes.

"When will you come back home?" I ask him softly.

"I don't know…" Alex sounds annoyed, and maybe just a bit sad. "Maybe when the trial is over."

I frown. I don't like that answer very much. God knows how many weeks that can take. "I feel so lonely at night without you there."

A few beats of silence ensue as my words sink into him. "Even if I wanted to move back in, I wouldn't sleep in the same room as you," he says, sounding formal and certain.

His answer smashes my heart in a thousand pieces. "Why do you hate me so much?" I ask with a lump in my throat from his words. Why does he have to be so hurtful?

He laughs bitterly. "You betrayed me. Do I have to keep reminding you of that?"

"You betrayed me too."

"To protect us. Big difference." Alex's voice is growing more and more annoyed, and I feel him start to pull away, so I tighten my arms around him and change the subject.

"If we sleep in separate rooms, would you consider moving back?"

He hums in his throat, considering the offer. "Let me think about it."

"That's all I ask," I whisper, finally able to relax against him now that our brief argument is over. I inhale deeply, filling my nose with Alex's unique scent, and eventually fall asleep.

* * *

Landing comes early, and it takes all of my energy to roll out of bed and get ready. I've brought another set of comfortable clothes, but to my surprise, Alex comes out of the bathroom in a shirt and tie, looking ready to go straight to work.

I don't question it. Maybe he is just trying to keep up appearances for the press if they're lurking around. I pull a brush through my hair and braid it before washing my face. I forgo any makeup, since my only plans are to go home and unpack. Alex doesn't comment on my overly casual appearance, only nodding at me as I join him in the cabin.

He really drives me crazy sometimes, especially now—so nonchalantly acting like we didn't sleep the entire flight wrapped in each other's arms. I know he misses me, he's just too stubborn to admit it.

We depart the plane together, but to my surprise there are two cars waiting on the runway for us. I turn to Alex, confusion written on my face. "Why two cars? I thought you said if we slept in separate bedrooms you'd come home?"

He barks a laugh. "No, I said I'd *think* about it. Plus, there are two cars because I have a meeting with Ryan I have to go to, so calm down."

Well, I guess that makes sense. Feeling defeated knowing that Alex isn't coming home with me, I give him a half-hearted hug, and I tell him goodbye reluctantly. So much for getting back together.

The driver loads my bags for me as I watch Alex leave in the second vehicle. I'm so depressed that our romantic getaway is over and that we have to return to the real world of work, trials, and being constantly at odds. I wanted more time in Venice and more time with him.

Lost in thought, I flip mindlessly through my pictures on the drive home. Zach isn't very chatty either, so the only noise in the car is the sound filtering in from the city and the soft jazz music on the radio. Suddenly though, a text pops up from Matt:

Hi P, How are you doing? Is everything alright? I'd love for you to join me at the library for a study session whenever you have time. X

P.S: My dad seems to want to talk to you. Call him when you can.

Jeez! I had totally forgotten about Matt and his dinner! I'm pretty sure the "*how are you doing?*" is a way to remind me I skipped the event without telling him why. I close the message without responding; Matt might have the best intentions in mind but talking to his dad is one of those things I don't look forward to. It's insane how Eric is so obsessed with this case. Jeez, he really is always on my back. I can't wait to get this done once and for all.

I look back down at my phone, almost responding to him but chickening out at the last minute. Matt and his dad will have to wait.

* * *

Stuffed from dinner, I relax on the couch, letting Maria start a fire in the fireplace while I read, my feet kicked up on the armrest. It's been such a long day. I'm absolutely ready to wind down for the evening.

Except...

Alex still hasn't come home. I know he told me he would just *think* about my suggestion of separate beds, but I really expected him to come. I had even told Maria to prepare the guest bedroom for him.

I can't stop myself from looking up from my book to peer at the closed door every few minutes. I even catch myself pulling up the security camera app and checking to see if his car is in the underground parking or out front. Of course it isn't, and as the clock creeps closer to 10 p.m., I begin to lose hope.

I'm getting ready to call it a night. The orange light of the fire is dwindling to embers when Alex finally arrives. It takes all of my self-control not to throw my book across the room and jump into his arms.

"You came!" I exclaim, walking in his direction.

"Yes. Sadly, my better judgement tends to leave me hanging when it comes to you," Alex grumbles, handing his coat to Maria as she rounds the corner, looking almost as happy as I am.

"Welcome home, sir," she gushes.

"Thank you, Maria," Alex responds, giving her the warm greeting he had denied me.

It doesn't matter. He came home. I can work with grumpy Alex if it means he will be here with me.

"There's some food from dinner leftover if you want, but I'm sure it's still fantastic. Maria made summer squash ravioli," I tell him with a smile, trying to lighten the mood.

But Alex just shakes his head. "Ryan and I ordered some food. There was a lot for me to catch up on, since I had to take a last-minute trip to babysit my wife in Venice."

I wrinkle my nose in disgust. Luckily Maria is no longer here to hear us. "Babysit?" I repeat, totally astounded at his word choice. "No one said you had to come."

"And have you waltzing around the masquerade in your panties alone? I don't think so. You continue to be a thorn in my side, wife, but I am morally obligated to keep you safe."

He waits for my response, but I just huff, turn my back on him and return to the couch, wondering why he is such an ass with me.

"Don't like to be reminded about your nearly naked Venetian adventure?" he asks as he seems to be following me into the living room. "Or maybe it's the fact that you've caused me nothing but grief for weeks on end."

What a fucking asshole! "Didn't seem much like grief when you fucked me in the red room," I shoot up standing by the couch and launch a throw pillow in his direction that he catches with a shocked laugh.

"Did you just throw a pillow at me? Pregnancy hormones are making you crazy," he says, mocking me, his eyebrows raised in surprise. The mention of the pregnancy makes me even more annoyed at him than before, and I stomp away toward the back of the condo.

"I'm going to bed," I snap back at him.

"Good," he responds stoically. "I'm sleeping in the guest room, anyway."

Well, damn. That takes some of the angry wind out of my sails. Still, I enter the bedroom and shut the door behind me, hearing some of the china in the kitchen tinkling with the force of it. Oh gosh! I didn't even realize I slammed the door with so much strength.

I shower, anger bleeding out of me and running down the drain with the water, leaving only resentment and sadness. I towel dry my hair, but any energy left in me is gone, and I head to bed with my hair still damp. I manage to pull an oversized t-shirt over my head to sleep in before I collapse on the mattress, feeling boneless and crappy. Groaning into the pillow, I regret my earlier deal with Alex. It's almost worse having him in the house, knowing that there is no way that he will hold or comfort me throughout the night.

I toss and turn, trying to focus my mind on something, anything, besides the fact that Alex despises me so much. I keep thinking back to all the loving, sweet moments we have spent together. Did I really make the wrong choice by siding with Eric and the Department of Justice? I've been telling myself so often that no matter what, I have to do what is right. So why does it feel so wrong during these long, lonely nights?

Enough! I will not lie here passively while my husband tries his best to pretend I don't exist. Alex slept in bed with me in the plane, and the night before we had even made love. I think I need to keep the momentum going if I want us to go back to normal.

Decision made, I get up and walk carefully into the hall. I don't turn any lights on, because I don't want to alert him of my intentions until we're face to face. The guest bedroom is a short walk away, and I pause with my hand hovering over the doorknob, briefly wondering if I should go ahead or not. What if it makes him angry, or makes him leave and not come back? Maybe I should just accept what Alex has offered and be content with him staying in the condo with me.

Nah, I have to try and be brave. If I managed to make him go to Venice because I held my ground, then I can do the same now. I turn the knob and ease the door open as quietly as I can, only the shushing noise of the door sliding over the carpet giving me away. I tiptoe to the bed, but as my eyes adjust to the darkness, I'm beginning to realize that the bed is empty. What the heck?

Turning around to check the adjoining bathroom, I'm not even able to take a step away from the bed before the light flicks on, scaring me half to death. "Ah!" I yelp and fall backwards onto the bed. I sit up, only to see Alex, still fully dressed, leaning on the wall beside the door. Somehow, I hadn't seen him in the dark.

His expression is thunderous, mouth drawn in a tight frown and forehead furrowed. "We made a deal. How did I know you were going to try and test my limits on the very first night, little Petra?"

I swallow, humiliated in the stark overhead light. "I'm sorry, it's just that I'm so lonely and—"

"I know. You've fed me that line before. Every time I give you an inch, you take a mile. I thought you were the more naïve of the two of us, but here I stand, the fool again." Alex scoffs, crossing his arms. "Get out. I need to rethink staying here."

I jump to my feet, holding my hands up in front of me. "No, wait! I won't do it again. Please stay. It won't happen again!" I feel almost sick with angst. One step forward and two steps back, just like always.

Alex closes his eyes, reining in his temper before he responds. "Fine," he grits out. "But if this happens one more time, I'll never come back to this condo again until the trial is over. Do you understand me?"

"Yes, I understand," I say quietly, coming forward to hug him but stopping short when I realize a hug must be the last thing he wants from me. There is a knot in my throat, and I try not to tear up as I walk to the door, rejected by my own husband.

Alex says nothing. He doesn't call me back; he doesn't reconsider, and he doesn't even tell me goodnight.

Tears are fully streaming down my face when I crawl back into bed, covering my head with my pillow as I sob. Even after Venice, I'm so starved for affection. My body and my spirit crave him, his voice, his touch, but even the brief reprieve of having him during the weekend wasn't enough to slake my need. He is so close, yet so far.

I finally manage to stop crying, and before I fall into a miserable, restless slumber, I reach my hand out and lay it flat on the cold wall. Maybe Alex is touching the wall in his room too, and in this way something still connected us a bit.

Imagining that I can feel the cadence of his heartbeat through the wall, I slowly fall asleep.

CHAPTER 17

Manhattan, February 22, 2021
Petra Van Gatt

To my greatest discontentment, I wake up this morning answering Eric's phone call. After my phone rang non-stop for at least five minutes, I could no longer stand his insistence and had decided to talk to him. What a big mistake that was. Eric now wants to meet me this afternoon in his office. I asked him why and, unsurprisingly, he said he'd only tell me once we met in person. I'm really hating him and his attitude to the core, but being his enemy is the last thing I need. Plus, the good news is the first court session has been scheduled for March sixteenth, which means once I testify, I'll be done with our agreement once and for all.

As I walk into his office, Eric welcomes me with a bright smile and shakes my hand wholeheartedly. Yet, something tells me his warm and friendly manners won't last long. Eric invites me to sit on the couch, while he sits in the armchair beside me. An uncomfortable silence settles between us as he ponders how to start this meeting with me.

"Do you know why are you here, Petra?" he asks out of the blue.

I want to laugh out loud at his stupid question. What a joke this guy can be! I literally asked him a few hours ago why he wanted to see me. Instead of laughing or giving him a piece of my mind though, I take a deep breath and just tell him the obvious. "Um, not really, no."

His expression switches and I can see how I didn't manage much to hide my mockery. "Where were you this weekend?"

His new question leaves a sore taste in my mouth, and the way he's looking at me isn't as soft and friendly as before. I can reply in a defensive way, or simply be polite and tell him the truth. He most likely already knows the answer, anyway. "I was in Venice."

"That I know," Eric snickers and I wonder why he asked me that in the first place, then. "Let me rephrase my question, did you attend a peculiar masquerade party over the weekend?"

My heart skips a beat and I do my best to conceal my shock. "How do you know that?"

"How?" he repeats, sounding irritated. "Please, Petra, stop playing that game, you know exactly how I know it."

"No, I don't," I tell him, left feeling totally perplexed. "What's going on?"

Eric frowns, wondering if I'm telling the truth or not and checks me out attentively. "One of my best friends called me from Venice, asking me to drop your husband's case."

What? My eyes widen in surprise at his revelation. "Why would your friend do that?"

Eric starts to finally believe me and decides to open up. "Well, let's say he was caught in a very compromising situation that could cost him *everything*."

His own best friend was at the ceremony with one of those girls? Damn! "And what did you do?"

"I negotiated," he says, keeping it short. Since I narrow my eyes at him in confusion, he explains further. "I dropped your mom's police report." While I'm celebrating inside my mind, I make a conscious effort to look indifferent to it. "Now, given the fact you and your husband were in Venice *together* this weekend, I'd love to know who the hell was blackmailing him."

"I have no idea," I reply, without blinking once.

But Eric shakes his head, huffing at my answer.

"Alex barely talks to me," I press on. "I didn't even know your friend was at the same party as us."

"Did Alex leave your side at any moment?" he asks.

I feel tempted to leave this meeting once and for all, but it's better just to go along with his interrogation for now. "No, he was with me the entire time," I answer, unable to keep my annoyance out of my tone.

"Was there someone else you knew at the party?" he keeps asking.

"Not that I'm aware of, no."

Yet Eric doesn't seem convinced, so he leans forward, getting closer to me. "I'm giving you immunity because I'm trusting you," he reminds me, his tone steady and almost threatening. "But don't try to outsmart me because I can take it away just as fast."

My patience with him is running low, but I'm trying to keep my temper in check regardless of his lack of manners. As I come to think of it, I understand now why Emma had a few issues with him when he went to interview her at her house. "I'm not behind any of this," I repeat once more. "I'm telling you the truth."

We keep looking in each other's eyes for a few more seconds, until Eric finally blinks, and leans back against his armchair. "If you say so." Then silence ensues as he ponders something through. "Did Alex move back into the condo yet?"

His question catches me completely off guard and the truth is I have got no idea. "Um, I don't know exactly."

"If he did, ask him who was blackmailing my friend."

"That's absurd," I snap, throwing all civility out of the window. "He doesn't talk to me, he literally hates me." I blow out a deep breath laced with frustration, and then say, "Look, I know you are going through a lot of stress because of the trial preparation, but my husband doesn't trust me. He knows perfectly well I'm taping our conversations so there's no way he'd tell me who was behind the blackmailing of your friend."

"It is worth a try," he answers nearly gritting between teeth.

I shake my head at how absurd his demand is, but in any case, I'm gonna do it for the sake of fulfilling our agreement. "Fine," I hiss. "I will try to talk to him."

"Good," he says before standing up. "I truly appreciate the collaboration, Petra."

***

After leaving Eric's office, I take my iPhone and text Zach to come and pick me up. To my greatest surprise though, I find a new unread message from Emma: *I imagine you wanna talk about Venice, huh?*

This was in reply to an SMS I had sent her the previous night, asking if she was back home.

Only if you want to. But yeah, I send in return as I step outside of the building.

Then looking around, I find my driver waiting for me at the curb, and as I approach the car, Zach opens the rear door and I get inside.

A few minutes later, a new message pops up: *Alright, come over.*

Immediately, I instruct Zach to change destinations and to drop me off at Emma's house instead. He hesitates for a split second, but finally complies.

I haven't seen Emma since the funeral but back then she most likely had already booked her trip to Venice, and yet, she didn't bother to say a word to me about it.

I wonder in which state I'll find her now that I know the truth; will she tell me the full story or will she just leave me in the dark—or even worse, lie to me?

After a forty minute drive, Zach finally pulls onto her estate and parks in front of her entrance. There's no one at the door to welcome me though. Not even the maid or the butler and I find it quite weird. I can only assume Emma's busy doing something inside. I leave the car, instructing Zach to wait for me, head to the door, and press the doorbell, waiting outside for someone to meet me. Finally, I hear footsteps approaching and the door cracks open.

To my surprise, it's Emma herself who stands in front of me. Her face isn't very welcoming though, and she doesn't even invite me inside. I can't help but wonder why.

"Hey," I greet with a genuine smile. "Are you okay?"

"I'm good, yeah," she answers back, like she's holding a grudge against me or something. "I imagine you came here to talk?" she asks, leaning against the doorway and folding her arms over her chest.

She seems very defensive, but I can't understand why. "Well, yeah, after seeing you participate in that initiation ceremony, I'd like to know why my best friend kept me in the dark."

"I see…" she nods, looking away for a moment. "Are you recording us?"

Wow. I see news runs fast. I didn't tell Emma I was taping conversations for the trial, so it must have been either Alex or his sister who told her. "I'm not," I say sincerely. "You aren't a suspect anyway so you're good."

Despite my answer, Emma frowns at me, and seems to be even more confused. "Because if I were one, you'd be pretending to be my friend and tape our conversations without my knowledge?"

Her question leaves me a bit on the fence, and I'm not really sure what to tell her. "Well, if you had killed my mom, I wouldn't be very pleased, and I'd want to know the truth."

She shakes her head, annoyed at my honest answer. "Alex told you he is innocent," she retorts. "Why are you still doing this to him?"

Her reaction catches me totally off guard. I can't believe how protective she is of him! Is it because she is having an affair with his sister or what? "How can you be a hundred percent sure?" I ask her.

"So you *don't* believe him?" she replies instead, her expression deeply astonished, like she's putting herself in his shoes. "Fuck, what happened to you?"

"To me?" *Now she's really out of her mind!* "Nothing; if I'm doing what I'm doing it's because of my husband's constant lies and secrets. That's all."

"Why didn't you tell me anything about the deal you made with Eric?"

Oh, so that's why she's mad at me.

"I can't believe you kept such a secret from me."

"Because it's completely confidential. I can't talk about it with anyone," I say, my tone getting louder.

"You know that it was Eric who told him, right? He doesn't give a shit that the whole world knows you're gonna testify against your husband."

This is something I didn't know, actually. I knew Alex had found out about my cooperation with Eric, but I didn't know it was Eric himself who had told him. I heave a long sigh and tell her the truth. "I didn't know, no."

Emma looks genuinely surprised that I wasn't aware of it, and after some pondering, she asks, "Do you regret siding against him?"

"I don't know," I answer as sincerely as I can. "Alex lied to me about my mom. He constantly told me he didn't know where she was and yet he knew." Emma remains on her guard, but I can finally see her face softening a bit. She must be thinking if I can do that to my own husband, then I can also do the same to her. "I love him but it's because of his lies and secrets that I had to side with Eric." And seeing how she isn't reacting, I add, "I'm sorry if I kept it to myself."

A gush of air rolls off her lips, and after considering me, she finally uncrosses her arms. "Did Eric tell you about the report?"

I frown at her question. "What do you mean?" I ask like I know nothing.

"He dropped the police report and won't use it in court or show it to Jan."

A million questions come to my mind, but as I want to get to know her side of the story, I simply ask, "Why?"

"Well, one of his mentors was at the ceremony and we caught him with a few girls—all minors—so he asked Eric to drop it as a favor to save his ass."

"Oh my gosh!" While Eric told me his friend was caught in a "compromising situation" I never thought it was something like that. "How do you know all that?"

"I helped Yara catch him," she says. All of a sudden, I smile up to my ears, thinking about an eventual reality. "So wait—that's why you were participating in that ceremony?"

"Yeah, of course," she replies promptly. "I mean, I had to play along, you know."

I wonder if she's telling me the truth or not, but I proceed nevertheless, "And, um, you and Yara…" Emma raises her brows, reveling in my uneasiness to tackle such a private matter. "Are you together?"

"We are just close friends," she tells me, even though I'm not really convinced. After all, if Alex didn't want to answer my question with a big resounding *no*, it's because it wasn't a negative answer to begin with.

Stepping closer, I open my arms wide and give her a hug. "Emma, I'm so relieved to know that. I thought Yara was grooming you to force you into that cult."

I release her and Emma just smiles at me in return, most likely wondering if my words carry an underlying meaning or not. And I truly hope she'll give it a thought if she's indeed having an affair with her.

"Nah, I was just doing her a favor to help your husband out," she answers, her expression more relaxed than before, but who knows if it's not a cover up. "Since you are siding with Eric, I couldn't tell you I was going there."

"Does Alex know what you and Yara did?" I ask.

"Yeah, of course," she replies like it's obvious. Well, not for me. "He didn't tell you, huh?"

"No, he no longer trusts me," I disclose, unable to hide my pain as I say those words.

"Well, yeah, you sided with the guy who wants to put him in jail," she reminds me once more. And I can tell how pissed off she is at me for having made such a decision. "Yara told me you are gonna testify against him in court, is it true?"

"Yeah, I have to fulfill my part of the deal if I want to keep my immunity."

"Wow," she utters, shaking her head in disbelief. "That's insane..." She cuts eye contact, looking down to the floor in order to hide her disapproving expression. "Well, I'm also gonna testify."

My eyes widen in surprise at her revelation. "Really?"

"But on the defense side," she adds.

"Of course." Not knowing what else to say or do, I smile, trying to conceal my astonishment. This is definitely Yara's request. I can't imagine Alex asking her directly to testify on his favor.

"Well, um, thanks for coming," Emma tells me, now that an awkward silence has settled between us. I never thought she'd kick me out of her house like that, and yet, here we are. She still seems to be holding a grudge against me for siding with the prosecution and I guess she'll need some time to digest it.

"If you need anything I'm here, okay?" I say, giving her another hug in the hopes that she will forgive me soon.

"I know."

* * *

Manhattan, February 25, 2021
Petra Van Gatt

To my surprise, Alex has finally accepted my invitation to have dinner together. Since we came back from Venice, he'd always arrive at the condo so late that I had already eaten. And yet this time, for some reason, he didn't try to find an excuse when I called him and asked him to have dinner with me. I didn't give him much of a choice either, since I told him Maria was preparing dinner for the two of us and she was expecting us to dine together. Maybe it's because we have the prenatal appointment tomorrow with Mariana that he decided to accept, or maybe because it was Maria's request. Despite all my excitement, the vibe between us has been colder than the weather in Antartica.

I might be sitting in front of him, but it feels like there's a wall in the middle of the table. Dinner has been quiet, so damn quiet that I find it infuriating. Alex, on the other hand, seems to be totally unbothered that we haven't been talking and keeps cutting and eating his food like I'm not even here.

Trying to find a subject of conversation, I say, "I'm glad Eric dropped my mom's report."

All of a sudden, Alex looks up at me, his lips in a straight line. "Was it him who told you that?"

"Yeah, he thought I was behind the whole blackmailing his friend thing," I tell him, before forking another bite of food.

"I see," he mumbles pensively as his gaze drifts down to his plate. Alex doesn't say anything further and keeps his attention on his meal.

After a few more seconds of silence, I ask, "It's Yara who blackmailed him, isn't it?"

"I'm not talking about it with you," he grits. Then he puts another bite in his mouth, and after swallowing it through, he adds, "As I mentioned before, our discussions will be limited to your pregnancy and that's it. So don't bother trying to get anything from me."

His freezing tone chills my bones and paralyzes me on the spot. I look down at my plate, feeling humiliated at his words. I don't find the will to say anything else. I'm just deeply hurt by his constant cold and distant attitude toward me. The rest of the dinner proceeds in silence and I suppose this is exactly how he intended it to be.

CHAPTER 18

Manhattan, February 26, 2021
Petra Van Gatt

Staring out the window of the car, it's easy to let my mind wander and zone out. The rainbow of cars flashing by on the shining wet streets, combined with the lack of music on the radio, and Alex's constant silence is making me sleepy despite the anxiety roiling inside of me. Since Matt had taken me to the last appointment, the idea of Alex being with me this time is making me even more nervous. Since he came back home, he's always been on his guard, barely saying so much as a word to me. It's such a weird relationship. I wonder if we will ever come back to what we used to be, if he will ever smile in my presence willingly again.

Heaving a long sigh, I lean my head against the cool window and close my eyes, focusing on the little lives growing inside of me. If they are okay, then I will be okay, no matter what. Alex or no Alex.

Still…

It's hard for me to not imagine what I wish this trip was like instead of the harsh reality. In my fantasy, Alex is holding my hand and dragging his thumb over my knuckles for reassurance. He holds me close on the way into the building and strokes my hair during the ultrasound.

Instead, it's almost like he's made of stone sitting next to me as he waits for the light to turn green. I'm lonely, even though I'm surrounded by people most days. Heck, even my bed is cold. I thought the prenatal appointments would bring us closer, but I was wrong. I scrunch my eyes tighter and fight off the sadness, but to my mortification, a little chirp of a sob escapes and Alex immediately looks over at me.

"What's wrong?" he queries.

"Nothing," I sniffle, wiping my eyes swiftly. "And everything at the same time."

Alex draws out a breath, tapping his fingers on the steering wheel. "I know what you mean. This is just the way it has to be."

You mean having a big wall between us and behaving like two strangers? I don't know if it's the hormones whipping through me or what, but I can't let this go. "It doesn't have to be this way, no! Just because I'm gonna testify doesn't mean you have to treat me like a pariah!" I hiccup another sob. "I m-miss you. And I'm scared."

Alex shakes his head, his shoulders tense. "Control yourself," he grits out. "It's not me who decided to side with the prosecutor. Choices have consequences."

I notice we are pulling into the clinic, and when Alex parks, I'm so annoyed at his heartless behavior, that I shoot out of the car like a rocket, slamming the door and stomping toward the entrance, heels clacking loudly on the pavement with my purse gripped white-knuckled in my hand. Alex follows behind me, rushing up to hold an umbrella over me. I want to tell him not to bother, but the last thing we need is some headline saying Alex left his wife out in the rain. We walk tensely into the breezeway, Alex shaking off the umbrella. I'm vibrating with anger, anxiety, and the precursor to grief.

I will not cry. I will not.

We check-in and take a seat in the leather chairs in the waiting room. I avoid looking at the other women, their bellies swollen and their faces alight with joy and gleeful anticipation. The men sitting next to them are rubbing their shoulders or fetching them cold drinks from the vending machines. One man is even stroking his wife's pregnant stomach with a look of worshipful awe on his face. Meanwhile, my husband flips through an old copy of TIME magazine, looking aloof. It's just not fair.

I blow out a breath and rest my chin in my hand as we wait. Eventually, a nurse comes out, clipboard in hand, and waves us back. It's the most high-end OBGYN facility in the city, and the hallways look more like something out of a million-dollar home than a doctor's office. The floors are white marble and the walls a rich, cherry wood. Pictures of smiling babies and luminous pregnant mothers line the walls, and if I was carrying a normal pregnancy, they may have made me smile. Instead, the pictures just add to the things I'm afraid I will never have.

The doctor, Mariana, has a warm smile on her face when we enter her office. She stands, taking both my hands in hers as she greets us. She glances at Alex, and I see a flash of confusion in her expression. Of course, last time I came here on my own, while Matt waited in the room. So I do a brief introduction between the two of them to clear off any misconceptions. Mariana and Alex shake hands and after some small talk, we refocus on the checkup.

"Before we go through the results from the lab, can we do an ultrasound to check their growth? It will give a better idea of where we stand with the pregnancy."

"Sure." I shrug, too downtrodden to even make any further comment. Mariana furrows her brow in concern, a little wrinkle appearing between her eyebrows. I give her a quick nod to reassure her I'm alright, and she leaves the room briefly so I can change into the ultrasound gown. Alex doesn't leave, though, and I turn away from him as I undress. I can feel his gaze boring into my back like two points of a laser, but I don't react. I shrug my jeans off and let them float to the ground before stepping out of them and pulling the gown over my head, hopping up on the table.

"I'm ready," I call, and Mariana re-enters.

I stare blankly at the ceiling as Mariana smooths the cold jelly over my stomach. Alex is watching the process, taking in every minor detail. She flips on the machine and begins the scan, rolling the wand over my slightly swollen belly while looking at the screen.

A few minutes pass, with Mariana marking a few areas of interest on the scan as she snaps photos. At first I didn't want to look at the screen, fear and guilt racking me, but I can't contain my curiosity and turn to watch, comforted by the two fluttering heartbeats on the ultrasound.

Mariana frowns, squinting and looking closer at the screen. She checks her notes and turns back to scrutinize the readout, blinking a few times.

"They haven't grown much since the last scan," she posts out, sounding a bit chagrined. "Baby B is very small for sixteen weeks."

I heave a sigh, because there isn't much more to say. I was already expecting her comments about Baby B, anyway.

Then she instructs me to get dressed while she returns to sit at her office table. Once I'm ready, I sit beside Alex and Mariana opens the file that is in front of us. "So, I have here the results from the tests, and…" she lets her words trail off, and I know at this point the results aren't good. I tense, my heart speeding up in anticipation. How much more bad news can I handle? "I know I said you were having identical twins. But, that was what I could see from the ultrasound. The cell-free DNA test is telling me a different story. According to the genetic markers, baby B is a girl."

My face falls at the news. "But that's impossible, no?" I ask just as fast.

"Normally yes, monochorionic diamniotic twins are identical twins. And she was male initially, but there was a genetic anomaly that caused the Y chromosome to fall away. Which, of course, means there is only one chromosome left. An X."

Full of shock, I turn to Alex, who also looks a little pale at the idea of a genetic anomaly.

Mariana clears her throat and continues. "Baby B has what we call Turner syndrome." After looking at our facial expressions, Mariana then asks, "Have you ever heard of it?"

"No," I whisper, and Alex shakes his head.

I've never heard of this disorder and combined with the Twin-to-Twin Transfusion Syndrome I suddenly feel as if I'm at the bottom of an insurmountable hill. How can I get through all of this?

"On its own, girls with Turner's Syndrome need some special medical care until they become adults, but they live a somewhat normal life overall. What throws a wrench into everything is the Twin-to-Twin Transfusion Syndrome." I try to keep my composure, despite feeling as if the world is weighing me down. Alex notices and, to my surprise, squeezes my hand quickly.

"Petra, take a deep breath," Mariana says, most likely knowing how I'm struggling inside to keep my composure. "I'm gonna get you some water, and then we'll talk more in depth about the results, alright?" Her voice is gentle and warm, but I can still see the worry on her face.

She leaves the room and I force myself to keep my shit together. Alex is still silent, of course. Jeez, I'd do anything to have him reassure me right now, or merely hug me so I didn't feel so alone, but he seems to be as lost as I am. And when he finally looks at me, all I can see is pity from his eyes. Jeez, of all the feelings I want from him, pity is definitely not one of them.

A few instants later, Mariana re-enters and hands me a glass of water, before giving us each a pamphlet from the Turner Syndrome Foundation. It's packed with info about the condition and the supportive care the girls need to go through to have a somewhat normal life.

After sitting back in her chair, she says, "As you know, male and female twins are ninety-nine point nine percent of the time not identical. They are called fraternal twins. Identical twins come from one fertilized egg and therefore have the same genetic information. So two embryos that start out as male with XY chromosomes and then develop into a male and female pair is exceedingly uncommon which is only caused by a genetic abnormality."

"So that's what happened to our babies?" I ask, trying to keep up.

Mariana nods. "Yes, exactly. In the case of your twins, the fertilized egg is divided into two embryos in the early stages of development. During division, one of the copies of the Y chromosome was lost, therefore your twins are now classified as male with XY in the case of Baby A, and female with a single X chromosome in the case of Baby B. As you know, a girl's normal genetic makeup is XX. Although Baby B will for all intents and purposes appear to be a girl, her cells only contain one copy of the X chromosome."

"What kind of complications can she expect in her life with this condition?" Alex asks. And I like the fact he's already thinking our little girl is gonna pull through.

"Developmental delays, nonverbal learning disabilities, and behavioral problems are very common," Mariana answers, keeping her tone as clinical as possible. "Heart defects, infertility, and short height are also other issues to bear in mind."

Jeez! Silence echoes in the room as we process the information. I rub my temples, feeling a headache coming on strong. Mariana allows us the quiet, knowing that it's a lot to process.

Alex is furiously flipping through the information packet, his lips drawn in a thin line. "So what can we do? Surgery? Gene therapy?" he asks, focused on the same thing as I—saving her.

Mariana sighs, turning her gaze to face her computer and typing a few things in, then her attention falls back on us. "I want you both to understand the gravity of this situation. Due to the TTTS, there's a very slim chance we pull both babies through this. On the other hand, there is a very good chance we can pull Baby A through. Each day that we wait, Baby B becomes weaker, and Baby A's body is overwhelmed by the influx of blood. It isn't just Baby B that is in danger as we wait."

"What are you suggesting exactly?" I ask, since I feel Mariana is just going around, mincing her words.

"Giving all the issues Baby B is facing and how it's putting baby A in jeopardy... I'd play it safe and do a selective reduction."

I narrow my eyes in confusion. "A what?"

Mariana takes a few seconds as she searches the best words to explain. "It means to terminate the growth of Baby B."

My heart sinks and I freeze immediately at the word *terminate*. "I can't just kill one to save the other. I just can't."

"I'm sure there's another way," Alex interjects in a more diplomatic manner than I did. "What about surgery or gene therapy?" Alex repeats. "Weren't we supposed to meet with a surgeon?"

Mariana shoots him an annoyed look. "Yes, I'll get you an appointment with the fetal surgery specialist. We need to handle the Twin-to-Twin Transfusion Syndrome before we can try tackling the Turner Syndrome. They can run some advanced tests for you, and maybe they can recommend a good geneticist. I'm not qualified in genetics, so I don't know if there're any treatments available. Meanwhile, I'll be looking for one too." She taps her fingers on the desk a few times, picking her next words carefully, and for some reason, she looks intently at Alex. "Also, when a mother feels stress, the cortisol from that stress is shared with the fetus. It's very unhealthy for them and can make even a usually healthy pregnancy experience problems. Your wife needs to be as comfortable and relaxed as possible."

Alex just snorts. "My wife already has a very comfortable and relaxed life, believe me. She is already far too spoiled."

My jaw drops at his comment, while Mariana flushes red despite doing her best to remain stoic. She then stands, slamming her clipboard down on the desk. "As you wish. Nevertheless, this is medical advice worth considering." She shakes our hands for the sake of courtesy, but the annoyance she feels for him is overly palpable. "Well, I think we are done for today. Our next appointment should be after you have seen the surgeon." She goes to exit her office, but stops, her hand on the handle of the door. She turns to look in my direction and then says, "Petra—think about everything we've discussed, and feel free to call me with any questions you have."

The door clicks shut behind Mariana and I rub my face with my hands, both embarrassed and upset at Alex's remarks.

What a fucking asshole! I'm doing my best to portray a united front with him when we are out in public, but with these type of comments everyone will see through it.

"Are you ready to go?" Alex asks, trying to sound soothing.

"Yep," I snap flatly. "The spoiled wife is ready to go." And I leave him at that. I don't want to start an argument here in the clinic over his stupid remark, but damn! What a dick he can be sometimes. The only thing I want is to go home and be left alone. I gather my things and we head out.

Alex hasn't said a word, but I don't complain when he holds the umbrella over me on the walk out to the car. He holds the door open for me and I slide in, remaining silent as he slips into the driver's seat and exits the parking lot.

I try to process everything that Mariana just told us. The complicated medical descriptions seem to meld together in my mind and make less sense the more I think about them. The only thing that keeps repeating in my thoughts is, why? Why did these things keep happening to me? It didn't scare me to know that I may have to raise a child with a rare condition. What frightened me was the possibility of having neither of my babies to raise at all.

"A little girl," Alex murmurs, more to himself than to me.

Looking at him quickly, I see him lost in thought, his gaze on the road. I assume I won't be getting any apology from him, so I pull out my phone and begin scrolling, searching up many things about Turner Syndrome, not even noticing that my cheeks are wet until a single tear splashes on the screen of my phone. I quickly wipe my face, but Alex has already noticed. He glances back and forth between me and the road, concern written on his features.

"Can we dine together this evening?" Alex asks, his voice humbled. I can nearly taste the remorse in it.

"Yeah, sure," I respond, looking back at my phone.

I can see out of the corner of my eye that he keeps glancing at me, but I don't have the energy to even entertain a conversation with him. It should perk me up Alex wants to have dinner together, but I know once dinner is over that he will leave like usual. I don't need someone sharing a meal with me out of pity or remorse. The fact I'm cooperating with the prosecution has given him an excuse to leave me high and dry, and that's exactly what he has done. Dinner is a shadow of the companionship and affection I really need from my husband right now.

Once we arrive, Alex parks the car in the underground parking and we take the lift together in silence to head to the highest floor.

After stepping into the condo, Maria crosses the hallway to greet us and seems quite happy to see Alex and I together. She beams, clasping her hands in front of her and asking if we are still having dinner tonight. Alex confirms, walking past the two of us to pour himself a drink. I settle into the couch to wait, continuing to look things up regarding Baby B's illness.

"Has everything been alright here? Are you comfortable?" Alex asks between sips of his drinks.

I look up, still distracted. "Huh? Oh, yeah. It's fine."

Since Alex stays at the condo sporadically, I don't see him as much as I thought I would once we got home. He won't even allow us to share a bed as husband and wife, which left me feeling bereft and bitter, but frustratingly, still craving his attention.

Maria breaks the tension momentarily by letting us know that dinner is ready. We head to the table, the tension palpable in the air between us. Dinner is pasta in a creamy, vegan-friendly sauce with roasted broccoli. To my biggest disappointment, Alex gets a roasted chicken breast with his like he couldn't care less about my thoughts on the matter, and a salad is in the middle of the table for us to share. I shake my head in displeasure, knowing he no longer bothers to keep meat out of my sight. My plate smells delicious, but my stomach is still in a tight ball of anxiety, and I pick at the food, forcing a bite into my mouth here and there.

"Hey," Alex inquires gently, "is the food okay? You really need to eat more for the babies."

"What's it matter?" I sigh, pushing the pasta around on my plate. "Every new appointment, there is something else wrong with them."

"Don't talk like that. We're going to see the surgeon. Things will get better. You'll see."

I'm mentally exhausted but fork a bite of salad into my mouth to both appease Alex and have an excuse to not answer while I collect my thoughts. I swallow, biting my lip.

"Do you think she will have a happy life with this syndrome?" I ask, entertaining the idea she could live. "If we can get the TTTS taken care of, of course." There is a slight wavering in my voice.

"We will give her a happy life, Petra. No matter what is going on between the two of us. We will give them both everything."

"But the complications…" I sniffle, tapping the corner of my eyes with the linen napkin.

"There are certain issues to look out for, but life won't be too much different from her brother. Mariana said there are difficulties, but she can live with it, remember?"

Alex tries to sound positive, but I don't remember Mariana sharing the same optimism. The words *heart defect* and *developmental delays* come to mind, and my face falls a little.

"We will have special schooling for her if needed, and top of the line medical care."

A smile plays at my lips seeing how confident and solution-oriented he is about our little girl, regardless of what Mariana advised us, I'm determined to fight until the end for her. I already lost one baby girl, I can't lose another one. "I'm glad you are not taking Mariana's side."

Alex rolls his eyes, cutting a bite of his chicken. "I respect her greatly as a physician, but she seems a bit too fatalist to me." As I keep looking at him, I can tell he's thinking about their interaction. "And that part about the stress just struck a nerve," he finally admits. "All my sisters were working while pregnant, and their children turned out healthy and fine. She was basically implying that a pregnant woman is some sort of incapacitated creature who can't deal with any stress from having an active life."

Despite his statement, I decide to test the waters a little. Maybe I can play it to my advantage and make him move back to our bedroom. "She's right, though, you know. It's bad for me to be stressed. The babies feel it."

But Alex raises his eyebrows at me, seeing my strategy coming miles away. "You know what's stressful? Having a wife that betrayed you."

Here we go again. "Alex—"

"You might have felt annoyed with my remarks, but this is nothing compared to what you have done to me," he interjects, before drawing out a breath, visibly hurt. I don't find the will to reply back, so we just keep quiet and resume to eat in silence.

Despite everything we are going through, at least he seems to have the best intentions for our little girl, no matter what condition she is born with. This is a start, this connection between us from our children. While Alex keeps cutting his food, I revel in the simple fact that he's here and determined just as I am to fight for the survival of our two babies. It's nice to have him here. I can't deny that... it almost seems like things are normal again.

"Petra," he says, warmth tingeing his tone. "It really will be alright, no matter what. I will not let you go through this alone."

I try to smile, but Louise's words filter back to the front of my mind. "*I only see death and misery.*" I swallow hard, the memory souring Alex's kind words. *How much more death and misery can I endure?*

"Thanks," I tell him, my heart not in it.

Maria clears our plates, and without being asked, sits a small plate in front of each of us. There is a small chocolate torte topped with ruby red raspberries. During any other time, I would have scarfed it down immediately. Instead, I push the plate away, but as soon as I do, something flutters in my stomach.

Eyes wide, I gasp, laying both of my hands on the small swell of my belly. The flutter comes again, feeling like the tiniest bubbles inside of me. I laugh breathlessly, and the table, torte and all, become blurry as my eyes fill with tears.

Alex stands quickly, but I hold up a hand to stop him. "Nothing's wrong. They're just moving that's all," I tell him, a tiny bit of wonder filling me despite all the bad news I have received today. Alex looks surprised, so he walks around the table and squats down in front of me, never taking his eyes off of me.

"Is that a good thing?" he asks me, and I nod.

"It is. I think—" I let out another airy laugh. "I think they want me to eat the dessert."

"Well, I guess you should dig in then." A quick laugh escapes us, and as I look at him, there's a glitter in his eyes I hadn't seen before. It makes my heart swell and aches at the same time. He then stands up, and, to my surprise, leans down to give me a long kiss on the head. It's a simple gesture, but I'd missed it terribly.

Feeling a little lighter for the first time since the doctor's appointment, I pull the torte back to me and eat it happily. And it tastes incredible.

CHAPTER 19

Manhattan, March 12, 2021
Petra Van Gatt

It has been two weeks since the appointment with Mariana and my spirits haven't lifted much. Alex has been in and out of the condo and just as distant as usual, except I can feel the pity radiating off of him. It's the last thing I want from him, but the only emotion he seems to be able to give aside from hatred.

With the jury selection for his trial taking the whole week, I'm positively surprised he's still coming home from time to time to have dinner together. I wish we could have a serious conversation about the trial and what my testimony means to our future, but there's so much tension between us that I haven't dared to tackle the subject.

As I come to think of it, I laid in bed awake last night, and I could hear Alex walking the floors every few hours. At one point, I heard glasses clinking and knew that he was up drinking. I was considering joining him, if only to have someone to sit with instead of worrying all night on my own, but when I was putting on my slippers, I saw the light glowing under the door disappear. Guessing he had gone back to bed, I did the same.

This morning he looks haggard. To anyone else, he'd still appear to be the perfect, put-together Alex, but I know better. I can see the stubble on his cheeks, a little longer than usual, and the dark circles under his cerulean eyes. I feel a pang of sorrow knowing that he is suffering, but at least I'm not fighting this battle completely alone.

Now, we are getting ready to exit the condo, and I check my purse to make sure I have everything I need for the appointment with the fetal surgeon. Anything to keep my mind off what is coming. Alex waits by the door, his uncomfortableness radiating from every pore. This is an unfamiliar battle for the both of us, and I know he's putting up a strong front for me. He checks his watch.

"Ready to go?" he asks me, shifting from foot to foot.

"Just about." I check myself in the mirror one more time before taking his outstretched arm to depart.

I've been putting extra effort into my appearance every time Alex is around, hoping that he'd have a moment of weakness where he couldn't resist my charms. The thought of him sweeping me up in a kiss brings a smile to my face as he helps me into the car.

"What are you grinning about?" he teases, trying to lighten the mood.

"Just thinking about... um... Venice," I say quickly, not wanting him to know my personal daydreams.

He scoffs, getting into the driver's seat. "You better be thinking of the sights."

"I am. A specific red sight, actually," I reply with a wink.

Alex curses, looking away from me, but I see a smile tugging at the corner of his mouth. It makes me feel a little lighter inside. As strained as our relationship currently is, there is still passion and attraction.

I lay my hands over my stomach as we drive. Alex is mostly silent as usual, and I can't really blame him. Whatever the fetal surgeon tells us will completely change our lives. There is the potential for hope, but also for heartbreak. We both have been doing a ton of research, but our case is so very rare that it is a medical anomaly. It makes it hard for us to find anecdotes from anyone else that has gone through the same thing, and it makes me feel even more alone. If I had just one other person to talk to, that understood... but I don't. Maybe in the future someone else could read my story in a medical textbook and not feel so adrift.

"You're quiet," Alex points out, keeping his eyes on the road.

"Just thinking... What are the odds that all of this happens to us and our babies?"

"You know nothing is ever normal or easy between us." His tone is almost sad. "I wish it was easier. For both of us."

"But we could get good news today. I'm still hopeful." I try to sound as upbeat as my words suggest.

"Of course. Me too."

Arriving at the Fetal Care Center, I feel my heart racing, so I hold my hand over my chest. The combination of dread and excitement are warring inside me as we check in. The babies must be able to tell that my emotions are running high, and they let me know with little flutters and turns inside of me. They've been moving on and off since the last appointment. Each little movement makes me more and more in love with my little ones, and at the same time causes the fear of losing them to grow bigger and bigger.

Baby B's Turner Syndrome is a huge hurdle, but it isn't threatening their lives like the Twin-to-Twin Transfusion is. I have an idea of what the surgeon is going to suggest after researching, but I refuse to think about it. It's an impossible choice and I will not make it today, no matter what the surgeon says.

"Petra Van Gatt!" a nurse calls.

Alex squeezes my hand, and we head back, following the nurse to the sterile room to await the surgeon. We settle in and a few minutes later, the surgeon follows. He's an older man, tall and thin, with a warm face. His smile is comforting and inviting.

"Hello, you two. I'm Dr. Bavarti. I've had a look at the scans from Dr. Torres' clinic, but I want to do a little bit more imaging, so I know exactly what our situation is. As you know, the situation with pregnancies this early can change day by day, if not hour by hour, so I need to ascertain exactly what's going on. I've also ordered an amniocentesis to confirm the diagnosis of Turner Syndrome and rule out any other maladies."

"Sure, okay," I say, feeling dazed.

"Wonderful," Dr. Bavarti replies.

The nurse returns with a wheelchair and a soft cotton hospital gown that is much more comfortable than usual medical gowns. After I change, I take my seat in the wheelchair, and I feel a little silly sitting in it as they wheel me around the surgery center.

First up is the MRI. It isn't too different from the CAT scan I had once when I was a child. The worst part about it is holding entirely still for so long. It takes around an hour, and my neck is stiff when they pull me out of the giant tube.

Following the MRI is the test that I had been dreading the most: the amniocentesis. While it's not a requirement, having a second diagnosis regarding Baby B's genetic makeup has been strongly advised by both Mariana and Dr. Bavarti. And despite being told it's not painful, anything with needles is pretty terrifying to me.

Dr. Bavarti himself performs the procedure with a nurse guiding him via the ultrasound machine. Panic is rising in my chest as I see the long needle on the sterile tray next to the doctor. My breaths are coming in shallow gasps.

"Just breathe," the doctor tells me as the nurse applies the ultrasound gel. "In through your nose, out through your mouth."

I do my best, but it isn't helping. I bite my lip to keep it from quivering, and turn to Alex, who has been sitting by my bed the whole time. "Please hold my hand," I breathe, looking at him through a haze of tears.

He takes my hand in both of his and kisses it. "It's gonna be okay, relax…"

I nod, hair falling in my eyes, and keep my gaze locked on his face through it all. Alex continues to plant soft kisses on my knuckles, and the simple sight of it soothes me.

The needle pierces my womb and I cry out, every muscle in my body tensing. It hurts, but not as much as I thought it would. The nurse walks me through everything as it happens, but Alex keeps by me the whole time. I see him clench his teeth and a new sheen of moisture in his eyes as they push the needle, and through the pain I'm touched that he seems to be affected by my pain just as intensely as I am.

Once everything is over, the nurse cleans the gel from my belly and leaves so I can change. I redress in my leggings and white tunic. An aid brings Alex and I some water and cookies as we wait in the private room for the doctor to review the tests. Eventually, he returns, still smiling, but I see the tension in his face that he is trying to hide.

"Well," Dr. Bavarti begins. "My colleagues and I have certainly discovered some potential problems. Please bear with me while I explain, and I'll do my best to answer any questions you have when I finish."

His explanation is incredibly scary, with a ton of jargon I don't quite understand. I try to keep up, and I can see Alex taking notes on his phone out of the corner of my eye. Each extra problem the doctor tells me is like a fist squeezing my heart. He speaks about partial placenta previa with the possibility of circumvallate placenta, intermittent absent end diastolic flow, possible amniotic bands, marginal cord insertion, double barrel placental cord insertion, and honestly, I'm sure I forgot a thing or two.

Once the doctor is done explaining everything, I try to swallow past the lump in my throat and take a few minutes to compose myself. He waits patiently while I try not to hyperventilate. I feel Alex rubbing my back to comfort me, but everything is being drowned out by my overwhelming sorrow. Once I'm calmer, I steel myself for the most important question.

"What about the surgery… the…" I wrack my brain for the scientific name.

"The fetoscopic laser photocoagulation?" Dr. Bavarti finishes for me.

"Yes, what about that one?" I ask.

"Well, let me show you the image of the ultrasound that is worrying me." Dr. Bavarti hangs an image from one scan on a back-light board, illuminating it for us. He's circled one area between the fetuses in red.

"What is it exactly?" I ask, squinting at the picture.

"This shows how close both of the umbilical cords are. From our estimations, they are less than one centimeter apart." The surgeon exhales and thins his lips before continuing. "I want you both to know that I very much want to be able to perform the surgery for you, but the fact of the matter is that it's simply too risky. If something goes wrong, you would lose both of them."

I clasp my shaking hands together. I have spent the last few nights lying awake, my hands on my belly to feel their tiny movements. When I close my eyes, it's almost like I can tell which baby is which, and it's breaking me apart to know that they are in danger and there is nothing I can do to help.

"So what are our options?" Alex inquires.

"There is only one option that I can see, and I'm afraid it isn't the one that you're wanting to hear. Our scans have confirmed that Baby A is strong and healthy, but as you know, even the recipient twin in a TTTS scenario eventually will be endangered. Baby B, on the other hand, is smaller and weaker, and is becoming more so day by day." The doctor pulls out his chair and lowers himself into it, so he is on eye level with Alex and I. "If we terminate the weaker of the two, we give Baby A the best chance to survive. As we know, the other fetus is already a genetic anomaly with the Turner Syndrome, and these things tend to progress negatively the longer the pregnancy goes on." He pauses, gauging our reaction. "Even if they both make it to the end, which is unlikely if we continue down the current path, Baby B could be much sicker than we thought after birth. In my professional opinion, the only way to give you a healthy pregnancy and delivery, Petra, is to switch our focus to preserving Baby A."

Silence fills the room, huge and suffocating. Mariana had already suggested exactly the same thing two weeks ago but hearing the surgeon himself giving us the very same recommendation feels like a hopeless nightmare.

"No," I say firmly. Alex leans in and gives me a kiss on the temple to soothe me. I scrub my face roughly with my hands before proceeding, "I'm not making this decision now."

Dr. Bavarti nods solemnly. "I understand. This is probably the most difficult decision you will face in your lives. Take some time, but don't wait too long to decide. Time is precious in these situations."

The doctor hands me a box of tissues and I blot my eyes, relieved that he isn't going to push me into a decision today. "I'll think about it."

He escorts Alex and me out into the lobby, and I go to the front desk to check out. I can see Alex shaking Dr. Bavarti's hand and the two men talking quietly while I finish the checkout process. Alex rejoins me and we exit the building. My adrenaline is high after such an emotional appointment, and I ball my hands into fists to keep them from shaking. For once, Alex is attentive to me, continuing to run his hand up and down my back as we walk to the car before opening the door for me and helping me inside.

"Are you hungry?" he asks once he gets into the driver's seat.

I know I should probably eat, but ever since the last appointment with Mariana, I have been too torn up inside to eat regularly. There were moments where I was starving, but as soon as Maria would sit down the perfectly prepared salad or my favorite avocado toast in front of me, my stomach would heave, and I'd have to leave without even a single bite. I ate the most in the middle of the night, standing in the kitchen in my underwear, stuffing my face in the dark, illuminated by the yellow light of the refrigerator.

"Petra?" Alex says after I've been suspiciously quiet.

"No… I don't think I can eat after that."

It's almost like I can feel him dragging his eyes over my thin arms and the dark circles under my eyes. He shakes his head. "You need to eat something," he presses on. "For you and the babies. Eating for three, remember?"

"Yeah, but three for how long?" I say quietly, my voice quavering. I lean my head against the cool glass of the car window, gazing blankly outside.

Looking back at him, Alex's face is pensive, but after a few moments, he seems to have an idea. "Let's go to that vegan restaurant you like so much. It's here in West Village, right?"

I frown, trying to find which restaurant he's referring to. There are so many I like.

"What's the name?" Alex asks most likely to himself as he keeps ruminating. "Something about a butcher…"

"Oh," I utter, a laugh rolling off my lips. "The Butcher's Daughter?"

"That's it. What a weird name for a restaurant…"

We share a laugh and I feel instantly lighthearted at his amazing suggestion. Alex remembering something as simple as my favorite vegan place in the area is so sweet that I can't help but grin.

"Actually, yeah, that sounds good," I tell him, mustering up a small smile.

That place is a little out of the way, but the detour doesn't bother me. I'm still not hungry, but I'm hoping that seeing all the delicious food and smoothies will change my mind. The store is tucked into a little road made of old red brick with creeping ivy crawling up the exterior. This entire part of town is old and quaint, and I used to love coming here to visit the little vintage thrift shops.

Just being here with him has already boosted my mood, and even if it's only temporary, I'm touched that Alex remembered. I'd eat anything if it'd make him happy. He holds my hand as we cross the road, and we start window-shopping a little. He even lets me drag him into a used bookstore, where he sticks out like a sore thumb. Impeccably dressed Alex in his designer suit among stacks of old novels is one of the funniest things I've seen, and I snap a picture of him with my phone.

As the sadness evaporates for the moment, some things that I have been too devastated to notice return. Even this early in my pregnancy, my breasts are a little sore, the skin of my belly is itching, and I am finally getting ridiculously hungry.

"Enough books," I announce. "Time for food."

Alex shuts a copy of *The Grapes of Wrath* that he had been perusing and puts it back on the shelf before opening the door for me as we step outside again. We walk a few doors down to The Butcher's Daughter, and my stomach actually growls at the scents wafting through the air.

I end up ordering the pancakes with red fruits and a strawberry smoothie while Alex only asks for an espresso. Then we go and sit at a table at the end, cornered between a wall and a window. Without further ado, I start attacking my pancakes, putting a big bite into my mouth.

To my surprise, Alex is intently looking at me, a smile hanging on his lips, and I can't help but wonder why. "Do you remember last time we came here?"

He's got that twinkle in his eye that makes my heart go wild. I glance around the place, swallow my food, and nod. "Like it was yesterday," I say, memories replaying in my mind. "You told me we needed to talk before going to Brazil and I suggested meeting here because they had the best smoothies in town."

"And I agreed to it because I knew no one from my entourage would come here," he discloses, his face lighting up with his growing smile. His eyes drop down for a moment as he thinks something through before they meet mine again. "When I walked in and saw you from afar, my heart nearly jumped." My lips part at his confession; he had never told me this before. "And all I wanted was to tell you how much I was in love with you."

His tone is laced with nostalgia, and as I keep looking him in the eye, I can only imagine the pain he's going through because of my decision to side with Eric and testify against him. How did we end up here? And why? Are we truly cursed as Louise and Mom had said?

Regardless of anything else, my heart does a little somersault in response and I can't help but lay a hand on top of his and say, "I love you." I know we haven't said those words to each other for a very long time and I'm not even sure if he still feels the same for me, but I wanted him to know my feelings for him haven't changed.

The corners of his mouth twitch into a grin. "I love you too." His voice is low and barely audible, but he takes my hand, and closing his eyes, gives it a long kiss filled with so much tenderness that I know he truly means it.

As the late morning bleeds into afternoon, we remain in the coffee shop enjoying each other's company, talking only about our best memories together. I lick the powdered sugar left from my fingers, content to listen to the sounds of the small cafe and watch the day pass by out of the huge shop windows. Eventually Alex puts his hand over one of mine, startling me out of my reverie.

"It's time to go," he tells me reluctantly.

I sigh. "When we leave, it's back to real life and the thought of losing the babies."

"I know." His voice is thick with emotion, and overly gentle. "But we can't avoid it forever."

"I wish we could." I stand, pushing my chair back in, and hold his arm as we walk to the exit of the coffee shop.

The veil of sadness settles more heavily over me each second until I buckle back into the car, and consequently, into reality.

* * *

"Dinner's ready," Maria announces. I jolt up from the couch, nearly knocking my laptop on the floor. Ever since we'd gotten home, I'd been doing more and more research on our babies' ailments. My mind is spinning from reading so much, and I must have flipped through the doctor's notes at least ten times. Rubbing my eyes, I stand and stretch my arms over my head.

"So much time on the computer is bad for you, ma'am," Maria admonishes as she pulls my chair out for me.

"There's just so much information. I feel like I'll never understand it all," I tell her. Maria clucks her tongue at me but says nothing else as she sets the table.

Tonight is a crispy fried tofu stir-fry with rice noodles. Alex joins me within a few minutes, only to see that I'm sipping my hot green tea and not eating. He looks annoyed.

"Do I really need to tell you to eat again?" he scolds.

"The tea is to settle my stomach. I just constantly feel sick," I say between sips.

"Don't worry, sir," Maria tells Alex when she brings him his plate. "I make sure she takes her vitamins every day at least."

"It isn't enough," Alex growls, but drops the subject. If I wasn't pregnant, I know he'd continue to complain, but maybe he's actually taking Mariana's advice on not stressing me out so much.

Besides the pregnancy, Alex and his grudge against me is my biggest stressor by far. I just hope after the case, he will turn the page and be the Alex he used to be. I miss my husband, the one who was always attentive and caring. This grumpy Alex is seriously annoying the heck out of me. Although I must admit it was nice to have him with me during the appointment and to pretend our lives were normal for a little while afterwards. I eat a few bites, feeling guilty that I can't stomach more. The sauce is delicately spicy, and the tofu is crunchy on the outside just how I like it. I wish I could eat everything, but the best I can do is half.

Suddenly, Alex's iPhone starts ringing, and after checking who's calling, he excuses himself, letting me know it's Ryan—his lawyer. I also leave the table given the fact I'm already done with my meal, and head to my bathroom to take a quick shower before heading directly to bed. For some reason, I'm craving the peace, quiet, and darkness of my room. I feel unnaturally exhausted, but just like every night recently, the second my head hits the pillow I can't shut my brain off. I close my eyes and I'm back on the table and they're doing the amniocentesis, or I'm back in Mariana's office when the word "terminate" rolls off her tongue. The picture of the ultrasound with the big red circle marking the impossible surgery area haunts me. I whimper, clutching the blankets, hot tears rolling down my face. If only I could just rest…

My eyes pop open and I raise up onto my elbows as the door slowly cracks open to reveal Alex, in a white t-shirt and gray sweatpants silhouetted in the doorway.

"What are you doing here?" I ask him, brushing my tears away.

"Something told me you needed some company." His voice is quiet and low.

Alex slides into bed beside me, pulling me into his arms for the first time in so long. I try not to cry into his chest, but the warm scent of his skin and the rise and fall of his breathing are so familiar. I've missed him so much, and needed him so badly, that I can't help but sob.

He shushes me softly as he holds me, my shoulders shaking. After what seems like forever, my sobbing tapers off into sniffles.

"I'm sorry," I whisper.

"Don't be," he presses a kiss on the crown of my head. "Listen, I was thinking it might help if something good came out of all of this. I'm going to plan a gala dinner to raise money for other kids with Turner Syndrome. It will be a black-tie event, expensive plates, the whole nine yards. What do you think?"

The idea of giving back to the community is appealing. It would channel my grief into something productive. There is just one thought that makes me hesitate.

"If we lose her by then, I think it might hurt too much for me to go through with it. It will be just like when we lost the first pregnancy," I tell him, my breath hitching.

"Don't look at it that way," he soothes, holding me tighter. It's almost like when he presses me so close, some of the terrible feeling inside of me transfers to him and he helps me to carry the weight. "If that comes to pass, the fundraising gala will be in her memory, like an homage to her."

I ponder his words more carefully. "You're right. It will hurt but… she'd want us to help others like her."

"Exactly," Alex says, "Now, time to rest." He gives me another kiss, this time on the forehead and I shut my eyes, reveling in his touch as much as I can.

"Okay. I'll try."

And surprisingly, having Alex here helps. He shares my pain, and I am able to rest. Counting his heartbeats, I slowly drift to sleep in his arms, wishing that he would be here for me like this every night.

CHAPTER 20

Manhattan, March 15, 2021
Alexander Van Dieren

Ryan and I have spent the whole day reviewing our defense and getting to know the jury that has been selected. Okay, mostly Ryan. I have barely managed to keep myself focused knowing that tomorrow my wife will testify against me. That's why I have decided to meet him at my private residence, away from the condo where we could possibly be in her presence. I still want to believe she won't testify tomorrow, but I know I'm just fooling myself. Ryan, on the other hand, seems quite confident of the jurors we got. Given the fact I have never done this before, I've got no reason to share the same optimism.

"How is Petra doing?" he asks out of the blue, most likely because I haven't been paying attention to pretty much anything the whole time. "You seem to be on another planet today."

"Not great," I disclose, which is also how I'm feeling. "We had high hopes for the surgery, so it was a big blow when the doctor told us it wouldn't be possible to do it."

Ryan winces. "So what are you gonna do, then?"

"Take it day by day," I say, before heaving a sigh. "There isn't much else we can do."

He nods, not knowing what else to say, then his eyes dive again to the sheets between his hands and he decides to change the subject. "Regarding tomorrow..." He looks back at me, removing his glasses for a moment. "Your wife is Eric's first witness. She will testify at eleven a.m."

That's the kind of info I didn't want to know.

"I have a really good strategy for her cross-examination, but I need you to trust me on this."

"You have my full trust," I tell him. "Just make sure I don't get a guilty verdict."

Ryan leans back on his chair, a smirk rising on his lips. "You won't." He then closes his file, stacks it back into his briefcase and rises from his seat. "Well, try to relax and get some sleep, alright?"

I nod, leaving my chair to escort him to the door.

"I will come back tomorrow morning and we'll go directly to the courtroom together."

"Thank you for everything, Ryan," I say as we shake hands for longer than usual. "See you tomorrow."

Once he leaves my residence, the silence hits me so I decide to put on some opera music before serving myself a glass of Macallan. I go and watch the sunset, which is now settling on the horizon behind the Hudson River, while taking another sip. My iPhone starts vibrating inside my pocket, most likely to announce a new SMS. I take it out and check.

Yep, it's my wife texting me.

Are you coming home tonight?

Not tonight, no, I text back.

Okay. Good luck for tomorrow. X

Good luck? I chuckle at her reply. Is she being sarcastic here or just genuine? What does luck have anything to do with it? Regardless of her intentions, I type two words in response: *You too*, and press send.

Manhattan, March 16, 2021

Despite taking a few pills before going to bed last night, I barely managed to get any sleep. Not even after drinking a stronger-than-life double espresso this morning can my spirit lift up, especially in the face of what is yet to come. To my surprise, Ryan is at the door at nine o'clock sharp and accompanied by the one and only Roy Van Gatt.

"I figured you'd need an old friend to cheer you up," Roy says as my eyes alight on him.

"Thanks for coming," I tell him, a grin hanging on my lips, before greeting him with a hug.

"Are you ready for the big day?" Ryan asks. As my attention switches to him, I can tell he at least seems to be in a much better mood than me.

"No," I answer, before we head downstairs and get into the car that is waiting for us.

Roy and I sit in the backseat, while Ryan sits in front with the driver.

"By the way," I begin as I come to think about a little detail. Then turning to Roy I ask, "When was the last time you saw your daughter?"

Taken by surprise, he ponders my question for a few seconds. "Um, something like two weeks ago," he answers. "Why?"

"And you haven't noticed anything different last time you saw her?" I keep asking.

"Well, she looked very concerned about you."

My lips curve up at his answer and I do my best not to laugh. "Anything else?"

Roy, on the other hand, remains just as serious as he tries to figure me out. "Not that I'm aware of," he replies. "But why?"

"Well, you might find her slightly different today," I tell him, reveling in his curiosity.

"How so?"

"Oh, it's nothing…" I do my best to conceal my growing smile. "You'll see for yourself."

Once the driver stops in front of the court building, I don't have the will to get out of the car as I see Eric from afar surrounded by microphones and reporters, most likely making a very inspiring speech about the case and how awful I am.

"Don't worry about him," Ryan tells me as he turns to look in my direction. "He might speak as much as he wants, but he has no evidence whatsoever that you are guilty."

That I know. But is it enough for the jury though?

We leave the car, escorted by security, and make our way to the entrance of the court.

As we climb the stairs, some reporters turn their cameras on us, and start screaming my name to catch my attention. I keep ignoring them, looking ahead of me. Unfortunately, they start rushing in our direction and following us. The police start stepping in, and I heave a long sigh in displeasure, shaking my head while reporters keep shouting at us to get an answer to their questions. Since I don't react, they start blocking the way we need to go, and soon enough, we can't even take a step without my security and the police making some space for us.

We head inside the courtroom and find Ryan's legal team already sitting there, waiting for us. After greeting them, Ryan and I sit in front at the defense table, while Roy keeps us company.

As I give a quick glance around the room, I notice a few cameramen are already here, standing against the wall and probably recording us. *Damn it.*

All of a sudden, noise emerges from the entryway and then from the door and not surprisingly a group of reporters walk inside to take a seat in the gallery. A few minutes later, Eric walks in, escorted by my lovely wife on his right and Matt on his left.

Despite hating Petra for siding with the prosecution, I can't deny how beautiful she is with her black blazer and matching fit-and-flare dress and stilettos. As I look at her face though, I've rarely seen her as serious and expressionless as now. While I'm shamelessly checking her out, she, on the other hand, is totally ignoring me.

"I don't get what changed," Roy whispers to me as his eyes follow her until she takes a seat beside Matt in the gallery. "She looks just the same to me."

Well, yeah, with her dress and blazer hiding her emerging bump, you definitely can't see shit.

"I'm sure you'll find out soon," I tell him discreetly before he goes and takes a seat in the front row.

"All rise," the bailiff asks as the judge comes in.

Once the judge goes to the bench and takes her seat, she then orders everyone but the jury to do the same.

The bailiff stands in front of the jury and says, "Please raise your right hand. Do you solemnly swear that you will truly listen to this case and render a true verdict and a fair sentence as to this defendant?"

"I do," the jury answer.

The judge then looks at them and proceeds. "Members of the jury, your duty today will be to determine whether the defendant is guilty or not guilty based only on facts and evidence provided in this case. The prosecution must prove that a murder was committed and that the defendant is the person who committed the crime. However, if you are not satisfied of the defendant's guilt to that extent, then reasonable doubt exists, and the defendant must be found not guilty." Her attention switches to the bailiff. "Mr. Gomez, what is today's case?"

"Your honor, today's case is The State of New York versus Alexander Van Dieren."

My stomach feels like it's tying in knots as I hear the bailiff saying my name.

"Is the prosecution ready?" the judge asks, looking at Eric.

His co-council and him stand up. "Yes, your honor."

After instructing him to sit again, her attention lands on us and she asks Ryan the same question.

Ryan also stands up. "Yes, your honor," he says and sits again.

Knowing it's time for the opening statements, Eric stands up, walks a few steps ahead, and turning to the jury, he starts his atrocious speech.

*　*　*

After Ryan finishes his opening statement, I give him a quick nod in acknowledgement, letting him know how much I loved it.

"Prosecution, you may call your first witness," the judge says to Eric.

He seems delighted to get started and I know exactly why. "Thank you, your honor. I call to the stand Petra Van Gatt."

Joyful whispers erupt from the gallery as the reporters were anxiously waiting for this precise witness to come forward and testify against me. And as I watch my wife being sworn in, all I can think of is how did we get here. From the moment I saw her at her dad's fifty-fifth birthday to now, I can't help but wonder what went wrong along the way to make her have the guts to do this without any shame or guilt. Is she really doing this to avenge herself because I lied about the abduction? Goddamnit! If she had just talked to me before making up her mind, I'd have told her it was me who had freed her mom and had even invited her to New York.

"Can you tell us a bit more about the relationship between your husband and your mom?" Eric's voice pulls me back from my thoughts and I realize her testimony has already begun. I just hope I didn't miss too much of it.

"They were enemies," Petra tells him. "My mom never liked him and was always trying to tear us apart."

"Did your mom attend the wedding?"

"She did not," Petra answers.

"Why?"

"Well, she didn't approve of our relationship in the first place, so there was no reason for her to go."

"And it was the day after your wedding that you received her first audio message?"

"Yes."

Eric then starts playing on the speakers the first audio message Tess left to her daughter.

Afterwards, he keeps asking Petra a bunch of questions about her mom's disappearance, until Carice comes in the picture.

"After Carice called you, did you follow her advice and talk to your husband about your mom's disappearance?"

"I did, yes."

"And what did he say?"

I notice how she never looked at me, not even once, since she arrived in the courtroom. Even though she's talking about me, her attention is always on Eric. "He assured me he had nothing to do with her disappearance and that I shouldn't worry so much about it."

"Did you believe him?" Eric keeps asking.

"A part of me, yes, another part…" To the delight of the reporters and cameras, her face carries the same uncertainty as her words.

Eric looks at the file in his hand. "On February sixth, you received a phone call from your mom, correct?"

"Correct."

"What did your mom say to you?"

"She said she was on her way to New York, that she didn't have much time to talk, and asked me to meet her at my dad's place the next day. She also requested me to keep our conversation totally confidential and to not tell anyone that she was on her way."

"Did your husband ask any type of question about your mom that very same day?"

"Yes, he did."

Eric nods, obviously pleased.

Damn it. I try to keep my composure but it hurts like hell watching her going along with his little game.

Everyone in the gallery starts whispering, but the noise fades away when Eric speaks again. "And what was that question?"

"He asked me if I had managed to talk to her."

Whispers erupt around the courtroom once more, and the judge starts shushing and requesting silence.

"Did your husband ever ask you about your mom before that day?"

"No, he didn't."

"Thank you," he tells her. Then looking at the judge, he says, "Your honor, no further questions." And he walks back to his chair.

Ryan stands up, a small smile on his lips that he's trying hard to fight, and paces slowly in her direction. "Ms. Van Gatt, when your husband asked you about your mom that night after she had called you, did you give him any information or details about her location?"

"No, I didn't," Petra answers promptly.

"Did you tell him about your mom's intention to go to New York and to see you the next day?"

"No, I didn't."

"What did you tell him, then?"

Petra pauses for a beat. "I told him I hadn't been in touch with her."

"So you lied to him?"

"Argumentative, your honor!" Eric snaps.

"Overruled," the judge answers. "You may answer the question."

Petra takes her time to reply, and I can hear some whispering emerging from reporters in the back. "Yes, but to protect her from him," she answers grudgingly.

"So coming from you, there was no way your husband could know your mom was on her way to New York?"

"Um, correct."

"How many people knew your mom was coming here, Ms. Van Gatt?"

"Objection, your honor," Eric shoots up. "That's beyond the scope."

"Overruled," the judge answers again. "Please answer the question."

Petra seems confused. "Um, I don't know."

"Maybe she gave you an indication, no?"

"Objection, your honor, the question is speculative!"

"Sustained," the judge replies. Then she looks at Ryan and says, "Mr. Steinberg, kindly rephrase the question."

"Did your mom tell you how many people she had been in touch with on her way to New York?" he asks again.

I smile, seeing Petra getting uncomfortable. She looks at the judge, waiting for her to do something.

"Answer the question, please," the judge tells her.

Her attention goes back to Ryan, and she says, "She told me she had called Eric and Carice."

"Eric?" Ryan repeats. Then pointing to where Eric is sitting, he asks, "You mean this Eric?"

"Correct."

Everyone starts whispering louder than before in shock at the revelation that Eric and Tess were friends and it takes a few bangs with her gavel for the judge to keep the gallery under control.

"So as soon as your mom allegedly escaped her abductor, the only people she called to let them know she was going to New York were Eric, here present, and Carice?"

"Speculative, your honor!" Eric is getting so damn annoying! Jeez!

"Your honor, I'd like to enter defense exhibit A." Ryan takes a document from our table and gives it to the court clerk who passes it to the judge. "According to the latest phone numbers Tess Hagen called, only Eric Bradford, Carice Knowles, and Petra Van Gatt make the list." He then walks back to where Petra is sitting and proceeds. "Has your mom, to the best of your knowledge, always been firmly against your relationship with Mr. Van Dieren?"

"Um, yes."

"Was it because she was against your relationship with Mr. Van Dieren that she refused to attend *your* wedding reception even after *you* invited her directly?"

"Speculative, your honor," Eric snaps.

"Witness had already confirmed those facts with the prosecution, your honor," Ryan steps in. "I'm just asking the same question here."

The judge looks at both Ryan and Eric and then says, "Objection overruled, you may answer the question."

My lips curve up, seeing how the judge is on our side today. Looks like being close friends with Tess Hagen isn't working in Eric's favor.

Petra doesn't look very pleased either, but she answers the question, nevertheless. "Yes."

"Yet, between your husband and yourself, only *you* knew that your mom was on her way to New York, isn't that right?"

"Argumentative, your honor!" Eric stands up, outraged.

"Sustained," the judge says. "Please either rephrase you question, Mr. Steinberg, or ask something else," the judge sounds pretty annoyed at Ryan's performance, but I'm loving it.

Ryan ponders for a moment. "Ms. Van Gatt, apart from lying to your husband when he asked you about your mom, what else did you do to protect her?"

"Um, I don't understand the question," she says, clearly confused.

"You said you lied to protect her from him, correct?"

"Correct."

"What else did you do to protect your mom from your husband?"

"I…" Petra looks down at her lap, lost for words.

"Did you call the police to go and check on your mom just in case he would find out that she was in New York?"

"No, I didn't."

"Why not? If you wanted to protect your mom from your husband surely you'd have taken extra prevention."

"Objection!" *Here we go again!*

"Overruled," the judge snaps. "Please answer."

"I…" Her eyes remain down as she considers his question. After a few more seconds though, she looks back at him, quite destabilized, and says, "I don't know."

Amid the emerging whispers, Ryan drops the comment of the century. "And yet, for some strange reason, here you are, with full immunity while my client is suspect number one."

* * *

"What a brilliant performance," I praise Ryan as we leave the courtroom. "You totally destroyed her."

"I only did my job," he says, playing it down.

Regardless of what he says, I'm feeling lightheaded and my mood has totally changed from this morning.

We stand outside the courtroom while Ryan shakes a few hands that come by to congratulate him. Heck, even some reporters are praising him and thanking him for the show he gave us.

"Alex," I hear someone saying behind me.

"I don't talk to you," I snap after turning and finding it's Petra. "If you have anything to say about the case, you have my attorney's details." Not wanting to draw attention to ourselves, I start making my way out of the court building, but she seems to be following me closely.

"All I did was be as impartial as I could," she says, nearly stumbling over her words.

"Good for you," I answer, wanting nothing more but to stay away from her. Reaching outside, I go down the stairs and try to ignore her as much as I can.

Yet Petra is now beside me and matching my pace. "Why are you being such a dick?"

"Me?" I stop in my tracks at her vulgar question, turning to face her once and for all. "Have you heard your testimony? You humiliated me." I can't help but snicker, because I'm pretty sure she doesn't even realize it. "Eric must be very proud of you." Shaking my head in disgust at the simple memory of it, I add, "You know what? I'm glad I have a really good attorney because your testimony was really despicable." Petra gasps in shock at my statement, but the real shocker here was seeing her testifying against me. "Now, if you'll excuse me, I don't want to look at you any longer."

CHAPTER 21

Manhattan, March 19, 2021
Petra Van Gatt

I'm spread out on the couch, my feet propped up on a few pillows from the bedroom to elevate them over my head. My pregnancy is still in the early stages, but since I'm carrying twins, I'm already starting to experience some of the less than stellar side effects, including my feet swelling in the evening. A few minutes ago, Emma had called me to tell me her testimony has been broadcasted everywhere, so unfortunately for me, my morbid curiosity makes me watch the news for the very first time in my life—but I flip through the channels each time a segment on the trial pops up. Their speculations about the trial and our relationship are just too ridiculous and far-fetched to watch any longer. Jeez, those presenters really love sensationalism, it's unbelievable. The more scandalous and melodramatic the better. It reminds me of the headlines about my own testimony from Monday, making my stomach drop, so I just turn off the TV, and try to forget about the trial once and for all. Following Mariana's advice, I haven't been to the courtroom since my testimony. Not only is my presence no longer required, but it's quite a stressful experience in itself, which can be hurtful for the babies.

Maria bustles her way into the living room, a cautious expression on her face. "It's dinnertime, ma'am. What can I make for you this evening? Any preference?"

I lift my phone up from where it is laying on my chest and check the time. It's a little past 7 p.m. I guess it really is dinner time. Except… I'm not hungry. It seems like I never am anymore.

"No, thank you," I say politely. "Maybe some hot tea and, um, a cookie?"

I can see that Maria wants to protest. She's warring between scolding me for not eating like a responsible mother-to-be and keeping quiet since I am technically her employer. She fusses with her apron for a moment, lips pursed, before she can't hold it in anymore. "Ma'am please. You have to eat something. It just isn't healthy to starve yourself."

"I eat," I retort. "Just not at normal mealtimes."

Maria wants to say something more, but she holds it back and simply nods. "As you say, ma'am."

A thought crosses my mind. I might actually be interested in dinner if I didn't have to dine alone.

"Maria?" I say loud enough for her to come back in. "Is Alex coming to dinner tonight?" I ask hopefully. I haven't seem him since the trial, but before Monday he at least used to join me for dinner more often than not. Maybe because it's Friday night, he'd have a change of heart and come.

Maria's face falls. She'd clearly been hoping to avoid this line of conversation. "Ah… no, ma'am. He called earlier this evening and said not to make a plate for him."

I sink back into the couch. Well, damn. "Just the tea and cookie, then."

Maria looks crestfallen, but she acquiesces and leaves. I pull out my iPhone, hellbent on texting Alex and asking how long he plans on avoiding me, but to my surprise, there is an unread message in my text inbox already from Matt.

Hey, P. I haven't heard from you since the trial and I'm starting to get worried. Give me a call when you're feeling up to it. X

Matt is so sweet. He's always been so kind, and it makes me feel a pang of guilt deep in my stomach. What have I ever done to deserve such kindness from someone like him? I know he has a bit of a thing for me, but even so, he is an amazing friend.

I take a deep breath and decide to call him. It'll be nice to hear a caring voice besides Maria's, anyway. The line rings a few times before Matt picks up.

"Hey," I start lamely.

"Petra! It's so good to hear from you. I've been worried that you were beating yourself up still about the testimony," Matt says, his voice filled with concern.

I'm quiet for a second before responding, "Maybe a little. I thought that the testimony would be the worst part and that everything would slowly go back to normal afterwards. Instead… I haven't heard from Alex all week."

There is an intake of breath on the other line, and then strained silence.

"Matt...?"

"Sorry," he replies tightly. "I'm just having a hard time understanding why a husband would leave his wife, who is going through a pregnancy—let alone with twins, alone for nearly an entire week. It's detestable." Well, he doesn't mince his words.

"He says I betrayed him," I confess, wanting to share this with someone. "That we could've gotten through anything as a team, but now I've left him to fight alone..." I choke down tears.

"Stop it, P. You followed the law. If he hadn't broken it in the first place, we wouldn't be here."

"He could still be innocent," I remind him. "I didn't manage to get anything stating otherwise."

"In any case, he shouldn't treat you like that." I nod, agreeing wholeheartedly with him. "Do you think he's spending the weekend away?"

"I don't know. I haven't seen him the whole week, maybe he's..." I sniffle, trying to contain the tears already falling. "Whatever. I don't care what he's doing. I'm so tired of this shit."

"Hey..." Matt's voice changes from annoyed anger to gentle worry. "Look, just because you're cooperating with the prosecution doesn't mean he has the right to behave like a dick to you. Why don't you come over?"

He really is too sweet. The invitation warms my heart, but I'm such a mess that I don't think I'll be good company. "Thanks, but I don't want to disturb you."

"Since when have you disturbed me? My dad is out, and I was about to watch a documentary and order a pizza. If you want to come over, we can watch it together. I'm sure you'll like it," Matt cajoles. He knows I love documentaries! What a sneaky way to tempt me over.

"What's the name?" I ask cautiously.

"That's a surprise." I chuckle, knowing that he'd say that. And to make me even more interested, he adds, "But let's say it's the type of documentary that's been banned everywhere."

Damn him! He's got me and we both know it. "Alright," I murmur in defeat. "I'm on my way then."

***

Matt is at the door to welcome me into his sprawling red brick townhouse located in Greenwich Village. I remember how I came here once with my dad for that private party Eric was hosting a year ago. Insane how time flies so quickly. As I get out of the car, Matt heads down the sidewalk to greet me and offers me his arm as we walk inside.

"I'm not suddenly made of glass, you know," I joke.

"I know, but I'm not taking any chances with you and your precious cargo," Matt tells me, motioning toward the small swell of my belly. It makes me grin a small bit to know he cares.

The inside of Matt's house is a split level, and we head down into the lower one to the dedicated movie room. It isn't a theater exactly, just a huge plush sectional and a ridiculously large television on a glass stand. In the cubbies beneath the TV, there is one of every gaming system currently on the market, all backlit like pieces of art. There are no cords to be seen.

"You play video-games?" I ask, surprised.

"My dad does," he answers.

My brows rise in surprise. Wow. I never imagined Eric, a fifty-something year old man, spending his time in front of a screen.

I settle into the couch while Matt gets everything ready. I had changed into some cozy black sweatpants and piled my hair on top of my head in a messy bun. *Top of the line movie night fashion*, I think with a giggle.

Matt returns triumphantly after a few minutes with a blank DVD in his hand, holding it in the air like a trophy. "Found it! My dad mentioned having it, but he hid it pretty well this time around."

"A DVD?" I ask sarcastically. "That must be so old. What is it called?"

Matt squints, trying to read the title written on the disk in sharpie.

"It says, uh, 'Royal Families'?" He looks skeptical. "That doesn't sound like something that would be banned."

"Who cares? Let's get started!" I say, patting the couch next to me. Matt inserts the mystery disk into the TV and takes his seat beside me as the screen turns gray, trying to read the DVD.

"It wasn't easy finding a vegan diavola pizza, but I managed. It should be here shortly," Matt says. I'm still not hungry, but greasy delivery pizza sounds a lot more interesting than Maria's perfectly prepared, nutritionally balanced meals.

"I'm really proud of you, Matt. Being a vegan isn't easy. If anyone knows the struggle, it's me."

I can see Matt blush in the dim light of the television. He clears his throat and keeps his attention on the screen. The BBC logo appears on the screen, and I look at Matt, confused.

"BBC?" I ask slowly. "Really?"

"Give it a chance!" Matt insists, but I can hear a thread of humor in his tone. "Let's keep an open mind, shall we?"

"Alright, alright..." I try to keep a straight face and pay attention to the movie, but it's harder than I thought. It's clearly old, probably filmed around the seventies, and as the minutes pass, I can tell it's a slice of life documentary about the British Royal Family.

The pizza arrives in time, and before I know it, I'm chewing on a slice, pulling the pizza away from my mouth as a long string of cashew mozzarella refuses to break. The strand of cheese finally snaps, and I have to slurp it up like spaghetti. Matt watches the whole time, and snorts in amusement.

About twenty minutes into the documentary, a young Queen Elizabeth is on the screen digging animatedly through her purse for pocket change to give little Prince Edward for candy. She trills in her charming accent about how the gooey candy will end up in the car, and it's at that moment the documentary is just too much for me. I howl in laughter, kicking my feet at the absurdity of it all. "Banned documentary, indeed."

"Oh, shut up, P." Matt sulks, but within seconds he's laughing alongside me, tears in his hazel eyes.

"Oh my god." I gasp as the laughter subsides. "What a stupid movie."

Matt wipes his eyes, looking back to the screen where Prince Edward is cramming a candy bar into his royal six-year-old mouth with gusto. Matt struggles to contain himself, catching my gaze with his mouth twitching at the corners.

"I guess I should apologize, but it really is a banned doc! I didn't lie!" he insists, throwing his hands up. I pat him on the knee comfortingly.

"It's fine. I needed that laugh," I reassure him.

Matt's expression becomes more serious, and I can tell from his roaming eyes he's taking in the weight I have lost, and the darkness under my eyes. I feel like covering myself up, but I resist the urge and let him see me for who I really am right now.

"I think you need more than just a laugh, P," Matt says gently, brushing a strand of loose hair from my face. "Why aren't you doing all of this with Alex right now? The pizza, the movie? It's nine p.m. on a Friday. Where is your husband?"

The sounds of the movie fade into the background as I try to come up with an answer. In reality, I don't have one. I don't know where Alex is, or if he's even worried about me. I dig up the only excuse I can think of that doesn't make Alex look like a complete monster.

"I guess my testimony left a pretty bad impression on him," I mutter, looking at the ground.

Matt raises his eyebrows. It isn't the answer he was expecting. "Look, you were very polite and respectful," Matt says. "You answered as honestly as you could, and I think you did a pretty good job. If he's butt-hurt because of it, that's his problem."

"Really Matt? Butt-hurt?" I shake my head, almost amused. "Anyway, he isn't quite as understanding..." the almost-amusement falls away. "I'm so tired of his attitude. He has said nothing for the past four days." I slouch down, my head falling against the back of the couch. "What kind of husband is that?"

Matt is silent for a moment, but he finally musters up the courage to ask me, "Do you, um, regret marrying him?"

His question takes me by surprise, and I feel an uneasiness taking over me as I think about it.

"It's hard to say," I mumble, still ruminating over Alex and I, our journey, the bad and the good, and everything that has happened since he got arrested. "I love him, but I think our relationship is ill-fated," I confess, shaking my head at how blind I was. "Everyone saw it but us." I pause, a small smile playing on my lips as Matt keeps quiet, listening. "We, on the other hand, thought nothing but death could tear us apart." I grin to myself, warm memories running through my mind, until I remember what happened to my mom. "And like clockwork, death came to tear us apart."

"Do you think he will ever forgive you for cooperating with us?" Matt asks, his tone heavier than usual.

"I have no idea, if I'm being honest," I say sincerely. "Each time I think we are getting closer to getting back on track, he goes back to calling me a traitor, an enemy, and whatever else crosses his mind."

"That's bullshit." Matt runs a hand through his messy brown hair and looks at me tenderly. I'm suddenly uncomfortable, realizing how close we are sitting—our thighs are touching, but I shouldn't worry. He has never tried anything, and he knows perfectly well I only see him as a friend. He turns his face from me, and the room suddenly darkens as credits begin to roll on the screen.

"Alright, let me drive you home," he says, already standing up. "It's getting late."

I take a deep breath and blow it out slowly. He's right, but for some reason, a tiny part of me wishes I could stay. Maybe fall asleep on the big sectional, curled up with a fleece blanket, content in the knowledge that there would be no Maria forcing vitamins on me at 8 a.m.

What if Alex came home to find me gone?

So what? He has left me in the dark for days. He deserves a taste of his own medicine.

Matt is still watching me expectantly, and I'm struck by how much I don't want to drag him into Alex and I's drama. "Alright. Take me home, then," I say reluctantly.

We head to the car serenaded by the chirping of crickets in the adjoining fields. Matt stops in front of a red Lexus and opens the door for me. Wait—he got a new car? Despite the question being on the tip of my tongue, I refrain myself from asking. As I climb inside though, I can tell how different this car is compared to his low-key, black Hyundai. "I didn't know you got a new car," I say. "It's nice."

"Yeah, the other one was getting old," he answers.

The drive home is unremarkable. I know Maria will tattle on me for having Matt take me home rather than Zach, but I don't care. I roll the window down to feel the night breeze on my face. The Goo Goo Dolls song "Iris" is playing on the radio, and Matt hums along, tapping his fingers on the steering wheel.

"Old song," I comment. "But a good one."

"I think everyone knows this song. It's timeless," he says, his brownish hair blowing in the wind.

The lyrics filter through my mind, the feeling is bittersweet.

If everything's made to be broken, I just want you to know who I am, the singer croons, and the words strike me hard. Does anyone really know who they are?

Matt shakes me out of my thoughts with a question. "I know you've probably got a busy weekend ahead of you, but do you want to go to the library with me Monday? I need some help to review my knowledge on ethics."

I rub my belly, thinking about the exams that are slowly but surely approaching and where those two will be by then. "Alright. I'll help you study if you help me pick out a few books for financial accounting."

"Deal," he says quickly as he turns onto the street of my condo. "Hey, P? Take it easy, okay? I want to see you way fatter on Monday."

I punch him in the arm, and he only laughs. I giggle too, despite myself, and take an extra-long time opening the car door. I don't want to ruin the happy moment, but my home looms behind me. I have to go.

"Bye Matt. Thank you," I say, reaching out to lay my hand on his quickly before exiting the Lexus. Matt waves as I go, and after closing my door, I stand on the sidewalk and wave in return until the motor starts roaming again, and Matt drives away.

What a great evening that was, I think to myself. His kindness is a balm to the raw wound of Alex's absence.

Reaching the condo, the sound of footsteps approaching can only indicate that Maria's still up, and, not surprisingly, she chatters anxiously at me, pushing my nighttime vitamins into my hands. I realize I don't care if she tells Alex I was out, or even the description of the car that brought me home. Maybe then I'd get a sliver of his attention.

I dutifully take the vitamins and head to the bedroom. I run myself a hot bath before turning in for the night, taking a bit of joy in feeling the babies rolling around inside of me in response to the warm water. They seem to love a bath just as I do. I fill the tub with bubbles and turn on some relaxing music. On a whim, I text Alex, asking him where he is, and if he will come home.

I love you, I type to end the message before sending it. Sighing heavily, I finish bathing and shimmy under my sheets. The silk is cool on my bath-warmed skin.

I check my phone one last time before putting it on the nightstand. Not surprisingly, Alex hasn't replied. With an extra pillow tucked between my legs for comfort, I eventually find slumber, as lonely as ever.

CHAPTER 22

Manhattan, March 22, 2021
Petra Van Gatt

I put the finishing touches on the painting and stand back, admiring my work. I spent the whole weekend finishing it, and being able to stand back and look at it finally done fills me with pride. I hear the door to my atelier creak open and Maria enters, holding a tray with a mug of steaming hot cocoa and a huge snickerdoodle cookie. She has sort of given up on getting me to sit down and eat a full meal and relented to my ever present need for sweets.

"What do you think, Maria?" I ask her brightly.

Maria walks over, sitting her tray on a side table. She gets a good look at the enormous canvas and gasps, holding both her hands to her heart.

"Oh gosh!" Maria breathes out. A chuckle escapes me at her shocked expression. "That's very, um, daring…"

I sit my paintbrush down, raising an eyebrow at her. "Well, yeah, but do you like the colors, the shape, the texture?"

Maria composes herself, brushing her hands down her apron. "Oh, you paint very well, of course! But it's such a... very... erotic portrait of Mrs. Van Lawick."

I glance back at the painting and try to see it through someone else's eyes. Okay, yeah, maybe I shouldn't have shown it to her, but I'm so used to see Yara's naked body for the sake of this painting that I've become totally desensitized to nudity, or at least to hers. But it's what she wanted, anyway. Yara had commissioned the portrait in this precise position—kneeling on the floor, legs spread apart—and lack of clothes, and I'm just following the photo I took of her faithfully.

While I refocus on the canvas, Maria keeps setting out my midday snack, occasionally casting worried looks at Yara's painting. I enjoy my cocoa right there on my painting stool, back pain be damned.

"Any word from Alex?" I ask, before she can leave.

"Unfortunately not, ma'am. Yesterday he came home late and left very early in the morning," Maria says carefully, not wanting to upset me.

I huff a frustrated breath. But really, I already knew that he hadn't said a word. Since the day I testified, I haven't seen him. But just as I finish that thought, my iPhone rings. Instead of Alex's name flashing on the screen, it's Matt's. I juggle my cookie to my other hand and answer.

"Still meeting at the library today?" he asks.

"Absolutely. I'll be there shortly," I chirp back, happy to have a reason to get out of the house.

I finish my snack and go to change out of my paint covered clothes and into something a little more proper for the college library. An ivory cable-knit sweater, brown riding boots, and dark blue jeans should do the trick.

I forgo Matt's invitation to come and pick me up, deciding to call my driver instead. I'm envisioning a brawl between him and Alex downstairs, if Alex just so happened to come home as Matt pulled up.

The trip through town is a long, boring drive, but I arrive right on time. As soon as I prop the door open to the library, the smell of old books hits me like a ton of bricks. I'm overcome with nostalgia, remembering being deep within these stacks searching for rare editions. I hold the memory close to my heart as I look for Matt, eventually finding him at a table deep within the maze of the second floor.

"Hey Petra!" he whispers enthusiastically.

"Hey!" I whisper back, adhering to the ubiquitous quiet library rule. "Nice to see you, Mr. Bradford."

Matt makes a face like he's smelled something bad when I utter the name, and it causes me to chuckle as I join him at the table. Matt fills me in on what he's studying, and even though Kant isn't my favorite philosopher, I stick with it and do my best to help him with Kant's deontological moral theory. I ask a few questions here and there, following his notes, and we fall back into a rhythm, just like old study days. It's obvious Matt didn't need my help; he knows Kant better than Kant knows himself. A smile filled with pride settles on his lips as he speaks so eloquently about the Kantian ethics and Kant's opposition to utilitarianism. And before we know it, we have reviewed everything about Kant and Matt seems to be finished for the day.

He closes the huge tome with a "thunk," exhaling in relief. "That really went so much faster with you here."

"I'm so glad I could help," I reply genuinely. These little, mundane things that Matt invites me to do make me feel like I'm living a normal life again. It helps to forget all the negativity in my life. Maybe we should do it more often.

"The only issue is, I blocked out so much of my schedule for this study session and we are done way too early." I laugh at his expression; Matt taps the pen he is holding on his lips as he considers the situation, looking around. His gaze lands on something and his whole face lights up.

"Oh, let's play chess," he blurts out excitedly.

"What, really?" I turn around to see the chessboard he is referencing. And sure enough, there is a set nestled under a window, flanked by two ancient chairs. I have never seen a chessboard here before, but maybe someone had just forgotten it there. Matt and I had played a few times throughout our freshman year, but mostly online, and as far as I could tell, we are pretty evenly matched. It makes for a fun, unpredictable game. At first I think it seems kind of silly to play the afternoon away, but the more I think on it the more I come to the conclusion it'll be a nice distraction from my real problems. I check my phone quickly to make sure my wayward husband hasn't tried to contact me, and when I see my notifications empty, I power the phone down and put it in my pocket.

"Sure, let's play." I smirk. "Unless you're afraid to lose that is."

Matt scoffs, taking my hand and leading me over to the dusty chess board. He brushes it off with his hand, the dust motes floating in the air and twinkling in the sunlight beaming through the windows. It's almost like a movie scene, the young couple whittling away long hours together in an enchanted library. Except, it isn't like that at all. I'm just the pregnant high-profile wife who made the news for testifying against her own husband, putting his future in total jeopardy, and Matt is my friend who probably just hangs out with me out of pity.

No, absolutely not. I am not going to think that way right now! The real world is too harsh, and these quiet moments with Matt in a forgotten part of the library are a respite I desperately need. I plop down in one chair, pushing past Matt so I can get the white pieces. Matt rolls his eyes and takes his place on the black side, and we get to work.

The hours pass quickly, the two of us filling the silence with memories and stories from our past. My cheeks start to hurt from all of my smiling. We set the pieces for a second game, when suddenly the lights go off with a mechanical click, the library only illuminated by the floodlights in the corners and the pale evening sun. But we keep playing. After all, we have a game to finish. Each move is more calculated and pondered than our last game. I take my tower decidedly and move it. Matt heaves, his face overly serious as he tries to figure out what I'm up to.

"Excuse me," I hear from behind Matt.

Looking above his shoulder, I see the librarian, her coat and purse gathered in her hands. "The library is closed."

Matt and I look at each other in shock, and, in a quick move, he glances at his watch before making a grimace.

"P, it's nine pm," he says, totally astounded. "I can't believe we stayed here so late." He jumps up and starts gathering his things.

His serious tone makes me laugh. "Mr. Bradford, I can't believe you'd take advantage of my precious time like this." I gasp, laying the back of my hand over my forehead dramatically. He shoots me a dirty look with a hint of a smile, and we head out of the darkened building. As Matt holds the door for me, my stomach rumbles audibly, and I groan in embarrassment.

Matt chuckles, "You want to go get something to eat?"

I do, actually, but I've wasted so much of Matt's time already today. "Don't worry about it, I'll just have Maria make me a sandwich at home."

"Nonsense. I know this outstanding Indian restaurant a few blocks away. They are open pretty late. What do you think?"

I power on my phone and wait a few moments to see if Alex has decided to contact me. As I suspected, there is no message. I mentally shake off the pang of sadness that pierces my heart and pocket the phone again. "Alright, Mr. Bradford. Indian it is. Let's go."

The inside of the restaurant is sparsely decorated, but the wonderful smells make up for it. I know that this food is going to give me heartburn later on, but oh well. Worth it. We seat ourselves in a booth with cracked red pleather seats and turn the single page menu over to peruse the offerings. I order the chickpea curry with a level zero spiciness, and Matt gets vegetarian tikka masala, level two spiciness. We also split an order of garlic naan bread.

I suck my mango lassi happily while waiting for the food. Matt is following up with a few emails on his phone, and I use the time to check my phone yet again for any word from Alex. I feel nothing—no sadness or anger—when the screen is predictably blank. Matt looks up from his phone to see my carefully neutral expression.

"Are you alright over there?" he asks.

"Yes. It's just…" I sigh, taking another long drink. "I've got some stuff going on, you know?"

Matt's gaze flicks down to my belly and quickly back up. "How is the pregnancy going? You haven't been telling me much."

I roll my glass between my two hands, the ice clinking as I figure out how to explain everything without spending the entire night here. "It isn't ideal. You know I'm carrying twins. One of them is stealing nutrients from the other, making the other baby weaker and less likely to survive. It's called Twin-to-Twin Transfusion Syndrome, or TTTS. We saw a surgeon that should have been able to fix the problem, but the umbilical cords are too close, and the surgery puts both babies at a greater risk."

Matt blanches, reaching out to hold my hands. "My God, Petra, I had no idea."

I squeeze his hands as I continue, "That isn't all. The donor baby, the one having nutrients taken from her, developed something called Turner Syndrome. It's a genetic condition that will cause her to be a little stunted growth wise, among

330

other things." I take a deep breath, feeling my emotions starting to get the best of me. "It's like the cards are stacked against us."

"Why didn't you tell me? I've been treating you this whole time like everything is normal, but you're going through so much."

"I haven't been thinking too much about the pregnancy, honestly. I'm so afraid I'm going to lose them both that I don't want to get too attached." I pull my hands from his and dash the tears from the corners of my eyes.

We sit in silence for a while, but Matt clears his throat and I look up to meet his hazel eyes.

"You know I'm here if you need anything. Seriously, anything. A ride to the doctor, a midnight craving, whatever you want I'm here for you."

My lips curve up at his kindness. "I know you are. It makes me feel even worse for not telling you all of this."

"Don't feel bad, it's an unbelievable burden for you, I'm sure." Matt's face is open and attentive, ready to listen to anything I have to say. "Didn't you say you had a doctor's appointment coming up? Do you need a ride?"

For a crazy moment, I almost tell him yes. Alex would be apoplectic if I had Matt take me instead of him, but it's what my husband deserves for leaving me alone like he has. But they are Alex's children too, and he deserves to know what is going on.

"Thank you, but no. Alex and I go to the appointments together. It's the only thing he has been consistent about."

Matt leans back in his seat with a pissed-off look on his face. No doubt thinking about how awful my pregnancy has been and how little Alex has been around. "Okay, if you say so. But if he lets you down, you know I'm just a phone call away."

The server brings our food, and even though my stomach has become very upset from the pregnancy talk, I tear off little pieces of the naan bread to dip in my curry, taking small bites until my appetite returns. I watch Matt from under my eyelashes, taking in his ruffled hair and clean-shaven face. For a split second, I wonder if Alex and I had never been more than godfather and goddaughter, if I'd have considered giving Matt the chance he so obviously desired to have with me. He has been a one-man support system for me lately, and my heart is admittedly softening toward him more and more. I want to do something for him, to show him he means so much to me.

"Matt?" I say, an idea springing to mind. "I'm… uh… Alex and I are holding a gala dinner to raise money for other families dealing with Turner Syndrome. I'd really love it if you came."

"Are you asking me to be your plus one?" There is a thread of hope in his voice, and it kills me to have to let him down.

"No," I say amid my laughter. "I'm sorry. Alex and I have to keep up appearances in public, even if he is ignoring me most of the time. Bring someone with you, maybe a beautiful girl you're interested in. Oh, why not Sarah? You guys used to be close friends, no? It's a big black-tie event so there'll be the media in attendance and most of our stakeholders." I try to sound lighthearted, but why am I so bothered picturing Matt with another girl on his arm?

Matt laughs ruefully. "Sure. I'll come and see if Sarah wants to join. She likes that kind of stuff so I'm sure she can make it." He takes a bite of his food before continuing. "When you say keeping up appearances, do you mean that you two are actually separated? I mean, do you think Alex is seeing someone else?"

The question makes me queasy. Surely Alex wouldn't go that far. "We are still married, not on a break or anything. I'm sure he'd never do that to me."

Matt shrugs, unconvinced. "If you say so."

I frown, knowing exactly what he's thinking. "Please don't put things in my head," I say, now that I'm reminded of how Alex met Amanda in her apartment last year without even telling me and it was Matt who gave me the unedited tape. "We'll be together at the growth scan in a few days, and I'm going to tell him I expect him to be here for me more often. It's been a hard time for him too, with the pregnancy and the trial and all," I find myself saying.

Matt doesn't respond, and we continue our meal awkwardly, the charm of the night long gone, killed at the memory of Alex's lies and secrets that filled my daily life even before our wedding. At least the food is tasty. I pack up my leftovers and call my driver to come pick me up. Suddenly, it feels wrong to let Matt take me home. We are getting too close, and knowing he had feelings for me just a few months ago, I don't want to give him any wrong idea.

When the sleek black car pulls up, I bid Matt farewell, feeling a little upset our fun day had ended on such an unpleasant note. Matt hugs me close, and we embrace for a little longer than necessary. It makes me realize how starved for touch I really am. He pulls back and stares deeply into my eyes, his voice low and serious.

"Keep me updated on everything and call me after the scan. Just because Alex doesn't see how lucky he is to have you in his life, doesn't mean I don't." He kisses my cheek quickly and I blush, hurrying out of the restaurant and getting into my chauffeur's car.

As we pull away, I take a last look at Matt's tall form standing outside with the lights of the restaurant behind him. I cover my cheeks with my hands, hoping to conceal the blush that still lingers there for much too long.

CHAPTER 23

Manhattan, March 26, 2021
Petra Van Gatt

I do a quick twirl in the mirror, the black and white tweed pleated skirt falling above my knees and covering perfectly well the lace of my black silky thigh highs. Next I throw on a black, cozy knitwear top and grab a pair of ankle boots to finish the ensemble. I've already curled my long hair into gentle waves and applied subtle makeup to enhance my big blue eyes and petal pink lips. The top hides the outlines of my growing belly, and I think I look radiant. What a difference from my usual pair of All Stars and white shirts. I want so badly to catch Alex off guard with my appearance, and to see a flash of want in his eyes. Secretly, I've been hoping he'd bring me roses and apologize for his long absence.

All of a sudden, Maria taps on the door frame, interrupting my daydreaming. "Alex is here, ma'am."

I check my appearance one more time before heading out to meet him. As soon as I see my husband, I'm hit with a wave of emotions. I'm so happy to finally see him, but at the same time so angry at him for having ignored me for so many days. His hands are empty of flowers. No matter, if I want his attention now, then I'm going to have to let it all fall by the wayside. He looks up from his phone as I enter, and I flash him my brightest smile, but his expression doesn't change.

My face falls. Okay, well, I guess that means I shouldn't have wasted my time putting effort into my appearance today.

"You ready?" Alex asks shortly.

"Yeah," I mutter, shoulders slouching as I follow him out to the car. And just like last time, it's him driving. I guess it's a way for him to have something else to focus on other than me.

We ride in silence for a while without even the radio playing. I can't take it anymore, so I ask him, "How have you been doing?" I try my best not to sound annoyed.

Alex simply says, "Fine," not taking his eyes off the road.

He's really getting on my nerves with his indifference. I scroll through my phone to keep busy until we get to the clinic, knowing that if I think about Alex's abandonment of me for too long, then I'm going to snap. We walk into the office as usual, and after a brief wait, we are escorted back to a room.

Like clockwork, they ask me to change into a gown and weigh me. I avoid looking at the scale, terrified that I've lost weight. A nurse draws my blood and checks all my other vitals before it's time for the actual ultrasound.

Mariana comes in with my file in hand, nodding curtly at Alex before greeting me warmly.

"We've got quite a bit to go over regarding the amniocentesis and MRI you had done at the Fetal Care

Center, but I'm going to go ahead and get an updated growth through ultrasound first."

"Okay," I say, trying to calm my racing heart. I really don't want to talk about any of the tests, because as soon as we do, Mariana is going to bring up that dreaded word again: *terminate*.

I hop onto the table, avoiding looking at Alex as Mariana rubs the wand over the skin of my stomach, holding still to snap images every once in a while. After about ten minutes, it's finished, and I clean up before changing back into my regular clothes.

"Doing okay?" Alex asks, as I sit next to him. His face still appears aloof, but I see genuine concern in his eyes.

"I'm scared," I whisper to him. He nods and places a hand on my upper leg, squeezing softly.

"We're going through it together," he promises.

Yeah, right...

When Mariana returns, I can feel myself panicking. I take deep breaths, slowly exhaling and counting the seconds to calm down. I can hear my blood rushing in my ears. Mariana types a little at the computer and flips through her paperwork before she looks up at us and clasps her hands together. Time for serious talk.

"First, let's go over the advanced imaging from the MRI. I had already assumed that this was the case, but it's now very clear to the doctors at the Fetal Care Center and myself that Baby A, the recipient one, is hogging most of the placenta, leaving Baby B with very little space and nutrients to thrive."

Keep breathing, Petra, I tell myself before asking, "But there are still two heartbeats, right?"

Mariana looks pained. "Yes, but—"

"Then let's continue like that," I interrupt before Mariana could step in.

Mariana heaves a sigh in resignation. "As you wish but be aware that the longer you wait to terminate Baby B, the more you are putting Baby A at risk as well."

There it is, that word. Terminate. It makes me go cold all over and my meager lunch starts to come up into my throat from nausea. I swallow hard. "I understand."

"I think it's important you get mentally ready that Baby B might not make it until the next appointment," Mariana insists. I'm still silent, staring at the ground, when Alex speaks up.

"I think she understood," he tells her, voice low.

"Very well." Mariana flips through her chart again before landing on the page she was looking for. "The amniocentesis and subsequent karyotype test confirmed the initial diagnosis of Turner Syndrome in Baby B. We won't know the severity of the disease until she grows a bit more. Baby A had none of the genetic markers, meaning he has no apparent genetic anomalies."

Okay, well, I already knew all of that. It's a bit of a relief to know without a shadow of a doubt what our obstacles are, though. "Understood. What's next?" I ask.

She flips to the next page. "The lab work from the blood tests earlier today, plus your weight, show a few areas of concern."

Alex looks at me and then back at Mariana. "Her weight?"

"Yes," she says coolly. "Petra has gained no weight since her last appointment. In fact, she's lost three pounds. That doesn't sound like much, but when you consider how little the babies themselves weigh…"

"I get it," Alex cuts her off. "Is she sick?"

I don't really appreciate them talking like I'm not even in the room. Mariana shakes her head no.

"Not really sick, per se. Eating a vegan diet during pregnancy is okay as long as the mother takes her supplements and eats a balanced, nutrient-rich diet. Petra has not only lost a bit of weight, but she is iron and vitamin D deficient, and the lack of iron has made her anemic."

My face burns with embarrassment, and I continue to look at the tiled floor.

Mariana continues, "Have you not been making sure she eats?" she asks Alex. He scowls, looking away from her.

"I have been… away," he admits.

"I see." Mariana grits her teeth but says nothing else to him. Instead, she turns to me. "Petra, since you aren't taking proper care of yourself, I'm going to appoint you a midwife. She will just check in on you and help you make smart choices in your diet, so the babies get everything they need. With the TTTS, you being anemic is very dangerous if you're hoping for Baby B to pull through. You need twice the iron as usual to make red blood cells for them."

Great, she is assigning me a glorified babysitter. Resigned to my fate, I agree to the midwife. Mariana then escorts us to the reception and sets our next appointment in three weeks time. So this is how long she thinks Baby B is left with? She then instructs us to wait in the room for the midwife to come and gives me a brief hug as she leaves, worry plastered all over her features.

"Why aren't you eating?" Alex asks tensely once we are left alone.

"Maybe because I'm forced to eat alone every evening," I retort. How dare he get on me about my eating habits when he hasn't laid eyes on me for ten days?

"Petra, you know—" Alex is cut off as the door opens again. A beautiful dark-skinned woman enters, wearing an amethyst-colored dress under her white medical jacket. She smiles at the two of us warmly, coming over to shake our hands.

"It's so good to meet you," the woman says. "My name is Lily, and I'll be your CNM."

"CNM?" I ask.

"It stands for Certified Nurse-Midwife," Lily explains. "We'll go through your eating habits, and then make a plan that will include food, sleep, mindset, and exercise."

When it comes to my alimentation, Lily gives the two of us some pamphlets and other materials going over a proper vegan diet for expectant mothers, as well as some free samples of different supplements for me to try. She isn't pushy, and she explains the importance of an iron-rich diet and how I can adjust my eating habits. I had expected to be annoyed by the midwife, but I actually like Lily a lot. She's focused, pragmatic, and to the point. It isn't until the end of our visit with her that things become uncomfortable again.

"I think that's all for today. I will do a home visit twice a week to check on you. Your address is the one I have on file, right?"

"Correct," I answer.

"Shouldn't we also talk about the birthing plan?" Alex asks. "After all, she's already twenty weeks in."

Lily's expression changes to become full of pity. "Next time, maybe. Mariana advised against setting up a birthing plan this early because…" She tries to find a careful way to say it, but I already know.

"Because she thinks I'm going to lose the babies," I finish.

Lily closes her eyes for a second before nodding. "Yes."

I let the wave of grief crash over me, tears filling my eyes, but as soon as the wave ebbs, I collect myself, standing. Alex follows suit.

"It was nice to meet you, Lily," I tell her.

"Likewise," she replies, still looking vaguely upset.

As soon as Alex and I get outside the clinic, I bury my face in my hands. No tears come this time, just an overwhelming sense of helplessness and frustration. I scream into my palms, venting all the feelings of rage, loss, and inevitability. How come Auntie Louise saw my future so clearly and there's nothing I can do to change it? Why is this happening to me?

Alex stands next to me and doesn't say a word. Instead, he loops his arm around my shoulders, walking me to the car so I can break down in private.

"Fuck!" I scream as soon as the car door closes, causing Alex's eyes to widen. "Why is this happening to me? Why?"

Alex, for once in his life, looks lost. "If I could do something I would."

Really? If he had meant that, he'd have been caring for me, not avoiding me like the plague. "I don't need your pity, Alex," I snap. "The only time I ever see you is here. If you're lucky, maybe both babies will die, and you won't have to go with me to these stupid appointments anymore." My voice gets louder, cracking at the end of my statement.

He looks shocked, and all the blood drains from his face. "Don't say that."

"Why? It sounds quite obvious that's what's going to happen, no?" I scoff, "Plus, you have been absent for the past ten days, no phone calls, no hellos, *nothing*." Alex looks like he wants to interject, but I don't give him the chance. "If it wasn't because of the pregnancy, you wouldn't even be here today," I point out, trying to keep my emotions in check, but my heart is too heavy. There's only so much a person can take. "When are you going to stop holding a grudge against me and turn the page?"

The silence stretches out between us, broken only by my heavy, tear-filled breaths.

"I haven't figured it out yet," Alex answers lamely. I can tell from his face that even he knows it's a bullshit answer.

I chuckle in disgust. I just want to leave the damn car and not see him ever again. He starts the car, and we leave, the air tense. My phone pings, and I open the message. It's a picture of the old chessboard in the library from Matt, with the caption, *Care for a rematch?*

The idea of escaping this car and Alex's careless company is irresistible. Fuck Alex, and fuck going back to his condo to sit like a caged bird, Maria clucking over me every few hours.

"Can you drop me at the library?" I ask him.

"Sure," he says without inflection. The only evidence of his feelings is the whiteness of his knuckles clenched on the steering wheel. He doesn't even try to invite me for dinner or anything. What a fucking asshole…

Alex pulls over in front of the library, not even bothering to look at me. "Don't forget we have a board meeting on Monday," he says, his voice clipped.

"I know," I bite back. "Bye."

I rush into the library, squinting my eyes at the change from the harsh daylight to the soft buttery light of the interior. I scan through the tables spread across the vast room, and head through the stacks to the haven of the chess corner and the only man who seems to care about me anymore, Matt.

I don't remember it being so far, but before I realize it, I am trotting, weird looks flashing past me as I do so until I reach the end of the shelves and the open area where tables are set up for studying. Again, there is no one there, except for Matt, sitting at the chess table under the window, exactly like last time.

He looks up in surprise at my dramatic entrance, and he stands. I quickly close the distance between us and throw myself onto him. He catches me with a surprised "Oomph!" and I squeeze him tightly, the familiar smell of his cologne unwinding the tension around my breaking heart.

My husband dropped me off on the sidewalk like yesterday's news. Fortunately, Matt is here holding me in his arms as I shove all the emotions from the appointment and my scant few hours with Alex down, locking them in a box deep inside me with all the other terrible things that have happened to me lately.

For a wild second, I think about breaking down and sobbing, knowing he will comfort me. But that isn't fair to Matt, who I know still harbors feelings for me. Instead, I put the pieces of myself back together as he hugs me, taking solace in the touch of another human.

I pull away first, and Matt looks down at me. His expression is filled with worry, mixed with heartbreaking affection. He's frowning, the corners of his mouth pulling down. *Please don't ask, please don't ask*, I think desperately, but it's no use.

"How was the appointment?"

"Good," I lie, displaying a polite smile as I try to play off the show of emotion that just happened between the two of us. I refuse to get into the details of the appointment. It was the same news that I told him at the Indian restaurant, anyway. Bizarrely, the part that has me most upset is Alex and his attitude toward me.

"You sure?"

"Yeah, let's play," I say, wanting to close the subject once and for all.

He agrees, but pauses, pulling a small brown paper bag out of the backpack he had brought. "I picked this up for you at the coffee shop. I know you can't have caffeine, but the barista couldn't stop raving about these."

I take the bag and open it. Inside is a brownie. It's dense, moist, and has a swirl of salted caramel on the top. Remembering Alex's empty hands when he came to pick me up today, I have to fight back tears. I sniffle briefly, clutching the bag close to my heart.

"Oh, thank you," I say, my voice watery.

"It's nothing, really," he replies before sitting down in front of the black pieces. "Go ahead, I know you want the white ones."

Touched by his thoughtfulness regarding the brownie, my preferred chess color, and just… me in general, I lean down and give him a quick peck on the cheek before taking my own seat. Matt blushes scarlet, patiently waiting as I move my first piece.

"By the way, I love your skirt, it's really nice."

My smile keeps growing at his compliment; at least he noticed the effort I had made today. "Oh, you do? Maria and I went to buy some new clothes."

"It looks great on you."

Well, at least the outfit is flattering and hides my emerging bump quite well. Not that I mind, but there's no need for the media to know about my personal life.

After our game of chess, Matt and I don't feel like going home. This little corner of the library is just too amazing to leave. Since he decides to study for ethics, I also decide to take a copy of the book I'm currently reading out of a shelf. That's the great thing about this library; they have a copy of nearly every book in the market. We sit beside each other and as soon as I open my book, Matt asks, "What are you reading?"

"Um, it's a book my dad recommended to me," I say. And then I show him the cover, knowing he's gonna hate it simply by the title.

"*The Virtuous Egoist* by Tara Smith?" A laugh escapes me at his grimace. "Really?"

"Well, he said it was good, so I'm reading it," I tell him.

"How do you find it so far?"

"I like it," I disclose and my smile keeps growing seeing him even more shocked than before. After all this is a book that advocates for objectivism—Ayn Rand's philosophy—and one of his biggest pet peeves. "Her philosophical views are interesting," I add to provoke him. "Similar to Rand's."

Matt shakes his head like he's extremely disappointed in my poor philosophical and literature choice, but I'm just reveling in his overly dramatic expression.

"I really need to know something…" He's got that cute little smirk on his lips and a twinkle in his hazel eyes.

"What?" I ask, quite amused, staring at him as he thinks something through.

"How can someone so beautiful can have such a poor taste in philosophy?"

I laugh under my breath at his stupid question, but I play along. "I guess taste is a matter of subjectivity," I say, my voice low and soft. To my surprise, my heart starts thundering because Matt is leaning in, and he's getting close, very close to my lips. "Like the fact you think I'm beautiful," I add, trying to conceal my growing nervousness. "It's also subjective."

Matt observes me attentively. "Mm, I'm sure there are objective parameters that I could use."

Containing another laugh, my lips part slightly at his humor, and I feel the heat rising on my cheeks. "Such as?"

I swallow when his eyes travel to my mouth, his head dipping down just inches away from closing the distance. "Proportions, symmetry…" He tucks a loose strand of hair behind my ear, and in the heat of the moment, slowly closes the small gap between us, pressing his lips on mine. He doesn't rush, but also doesn't vacillate. And, for a split second, I forget everything, letting myself revel in his tenderness and touch.

Fortunately, consciousness hits us right back, and we pull our lips immediately apart.

"Oh my gosh," I utter in shock at what we just did.

"I—I'm… so sorry," Matt mumbles, unsure what else to say or do. Yet, I keep looking at him, totally speechless, livid, and numb at what happened. "I shouldn't have done that."

I ponder his words, replaying exactly what happened and how. Unfortunately, he's not the only one to blame. Having someone who cherishes you feels good, and maybe there was a part of me that wanted to know what it felt like being kissed by him. "I think we are both guilty." My eyes meet his again but all I can feel is a huge weight of shame and guilt, so I rise from my chair and add, "I should get going, um, it's getting late," I find myself saying, which is not even true but it's better for me to go.

Matt just nods at me in return. Despite being as shocked and embarrassed as I am, he still asks, "Sure, um, do you want a ride?"

"That's okay, I'm gonna call Zach." Then I simply wave at him and leave the library.

* * *

On my way back home, I can't stop replaying what happened between Matt and I. What a horrible, horrible mistake that was. If Alex and I are already so estranged, this is gonna make things even worse. I shut my eyes and press my lips tight, hitting the back of my head against the headrest again and again. Fuck! Fuck! And fuck! I should've slapped him, told him no, pushed him back, but I didn't. I leaned in just as much as he did and let him kiss me. I have to talk to Alex about it and we have to put everything behind for the sake of our marriage. The fact he's also treating me like I'm his enemy and his estranged wife, isn't helping either. For fuck's sake we are living under the same roof, yet he doesn't sleep with me and we barely see each other! I take my iPhone and call him so that we can meet. Yet, he doesn't pick up his phone. Of course… So I go to the message app and type in: *I really need to talk to you. Please, can we meet at the condo? It's really urgent.*

My legs start quivering impatiently as I remain here sitting in the car and waiting for his answer. Fortunately, a few minutes later, a new message pops up: *Okay, let's meet in the dining room.*

That's it? No questions asked? Wow. He must already be at home to reply with such an easy going attitude.

I'm trembling at the idea of what could happen to us. Is he gonna divorce me because of a peck? Oh jeez, I hope not! But I won't keep the truth away from him. If we want to move forward, we need to be honest with each other.

Suddenly, another message pops up. *Are you mad at me? I'm sorry for what I did. X*

Am I mad at Matt? Well, I should be mad at me first and foremost. After all, I'm the one who's married, not him. But Matt knows I'm currently going through a bad phase in my marriage due to the trial, my testimony and so much more, and yet, that didn't prevent him from doing what he did.

I'm not mad, but we shouldn't have done that, I text him back.

I know. I'm sorry, I fucked up. I won't do it again. X

Yeah, well, it's a bit too late for that. What a fucking mess I put myself in. I close my eyes again, breathing in and out, but all I can think of is about that stupid mistake. I don't even know why I did it. Is it because of the pregnancy hormones? Because of the lack of intimacy between Alex and I? I don't know, but I only see Matt as a friend, which is why it doesn't make any sense. Heck, I never pictured myself having something more with him.

Reaching our condo, my heart is in my throat and I'm not even sure how I will be able to look Alex in the eye and tell him the truth. *What a monster I am...* But I have to. I walk slowly to the dining room and my heart falls to my knees as I see the dining table beautifully decorated with a romantic place setting for two.

"Maria's idea," Alex says immediately. Yet, I'm pretty sure that's not true. Maybe he finally realized he was being a dick to me.

The guilt and shame weight on me and I feel devastated. My eyes start watering and I sniffle, pushing the first tears back.

"Are you okay?" His voice, warm and caring, makes my heart reel.

Oh Petra, what have you done?

"I... um..." I barely manage to articulate, staring at the floor as I speak. I'm scared, so freaking scared of telling him the truth. My heart is hammering inside my chest as I pull my chair and sit in front of him. I don't manage to look him in the eye though. I did something absolutely horrible and all I can do is stare down at my lap in total embarrassment. Then I take a deep breath and for better or worse I say, "Matt kissed me."

And then, nothing…

No words, no screaming, no loud breaths, no tears, nothing. So I slowly drift my eyes up and dare to look at him.

Alex doesn't even blink, he just looks at his empty glass of wine, playing with the base. "I see," he mumbles, like he's barely here. His face is totally emotionless as he keeps observing his glass. Then his gaze finally lands on me, and he asks, "Did you slap him back?" My lips part at his question and I don't find the will to answer it. "Tell me the truth," he says gently.

I breathe in and out, my gaze traveling back down to my lap, before I mutter a mere, "I didn't, no."

Another beat of silence ensues, so I look up again and find Alex nodding as he thinks something through. "Did you push him away, maybe?"

My eyes drift down again, quite ashamed of myself. "No…"

"Did you tell him to stop, at least?"

And yet I shake my head, giving him a third negative answer.

"So, did you just… let him do his thing?"

The disappointment in his voice petrifies me. I swallow the lump in my throat, barely able to face the truth. "Yes." My tone is barely audible, but Alex just chuckles in return before rubbing his eyelids tiredly. "It's not what you think—"

"Oh, it's exactly what I think," he snaps, glaring at me with disdain. Then he heaves a long sigh filled with sorrow and looking me in the eye, he asks, "You liked it, huh?"

I close my eyes for an instant because I don't even know what that kiss meant. "You have been so distant with me and —"

"Did you like it or not?" he asks again, cutting me off.

"I don't think so," I answer, my voice broken and low.

"You don't *think* so?" he repeats, sounding deeply disappointed. "Did he place his tongue inside your mouth?"

His unexpected question makes me gape at him. "Argh, you're being disgusting," I rebuke, shaking my head.

"Answer me!" he grits between teeth. I've never seen him like this before, I wanted to talk rationally but this is becoming ridiculous. "Petra, answer me," he repeats, his tone demanding.

Tired of his attitude, I stand up, ready to leave this conversation behind before it escalates, but Alex steps in. "Don't you dare leave this table!"

"Or else what?" I snap back, already standing tall in front of my place setting.

Alex does the same, and the way he jumps from his chair and marches around the table to meet me is making me reconsider my manners just as fast. I cross my arms over my chest as Alex stands behind me. I can hear his breathing growing louder with disdain and hate as he looks down on me. "Did he touch you while he was all over your mouth?"

I blow out a breath, irritated by his attitude. "I'm done with this." I take a few steps to pass him, but Alex stands in front, barring my way.

"Oh we are just getting started here, believe me," he says, his gaze filled with anger.

"I'm not answering your filthy questions," I hiss back.

In the blink of an eye, Alex turns me around and snatches my back against his chest, his arms holding mine, and leans down just enough to reach my ear. "Answer me," he growls.

Since I keep my mouth shut, not giving anything away, his hand goes up to my chest and under my top, and a quick gasp escapes me as he starts fondling my left boob, slow and soft, the gesture feels odd and good at the same time. As I come to think of it, he hasn't done that for a long, long time.

His lips start brushing around my cheek, and my heart parts in fury at the feel of his warm breath on my skin. "Did he touch you here?"

I gape instantly, unsure what to think of his question and touch. His hand lingering under my top reminds me of us and what we used to do together. "Of course not."

His lips pull my earlobe softly, before they go down on my neck, exploring every inch of my skin, then his mouth starts tugging and sucking my flesh, and I release a quick moan at the suction. "And here?"

"No!" I whisper in outrage. I'd never let Matt do anything of the sort, fondling my boobs while sucking my neck? Jeez, even when we kissed, he never dared to put his hands anywhere else than on my face.

Alex then removes his hand from my top, and as he does so, I feel an inch of sadness, but I don't dare to tell him. Then his hands go down to my skirt and to my surprise he unzips it and lets it fall on the floor. I feel quite self-conscious now that I'm here standing in front of my place setting without my skirt on. I can only hope Maria isn't coming over any time soon. All of a sudden, I feel his hand sliding under my panties and then… "Ahh!"

"And here?"

I haven't felt his fingers between my legs for so long that my face must have gone red up to my ears. My breathing becomes louder and ragged, and I start drenching faster than I should. "Alex…"

"Answer me," he demands.

"No, he didn't…" His fingers start rubbing around my clit in circle movements and I've got to close my eyes, to forget that I'm here, standing in the dining room, no skirt, while Alex is fingering me. "Ah!"

"Did you want him to fuck you?"

"No!" His question makes me want to puke. I'm about to tell him a word or two about his repulsive questions when…

"And me?"

I gasp, sucking in the air, my eyes widening in surprise. "Yes," I breathe instantly. My heart pounds, prickly heat coats my arm, and I'm sure my blood pressure is steadily rising.

"Bend over."

I blink twice at his request. "What?"

"I said bend over."

Quivering, I do as Alex says, stretching my arms out in front of me over the table. Alex hikes up my top until I'm pressing my bare breasts against the cold glass. The chill of it is hardening my nipples when I feel Alex kneel behind me, roughly yanking my underwear to the floor. Within seconds, I can feel his hot breath on my butt-cheeks, and my face flushes crimson.

"What are you—" I try to ask, but I'm cut short when his tongue flicks out to spread the folds of my pussy, licking off the juices that have coated my nether lips and upper thighs.

He makes a rough noise at the taste, and pulls me backwards, closer to his face.

"Look how fucking wet you already are."

I cry out softly as his tongue spreads me open again, dipping into my channel from behind, lapping at me as I become wetter and wetter. His beard is scratching my ass, and his fingertips are digging into the soft flesh of my hips.

How did this happen? We were arguing two minutes ago, nearly at each other's throats, and now Alex has me bent over the table, tongue fucking me while I push table settings out of the way. I'm not sure if this makes us more dysfunctional or less, but the thoughts of the fight are rapidly leaving my mind at the feeling of his tongue slithering around inside me.

"Alex... ah!" I cry out as he pushes his face deeper, forcing my legs further apart and finding my aching clit, wrapping his lips around it, and sucking. My legs are shaking, and he wraps his powerful hands around them to hold me upright as he plunders my pussy with his mouth.

Each pass of his tongue is a wave of ecstasy cascading over me. The way he is eating me out is nearly frantic, devoid of any teasing or gentle touches. Just a direct, focused onslaught aimed at making me as crazed as possible.

And it's certainly working, holy moly! A tornado could descend from the sky and rip the roof off of the house, and I wouldn't notice. All of my attention is on my husband and his incredible mouth. With a low cry, I push back against him, my fists clenching with the need to grab on to something, anything, to ground me before I fly away.

"You're going to make me come," I keen, hearing him rumble in his throat with his tongue still deep between my folds. To my shock, he smacks my ass with a sharp slap. I jump, but the quick sting fades almost immediately, unfolding into a heat that exacerbates my pleasure.

"Oh…" I moan, surprised at how good the brief spanking felt. Alex repeats the motion, a quick stinging slap followed by a wave of heat. The rough caress kick starts my orgasm, and before I know it I'm coming all over his face. I just know I'm covering him in my juices, but I'm too far gone to care. I grind against him as I climax, and it's only his firm grip that holds me upright as my insides spasm, clenching and unclenching, desperate to be filled.

I'm still panting when Alex pulls away, still helping to hold me upright. He leans his body over mine, and it makes me feel even more flushed to realize he is still fully dressed. His lips are damp as he nips the shell of my ear, whispering, "Who just made you come that hard, Petra? Tell me."

"You, Alex." I breathe, my heart thundering against my ribs.

"That's right. And I'm gonna make sure you don't forget that," he grits out, voice strained with arousal. Alex clamps both of my wrists within his hands, stretching me out before leaning to tell me roughly, "Stay just like this. Don't move."

I nod, and I can hear him as he reaches down to work at his belt. The sound of the metal buckle coming undone fills me with rapt anticipation, even so soon after my previous orgasm. I can't get enough of him, and it has been so long since he's put his hands on me, making me feel like this. I've missed it so much. I wish he would kiss me, cradle my face in his big hands and tell me he loves me, but instead he is working my body over almost coldly.

Still, I want it. I want him however he will have me, and if that's half naked bent over this table then I'll take it.

I hear Alex's pants hit the floor, and then I feel the head of his cock parting my swollen pussy, rubbing over my clit and back to the mouth of my channel, wetting himself with my cum before he pushes in, slowly at first, and then without warning, burying himself completely. I suck in a surprised breath at the sudden feeling of fullness, but Alex doesn't give me a moment to breathe. He pulls out before slamming back in again fully. My mind is reeling but my body is celebrating, coming alive under his touch, relentless as it may be.

We fill the dining room with the wet, slapping sounds of him pulling out and driving home in my pussy again and again. It all blends together for me. I can't keep track of the individual movements he makes within me, only the overwhelming sensations building inside as he kisses my womb with the head of his manhood at the apex of each thrust.

Like an exploding star, my orgasm builds deep in my stomach, growing hotter and hotter with each passing second. It's too much, too soon. I try to pull myself forward on the glass table, but Alex stops me.

"Don't even think about moving," he bites out, fucking me even harder, until my toes are barely touching the floor.

"Alex, please!" I cry.

Suddenly, his hips stutter, and he pulls out of me, his cock still hard as iron and glistening. With a gentler touch than before, he turns me around, lifting me until I'm sitting on the edge of the table.

Alex wraps my legs around his hips and slides back into me. He buries one hand in my hair, and palms my breasts with his other hand, keeping my blouse hiked up around my collarbone as he pulls and plucks at my nipples. Once he is deep inside of me, he holds still for a moment before starting up a smoother rhythm than before. Instead of a punishing race to the finish line, he's giving me his cock in a more controlled pace. I take in his expression as if it was the last time I would ever see him. There is a vein sticking out in his neck, and I can tell by the set of his jaw that his teeth are clenched.

Little sparks follow his hands as he caresses my tits, stomach, and back. Alex grabs one of my legs and throws it over his shoulder, and the new position has him pressing right into my g-spot. Pleasure crawls up my spine, and I groan, throwing my head back.

"Just like that," I whisper to him.

He exhales between his teeth, sweat beading on his forehead. He jerks my torso more upright, crushing his mouth to mine finally. I had been afraid he was too angry at me to kiss me but tasting myself on his lips and tongue and filling my nose with his familiar scent calms my worries. He still can't resist me, just like I can't resist him.

Our tongues tangle, teeth clicking together as he keeps pumping into me, as steady and sure as the tides. It will be okay; everything will be okay if he still needs me like this. We will be alright.

I throw my arms around his neck as he peppers kisses on my jawline and neck before returning to my mouth. My heart is at his mercy and I can only succumb to the addictive sensation of being his. He nips at my bottom lip, teasing me hard, before plunging his tongue back into the cavern of my mouth. We are so close, that I'm unsure of where he ends, and I begin.

The supernova orgasm building in my stomach is reaching the point of no return. My focus is single-minded. I want us both to come together, as one.

"Come inside of me," I beg between kisses.

"Is that what you want?" he demands, unyielding. His tone sends a shiver through me, but it's hard to concentrate. I force the words out, locking my gaze with his, desperate.

"Yes, yes, more than anything." I have missed this so much, him and me, making one in perfect harmony, as we put aside our fights, what divides us, and focus only on the now. Something fierce flashes in his ocean-colored eyes when I speak. My hips and thighs are shuddering, and the first ripples of my climax break free. My inner muscles clench down on Alex's cock, and I can hear him gasp roughly. Before I can scream with pleasure, he has his mouth on mine again, and I cry out against his lips. He crushes me to him, hard, and I feel the hot stream of his cum shoot inside of me as he continues to fuck me, refusing to stop until he has spilled every drop inside my pussy.

He leans his forehead against mine as we both struggle to catch our breath, periodically kissing languorously.

"Did you enjoy it?" he asks, his lips pulling my earlobe.

My breathing is still ragged, making it hard to talk, but I drag some precious air into my lungs as I slowly recover my senses. "Yes," I say in a whisper.

"Good," he then gives me a quick kiss on the head before pulling himself out of me, letting his cum drip down my thighs. "It was my way of telling you goodbye."

"What?" My heart freezes at his last words. He didn't say that, no, he didn't!

"From now on, we are on a break," he announces flatly as he dresses himself back.

I push my underwear up and stand in front of him. "You can't be serious!"

"I'm very serious," he answers, his tone steady. "You seem to be very confused about your vows. So I'm gonna give you some time to think about them and what you want in life."

"I want you," I say through my despair.

"No, you don't," Alex retorts. "Your testimony against me and the kiss with that boy tell me the precise opposite."

"It was a mistake." My mouth remains wide open to breathe as I say those words. "I won't see him again."

"Why not?" he asks promptly. "Are you afraid of not being able to resist him if you do?" Instantly, he grabs my mouth between his hand, looking me straight in the eye. "Are you afraid of not having a damn backbone to tell him no?"

I can't talk because my lips are squeezed between his fingers, but I'm hating his attitude to the core. Once he finally releases me, I fold my arms over my chest, and ask, "What are you gonna do during this break?"

"I'm moving out," he announces.

I gasp instantly at his answer. "Why? You can stay here. Please."

"No," he replies sternly. "I'll go back to the residence where I was staying. Take this time away from me to reflect about your life and if you really want me as a husband or just as a father to our kids."

I swallow the lump in my throat at his statement; he can't be serious!

"Alex, I want you in every sense." I sound desperate but that's because I am, he's about to move out and I can't fathom having to live here the next few months without him. "What about the pregnancy? What if I need help?"

"You have Maria twenty-four-seven. She literally lives here. Your dad lives a few blocks away with Janine, and you have also the midwife available at your fingertips."

"Are you gonna have an affair or something during this break?"

"What?" He looks at me with narrowed eyes like I asked the most stupid question in the world, but I couldn't help it. "I'm not the one here who kissed someone else. Unlike you, I don't go to the library to pretend I'm studying when in fact I'm there to meet with someone that I kinda like but can't admit it because I'm married."

His comment hits me to the core. Is this really what he thinks of me? "Matt and I are just friends," I repeat, tears brimming my eyes. "That kiss was a mistake. It meant nothing. It'll never happen ever again."

"Friends don't go around kissing each other on the mouth, Petra. Stop fooling yourself."

I shut my eyes for a moment, reality being too hard to face. And while I do so, I hear Alex walking out of the dining room. I put on my skirt, and go lean against the doorway of the dining room as I watch him grabbing his coat, getting ready to leave. "Are you gonna ask for a divorce?"

"I should. But I won't," he snaps, putting his coat on. Then he walks back to where I'm standing and starts stroking my cheek softly, considering me. "This break is for you to understand once and for all what your priorities are in life. And especially what you want from us." He takes a deep breath, his chest rising and falling as he does so. Afterwards, a heavy silence falls between us as he thinks something through. His gaze goes up to meet mine, and all I can see is the sadness and disappointment in his eyes. Oh gosh, and it breaks my heart in two. "I want you as my wife, but I can't have you if your heart is elsewhere." I shut my eyes tight, the weight of my actions falling on me like an avalanche. Then Alex presses his lips on my forehead in a kiss filled with so much sorrow that silent tears start falling down my cheeks. "Goodbye."

I freeze at his last word, my heart skipping a beat, but I press my lips tight and with my eyes shut, all I can hear is his footsteps going away from me, the front door opening and then slamming behind him.

I don't retain my tears and I cry my eyes out, because I hate myself. I hate what I did to him and I can't for the life of me believe I let Matt kiss me. I want to punch walls and break glasses, but I don't do any of that. It won't fix anything. So instead, I take a deep breath in and out, go back inside the dining room, and call Emma. I need to speak to someone. I need to cry on a shoulder. And she's the only one who I trust enough to do that. The ringtone goes on and on until...

"Hey," Emma's voice makes me smile amid the pain that I'm going through. "What's up, girl?"

"Hi," I breathe as I sniffle. "Um, I was wondering if you are around..."

"Yeah, I'm at a party. You wanna join?"

I chuckle at her invitation; this Emma never changes. "No, um, I just wanted to talk to you and hear your voice."

"What's going on?" Her tone switches, becoming deeply worried. She knows me well, but I don't find the will to tell her the harsh reality over the line. "Petra? Are you okay?"

I sniffle in return, and finally manage to say, "It's, um, it's Alex and I…"

"He did something bad?" she asks immediately.

I shake my head, unable to vocalize the words. "I did."

I hear nothing on the other side of the line, but a loud gush of air. "Are you at home now?"

"Yeah… And he moved out," I tell her.

"He moved out?" she repeats in outrage. "Fuck… Okay, um, I'm on my way. Gimme a few minutes, I'm gonna call my driver and I'll go there to see you."

"Oh, Emma, I…" I glance around, feeling so shitty that I don't know what else to say. "I'm sorry to ruin your evening."

"What the fuck? Are you serious? I'd rather be with you. I'll be there soon."

"Thanks, I—I really appreciate…"

"Hang on, alright? See you in a few minutes."

After she hangs up, I plunge my head between my arms as they rest on the table. I never in my entire life imagined I could have done something like that to him. It never occurred to me. But after feeling so rejected, hated, and completely ignored by my husband, I let Matt kiss me, reminding me that I too deserve to be loved and cherished. Now that I can think with more clarity, I realize that kiss has never been about Matt, but about the man I love not giving a damn about me.

"Ma'am?" I hear Maria saying as she walks in.

I straighten myself and wipe my tears away. "Yes?"

"Shall I serve dinner for you?"

"Oh, um…"

"You have to eat," Maria reminds me just as fast.

"Yes," I say, sniffling and rubbing my eyelids tiredly. "I'll have dinner." I've got no appetite, but I will eat slowly and make an effort. Then Maria walks out of the dining room, and I'm left sitting alone, the chair in front of me empty.

* * *

Twenty minutes later I hear the bell sound through the condo. I smile on the inside knowing it's Emma, but I keep eating my soup, waiting for her to walk in.

"Whatever you are going through, I'm sure it's gonna pass," she states as she enters the dining room. I stand up and give her a hug so strong that I let my emotions overtake me. "Hey," she purrs, her hand stroking my hair. "It's gonna be okay."

"Oh, Emma, I did something so bad," I tell her amid my tears. Emma wipes them with her thumbs and keeps waiting for me to say the rest. "I'm so scared he'll never forgive me."

"Look, whatever you did, I know how much Alex loves you. Even after you testified against him, he never stopped loving you."

Despite everything I'm going through, her words bring a much-needed warmth to my heart. "Yeah, but now it's even worse," I confess, my head dipping down in shame.

"Alright, fess up," she says, lifting my chin so that my eyes can meet hers again. "It's better you tell me the truth if you want me to help."

I take a deep breath in and out, trying to regain my composure. Emma is right; if I want to move forward and heal, I need to face my mistakes once and for all, even if I'd rather dig a hole and throw them in there. "Alex has been so cold, distant, and such a jerk with me, that I let Matt kiss me."

Emma's eyes widen in surprise and she doesn't even hide her astonishment as I tell her what I did. "It was short and innocent, only a peck," I tell her like it matters. "Then I left the library, came home and told him immediately."

"And how did he react?"

"He had a romantic dinner prepared." I nearly sob as I remember that. "He asked a few questions and then told me from now on we were on a break."

Emma winces and is rendered totally speechless. For the first time since we have been friends, she doesn't seem to know what to say or do, which makes it even worse.

Her eyes dip slowly down as she thinks something through and then for some reason, she frowns. "You might hate me for what I'm gonna say, but I think you both need to heal before you can get back together."

I frown in confusion. "What do you mean? You think we are better off separated than together?"

"You guys have been going through so much shit this year, like, I think you both need your own space to heal before trying to turn the page without resentment or bitterness for each other."

Living separate from him is the last thing I want, but I don't want to sound selfish, so I remain quiet, pondering her words. Maybe after everything we went through, giving space and time to each other would help the wounds we have inflicted on each other to heal.

Silence fills the space between us, not knowing what else to tell her. Then as we look at each other, I wonder if she has found out about my pregnancy or not, but by the look on her face, I don't think she has. This skirt combined with the black blouse is perfect to hide my bump. I'd love to tell Emma, but I don't feel comfortable enough at twenty weeks to let her know. After all the bad news and premonitions, who knows if it's gonna last. "Thank you for coming." I give her a bright smile in appreciation. "You have no idea how much I needed to talk to you."

CHAPTER 24

Manhattan, March 29, 2021
Alexander Van Dieren

"You are what?" Roy repeats once more, annoyance thick in his tone.

I'm already regretting to have told him the truth, but given the fact we have a meeting with Petra in a few minutes, I thought it'd be better to let him know we are on a break. A lesson to remind myself I should keep my private life *private*.

"On a break," I tell him once more, despite the outrage on his face. "She's not only cooperating with Eric to put me in jail but she and Matt…" I let out an exasperated breath, not wanting to face reality—it still hurts like crazy.

"She and Matt?" Roy asks, impatiently waiting for me to say the rest.

I tap my pen steadily on the notes I have in front of me, still pondering if I should go ahead or not. Each time I think about what she did though, the pain in my chest comes back and I remind myself how disappointed I felt, how angry... "He kissed her and she didn't seem to mind it," I finally fess out.

"He kissed her?" Roy repeats, barely believing it. "I'm sure Petra wasn't expecting it and she was just shocked at his behavior." Roy innocently tries to protect her, which is understandable since at the beginning I thought the same— no, Petra wouldn't do that. But Zach told me she has been meeting him a lot over the past weeks. She might not call going to the library or having dinner with him a date, but if they end up kissing, to me, it's a date.

"The truth is I'm not even remorseful," I lie. "I don't hold a grudge against her," I lie again. "I just want her to be happy." At least this last part is true. "Maybe this marriage was a mistake." Then I just stand up and walk in the direction of the window to avoid his disapproving gaze.

"You have lost your mind," Roy comments promptly. I'm not surprised by his indignation; it's a lot to take at once. Then he rises from his seat, and walks toward me, before putting a hand on my shoulder. "She loves you, but this trial is creating a myriad of friction between you both." I remain quiet, standing in front of the floor-to-ceiling window as I take in the view. "You are becoming distant and frigid with her in a period of her life where she needs the precise opposite."

I turn to look at him, intrigued by his set of words. "What do you mean this period of her life?" I ask, wondering if he already knows about the pregnancy. I for sure didn't tell him.

"She lost her mother a month ago and now the trial is creating a lot of stress for her," he explains further. Roy pauses to take a deep breath and then says, "You have to forgive her."

"She betrayed me," I remind him. "*Twice*."

"And you lied to her too," Roy shoots back. "You broke several promises and disappointed her. Marriage is about forgiving each other over and over again."

"I can't forgive her for that…"

"You can't forgive your wife for a kiss that she regrets and didn't initiate?" he asks, visibly surprised.

"Don't make it sound like I'm being the asshole here," I tell him straight away.

"Well, maybe if you were less of an ass with her, she wouldn't have let Matt kiss her."

"She is cooperating with them," I snap, my tone rising unexpectedly. "And she literally testified against me." I shake my head not wanting to recall that day. "I can spend the rest of my life in jail. You know that, right?"

"She did what she had to." Roy keeps protecting his daughter like she's some sort of saint. "Look, she's your wife, and yet you hid the fact you knew about the abduction and then her mom died because of that."

I decide to focus again on the city that stands in front of me. I'm really done with this talk.

"The more you keep your distance from her, the worse it will be in the end."

Fortunately we hear a few knocks on the door and we turn immediately to check who's there. "Excuse me?" Cate asks as she stands in the doorway. "The rest of the board is here, can they come in?"

"Sure," I utter, trying to hide my discontentment to have to see Petra again after only two days from her betrayal.

After shaking hands with Joshua, Mike, and the rest of the board, Petra walks in, and against our better judgement, we glance at each other, knowing we just have to silence everything we are going through, and shake hands for the sake of politeness. While I know Petra's pregnant, I notice she always dresses in a way that makes it impossible for those who don't know to find out. Plus, since she is underweight, her bump is barely visible through her fit and flare blouse which is covered by a scarf and a black blazer. I glance at Roy to see if he noticed anything, but nope. There's absolutely no confusion or astonishment coming from his face as he gives her a hug and a kiss on the cheek.

We all take a seat around the glass table, and, for some reason, Petra has decided to sit right in front of me. I do my best to appear unaffected, but why does she need to be front and center in my field of view? Is it some sort of twisted desire to remind me of what she has done?

Fortunately, Roy, who is sitting at the head of the table, starts the meeting about all things I love: performance of our several portfolios and the need to expand the one in biotechnology.

Yet as we start talking about several strategies to pitch our current investors and how much we'd need to raise to expand our favorite portfolios, a few concerns come in.

"With Alex's current trial and reputation, we can't expand any portfolios," Joshua points out. "We need this whole thing to be a distant memory in the minds of our investors."

"Speaking of reputation," I begin. "Petra and I were thinking to plan a charity dinner for a children's foundation in order to water down the current headlines a bit," I say in order to discreetly mention the gala dinner I had in mind for the Turner's Syndrome foundation in honor to Jasmine. Mariana and Petra might call her "Baby B" but to me she has been Jasmine since the day I saw her in the scan.

"That's a great idea," Roy points out. "Everyone likes children, it will be good PR."

"I agree," Mike seconds. "This will score points with every editor that has been tarnishing your reputation."

"Petra and Alex," Joshua says, looking at us. "Needless to say, if Gatt-Dieren hosts the event we need you both to keep up a loving appearance." We look icily at each other, but don't say a word. "From Petra's testimony to the argument outside the court, you'll need to be very convincing."

"Do you have any non-profit in mind?" Roy asks, bringing my attention to him. "If not, we work with—"

"I'm thinking the Turner Syndrome Foundation," I interpose.

Roy blinks twice in confusion. "The what?"

"It's a foundation that helps kids with Turner Syndrome. It's a rare condition that affects only girls but I think it deserves some awareness," I mumble, giving a quick look at Petra as I say so. Since no one seems to see the point to bring awareness to something they aren't even familiar with, I add, "It's a favor I'm doing for a client who has a child with this condition."

"Ah!" Everyone nods, smiling in understanding. "Sure, that works fine."

"Do you have any specific date in mind?" Celia, the head of investor relations, asks. "We need at least a month ahead to make sure people can attend."

"What about holding it on May fifteenth?" Petra suggests. "Gatt-Dieren is known to do black-tie events in May given the fact it's when my dad's birthday is. Everyone will be more likely to accept the invitation, if it's also my dad's birthday."

"That's true," Joshua comments. "Even those who would see the charity event as nothing more than a mere PR move won't say shit if we combine it with Roy's birthday."

After agreeing to fix the gala dinner for May fifteenth, I can't help but share a small smile with my wife even though I know I shouldn't.

Once the meeting is over, I stand up like everyone else, but instead of staying, chit-chatting with the other members in the conference room, I walk toward the door and leave. I don't want to stay any longer in the same room with her. It reminds me of what she did on Friday while I'd asked Maria to prepare a romantic setup for the two of us. Jeez, what an idiot I was. I don't need this kind of reminder on a work day. Reaching my office, I close the door behind me and go to my desk chair. Yet, just five minutes later, I hear someone knocking on the door and even before I could ask who it is, the door cracks open.

What a lack of manners! I want to say a word or two for not waiting my instruction, but the sight of my wife prevents me from doing so.

"Oh," I utter in surprise as she comes in.

"Um, Cate told me you were here," she says like it's a valid excuse to enter my office without permission.

"Is everything alright?" I ask, rising immediately from my seat.

"Yes," she answers, a bright smile on her lips that I can't help but mimic. "I just wanted to thank you for not telling anyone about my pregnancy." Her voice is unusually sweet and gentle as she paces in my direction.

I observe her attentively and notice how beautiful she is today. Not sure if it's because I haven't seen her for two days, but her simple presence has such a mesmerizing impact on me. Unfortunately, my mind reminds me of her betrayal just as fast and my heart dies a little more. "You're welcome. It's none of their business, anyway."

"Indeed," she says quietly, standing in front of my desk.

"What about your dad?" I ask as I walk to meet her. "Do you intend to tell him?"

"I will before the gala dinner, that's for sure. By then, my bump will be too big to hide."

Her Jasmine perfume permeates the air between us and it takes everything in me to keep a stoic face and my hands to myself. "It's gonna be one hell of a birthday gift."

She starts laughing at my comment, and jeez, I had missed so damn much the sound of her laughter. After hearing it so many times, I should've become totally indifferent to it. Yet, it's precisely the opposite. Seeing her laughing and happy is my greatest weakness. Her gaze drifts down for a moment as she thinks something through before it meets mine again.

"I really want you back in my life," she says in a whisper.

Her words hit me like a hammer and I'm not sure how to tell her I'm simply not ready for that. Not wanting to start an argument, especially here in the office, I decide to close the subject even before getting started. "We have already spoken about it."

"But this distance is just so unnecessary," she presses on. "We are married. I love you and I want to be with you."

I heave a long sigh at her insistence. Somehow I knew she wasn't coming into my office just to thank me. "Petra, your actions say the precise opposite; *you* sided with the Bradfords, *you* testified against me, *you* taped conversations between us, and now *you* kissed someone else." I close my eyes for a moment, letting the reality of my words sink in. I reach for my eyelids and massage them with my fingers to alleviate the tension. Then I look back at her and say, "I seriously think you should reflect on what you truly want in life, because to me you seem very confused."

Petra frowns, looking away as she seems to sulk for a bit. "You know perfectly well that I love you."

Before she can even place one more word, I step in. "That's not what your actions are telling me." My voice remains low, filled with disappointment. "I'm not even sure if what you feel for me is love." Her mouth gapes at me in shock but I continue, "Lust yes, but *love*..."

"I can't believe you are doubting my feelings," she says, her tone growing louder. "I'm going through the shittiest time of my life, through a pregnancy where one of the babies or even both might die, and instead of being supportive you are doubting us? What am I to you? A heartless monster?"

"That's not what I said." I can see the frustration in her eyes, and how much this whole thing is affecting her, but I proceed, "I don't see you as a heartless monster. On the contrary, I love you, deeply."

"So why don't you come back?" she asks, on the verge of tears. "Why don't you move on?"

"Because you betrayed me," I remind her. "Don't you get it?"

Eye to eye, we remain silent for a moment, letting the truth hang in the air.

"What if I stop talking to Matt? Would you come back?"

I snicker at her question. "I don't need you to stop talking to that boy. I need you to be loyal to me," I explain. "This didn't start with that kiss, Petra. It started the day you got me arrested." Letting my words sink in to her, I walk back to my office chair and sit, grabbing a file to focus on. "Now I have work to do." I put my glasses on and lower my gaze to the document in front of me. "I'll see you for your next appointment."

"You don't have to go," she retorts promptly. "I can do it on my own."

"I insist on going," I tell her, my voice steady. "It's on the sixteenth of April, correct?"

Petra just nods, and since everything has been said, she finally leaves my office.

CHAPTER 25

Manhattan, March 29, 2021
Petra Van Gatt

On my way back to the condo, I try to fill my mind with positivity but all I can think of is the poor state of my relationship with the man to whom I swore vows of love and fidelity. How did we end up here? Why did he need to lie so much and create this big wall between us? I look out of the window with a wistful time as I see a couple kissing on the sidewalk. Yeah... Alex didn't even give me a kiss today. Nothing; just a very polite and professional handshake... I heave a long sigh, unable to contain the pain for being on a break. This is even worse than before; at least before he could be grumpy but he would come home and we were still together. Now, no matter what he says, we are truly separated. My home is empty every evening and every night, and for now, I can only dream of the day he will come back and forgive me.

Reaching the door of the condo, Maria opens the door for me, her expression a tad more serious than usual.

I'm about to ask her what's wrong, when I hear footsteps approaching from the hallway and I instantly follow them with my gaze.

"Ah! Finally! Here you are!"

"Yara?" I ask, unable to contain the shock in my tone as I see her standing in front of me. "What are you doing here?"

"I came here to collect my painting," she says like it's the most natural thing in the world.

"But why?" I keep asking, not convinced. "You could've just texted me your address, and I'd have shipped it to you."

"I wanted to collect it myself," she says. "Shall we?"

"Sure," I answer, still confused, but I walk past her and lead her to my atelier. "Did you travel all the way from the Netherlands just to collect it?"

"I also have a few things to do here," she answers, playing with the pair of black leather gloves she's holding in her hands. I notice they match her equestrian boots, contrasting with the white of her breeches and polo shirt.

Then, to my biggest surprise, I stumble upon two men I had never seen before standing in front of the door of my atelier.

I turn to Yara and before I can even ask her who they are, she says, "My driver and my security agent; they are here to help me take the painting out."

And she is not even embarrassed they would see her naked on the painting? I fail miserably to keep the astonishment out of my face, but I force myself to focus as I open the door and welcome her inside. While Yara walks into the room, and to the canvas that is lying against the wall, I can't stop wondering why she wants to take the painting in person. That doesn't make any sense. And what kind of things does she have to do here? While my mind keeps ruminating about her stay in New York, I hear Yara's gasping and uttering a big and resounding, "Wow! It's so beautiful!"

"Thanks," I tell her as she stands inches from the painting to admire it more closely. With so many questions buzzing in my head, I shut the door behind us, so that we can have a moment for ourselves. While I observe Yara entranced with her painting, my mind starts putting a few pieces of the puzzle together, and as I do so, an immediate urge to talk about Venice and especially about my best friend hits me.

"What kind of relationship do you have with Emma?" My question echoes through the four walls of my atelier and I can see how it caught Yara off guard. And before she can give me some bullshit answer, I add, "I mean, if you invited her to participate in such an exclusive initiation ritual and had her helping you catch Eric's friend, surely you must be very close."

She turns, a smirk rising on her lips, and starts pacing in my direction. "We are very close friends, yes."

"What a great *friendship* that is," I say, unable to keep the sarcasm off my tone.

Her smirk keeps growing across her face despite the seriousness of the conversation. "Are you getting jealous?"

"Rather concerned," I disclose, looking her in the eye.

Yara stands inches from me, her expression filled with amusement. "Emma is a big girl, you know. She doesn't need your concerns."

"Emma is human like everyone else," I say, my tone steady. "And like everyone else, she can get deceived and overly attached to someone she shouldn't."

Yara's dark eyes start narrowing on me and she takes one step forward, while I take one backward. "Are you trying to imply I'm deceiving her?"

Despite her tone getting more and more aggressive, I do my best to keep my nerves under control. "I'm not implying it, I'm literally saying it." She might be clenching her jaw, and straightening her posture to look more intimidating, but I'm just too tired of her little games to mind. "Don't try to groom her into your cult, or whatever that is."

"Or else what?" Yara snickers. "What is a little girl like you gonna do?"

I huff at her question. Damn… She is such a fucking psycho. I'm pretty sure her relationship with Emma isn't only a "close friendship" like they've both told me. "I can ask Emma to stop talking to you," I warn.

Yara bursts out in laughter. "And you think she'll listen to you?" She shakes her head, still laughing at the idea. "You're so delusional. You think what? That Emma is gonna bow to your every demand?" We keep staring at each other but I don't give her an answer. She simply doesn't deserve one. "Now, I'm gonna take my portrait and we are gonna close this subject once and for all."

She goes outside the atelier and calls the two men who were waiting in the hallway to come in. They pack the canvas inside a clear poly bag, with bubble wrap corners, and then into a box that can get easily carried out of the condo.

Yara puts her black leather gloves on and gives me a quick, "Goodbye," before leaving my atelier with her staff.

Maria escorts them all the way to the front door and I'm glad she does so, because my manners with that psycho are running pretty low.

Once I hear the front door shutting down again, I close the one of my atelier, take my iPhone, and call my driver.

"Zach? Are you in the parking lot?" I ask, thinking something through.

"Yes, ma'am," he says.

"Can you please get the car ready to follow the woman who just left the condo?"

"Yara Van Lawick?"

My lips curve up at his unexpected answer.

"Correct," I answer.

"Uh, okay, should I ask our security agents to track her car too?"

My eyes widen in surprise. Damn! I didn't know they were trained to do that.

"Oh, um, yes, why not?" My heart starts racing at the plan I have in mind, but I'm just too curious not to go through with it. "I'll be right there."

After hanging up, I head outside the condo, and go to the parking lot where Zach is waiting for me.

I speed up my pace and once I slide inside the car, I instruct him to go and follow Yara's car.

Zach seems to be in touch with Alex's security team as they are sharing info about where her car is heading to. I never thought a team who spends all day long watching security cams could be so helpful!

Zach starts to speed up and after a few turns right and left, we find ourselves crossing the George Washington Bridge and exiting Manhattan. Damn, where on earth is she heading to? As I look at our location in the GPS of my iPhone, I start to realize Zach is driving north, along the Hudson River. This is the same direction to go to Emma's place. At this point, unless Yara has something to do in New Jersey, it's clear she's going to meet her.

This is really weird; Yara travels all the way to New York from the Netherlands to pick up the painting herself and then goes straight to Emma's place with it? Yeah, something is definitely off.

After half an hour on the road, it's clear as water we are going to Emma's place. Zach decides to speed up and thanks to him, we manage to arrive just in time to see the gates of Emma's property opening wide and Yara's car getting inside.

"What should we do now?" he asks.

"Can you park two blocks away so we don't get caught by her cameras?"

"Sure."

Once we are parked, I ponder my next move.

Zach turns and looks at me as I remain sitting pensively on the backseat. "Ma'am, if you tell me exactly what you want, we can help you out."

"I need to know if the painting is still in the car or if Yara took it with her." That's the only way to find out the truth. If that painting was truly for Elliott or if, as I'm currently thinking, it is a gift for her lover—Emma. Jeez! The fact they both lied to me to cover up their little affair is just so damn infuriating. I tell Emma everything, and yet, it seems like this isn't mutual.

"Did you hear that?" Zach asks looking down at his phone who is currently in a call with a member of the security team.

"Yep, we can try to hack the security cameras of that estate. If we don't manage, we can always follow the car back until we get to see the truck," I hear from the speakers.

"Okay, that's good," I tell him. "Let me know if you manage."

Once the call ends, I wait patiently inside the car for an update. Yet, after an hour trapped in here, we haven't yet heard anything back from the security team. I keep glancing at my watch, impatient for some news, but at this point, I'm starting to lose hope.

"Ma'am?" Zach says, his phone against his ear. "It seems like Yara's car is leaving the property."

"Please, tell them to follow the car and to find out if the painting is still inside."

"That's what they are doing since they didn't manage to hack the security cams," Zach explains.

All of a sudden though, my own iPhone starts ringing and my heart freezes as I check who's calling me.

For better or worse, I decide to take the call and I put the phone against my cheek.

"Yes?" My voice is low and barely audible.

"What do you want, Petra?" *Shit!*

"Um, what do you mean?" I ask Emma like I know nothing.

"Someone tried to hack my security cams, and it appears that you and your driver are parked two blocks away from my property. My agents have access to street cams and can read plate numbers. You know that, right?"

I shut my eyes at my own stupidity. Of course Emma would find out about my little investigation.

My eyes dip down at my lap, not knowing what to say or do. "Uh, I—"

"Were you following Yara?"

"No!" I snap instantly. But then I realize how stupid it is lying to her like that, so I heave a long sigh and say, "Yes, um, whenever you are free, can I have a word with you?"

"Well, she just left, so help yourself."

Although I'm slightly apprehensive in meeting her face-to-face right after she caught me in the act, I instruct Zach to drop me at her house.

She must think I'm pathetic or crazy to follow my sister-in-law, but Emma doesn't seem to realize how dangerous that woman is.

As I arrive in front of her entrance door, Emma is standing in the doorway, arms crossed over her chest, an annoyed look on her face.

While I know she's doing it to make me feel ashamed of my behavior, I truly am not.

"Are you mad at me?" I ask once I get close enough to her.

"I'm not mad," she answers, her tone unusually chilled. "But what the heck is wrong with you? Why are you following Yara?"

"Well, because I'd love to know what's going on," I say, looking her straight in the eye. "See, I saw my best friend participating in a very humiliating ritual after being invited by that woman and now that very same woman came all the way from the Netherlands to pick up the painting I did for her and goes straight to your house." Instantly, Emma cuts eye contact, looking down to the void. Is it because she knows I'm right? Or is it because I'm forcing her to do some introspection about her personal choices? "So, yeah, I'd like to know why you are keeping secrets from me."

"We all have secrets," she says, her gaze meeting mine again. And at this point, it's clear Emma and Yara are a thing. I'm not sure how deep her feelings are for her, but one thing is sure…

"This is a toxic relationship," I snap as I try to bring some common sense into her. "You have to end it."

"Oh, I sure as hell don't have to!"

She's about to go back inside, but I hold her wrist, forcing her to face me again. "Don't you see how she is manipulating you?" I ask, annoyance thick in my tone. "She's exploiting your vulnerabilities and—"

"Alright, look," Emma pulls her arm away and releases herself from me. "I appreciate your concern over my wellbeing, but I don't need your unsolicited advice."

"Emma," I begin, this time holding both of her arms. "Whatever is going on between the two of you, you don't have to be part of this type of cult. This will fuck up your mind."

But Emma takes a few steps back and seems to get more nervous and irritated than before. "You know nothing about us, so stop interfering." She turns and walks back inside the house, but I follow right behind her.

"I have never seen you like this," I say while she keeps walking in front of me down the hallway, but I speed up my pace and start running to reach her. "Like, how is it even possible that you let yourself go down that path?" Once I'm close enough, I stand in front of her, barring her way. "Seeing you naked, collared, was…" I take a deep breath, shutting down those images. "It was so degrading that I couldn't look any longer."

"I did it to help her," she presses on, but it feels like she's just trying to close the subject.

"Wasn't it just an excuse for her to persuade you to do that?" Despite her many attempts to avoid me, I keep standing in front of her, making sure she considers my question. "What's going on with you?" I keep asking as I hold her shoulders so that she can't go anywhere else. "Tell me."

She finally looks me in the eye, and I can't tell if she's angry or just annoyed. "Not everyone is lucky in love. Okay?"

"Lucky or not, you deserve so much better than her. She's a manipulative and violent psycho."

"I know that." Emma heaves a long sigh, filled with so much sadness that it squeezes my heart tight. "But she also has some good moments."

"She's taken," I remind her. "There's no future between the two of you."

"I know, but she was there when I was at my lowest, and that's good enough for me."

"At your lowest?" I repeat, totally astonished. "How come I know nothing about it?"

Emma just shrugs in return. "Because you already have enough on your plate."

"You are my best friend," I remind her. "I am here for your highs and lows." Her chin remains dipping down as she tries to avoid looking me in the eye. I must say, I have never seen my confident Emma like this before. It feels like she's gonna cry from everything she has been holding back at any second. "What's going on? Please, tell me."

"Fine!" she hisses, before taking a deep breath in annoyance at my insistent nature. "You remember that day in ninth grade when I tried to kiss you?"

"I remember that, yeah? Wait," I say as I think something through, "are you still holding a grudge because I slapped you?"

"No, I deserved it," she answers, brushing that off. "I shouldn't have tried in the first place." She pauses, measuring her next set of words. "But, um, I tried to kiss you that day because I was in love with you." I keep quiet, looking at her as she seems to struggle to say the rest. "And what sucks the most is that this feeling never really went away." I press my lips tight as if I could taste her own struggle. She glances around trying to steady herself before proceeding. "Yara found out I was still struggling with it at your engagement party and from there she has been *helping* me."

"Emma, I..." My gaze is on the floor as I try to find the right words to say, but despite my many attempts, I don't find anything worthy. A few seconds of silence ensue, until all I can say is, "I'm so sorry."

"Sorry for what?" She shakes her head in amusement. "It's not your fault. I just have to learn how to deal with it."

"Being with someone who is using you isn't a solution though," I tell her.

"I know but it helps."

"You deserve so much better. I mean it." She snickers, and I frown, wondering if her attitude is because she doesn't believe me. The Emma I know used to be full of confidence and always sure of herself. Heck, she was always a bit intimidating and her presence commanded respect. But now? She seems to be totally under Yara's dominance, filled with insecurities I didn't even know existed. "Please, for the sake of our friendship, stop seeing her," I plead. "She is dangerous and manipulative."

"I can't do that," she answers with a fatalist tone.

"Why not?"

"Because I like her. Regardless of what you think, I like being with her."

Damn! Yara was right; she really got Emma under her skin. "If I ask you something can you answer me truthfully?"

She raises her eyebrows and ponders my question for a bit. "I can try…"

"That painting was for you, wasn't it?"

Her chuckling tells me exactly what I needed to know. "Yeah, it was a gift in return for helping her to catch Eric's friend. You're very talented, by the way. That painting is pretty good."

Despite her compliment, I'd have preferred not having painted it. "But why a painting with her kneeling with a collar and wrist restraints?" I keep asking.

"Those are mine actually," she discloses. "I wanted to reverse the roles for once."

What? So Yara is her Dom? Fuck! My cheeks must have gone a sharp shade of red at the revelation. I never thought they were in that kind of dynamic, and I'm left with the impression I invaded their privacy with so many questions. I feel rather uncomfortable to have been exposed to the whole truth.

"Now that you know everything do you mind leaving me alone?" Somehow I'm actually glad she asked me that. Their relationship seems much more complex than I thought, and while I'm sure it's not a healthy one, at the end of the day, Emma is a big girl, and I did as much as I could to share my concerns with her.

"Sure, um, thank you for telling me all of this," I say, before taking her into my arms and squeezing her tight. A quick silence emerges while we enjoy our hug. As I release her, I can read the nostalgia laced all over her face and it really feels my Emma today isn't having one of her best days. "But please, promise me you'll be careful with her."

Her lips curve up at my request. Yes, I'm insistent and yes, I'm still pretty worried with her. "Alright, I promise."

CHAPTER 26

Manhattan, March 30, 2021
Alexander Van Dieren

"Your invitee has just arrived, sir," Wang, the butler of my private residence, announces.

"Ah, perfect," I answer as I remain sitting in the living room, an opera playing in the background, finishing up some work on my laptop. "You can let him in." I keep myself focused on the screen when I hear a new pair of footsteps approaching. Then, I shut down my laptop, and look at my guest standing by the doorway. "I'm glad you called me," I tell Matt as he finally walks in. "I was about to do it actually, but I'm glad you did it first."

"Um, thanks for inviting me in," he says, slowly pacing in my direction. I gesture for him to sit on the sofa but the boy sits as far as possible from me. The fact he's so scared I'm gonna do something to him makes it all too funny. "I, um, I think I owe you an apology."

"Really?" I ask, sarcasm laced in my tone as I remove my reading glasses. Then I take a sip of my drink, reveling in his nervousness. "How so?"

"It was not my intention to do what I did."

I cross a leg, leaning back on my armchair, observing him attentively. "What did you do exactly, Matt? Tell me."

While I'm thoroughly enjoying our little chat, Matt, on the other hand, doesn't seem to be as entertained. "You know what I did."

"That doesn't mean I don't want you to tell me to my face." I pause, my gaze focused on his shaky hands. "Go on."

"I kissed her." His voice is barely audible, and he doesn't even look me in the eye when he says those words. "And it was a stupid mistake."

"And you think that's it?" I ask, suppressing a laugh. "You walk in, say I'm sorry, and think that's all forgotten?"

Matt frowns, his eyes narrowing on me. "Uh, what else do you want me to do?"

That's exactly the question I wanted him to ask. "If you want to remain friends with my wife, you're gonna have to not only stop taking advantage of our marital problems but also find someone else to love."

"Okay, I'll do that." His tone is hurried and laced with fear. He then just lets out a breath and says, "I don't have many friends, and she's really like the closest I have to a best friend."

"I have noticed that," I reply, before taking another sip of my glass, pondering something. "One more thing," I say, looking him straight in the eyes. "You'd better make sure that your dad leaves me and my family alone once and for all."

I notice Matt getting slightly uncomfortable as he breaks eye contact and heaves a long sigh. He fidgets slightly before opening his mouth to speak. "Fine," he hisses. "I'll have a talk with him."

I can't help but let a quick, quiet chuckle escape from me as I picture Eric's reaction seeing how Matt is now on my side. Pleased with how the conversation is going, I decide that it is time to move to another subject.

"So, I imagine Petra has already invited you to the gala dinner we are hosting in May?"

"Um, yeah, she did. And she also requested that I bring a plus one."

I nod pensively, thinking about the plan I have in mind. "You could invite Sarah Leniski," I suggest, although it's more an order than a suggestion.

Matt seems hesitant. "Yeah, but it's complicated."

"Why?"

"Well, because she wants more than just being friends with benefits you know…"

And that's perfect! "Why not give her a chance?"

"It's just…" Matt pauses, trying to find the best words to put on. "My heart isn't there."

"I'm sure it can get there if you give her a shot," I press on. "And that would help your case, because right now…" I let my words trail off, letting him know he might never see my wife ever again if he doesn't comply.

"If I give her a shot," he begins, considering me. "Do you promise I will remain in Petra's life?"

"If Sarah becomes your girlfriend, I'll even invite you two to the baptism of our kids."

His eyes open wide in surprise. "Really?"

"Really," I repeat, and after finishing my drink, I just say, "I'm not interested in wars, Matt. Unlike what you and your dad may think, I'm very much a pacifist." Plus, let's be honest, if I wanted my wife to never talk to Matt ever again, she wouldn't even mind since she suggested it herself. But there's something about this boy that makes me want to help him. Maybe it's because he cares so much about her and the babies? I don't know. But what I do know is that I'd rather keep my enemies close by and under my watch than sending them away.

Matt ponders my offer more seriously. "Okay, so, um, I will take Sarah with me to the dinner and we'll take it from there."

"Great." My lips curve up, knowing we've finally reached an understanding. "There's one more thing you'll need to do to seal our deal though…"

***

Manhattan, April 8, 2021
Alexander Van Dieren

I shouldn't be surprised that my wife wasn't coming to watch the closing statements. After all, she has never attended any other court session aside from the first one where she had to testify as a witness. Her absence has fed the media the most creative headlines and stories; some are already speculating a divorce post-trial, while others have correctly guessed that we are on a break and living in separate houses. Yet, none of them, fortunately, have found out about her pregnancy.

"The jury will now deliberate," the judge informs. "This court is adjourned until a verdict is reached." And she finishes the session banging her gavel.

Amid the noise of the gallery, I remain quiet, engrossed in my own thoughts. Jeez, I can't wait to get this done once and for all. My legal team and I leave the courtroom, and while they are chatting between them, I haven't said a single word yet.

"Are you okay, Alex?" Ryan asks.

"Of course," I tell him, despite feeling exhausted after such a long day. "Do you know how long the jury will take?"

"I don't know, it can take a few hours to a few days. Who knows... They all need to agree unanimously with the verdict." While I nod at him, Ryan smiles and puts a hand on my shoulder. "You are good. Eric failed to prove beyond a reasonable doubt that it was you. Relax." Yeah, easier said than done.

"May I invite you out for a drink?" I ask him.

Ryan seems surprised at my invitation, but he checks his watch and ponders for a second. "Alright, but I have to be home in two hours. I promised the kids we'd watch a movie together."

* * *

"I wasn't expecting to drink at your place," Ryan points out as he walks into the hallway of my private residence.

"Yeah, I wanted to go somewhere quiet." Since this case has been all over the news, I'm definitely not in the mood to go to a bar and feed the rumor mill.

I go to the bar cabinet to prepare us a glass, while Ryan paces around the living room until he stops in front of the floor-to-ceiling windows and checks the skyscrapers, all lit up against the night sky.

With a glass in each hand, I go where he is standing and give him his drink.

"Thanks," he says. "To a not-guilty verdict."

His toast brings a much-needed smile to my lips. "To a not-guilty verdict," I repeat, and we clink our glasses.

After taking our first sip, I hear him asking, "What's troubling you? The verdict?"

"Of course," I tell him. "Despite the great work you did, what if they are not convinced?"

Ryan shakes his head, a small smile playing on his lips. "Relax," he says once more, his tone steady and confident. "I know how horrible it is waiting for such an important decision, but I know they won't convict you."

I heave a long sigh, and decide to share my biggest fear with him. "I just can't risk not seeing my kids grow up, you know?" My gaze goes to the view of the city for an instant, and while I let myself dwell in my thoughts, the most amazing memories with my wife start replaying in my mind. "And Petra," I say just above a whisper. Then my eyes drift back to him and I tell him the rest, "Despite everything that happened between us, I don't want to lose her."

Ryan puts a hand on my shoulder, trying to comfort me, and says, "I saw their faces during my closing statement. The jury knows you aren't guilty. They know Eric is doing it for private reasons. I was very clear on that and was also very clear how your wife was granted immunity even though she had the same motives as you."

"So why are they taking so long?" I keep asking.

"Maybe because they need to convince a juror or two, who knows." His lips curve up seeing me so serious. "Don't worry. It's gonna be fine."

I nod at him, and take another gulp of the whiskey in a failed attempt to decompress.

"I have a question for you," Ryan suddenly says. "But feel free not to answer it, if you don't want to."

"Sure," I reply. "What is it?"

"How come there was no prosecution against you or your family in the Netherlands?" His question catches me off guard, but I find it interesting, nevertheless. "No prosecutor dared to press charges against them for Tess's abduction?"

A quick smile spreads across my face and I bring the glass to my lips, trying to hide it. "Because they know going against my family wouldn't be a smart move for their careers," I tell him bluntly. "And let's not forget that one of their main suspects would have been a judge of a court of appeals, so I think it's more prudent for them to rather leave us alone."

"Understandable." His gaze drifts back to the view and we remain quiet admiring the darkness of the night settling upon us. The sound of a ringtone breaks through the room, and

Ryan apologizes immediately while reaching for his inner pocket to take his phone out. "Oh, now that's strange," he says, looking at the screen.

"What?"

"Your wife is calling me." Ryan hands me his iPhone, and I take a few steps away, before I answer the call myself.

"May I know why you are calling my attorney?" That's also a way to say hello.

"Well, because you said if I wanted to talk about the case to contact him, so that's exactly what I did," Petra reminds me.

"What do you want?" I ask, trying to keep my tone courteous and not too irritated.

"I just wanted to know if the jury reached a verdict yet."

"You know perfectly well they didn't, otherwise it'd be all over the news," I tell her. "So why are you calling him?"

Petra draws out a breath and a few seconds of silence ensue before she finally tells me the truth. "I just wanted him to let you know that the only reason I wasn't present at your trial was because it gives me a lot of stress and anxiety and it can be unhealthy for the babies."

I heave a long sigh, softening at her words and at her smooth voice. Gosh, I had really missed it. "How are they doing?"

"Kicking from time to time, actually," she says with a quick laugh. "Especially when I'm in the shower or taking a bath."

I wish I could be there to see this, but she has caused me so much pain that for now all I want is to keep my distance from her. "I'm glad to know that." My tone is matching hers, warm and gentle.

"Do you… um, do you have any plans for this evening or tomorrow? We could—"

"Yes, I do," I interpose immediately. "We'll see each other next week at the appointment."

Petra doesn't say a word, but I can hear a gush of air rolling off her lips, filled with a sadness that squeezes my heart tightly. "I see… it's just…" she stops mid way, hesitating whether to proceed or not. "Never mind, see you next week, then." I can taste the disappointment in her tone, but this is just a consequence of all the bad decisions she's made.

I shut my eyes tight—rejecting her hurts more than I thought it would, especially when I see how hard she is trying to have me back in her life.

CHAPTER 27

Manhattan, April 15, 2021
Alexander Van Dieren

After everything—the arrest, the arraignment, the trial, and now the days-long deliberation—I thought I could not be nervous anymore. Yet, as I take my seat and adjust my tie, I can feel sweat beading on my forehead and acid churning in my gut. I am nervous. Petrified, even. And I hate it.

The lights overhead are stark as always, and as I try my best to ignore everyone filing in behind me, I can almost imagine the lights illuminating all of my sins, and God knows there have been many. But this murder isn't one of them, dammit, and I'm minutes away from knowing if I will spend the rest of my life paying for someone else's crime.

It's a fight not to turn around and see all the faces that have shaped my life. Two of them, especially. Yara, my little sister who has been trouble from the start, and Petra, my wife, betrayer, and mother to my children who graciously decided to also attend the verdict. I can feel them there, judging me, and it just makes everything more difficult. I wish I could do this alone, instead of in front of the world.

Ryan takes a seat beside me, setting his briefcase down and giving me a stern look. He's fought for me like a lion, never backing down or giving up as time went on, and now we get to see if all the turmoil was worth it.

"How are you feeling?" Ryan asks.

I shrug, holding all of my emotions in. "As good as anyone in this situation can feel, I guess."

"We've won this thing, Alex," Ryan tells me, his voice level and confident.

I nod once, not wanting to speak anymore until the judge reads the verdict. Ryan had done his part, and all we have left to do is play the waiting game. The twelve jurors file in, every one of them looking haggard. Seven days is a long time to deliberate. I'm not sure what had held them up, but the extended time didn't bode well for me. It at least let me know I wasn't a unanimous "guilty," but it also tells me that someone up there thinks I did it.

I see Eric and his co-counsel take their seats at the tables adjacent to mine, doing their best to ignore Ryan and I. Fine by me. The sooner this public circus is over, the better. Finally, the judge enters, a neutral look across her face.

"All rise for the honorable Judge Stanton," the bailiff intones loudly. We all stand until the judge takes her seat.

"You may be seated," she tells the room.

Everyone sits. I do my best to keep my breathing even.

Judge Stanton doesn't smile as she looks over her courtroom, taking in the full rows of attendants and the media jostling each other for spaces against the back wall. "Good evening everyone," she begins. "We're here today to read the verdict in the case of The State of New York versus Alexander Van Dieren. After a seven-day-long deliberation, the jury has reached a final decision. Bailiff, will you please bring me the sealed envelope?"

The bailiff retrieves the envelope from the jury's foreperson, walking it over to the judge. There is a hushed silence blanketing the courtroom. When I look down at my hands, I see that I'm clenching my fists hard enough to leave marks in my palm. Ryan squeezes my shoulder reassuringly as the judge opens the envelope and clears her throat before speaking.

"Members of the jury, I'll now read the verdict as it'll appear in the permanent records of the United States District Court for the Southern District of New York," the judge says, before her attention returns to the sheet in her hand. "State of New York, county of New York, district court for the Southern district, State of New York plaintiff versus Alexander Van Dieren defendant, Count one court file 242321201 we the jury in the above entitled matter as to count one intentional second-degree murder find the defendant not guilty, verdict agreed this fifteenth day of April 2021 at five thirty-five pm." I heard not guilty, right? I can barely breathe at this point, but I remain as focused as possible as I listen to the rest. "Members of the jury, I'm now going to ask you individually if this is your true and correct verdict. Please respond yes or no. Juror number nineteen, is this your true and correct verdict?"

"Yes," a young woman says amid the jury.

"Juror twenty-five, is this your true and correct verdict?" the judge asks again.

"Yes," a man replies.

She asks each of the ten remaining jurors one by one, and each gives the same answer. I search their faces as they do so, memorizing the people that decided my fate. Two of them, an elderly man and middle-aged woman, seem reluctant in their answers, but there is no hung jury. The decision is unanimous.

"Ladies and gentlemen of the jury, is this your verdict, so say you one, so say you all?" the judge asks once everyone has given their answer.

"Yes," they all answer in sync. It gives me goosebumps.

At first a quiet descends over the room while everyone absorbs the verdict, and then the murmurs begin, building to a buzzing crescendo until it forces the judge to call for silence, hitting her gavel against the sound block. Cameras from the media snap endlessly, no doubt capturing the stunned, empty expression on my face.

I hear none of it.

Images flash in my mind, things that are suddenly in my reach again that I was for sure I had lost. There were still places in the world I hadn't seen, changes in my own life that I wanted to make, and most of all, the birth of my children. As much as Petra had done me wrong, the idea that she might have to finish out this high-risk pregnancy and give birth alone was like a nightmare. I had to be there, and now I could.

Ryan pumps his fist, triumphant, before patting me a few times on the shoulder.

"Congratulations, Alex. We did it," he says, his voice thick with emotion.

"We did it," I reply, still in a daze of sorts. I blink rapidly, trying to clear the mist of tears threatening to haze over my vision.

"Order!" the judge calls again, the crack of the gavel ringing out over the rising voices of the media and attendants. Finally, everyone begins to settle down.

"Thank you. All right. Ladies and gentlemen of the jury, I want to thank on behalf of the State of New York and the Borough of Manhattan for your service in seeing justice being served today. I'm now going to excuse you from your service on this case. This will absolve you from your vows of silence. Court is adjourned!"

Ryan pops from his seat as if it was spring-loaded, seemingly incapable of acting stoically after such a big win. He makes his way over to the prosecutor's table, shaking hands and leaning in to talk to them. I can't hear anything over the noise coming from the attendants, so I gather my things and stand, plastering on my public persona over the torrent of emotions I'm experiencing. With a wide, fake smile on my face, I go to exit the courtroom, ready to make the rounds.

The next hour is a blur of shaking hands with Ryan's team, the visibly annoyed Eric's team, and answering questions from the reporters with vague, unproblematic statements.

"Yes, I'm thrilled. I was innocent, and I knew justice would be served," I told one media personality after the other when they'd ask how I was feeling.

"We are just glad to be able to move past this," I would say to each one that asked about Petra, my smile never breaking. These sharks would never see beyond the surface as long as I could help it.

From the other side of the crowd, I can see Eric in the distance, still entertaining a few interviews. I ponder for a moment if I should go and have a word with him. Though I guess I have to assume his son has already done it for me, and I refrain from approaching him at all.

"Congratulations," Yara says, finally appearing from the crowd as she gives me a hug. "We are so happy for you."

"Thanks," I answer, brushing that off. "You didn't have to come all the way from the Netherlands just for the verdict, you know."

Yara gives me nothing but a smirk—she's perfectly aware I know she isn't only here in New York for that. "I don't mind coming over here."

Lowering my voice, I discreetly ask, "When are you gonna put an end to it?" I can't keep out the annoyance lacing my tone.

She chuckles in return, knowing exactly what I'm referring to. "Whenever I want to." She then gives me a kiss on the cheek. "Well, enjoy your evening. You deserve it." And without further ado, Yara disappears from my sight, fading away into the crowd.

As the madness dies down, there is one person left standing that I haven't spoken to: Petra, in charcoal gray pants and a white blouse. She is still waiting for me at the top of the courthouse steps. She looks like she's feeling a similar riot of emotions as I am, relief and nervousness warring on her face as she rests her hands in her pockets. I know she's been there the whole time, but I knew I'd need more than a scant thirty seconds to talk to her between the rush of the media. I make eye contact with her, and she takes the cue, coming down the stairs to stand at my side.

Her eyes shine as she looks up at me, her expression open and hopeful. "Can I hug you?" she asks shyly, and despite my better judgment, I wrap my wife in my arms, breathing her in for just a moment. We aren't okay, but now we can at least begin to heal.

I can hear her breath hitching as we embrace, and when we separate, she dashes a few errant tears from her cheeks. "I'm sorry," she murmurs. "I'm just so relieved it's over."

There is so much I could do, and so much I wanted to say, like how this could have been done a long time ago had she not testified, but picking the scab from the wound of our relationship would do nothing but stress my pregnant wife out. I'd have to leave the past buried if I wanted to move forward.

"This is a bit of an understatement, but I'm relieved too," I tell her, sarcasm in my voice.

Petra gives me a watery smile and sniffles. She's so damn cute, and it takes all of my brainpower to remember that I'm still angry with her. Over the past months, she has seemed to do everything in her power to trip me up. Testifying at my murder trial, kissing that little rat, and being stubborn as a mule about the pregnancy, forcing herself to suffer if it meant carrying both babies to term. But if I think about it, as both babies continue to grow, was it stubbornness, or a mother's love and bravery, that had kept her going?

"I don't know what to say, other than I'm sorry, and I love you." Petra's voice quavers, but she holds her chin high. She's clearly been building up the nerve to say her piece. "Let's have dinner tonight. We can turn over a new leaf, and I've really missed sharing meals with you. We can go to that steakhouse downtown that has the alternate vegan menu, or Maria can make us something and we can eat on the terrace if it's warm enough, or—"

I hold up a hand, stopping her before she can get too far into her speech. "I'm sorry, I can't, at least, not tonight."

Her jaw snaps shut, and I can't help but notice the wobble of her bottom lip at my refusal. "Oh, um, okay, It's fine. No problem..." She looks down at her hands, twisting her wedding band as she tries to shrug off the rejection. "I guess I'll get going."

I want to stand my ground, I really do, but I need to stop capitulating to Petra if I want her to understand how much her kiss with Matt had hurt me. I have every intention of sending her on her way and enjoying my party tonight with my lawyer and his team, but the look she's wearing actually squeezes at my heart, damn her, and once again I go against my instincts to ease her hurt.

She's just turned on her heel to walk to the black sedan our driver Zach had pulled up in, but I grab her shoulder before she can leave.

"Petra, wait," I say. She stops in her tracks and turns to face me, her expression filled with genuine sadness. "I've already planned a dinner party tonight to celebrate with my lawyer and his team, to thank them for their hard work. We can't have a private dinner tonight, but you can join us if you'd like."

She perks up immediately. "Really? Sure, I'd love to!"

I nod, taking her hand in mine and walking her to the car. "I'll send Zach the address. It's at nine pm, and dress is casual."

Her smile is like the sun as she slides into the back seat, moving a little more slowly because of her belly. "I can't wait."

I kiss her cheek and shut the door, sighing heavily as it pulls away. She's really got me under her thumb, and the cold-hearted man I want to be just continues to melt under her gaze. I rub the back of my neck and exhale. Time to go home and prepare for the party, I guess.

As I'm entering my own car, my cell rings, echoing loudly in the parking garage.

"Hello?"

"Now that the nonsense is over, can I finally have my business partner back?"

I grin at the raspy voice on the other line. "Roy. Good to hear from you."

"Better to hear from you, Alex, especially on your own phone and not through the visiting glass at the jail," Roy says sardonically.

I huff out a breath. "Very funny." Things have been more tense between Roy and me since I've been on a break with his daughter, but time has smoothed out some of the awkwardness. "What can I do for you?"

"I should be offended. Can't an old friend just check up on you without an ulterior motive?" Roy tries to sound sad, but I could hear the laughter in his tone.

"Enough of that. I'm headed home, but I'm hosting a party tonight to thank my lawyer and his team. Why don't you join us? It'll be nice to talk without the case hanging over our heads."

Roy sighs. "Ah, Alex, you know I would love to, but since my business partner has been MIA, I have a meeting with some hedge fund officers from Singapore tonight."

I wince. "I promise I'll pick up my slack and then some now that the trial is over."

"You know I'm just yanking your chain Alex, but wait a second. You were so confident in the verdict that you had a party pre-planned to celebrate?"

"I didn't kill her, Roy. So yes, you could say I was confident." My voice is stern. "And even if I had gotten fucked over, Ryan and his team might as well enjoy what I wouldn't have been able to."

"I'm sure that would have been a fun party, celebrating losing your case." Roy chuckles. "Good thing it went the other direction! I was actually calling to see if you'd come to dinner at my place tomorrow evening. You and…" he pauses, before continuing hopefully. "You and Petra. I've missed you both terribly."

Touched, I lean against the car with a smile. "We'd love to."

"Are you sure you can speak for my daughter? She has been avoiding me like the plague since our last board meeting."

I wonder if it's because of the pregnancy that she has been avoiding him or because of some argument that she might have had with him. Regardless, Petra needs to see her father. "Don't worry, I'll talk to her."

Roy hums on the other end of the line. "Well, it's your funeral. Regardless, it will be wonderful to see you both."

"Looking forward to it. Let me know if I can bring anything," I tell him with warmth in my tone.

"Roger that. Have a good evening."

"You too." I hang up, pocketing my phone and considering how busy the next few days were going to be.

The drive home is uneventful, but my mind is racing with the morning's events. I told Roy I'd been confident about receiving my not guilty verdict, but in reality, I had been sick with worry. It was only now, as I'm sitting alone, that the dark thoughts consume me. Part of me is still afraid that this is a dream, and that I'll wake up tomorrow in a prison cell.

Other thoughts that occupy me on the drive are seeing Roy so soon, while Petra and I are still slightly at odds. With a jolt, I remember that Roy doesn't even know Petra is carrying twins. It's hard to believe how much the twins have changed our lives so far, that Petra's pregnancy isn't common knowledge. Despite being already twenty-three weeks in, she doesn't look overly pregnant yet, so with the right outfit, she can still hide it for the time being. Although... Even if she and I are still on a break, I think we should let her dad know about the pregnancy before he reads it somewhere.

* * *

Having the house full is a bizarre but exciting experience. Ryan arrives first, and, despite his protests, I pour him a glass of my most cherished edition of Macallan before we go and sit out on the terrace as the staff finishes setting everything up inside. Thank God Maria had come from the condo, because even though I consider myself a capable man, few can hold a candle to her when it comes to supervision.

I had changed into a pair of comfortable, worn, dark-wash jeans and a plaid button up. It's nice every once in a while to ditch the suit jacket, and with no paparazzi knowing where my private residence is located, I can finally relax. Despite this residence being smaller than any of my other properties, the open floor plan is perfect for the party this evening. It's chilly out, but the whiskey burns pleasantly down my throat as I enjoy the silence with Ryan.

After a few moments, I speak up. "You saved my life, you know."

"It's my job, and you paid me, so no problem," Ryan says, amused. "I'd be a terrible attorney if I couldn't get my innocent client off the hook, anyway." He takes a sip of his whiskey and sighs in pleasure. "Damn, this is good."

It isn't long until everyone else arrives. I've invited every employee at Ryan's law firm, down to the secretary and janitor, and a good number of them have shown. Everything feels lighter that it has in weeks. Everyone laughs easily and mingles among themselves.

Petra arrives eventually, and I can see that she looks uncertain at all of the strangers crowding the place. I remember she hasn't even seen this property yet, so her anxiety with the situation makes sense. I make my way through the crowd to her, raising my voice over those of the partygoers.

"You made it," I say simply.

"Of course I did. I want to celebrate with you." She looks around the open floor. "Who are these people?"

"Ryan's crew." I search her face, wondering if I have made a terrible choice by inviting her. "Are you sure you want to be here? We'll see each other tomorrow, regardless."

She shakes her head. "There's no place I would rather be."

The two of us make the rounds as a couple, chatting and socializing with everyone we come across. Ryan seems surprised to see my wife here but doesn't mention it. I get it though. She was one of the key witnesses, and it must look strange to someone that knows the fine details of the case to see her standing by my side. When we sit down for dinner, which is chicken parmesan for everyone but Petra, which has been substituted with eggplant and vegan cheese by Maria, my wife sits next to me and interacts happily with everyone around the table. It doesn't take her long to fall back into her cute and pleasant persona, and soon she has charmed all the guests with her sweet demeanor.

It's past 11 p.m. when the party finally winds down, and once everyone has exited the house, Petra flops down on the couch with a heavy sigh. "What a day," she comments.

"No joke." I sit down too, but don't touch her. "You want me to call the driver so you can head back to the condo?"

She looks at me sadly but seems resigned. "Sure, go ahead." She pauses for a beat, thinking something through. "I just wish I wasn't completely alone all night before these appointments. My nerves don't let me sleep."

I know what she's trying to do, but I can't blame her. Every appointment with Mariana is more of the same: doom, gloom, and talk of how dangerous the pregnancy is to Petra, Jasmine, and Baby A. I know the appointments are necessary, but Petra becomes more and more stressed with each one. Not to mention more bull-headed in her decision to keep both children.

Lily is gentler, but she still skates around the birth plan talk whenever Petra brings it up. Thankfully, her regular visits to the condo and her positive disposition have helped Petra to eat on a more regular basis, and she doesn't look quite so pale and drawn.

I'd never tell Petra, but I think she already has an inkling of an idea that I walk the floors before the appointments, too. If things were different, we would hold each other to get through the nights, but it is what it is. At least we are still moving forward.

As I keep observing her, sitting on the couch and playing with her glass of water, she looks like a kicked puppy right now, and the idea of sending her out into the night with her heart aching just doesn't sit right with me. Suddenly, a thought crosses my mind. The doppler! I've bought her a portable doppler so she could hear the babies' heartbeats whenever she wants, hopefully to ease her mind when she worries about little Jasmine. I was going to give it to her tomorrow after the appointment, when we confirm both babies are indeed still living, but Petra seems in good health. Hearing the babies' heartbeats tonight will lessen the dread she's feeling, I'm sure of it.

"Wait here," I tell her, heading to my room and grabbing the powder pink gift bag with blue tissue paper I had put the doppler in, bringing it out to her. She gasps when she sees the bag, covering her mouth with one of her hands.

"Alex!" she exclaims, eyes alight. "You got me a gift? Why?"

"Actually, I think it will do us both some good. Open it," I say, handing her the bag and sitting down next to her as she opens it. I had the forethought to remove the device from the box and put batteries in it already, so when Petra pulls it out, she looks at it in confusion for a moment. The machine looks like an intercom you might see on a hospital wall, with a wand a little larger than a tube of Chapstick connected by a spiraling cord.

"If you can't figure it out, the instructions are in the bag too," I tell her, amusement apparent in my tone.

She turns it one way and the other a few times, before relenting and digging out the instructions. It takes her only seconds to read the first line and figure out what's in her hands. She looks at me with wide eyes, an odd mix of happiness and apprehension on her face.

"A doppler? Alex, I…" She's grateful, but not quite as excited as I thought she would be.

"Is something wrong?" I ask, concerned.

"No! It's just… what if we listen and… and there's only one heartbeat?"

Shit, I hadn't even considered the possibility. Only hearing one heartbeat here in my living room would be considerably worse on her than it happening in the hospital.

"Have you felt them both move today?"

She thinks for a moment before nodding. "Actually, yes." She takes a deep breath. "Okay! Let's do it. Let's listen."

She pulls up her shirt while I power the little machine on, and it beeps to life. Petra is grinning nervously as I pass it over the bump of her belly, and I take a moment to locate the first heartbeat. The watery metronome of it rings from the speaker, and Petra lets out a high-pitched, elated giggle.

"There, Alex! There it is!"

Joy rises in me like the tide, and I have to swallow hard to keep the lump out of my throat. "One down, one to go."

We listen to the first heartbeat for a while before I hunt for the second one with the wand. It's the longest two minutes of my life, but finally, low on Petra's stomach, we hear the quickly fluttering second heartbeat. Petra makes a noise that is half laugh and half sob, covering her mouth again. The anticipation and the sweet relief that came on its heels have me choked up again. I have to clear my throat before I can speak.

"Our two little fighters and their strong hearts," I tell Petra. She throws her arms around my neck and in this moment, everything clicks together again. I'm holding my wife. Our babies are okay for the moment, and I'm a free man.

We both move in slow motion, the perfect energy between the two of us undeniable. I cup her face with my free hand, and she moves toward me, pressing her lips on mine softly. The touch of her lips spreads a wave of warmth through me. Gingerly setting the doppler aside, I return the kiss fully, reveling in the taste of her. My mind shuts down for a few seconds while my heart takes full control and I deepen our kiss as nothing else mattered, just her and I.

My reason kicks in and the golden moment ends when we separate, but the sweet expression on her face remains. She snuggles into my arms, and I relent, holding her for a while. It's been one hell of a day, and the quiet reprieve is nice.

I hear her breathing slowing, and before she can doze off, I give her a gentle shake.

"Petra, you have to go home," I say in a whisper, trying to extricate her from my body. "Zach is on his way."

"Just let me stay," she groans, refusing to rise. "We're going to the same place in the morning, anyway."

I knew she'd say that.

"I can't." I stand, leaving her sitting on the couch and keeping a safe distance between us. I'm already too tempted to give her what she wants. Fortunately, Zach should be here anytime soon. Then putting on a formal and steady tone, I say, "The court case is over, but that's not the only way you've wronged me and you know it. I'm not ready to begin anew yet, so you need to leave."

"Wow." Looking hurt, Petra silently gathers her things. "Fine, I'll wait outside, then." She stands, her expression filled with a mix of anger and sadness, and starts marching toward the front door.

I want to retort, but I know it's useless. She isn't looking to hear sense or reason. She just wants us to get back together. As I watch her leave out the door without even a goodbye, I can't help but dwell on the fact that I, too, want us to get back together.

CHAPTER 28

Manhattan, April 16, 2021
Petra Van Gatt

The ride to the pregnancy center is a bit chilly between Alex and I, probably stemming from the fact that I had stormed off last night after he had given me such a thoughtful gift. Admittedly, I feel a little sheepish about my behavior, but the constant back and forth of Alex's treatment of me is giving me whiplash. As I come to think about last night, one moment we were kissing and the other he was kicking me out. Make it make sense!

I look at him out of the corner of my eye. He looks more relaxed than he did for most of these appointments, and I feel the same way. Hearing both heartbeats last night really had bolstered my mood and allowed me to sleep. He had brought the little machine with him when he picked me up this morning, which meant that every night before bed I could check on Jasmine and her brother and sleep peacefully knowing they were alright.

Gosh, I guess I really should apologize. The doppler would give me the thing I needed most to make it through this pregnancy; a constant way to reassure myself of my babies' health. Alex has to forgive me. I'm pregnant and unbelievably hormonal.

"Hey, uh, Alex?" I ask nervously.

"Yeah?"

"I'm sorry about storming out last night. It was childish," I tell him sincerely.

"It's alright. I understand." He chuckles a bit. "I'm just glad to know you aren't still pissed at me."

"It's just… this is really hard. I want our old life back." I look down at my lap, twisting the hem of my blouse in my fingers.

"Rome wasn't built in a day, as they say. Plus, once the babies are born, it won't be our old life, anyways. It will be our new one." He looks over at me briefly before turning back to watch the road. "We'll get there. We have time."

"That's true, I guess." I sigh, not loving his answer, but still knowing he's right.

We arrive at the clinic and go through the usual check-in process. A nurse takes us back and I go through the usual rigamarole of changing into the hospital gown and waiting for Mariana. It's nice this time around that things aren't so strained between Alex and me, but even with the reassurance from the doppler last night, I'm anxious.

Mariana comes in eventually, greeting us both warmly despite her previous arguments with Alex. The ultrasound is pretty routine, and I feel intense relief when Mariana tells us both heartbeats are present and that the babies are growing, though once again Baby B is not as much as she'd have liked.

After I get cleaned up, Mariana comes back in, looking tired and resigned as she removes her gloves and takes a seat.

"Everything looks as well as one could hope for in a situation like this. I read the reports that Lily has been sending in and you've put on some weight Petra. Good job on that." She rubs the bridge of her nose, clearly reluctant to talk about the next part. "Should I even try to convince you of my opinion in the matter? You know I think the best thing for you and Baby A is the termination of the second fetus."

"Not an option," I say, my tone clipped.

"You are taking a big risk here, but if that's your final choice, I will respect it." Mariana sighs. "Let's talk about your delivery options, then."

I'm a little shocked because Mariana has been completely tight-lipped about birth and delivery plan for the last few appointments. I know she doesn't want me getting attached to the idea of having both babies successfully, but she will not change my mind.

"I'm ready," I tell her, trying to sound enthusiastic.

She shuffles her papers around, flipping through them until she finds what she's looking for. "Since you are still so high risk, we will continue with bi-weekly checks until you reach twenty-eight weeks, at which time we'll have you admitted to Mt. Sinai hospital for observation."

"Admitted, as in there full time?" Alex asks, sitting forward in his chair.

Mariana nods. "Yes. It's inconvenient, I'm sure, but the benefits greatly outweigh the negatives. For one, you'll be minutes away from an operating room if an emergency c-section is needed. Most importantly, we'll have you hooked up to monitors so that even the slightest change in the babies will be noted and we can react as quickly as possible."

It makes sense, but it still sounds terrible. "Is that really necessary? At twenty-eight weeks delivery would be dangerous but not hopeless, right?"

"Correct. But the farther on in the pregnancy that we get, the more nutrients Baby A takes from Baby B, meaning Baby B's placenta is likely to shrink significantly. A deficient placenta puts Baby B at risk for something called reverse cord flow. It basically means that the flow of Baby B's blood coming from the umbilical vessels isn't strong enough and in some situations can even 'go-backwards,' hence the name. If this happens, Baby B won't be getting sufficient oxygen and delivery would need to happen as soon as possible, otherwise, the condition has the potential to be fatal."

Of course, there is a chance for another abnormality. I'm so numb to all the scary diagnoses coming my way that Mariana's words didn't affect me as badly as I expected. At least the plan was to be on the lookout constantly for a problem, so it could be fixed right away.

"Fine. I don't like it, but if it's the best way to keep the babies safe, then I'll do it. What do you think, Alex?" I ask him. He should have a say in the situation, too.

"I agree. Anything that will keep the babies safe is good for me. As long as Petra is comfortable while she's admitted."

"It's a wonderful hospital for expectant mothers. It might be a little boring, but it won't be too awful." Mariana gives me a reassuring smile. "Just keep in mind that if you deliver by then, the babies will be quite premature, and will need a stay in the NICU for around two months."

Thinking about my children in the NICU and not being home in my arms for so long is awful, but I just want the best for them. It's so hard to walk the line between what I want and what's best.

I exhaled a tired breath. "I understand. We'll be prepared for that outcome if so."

"Great." She makes a few notes on her clipboard before sitting it in her lap and looking at me seriously. "I just want to reiterate that I think this is not the best choice. No one will think any less of you for choosing the other option and only carrying Baby A to term."

"You're wrong," I exclaim, sick to death of this line of conversation with every appointment. "*I* would have to live with it for the rest of my life. *I* would have to be reminded, every time I looked at my son, about his sister that I sacrificed."

Mariana winces, holding her hands up in front of her in a "stop" motion. "I understand," she says, with a more humbled expression. "We'll lock in the hospital admittance for May twenty-first. Until then, I'll see you every two weeks." She stands and opens the door for us, and we leave the stuffy, sterile room.

"Hey," Alex questions, laying a hand on my shoulder. "You alright?"

"I'm fine. I'm just so over talking about termination and what the right decision is. No one can decide what's right for my pregnancy except for me," I vent.

Alex gives my shoulder a squeeze. "I'm with you. Make your own decisions and I'll support you, as long as you aren't being too reckless."

"Thanks," I mutter, still annoyed as I get into the car, rubbing my belly protectively. Baby B… Jasmine, I mean, is real and alive. I absolutely hate talking about losing her, especially after I feel her and her brother moving inside of me.

Despite the babies being alive, it's clear to me that Mariana doesn't believe that she's gonna make it. Her concerns aren't reassuring. She seems so freaking sure something is gonna go wrong, just like Auntie Louise and my mom did. And yet, here I am once again not listening to any of them. Jeez, a delivery at twenty-eight weeks would be way too early though. This cannot happen.

What a conundrum. Under normal circumstances, I'd never want to have a premature birth, but with Jasmine's health being so shaky, it might be nice to have her in the world and getting treatment as soon as possible. On the other hand, the longer I wait to give birth, the stronger the twins would grow.

"Don't you think we should tell your dad about the pregnancy?" Alex asks, halting me from my thoughts.

What a random question, I think. "Next time I see him, I'll tell him."

"Great, then I can't wait to see his face at dinner," Alex declares, looking smug.

"What?" I twist in the seat to look at him. "What do you mean, *dinner*?" I wonder out loud.

"We're having dinner at his place tonight," Alex explains, a smirk on his lips. "It's going to be great."

I hesitate. It all seems so sudden. "But what if something goes wrong before the delivery day?"

"Up until now, the babies have defied all odds. And our little Jasmine is still alive, so we can at least tell him about them." Alex taps his fingers on the steering wheel. "He deserves to know about his grandchildren, don't you think?"

I guess he's right. I just hate the idea of letting anyone, including my dad, in on our little secret until we are sure both babies are going to make it. "Does Dad know we are having dinner with him at least?"

"Of course he does," Alex laughs. "It'd be quite the rude surprise to show up and expect dinner from him. He invited us over last night, after the verdict."

"Oh. In that case, I can't wait either," I reply.

As unsure as I am about sharing our big news, seeing my dad tonight would be a bright spot in the last few weeks.

* * *

"Are you sure I don't look, like, insanely pregnant?"

Alex chuckles and wraps an arm around my shoulders. "You look fine. Stop asking already."

"I just don't want to give away the surprise too early," I insist.

"We can just tell him you're getting chubby." Alex retorts with a teasing grin.

I slap him on the arm. "Shut up and ring the bell."

With an amused huff, he does so. I'd chosen a turquoise casual A-line dress that hid the swell of my stomach well enough that we should be able to keep our secret until we are ready to share. I'm buzzing with anticipation, not only to tell Dad about my pregnancy but just to see him and Janine without the cloud of the murder trial hanging over our heads. I also shove away the thoughts about the twenty-eight weeks plan, determined to spend a lovely night with the family.

Janine answers the door, and she squeals when she sees us, bypassing Alex completely to embrace me tightly.

"Oh, Ms. Van Gatt, it's so wonderful to see you again," she gushes. I can see Alex over Janine's shoulder, and he raises an eyebrow at the show of affection.

"Hello Janine," he tells her, and she releases me, turning to Alex. Her expression turns carefully neutral.

"Good evening, Mr. Van Dieren," she says curtly. "Mr. Van Gatt is inside the dining room. Follow me, please."

We trail behind Janine, and Alex leans down to whisper, "I believe you've turned everyone against me while I wasn't paying attention. Mariana, and now Janine. How could you?" His quiet tone is teasing, and I giggle.

"Maybe it's because you seduced Janine's favorite child away at the tender age of eighteen," I tease right back, and Alex holds his heart, pretending to be shocked.

"You wound me, wife. You know it was you that did the seducing."

He gives me a wink and I have to hold back a full-on laugh as we approach the door to the dining room. Janine opens the door and I brace myself for seeing my dad. It has been a while, and I have to admit that I've missed him quite a bit.

Dad isn't one for overt affection, but when I see him sitting at the table waiting for us, I can't help but hurry over. He stands and embraces me, and I lay my cheek on the soft fabric of his sweater, closing my eyes. It feels like home, for a minute at least. I pull back and beam at him.

"Hi, Dad," I offer.

"So wonderful to see you again." Dad is grinning with joy as he observes me. "Wow, look at you, you're glowing," he comments happily before looking over my shoulder at my husband.

"Alex," Dad says simply with a nod that Alex returns.

"Roy," he replies with a smile.

After patting me on the back, Dad heads over to talk to Alex more privately. Business chat, no doubt. I'm still stuck on Dad's comment about me "glowing." He couldn't know about my pregnancy yet, could he?

Feeling self-conscious, I hurry to sit at the table, arranging my dress. Janine bustles over to bring me cucumber water and clucks her tongue at me.

"You look thin. Have you been eating?" she chastises.

Ha! If only she knew how late to the Petra-needs-to-eat-more party she was. Maria, Lily, Mariana, Matt, and Alex were already members.

"Yes, Janine," I assure her, "I'm eating plenty. In fact, I had a doctor's appointment today, and they said I had gained a few pounds."

She looks unconvinced. "If you say so," she says, patting my hand and heading off.

Dad and Alex eventually sit down. It's a picture of semi-domestic bliss, all of us sitting here. The room is lit by a Tiffany chandelier hanging overhead, and the light is dim enough to seem intimate. We chat about everything—work, my paintings, and Venice. Dinner is wonderfully prepared, as always, and Janine has made some of my favorites, including a delicious vegetable risotto and steamed garlic asparagus.

After dinner is finished and we all have a little bit of in-season fruit with fresh whipped cream, Dad stands and stretches. "I've got a great Bordeaux we can crack open to celebrate the verdict, and I'll have Janine light us a fire in the library. How does that sound?"

Alex and I share a look and I want to explode with excitement. It's time to share the news! "Actually, Dad. I can't drink. You might want to sit down."

Dad frowns but retakes his seat. "Alright… is everything okay, you two?"

"Four." Alex inserts cryptically.

Dad turns to look at him. "What? Four?"

"There's four of us, Roy," Alex clarifies, barely able to hold back a grin.

Dad looks between the two of us, not catching up for a few seconds, but soon enough, it all makes sense to him. He leans back in his chair, agog.

"What exactly are you saying?" he asks hoarsely.

"I'm pregnant," I breathe.

First he goes pale, and then bright red, and then pale again in a matter of seconds. "But… four?" he croaks.

I feel my eyes filling with happy tears. "Twins, Dad."

He puts a hand to his heart and looks shocked enough that I have a brief moment of worry that he's having a heart attack. I'm about to ask if he's okay when he breaks out in an ear-to-ear smile, laughing loudly enough that Janine comes running.

He jumps from his chair and grabs the poor maid's hands, and she looks rather alarmed.

"Twins, Janine!" he exclaims, and Janine furrows her brow.

"What are you on about?" she queries.

"We're having twins. Alex and I, that is," I explain again, tapping the corner of my eyes with my napkin.

"We're having twins!" Janine blurts with the same vigor as Dad, shuffling over to embrace me.

I hug her back, feeling a rush of gratitude to the maid turned governess of my youth. Her body is soft and soothing as she holds me, and the comfort it brings me is immeasurable.

After a bit, Dad trades her places. He hugs me as if I'm made of glass, paying extra attention to my belly.

"But how?" he asks, still confused. "I thought you and Alex were on a break?"

"Petra is twenty-three weeks in," Alex explains further.

"Already?" His jaw drops and hi eyes widen in total disbelief.

I nod at him, suppressing a laugh.

He looks immediately at my bump, hidden behind the textured turquoise dress, but doesn't dare to touch it. "You were hiding your little secret very well. Not a single word about the pregnancy on the news," he says, giving me another hug and a kiss on the forehead. "We need to celebrate! Janine, how about that Bordeaux?"

"Uh, Dad…?" I remind him.

"Oh, of course. No wine then. What do we have that Petra can enjoy?"

"I just made a fresh strawberry lemonade, and we have a few bottles of sparkling grape juice from New Year's Eve when you were entertaining your clients and their children. We could have mimosas of sorts," Janine suggests, and Dad claps his hands together once.

"Sounds perfect," he concludes.

We toast the pregnancy in beautiful crystal champagne flutes filled with virgin strawberry mimosas. Even Janine lets go a little and has a glass. The virgin mimosa bubbles pleasantly in my mouth, tasting both tart and sweet.

"To Alex, Petra, and the twins!" Dad bellows, and we clink glasses with a laugh. "Have you thought of any names?"

"Since we're having one of each gender, it's been a little harder, but I think we've chosen Jasmine for our little girl," Alex says, looking at me affectionately.

"You know," Dad cajoles, "Roy Jr. is a noble name."

I roll my eyes, walking over to him and kissing him on his rough, whiskered cheek. "I'll keep it in mind." *Not.*

* * *

Being in my childhood home is comfortingly nostalgic, and I walk the empty halls, imagining the laughter of my children as the future comes. Alex and Dad have been boring me to death talking about portfolios and expansions, so I've snuck away to do a little wandering and thinking.

At the very top of the stairs, I crack open the door of my old atelier, awash in the memories of all of my hours whittled away here as a child. The air in the room is chilly, but I can still smell the turpentine and oil paints. It's dark, but the light is blindingly bright when I flick it on. I rub at my eyes, feeling silly that I didn't remember the violently luminescent overhead lamp I had loved to paint beneath.

The paintings are a tour of my life, ranging from my works as a small child to the pieces I had made days before leaving. I can see all my different phases and styles, some of them cringeworthy and others better than I remembered. I run my fingers over them as I pace, lost in thought.

Hidden in a corner behind a few still lifes is a painting that makes my heart ache. I pull it out carefully, not wanting to damage the old canvas. My chest feels tight as I look it over, remembering the embarrassment and guilt I had felt when Dad had hidden it, refusing to give it to Alex when I had asked. I had only been seven, and I couldn't yet understand why what I had painted was so inappropriate.

Two adults and two children stand in front of a sunset background, the man in what appears to be a black suit and the woman in a powder blue dress. Both adults hold the hands of one of two small children, a normal sized boy, and a tiny, petite girl. It's Alex, myself, and our children. Somehow, at seven years old, I had made this painting and inadvertently foretold my own future.

I hold it like something precious, but I'm startled when a knock comes from the door frame. I spin around, frightened, only to see Alex leaning there. He takes a slow look around the atelier, memories running through his mind.

"I still think you should have a gallery downtown," he declares, striding over to me with his hands in his pockets. "What have you got there?" he asks, nodding toward the painting I'm holding.

Swiftly, I go through my two choices. Play it off as nothing or give it to him all these years later. Gathering my courage, I hand it over, letting him examine the painting.

"It's a gift I made you when I was seven," I confess. "Dad never gave it to you, but, um, I want you to have it now."

His eyes scan it for a moment before his eyebrows rise far on his head.

"Is this what I think it is?" he asks incredulously.

I nod with a shy laugh. "Ha, yeah. In case you didn't know, I've had a thing for you since forever."

He looks touched, dragging a finger down the front of the canvas. "It's almost like you knew, even then, that we'd be a family."

A memory rushes back to me, of Alex, looking nearly the same as he does now, when I invited him into my atelier for the first time. It was right after my dad's fifty-fifth birthday. He was scanning across my work, nodding at it, impressed. Jeez, I remember how giddy I felt, how nervous... I had never felt so honored by anyone's praise before.

Alex sits the picture against the wall before gathering me in his arms and stroking my cheek. "Thank you, little Petra. It's incredible."

Eye on eye, he leans in slowly and I do the same until we close the small gap between us for a kiss. Oh gosh, there are no words to express the rapture that washes over me as our lips collide together. The kiss is slow and soft but growing more heated as I melt into him. I can smell his cologne and the spicy scent of him beneath it, and I try to deepen the kiss, but he pulls away with a groan.

"Petra," he growls, holding me at shoulder length. "We are on a break, remember."

I smirk at the effect I have on him, pushing forward and laying a last peck on his lips before he escapes. Alex picks his painting back up, wrapping it gently in one of the white painting clothes that were still folded on the shelves. He tucks it under his arm.

"I'm ready to head out. Are you sleeping over here, or do you want me to take you home?" he inquires.

The idea of staying here is tempting, but I'd rather spend more time with my husband and try to persuade him to go home with me. "Home, please."

We tell Dad and Janine goodbye, promising to visit again soon. My family is healing, and it's a wonderful feeling. Alex rolls the windows down as we drive, the cool air bracing. Modern jazz is playing on the radio, and between the smooth ride of the car and Alex's humming along, I feel happier than I have in days.

Finally, we reach the condo. My heart pounds when Alex opens my door and walks me inside without being asked, and after the success of dinner, I'm confident he's going to sleep over with me. I soften my body language, swinging my hips when he walks behind me. I step into the condo, take my shoes off, but notice Alex is still standing by the door.

"What are you doing? Come, take your things off and relax," I suggest, waving him toward me, but he shakes his head.

"I'm going back to my residence," he says, a hint of sadness in his voice. "I just wanted to drop you off."

"But—" I start, yet before I can finish, he saunters over and lays a finger on my lips.

"Shhh. No arguing."

He plants a chaste kiss on my cheek, lingering for a moment too long before retreating.

"Alex, please just stay," I beg, but he stands firm, stroking my cheek a final time before heading back to the door.

I want to protest more, or maybe grab him and try to convince him, but feeling deflated, I let him go. So much for a grand finale to a wonderful evening.

"Goodnight," Alex soothes before shutting the door behind him.

After waiting some time to see if he'd change his mind, I plop on the couch and pull out my phone.

Goodnight, x, I text him before heading to our bedroom.

I'd have loved my husband to take me to bed, but all in all, I'd still say it was a successful night.

CHAPTER 29

Manhattan, May 15, 2021
Petra Van Gatt

I've been keeping a very low profile for the past four weeks since my bump has become too swollen to hide. After our last appointment with Mariana, and knowing that so far the two babies are still alive, Alex and I have decided to make a big announcement at the gala dinner tonight. At least it'll give a good perception of unity to the media and change from the bitter headlines speculating an eventual divorce.

Looking at myself in the mirror, my lips spread in a wide smile as I observe the gown I'm wearing. It's an off-shoulder piece, fit at the breast, and it flares out toward the bottom. I've opted for a sapphire blue color matching with my eyes and engagement ring. I'm sure Alex will notice my choice given the fact that the first dress he bought me once I moved in was the same color.

My heart is speeding up apprehensively; after all, I'll see Matt for the first time since we kissed, and he might end up at the same table as Alex and I!

A few quick knocks on the door pulls me back from my thoughts and as I shout to come in, Maria steps in and says, "Your husband is waiting for you downstairs."

"Thank you, Maria," I answer politely. Yet, I can't stop wondering why Alex didn't come upstairs instead of sending Maria to do the job?

Never mind. Tonight hopefully things will get better. I take my clutch, spread some Jasmine perfume on my neck, and head downstairs.

I find Alex's car parked at the curb, and him waiting for me as he leans against it, just like he used to when we'd go and visit art galleries in the city. Nearly two years might have passed, but once my eyes alight on him, on his beautiful smile, striking blue eyes, and sun-kissed skin, I feel the very same butterflies in my belly as before.

"Ready?" he says, checking me out from top to bottom. He tries to appear unaffected, but a quick smile settles on my lips as I catch him looking at my cleavage. He did it for a split second but the simple fact that I can still draw his attention makes my heart flutter.

"Ready," I answer, walking in his direction.

Alex opens the door and helps me to get inside. He then walks around and sits beside me. The driver starts the engine and we finally leave en route to Gotham hall.

Silence settles between us, letting only the jazzy beats from the playlist fill the air. I notice how Alex is trying hard not to look in my direction, but after a few minutes of averting his gaze, he finally looks my way, and breaks the silence. "I need to talk to you," he says, his tone steady.

"Well, go ahead," I answer, feeling quite amused.

Alex heaves a long sigh as if he's getting ready for a serious conversation. "As you might know, my dad will be attending and—"

"And I suppose you want me to pretend everything is fine between us?" I ask him.

"Exactly," he breathes, his lips curving upwards. "Tonight we are the perfect couple—very much in love and looking forward to the arrival of our babies."

"But I am very much in love," I tell him, my face lighting up with a grin. "Aren't you?"

"Of course." He sounds sarcastic. "With such a faithful wife how couldn't I be?"

I huff at his sarcasm, turning my face to the window.

"News editors are gonna be there and they are gonna watch our every move to write whatever the crap they want," he warns. "So we need to be somewhat affectionate."

My attention goes right back to him. "You're gonna kiss me?"

"Not on the mouth, if that's what you want to know." I can't hide the disappointment on my face at his reply. "But we should be holding hands and so on."

I shrug. "Fine…" And I turn my head back to the window, yet internally I'm bouncing with joy knowing he's gonna be affectionate with me. He can say as much as he wants that it's only because of the media, his image, or whatever, but I'm sure this is just an excuse to cover what he truly wants: me.

* * *

Reaching Gotham Hall fills my head with nostalgic memories; just two years ago, I was in a very similar black executive car accompanied by Emma when I saw the majestic building standing in front me. Jeez, little did I know that night would change my life forever.

The organizers truly did a brilliant job—just like last time, we see multi-color lights bouncing on and off the façade and columns, a big red carpet at the entrance and two doormen welcoming guests.

As we stop in front of the entrance, a valet opens the door for me and helps me out to exit the car. With a twenty-seven weeks belly, I hold on to his hand and do my best to gracefully get out and land on my two feet.

Alex comes in and offers me his arm for support. I gladly accept it and hold on to it before we head inside.

Stepping into the ballroom, we are welcomed by the immersive atmosphere, a game of dark blue and purple lights flicker around the walls, round tables are spread across the room and a big jazzy orchestra is playing on the other side just in front of the dance floor. Photographers stand in our way to take a few pictures as we head to greet my dad, who's already entertained by his friends and Hendrik himself.

"Happy Birthday, Dad," I say as we reach him and the group he is with.

Everyone turns to check us out, and before my dad can say anything, Hendrik opens his arms wide and gives me a big hug. "I can't believe it!" he says, holding me tight. "I can't believe it," he keeps mumbling while hugging me.

Needless to say, my pregnancy caught him totally off guard. I thought Alex would have told him something over the phone but apparently not. Once Hendrik releases me, I see some tears streaming down his cheeks, and a big smile hanging on his face as he affectionately holds my jawline.

"I'm so freaking excited."

His tone surely is. I do my best to keep my emotions under control, but his happiness is very moving. As I come to think of it, he never experienced a pregnancy announcement since his daughters have always excluded him from their lives, and I can only imagine all the emotions he is going through right now. Then Hendrik goes and hugs his son and I finally manage to greet my dad, Joshua, Mike, and the rest of the group who don't waste time to congratulate me for the pregnancy. With such a bump, obviously one doesn't need to say anything. Needless to say, they are all on cloud nine given the fact a pregnancy will help to silence the negative press that has been going on.

"How many weeks are you?" Hendrik finally asks.

"Twenty-seven," I answer. "I'm expecting twins. A boy and a girl," I add already anticipating the next set of questions.

"Do you have names already?" Hendrik keeps asking.

"Jasmine for the girl," I tell him. "And for the boy, we are still searching."

"This is incredible," Hendrik mumbles, still visibly emotional. Then looking at Alex, he says, "This is honestly one of the best days of my life."

To my surprise, Alex wraps an arm around me and pulls me closer to him, before planting a kiss on my temple. And for a split second, I close my eyes, reveling in his tenderness.

* * *

A few minutes later, I glance around the ballroom trying to find Emma, but to my greatest disappointment, I don't see her anywhere. Yet she had told me she'd attend the event. She doesn't know about my pregnancy and this would have been the perfect occasion to tell her. Jeez, I just hope it wasn't Yara who dissuaded her from coming. I leave the ballroom and go to the lobby area where the music isn't too loud. There, I take my iPhone and call her. The ringtone goes on and on…

"Are you trying to call me?"

Recognizing the voice, I immediately turn around to greet her.

"Oh, wow," Emma shouts as her eyes land on my bump. "Now, that was… unexpected."

Regardless of her astonishment, I take her into my arms and squeeze her tightly. "I'm so glad you came," I whisper to her.

But Emma is still under a wave of shock, so she releases me just as fast and keeps observing me. "Holy shit…" I think now she realizes this isn't her imagination fooling her. "Why didn't you tell me anything before?"

"Well, because it's a high-risk pregnancy," I disclose. "The doctors thought it wouldn't last this long." Actually, I'm pretty sure deep inside, Mariana is still believing something is gonna happen sooner or later with Jasmine.

"Jeez!" Her gaze remains glued to my bump, and I can't help but laugh at her expression. "How many weeks are you in?

"Twenty-seven," I answer.

"It's a boy or a girl?"

"Both," I say. "I'm expecting twins."

"Oh fuck!" A quick laugh escapes me at her reaction. "That's insane!" Then as she thinks something through she says, "So wait—the fundraising for kids with Turner's Syndrome—"

"It's my daughter who has it," I tell her, quite moved that she made the connection so quickly between the foundation and my pregnancy. Somehow none of the gentlemen who congratulated me earlier made the link. "We are raising funds to bring awareness to her condition."

"Shit," Emma utters, her face laced with concern. "And can she have a normal life with it?"

"I hope so," I tell her. "She'll need ongoing medical care from a variety of specialists, but apart from that, she should be fine."

"And you kept it all to yourself?" she asks, surprised.

"Alex knew it too, and, um Matt."

"How are things between Matt and you?"

I glance around, making sure no one is listening to us and take one step closer, before lowering my voice. "I haven't seen him since that day in the library."

"Did he try to talk to you afterwards?"

"Yes, we spoke over the phone and he apologized over and over again but that's it." I pause for a beat, pondering a few things. "And worse: he's supposed to come tonight. I told Alex I could withdraw my invitation, but he didn't want to."

"I don't think Alex sees Matt as a threat," Emma says. And somehow I think she might be right. "I mean, you guys are having twins. I'm pretty sure Alex knows that kiss meant nothing to you." She then puts a hand on my arm, giving me some comfort. "One day or another, he's gonna turn the page on this, believe me."

"I hope you are right, but seeing Matt again is gonna be so weird…"

Emma seems to be intently looking over my shoulder to the entrance of the building, and then says, "Speaking of the devil."

I turn and look in the same direction. Jeez! My eyes alight on Matt and Sarah, perfectly dressed in a tux and a gown, respectively. Sarah's holding Matt's arm and the way they interact and smile at each other, tends to imply they are more than friends.

Sarah notices us first, then Matt, and starts waving at us. "Hey, Petra!" Sarah's over-the-top excitement and lively voice makes Emma roll her eyes in disgust.

"Behave," I whisper to Emma.

"Gonna try," she mutters. "But bubbly girls aren't my thing."

"Oh my God!" Sarah shouts, looking at my bump. And it takes everything inside Emma for her not to snap a thing or two in response. "I didn't know you were pregnant! Congratulations!"

Matt and I look at each other filled with shyness and decide to just exchange a quick nod in acknowledgement. That would do to say hi. My attention returning to Sarah, I say, "Oh, thanks, I appreciate it."

Then we speak a bit about the pregnancy, how many weeks, the sex of the babies, etc.

"This place is so wonderful," Sarah praises, taking in her surroundings. "You couldn't have picked a better location."

"Shall we go and see the rest?" Matt asks Sarah, most likely impatient to leave my company.

She agrees to it, and we watch Matt promptly walking away with Sarah as they head to the ballroom.

"Didn't that chick come to my house for your eighteenth birthday?"

"Good memory, Ms. Hasenfratz," I say, my lips twitching into a smile. "Yep, she did."

"She and Matt are a thing?" While I'm quite shocked at her question, Emma, on the other hand, remains observing them as they stand by the entrance of the ballroom.

"Um, I don't think so," I answer in confusion. "Like, why would he kiss *me*, then?"

"I mean, fuck buddies or something? They touch each other like they are used to it."

I frown, not convinced at her explanation. "No, I don't think Matt is into that."

Emma snickers just as fast. "Yeah, right. Don't be naïve. Just because he behaves like a saint with you, doesn't mean he is one."

I'm left speechless at her statement, so I just stupidly keep looking to the void, pondering what she just told me. Matt and Sarah? Nah, I don't believe it.

"Alright, I need to get drunk, let's go," she says as she takes me by the arm and drags me to the ballroom.

* * *

The worst part of the dinner is realizing that the friend who kissed me on the mouth is sitting at the very same as than my husband and I. I don't understand why Alex decided to let him come to the event in the first place. It's just so…awkward. As I come to think of it, is it just to make me feel uncomfortable? To remind me of my past mistake and make me feel terrible about it all over again? Looking up, I notice the smirk rising on Alex's lips as he stands on the other side of the table; to be smiling like this, he must know what I'm thinking. Jeez! And that's so infuriating! Suddenly, he paces around the table and as he stands close enough to me, he leans in and whispers, "Aren't you happy to have your little friend here?"

"Of course I am," I reply with a polite smile. "Why are you asking me that?"

"You seem rather displeased," he says discreetly in a low voice. "Is it because he brought Sarah with him?"

"What?" I utter in shock, but I keep my composure not to draw attention. "Stop being stupid," I snap in a whisper and I give him a quick slap on the chest. Meanwhile Alex is just having a blast and laughing his ass off at how annoyed I am.

"It's truly a pleasure to piss you off," he shamelessly admits. His mouth is getting even closer to my earlobe and then he adds, "His presence is a good way to remind you why we are on a break. Isn't it lovely?"

I huff, shaking my head, and decide to take a chair to sit beside Emma instead of giving Alex any further attention.

"Do you need help with sitting?"

Argh! His question makes it even worse! "No, I can do it just fine." Not really, but I'd rather take my time to sit on my own than having him help me out.

What a fucking asshole he can be! Despite sitting beside my best friend, she seems busy and rather quite entertained on her phone, texting someone.

"Yara?" The question rolls off my tongue.

She gasps, not expecting a sudden voice in the first place. "Oh gosh!" She puts a hand on her chest to calm herself down. "Still spying on me? Damn, get over it."

"I'm just asking," I say softly. "I hope she is treating you well, that's all."

Emma smiles, putting her phone back in her clutch. "I was just telling her about your pregnancy."

My jaw drops at her answer. "Why?"

"Why not?" she answers, unbothered. "It's gonna be on the news, anyway. Or maybe it's already in the news."

"Well, at least it's gonna change from the headlines saying that Alex and I are gonna get a divorce."

Emma seems surprised. "Have you been following the news?"

"Not me, but the PR team at Gatt-Dieren told me," I tell her, my voice lower than usual. "It's crazy how they can come up with so much bullshit."

"Do you think it's because they haven't seen him coming back to the condo for over a month?" she asks discreetly.

"I don't know, either that or because I wasn't present at the trial, and they might have thought I didn't care about him or something."

Emma nods in return, and her eyes dip down to her lap as she fills her head with something that seems to be troubling her. I take a deep breath, worried that it has to do with Yara. "Is she treating you right?" Somehow, as she looks at me, pondering my question, I already know the answer is no.

"Well, if I tell you the truth you're gonna make a big fuss about it, so…"

"So tell me anyway," I intersperse, suppressing a laugh.

Emma smiles at me in amusement and says, "She's okay, but sometimes she's just a bit too demanding."

"Like what?" I ask, curiosity laced in my tone.

"Um, like…" Emma looks down at her lap again, searching for the best words to put on. "I don't know, that's rather private…"

"Emma, I told you a lot of private things, remember?"

Eye to eye, her chest rises and fall as she considers me. "She wants us to both get piercings…" Her words trail off until she finally adds, "Down there."

I blink twice, unable to vocalize a word for a good second. "What?" I pull off my chest, shock deep in my eyes. "She wants you to pierce your clit?" I ask, wondering if this truly what I heard.

"Yeah, like not the clit itself but it's close enough." And while I'm doing mental gymnastics to control my temper, Emma proceeds. "She wants to get one, and wanted me to have one too."

"Fuck," I snap in disgust. "Emma, don't do it to please her."

"I know, I know," she answers hurriedly as if she's trying to appease me. "I mean, she's just batshit crazy and I like that, but I think for me that is just too much." I can't help but shake my head at what I just heard. What a psycho! I knew she was one the day she grabbed my arm. "But apart from that she is fine."

"Fine?" I repeat, unable to play it cool. "She is pressuring you to pierce your private parts!" Noticing I'm getting a bit too loud despite the music, I lower my tone and say, "There's nothing fine about that." Emma looks down, not knowing what else to say or do. So I ask, "What happens if you don't do it?"

"I can't tell you that," she snaps right away.

"So she is coercing you?" I try to keep my voice low, but damn, Yara's behavior is testing all my limits. "You have to end this relationship," I tell her once more. "This is becoming dangerous."

"Don't exaggerate things." She brushes it off. "I'm gonna have a talk with her and we will see."

Before I can add my two cents, a wave of applause takes me by surprise, and as I glance around the room, I notice how everyone is already seated, starters being served, and my dad is on stage, a smile on his lips, welcoming everyone to his fifty-seventh birthday.

* * *

Dinner's subject has been, for the most part, about finance and markets. Everything that Matt hates and everything that Alex and my dad love. Emma and I didn't speak anymore about Yara. After all, Emma knows perfectly well that I'd try to persuade her to wave goodbye to that woman once and for all. She wants her to pierce her genitals for fuck's sake! How twisted she can be! She's turning Emma into a sex slave under the guise of healing her and I'm not sure what I'm supposed to do; call Yara? Well, if I do that, Emma is gonna be mad at me for sure, and even worse, nothing guarantees me that Yara will stop seeing Emma. Does her husband know she is having an affair? Maybe it's worth talking to him instead…

Suddenly, I see Alex standing up and walking on stage at the demand of the presenter. Is he gonna make the announcement now? Oh gosh, of course he is! Dessert has been served and now everyone is getting their flutes of champagne refilled to do a toast. At the same time, I notice Matt discreetly standing up and getting ready to leave the table.

"Where are you going?" I ask, curiosity getting the best of me.

Matt smiles. "I'm just going to the bathroom."

I wonder if he is going right now because Alex is gonna talk about our marriage and my pregnancy and prefers not to listen to it. Nevertheless, I nod at him, and my attention returns to the podium and especially to Alex.

"Good evening ladies and gentlemen," he begins. And damn it, his voice shouldn't leave me all giddy inside. "I hope you're all having a good time." Guests cheer, raise their glasses, and applaud him in response. Alex gives us one of his irresistible smiles in return.

Oh gosh, is it getting hot in here or is it just me?

"We are all gathered here tonight to celebrate a few things. First is the fifty-seventh anniversary of my best friend who also became my father-in-law last December… Jeez, that last part is still weird to me but I'm getting there." A quick laugh escapes me and looks like the rest of the guests too. Alex then turns his attention to me and I swallow the lump in my throat. "But also to raise a toast to my wife, who is going through a very challenging pregnancy as we speak and has been nothing but brave."

Oh gosh, this is it. All eyes are now on me and I feel myself flushing with embarrassment. Guests start whispering and commenting and all I can do is smile out of politeness.

"My wife and I are expecting twins. Both were supposed to be boys but one of them lost his Y chromosome and became therefore a girl. Though, with only one X chromosome rather than the normal two she has a condition called Turner's Syndrome. Our little Jasmine will have to live with that for her entire life."

Jeez, I can almost taste the pity in the gaze of the crowd.

"One in every two thousand baby girls suffer from this condition, and yet when our obstetrician told us about it, we had no clue what it was."

My goodness, I take some deep breaths, trying not to let my tears fall in the middle of his speech as I recall that day vividly. While Alex is explaining what the health problems are that girls with Turner's Syndrome might face in their lives, Emma wraps her arms around my shoulders, giving me some strength.

"Which is why we truly appreciate all the support and donations that have been made tonight for the Turner Syndrome Foundation." Alex then raises his flute of champagne and looks especially at me. "A toast to my dear wife—thank you for keeping your head high despite all the adversities you are facing. Jasmine is very lucky to have you as her mother."

Since everyone is standing up to raise their glasses, I do the same and raise my cold-pressed juice. Emma helps me out without saying a word, and I feel slightly embarrassed that I took so long to stand on my own.

Everyone takes a sip of their champagne before a storm of applause fills the room and I'm left an emotional wreck. Is he just pretending for the sake of his image or did he truly mean every word he said? No matter what we are going through, I truly hope it's the latter.

Vibrant music starts playing before the presenter jumps on stage to congratulate Alex for his speech.

"Well, that was one hell of a speech," Emma praises. "I'm gonna go to the bar to get another gin. Do you want me to bring you something?"

I consider whether to go all the way to the other side of the ballroom with Emma or if I should just remain standing here and wait for her to come back. "Um, I could use another cold-pressed juice if they have that there."

"Alright, I'll be right back."

My eyes follow Emma as she gets immersed in the crowd and disappears from my sight.

"Your little friend left you alone?"

My eyes travel instantly to my left, following the voice. For a split second I had totally forgotten Alex is still tormenting me about Matt.

"He just went to the bathroom," I say as my eyes alight on him. "Congrats on the speech, by the way," I say, keeping my tone proper and formal. "I'm sure everyone loved it." Then I take another sip of my juice, and look elsewhere, trying to appear unimpressed at how attractive he is tonight and how moved I am by his wonderful speech. I don't know if it's because we are on a break or because of the hormones or both, but everything about him makes me weak. Despite looking away, I hear him approaching in my direction and standing tall in front of me. I want to leave his presence, but I'm stuck between two chairs and the table behind me.

"How are things between the two of you?" he asks in a low voice.

"There is nothing between the two of us," I tell him, annoyance thick in my tone. "We are friends."

"That's not what I saw…"

Now I'm totally in shock at what he's saying. "What did you see?" The aggressiveness in my tone makes him smile, like he's teasing me again or playing me.

"I saw the way he looked at you," Alex says. Then he steps closer to me, and as he leans in, he continues, "How he looked at your chest softly rising and falling, at your fingers playing with your hair, at your laughter when Emma told you some joke…" His voice makes my heart thunder faster at every beat, but I was imagining him, not Matt, seeing all those things. "And I know right now he's fucking his little Sarah while thinking about you."

"Argh," I utter, looking away. "You're being disgusting."

"Because I'm stating the truth?"

"Matt and Sarah aren't even together," I retort. "They are just friends."

"Oh, yes, they are…"

"You are lying," I hiss.

Alex doesn't say anything else. Instead he just grabs my hand and leads me outside of the ballroom and into the hallway. I try to keep up his pace, despite going faster than I'm used to. He puts a finger on his lips, instructing me to keep quiet. Then we stand in front of a door and despite it being closed, I can hear the moaning and slurpy sounds coming from the other side, and that makes my heart reel at the realization that he and Emma might have been right.

Alex twists the handle, pushing the door wide just as fast. A gasp rolls off my lips and my cheeks go red as I find Matt, his pants down, leaning against the wall while Sarah is on her knees in front of him doing you-know-what. I look away, the view being too graphic and disgusting to watch.

"Oh shit!" I hear Matt saying once he finally sees me.

"You don't even say hi, Petra?" Alex's sarcastic question makes me huff instantly. What a jerk! I bet he's reveling in my discomfort and humiliation. I just turn my back on them, marching toward the hallway in order to leave this stupid event behind.

A few seconds later, I hear Matt's loud voice approaching. "Petra, wait!" But I keep walking, speeding up my pace, despite hearing his footsteps running in my direction. As he reaches me, he holds my wrist but I pull it back and release myself just as fast. "Petra, look, I'm so sorry for what you saw, I—"

"You don't have to justify yourself, okay?" I snap, turning to face him. Before he can bring some more pathetic excuse as to why he was letting Sarah go down on him, I add, "We are just friends. That kiss was stupid and wrong. You should have never done it!"

"I know it was wrong, but…"

"But nothing," I interpose.

As I'm about to leave, he tries to grab my hand again. "Petra, please, listen—"

"Stop it!" I pull my arm from him so that he doesn't touch me. "We are just friends, Matt," I say louder. "Get over it." And I keep walking away, making my way toward the exit.

Then I reach outside, and start looking for Zach to bring me back home, but Matt keeps following me closely.

"Matt, please, just leave me alone."

"Can we talk, please?"

But I just shake my head, displeased at his insistence, and keep glancing around for my driver.

"I think she made it quite clear, no?" I turn back to the entrance, my gaze following the stern voice, and find Alex standing behind him. "Sarah is looking for you." I press my lips tight containing a laugh as Alex says that. "You should check on her, it's not very gentlemanly leaving her alone in the vestibule."

Matt mutters something under his breath, but finally decides to return inside.

Being left alone with Alex, I fold my arms over my chest, stiffening at him. "Thanks," I say politely. "But there was no need, I was managing the situation just fine."

"I saw that," he replies with sarcasm, before passing me. Then he glances up and down the street and beckons to a driver to bring the car over.

"You are going back home?" I ask, without keeping the disappointment off my tone.

"I am," he answers. His piercing blue eyes fall on me and his face softens with a small smile as he thinks something through. "I can drop you off if you want. It might be safer than going alone."

My eyes widen in surprise at his invitation, and even a flutter hits my stomach, but I just shrug nonchalantly, concealing my excitement. "Um, okay."

The car stops in front of us and Alex opens the rear door, inviting me in. I hold his hand for support to slide inside, and for some stupid reason, I put in extra effort to sit like a lady in front of him. Once he closes the door, I heave a sigh of relief, because my back is hurting and my feet are swollen. Jeez, those heels are a serious reminder of what hell is like on earth.

I hear the door opening from the other side, and Alex gets in, before instructing the driver to drop me off first at my— *our*—condo. His cologne fills the space between us and I wish my heart wouldn't recognize it, but I inhale quietly, because it reminds me of everything I miss: him, us, and the fond memory of being together.

The car starts moving and all I can hear is the engine and some street noise. Despite my best attempt, my heart is hammering inside my chest from the excitement of being here just with him. But I make the conscious effort to appear just as stoic as he is.

"Did you have a good evening?" His question breaks the silence between us and I turn to meet his gaze, only to feel a wave of warmth spreading through me as I look into the deep blue of his eyes. "I mean, except for that last part."

"I did. Thank you for organizing the fundraiser." My voice is sweeter than I aimed for, so I steady it a bit before adding,

"I'm sure the foundation will appreciate it." I keep observing him attentively, like I'm trying to memorize every little feature of his face. I wish I could get closer to him, but who knows how he will respond to my touch. After all, we are still on a break. "And you? Did you have a good evening?"

"I did, it was lovely," he answers matching my tone, the corner of his mouth pulling on one side. "Especially seeing Matt's face at the end, that was priceless," he says, chuckling. "The poor boy is so in love with you."

I huff instantly in disbelief. "Yeah, it must be because he's so in love with me that he was with Sarah in the vestibule," I reply in annoyance.

"Well, for some people, love and lust are two separate things. They can have sex without being attached."

"Are you talking by experience, perhaps?" I ask, my eyes narrowing.

Alex ponders for a second before saying, "I used to be like that, yes." And, for some reason, something in his gaze switches. "Until I kissed you in Rome."

I smile tenderly, recalling such cherished memories. "It feels like it was an eternity ago."

And for a moment, our eyes lock and everything else fades away. My heart is thundering so fast that I'm sure he can hear it and I wish for once we could forget everything else and be like we used to be—a couple. But Alex breaks eye contact, clears his throat, and turns to look outside of his window. "It does, yeah."

Jeez, I feel so embarrassed to be drawn to him like that. My cheeks must have gone red as he caught me staring at him like an idiot. "Matt loves me as a friend or like a sister, that's it," I tell him to return to our conversation about Matt, instead of us. "He's just confused about his feelings."

"I don't go around kissing my sisters or friends on the mouth, though." His lame comment makes me hate him on the spot.

"We've already spoken about it," I say in defense.

"Yeah, but it's a hard pill to swallow knowing your wife went along with it." I can hear the sorrow in his voice and it makes my heart ache. I press my lips tight, embarrassment flooding me. My gaze drops to my lap as I recall that day and that terrible mistake. I could argue back, find a few excuses for my behavior and blame it on him, but what for? Despite wearing our wedding bands, Alex and I are officially on a break, living in separate houses for almost two months now.

"I messed up, I know." My voice is barely audible, the shame of my actions weighing on me and making it difficult to even speak. "If I could go back in time and change what happened, I would. But I can't." I sniffle, pushing back the climbing tears. What I did hurt me as much as it hurts him and the simple memory of it makes me want to dig a deep hole and stay there forever. I don't dare to look him in the eye though. If there's only disdain and hate to be found there, then I prefer to quietly stare out the window as I wait to arrive home.

A heavy silence settles between the two of us, but to my surprise, I feel his body sliding over to the middle seat and without saying a word, Alex just drapes an arm around my shoulders, pulling me against him. My head falls into the crest of his neck, and we quietly stay like that, enjoying each other's presence, free of guilt, shame, or judgement. I shut my eyes, reveling in his warmth, and let his energy soothe me. Oh, I have missed him so much. His hand starts stroking my hair, and to my great surprise, he plants a kiss on my head. My heart is full and warm at the gesture and I wish he could do more, I wish he could forgive me and move on…

"Here we are," the driver announces.

My heart dies a little as the car stops in front of our condo. Rolling my lips between my teeth, I ponder how to make him come upstairs with me. Then my head leaves his neck, and after straightening myself, I look him in the eye and say, "Um, do you mind helping me until I'm settled in bed? I know it's stupid but I struggle quite a bit moving around." Which is not entirely untrue; my bump is making it harder for me to take off my dress and shoes by myself.

Despite keeping a straight face, I can see his full, kissable lips pulling at one side as he considers my invitation. "Of course. I understand," he says, his tone lower and softer than usual. It's the same tone he used to use when we were happily together and the memory of it makes me smile. After all, we haven't been so close in a very long time. "It must be hard for you at this stage to undress…"

I wet my lips at the word *undress*, and as our eyes lock, I find myself lost in his blue eyes and into the once-forgotten moments that bonded us together. My heartbeat speeds up as I find myself drawn to him. I wish *he* would have been the one inviting me for a chess game, I wish *he* would have been the one inviting me for pizza and to watch a documentary, and I wish *he* would have been the one kissing me on the mouth. I notice how his gaze slowly drifts down to my parted lips, and my heart is hammering anxiously in my chest at the idea he could finally kiss me. Alex leans slowly in, and he's close, so damn close that my stomach flutters in excitement…but the sound of my door opening breaks the spell between us and his attention goes to the person standing outside, and he nods at him in appreciation. "Well, let's go."

Shit! I curse under my breath as I watch Alex leave the car effortlessly. A no-brainer for him, but a big challenge for me. Fortunately, the doorman gives me a hand and pushes me outside so that I can land on my two feet.

"Thank you," I say, smoothing down my dress and making sure I'm decent.

Then my gaze sets on Alex who stands tall in front of me, and my heart gives a little jump as he tenderly smiles, our eyes locking again. Oh gosh, how am I supposed to resist him? Why does he have to look so handsome? And most importantly, why can't I stop loving him after everything he has done? He breaks eye contact and gestures me to go ahead, so I walk past him and lead him into the building.

After getting into the lift, an awkward silence fills the space between us as we wait together like two strangers in this small compartment. I wonder if I should make some small talk or not, but fortunately, the doors finally open wide, and we get out.

As Alex steps into the entryway, I realize he hasn't been in our condo for a month and it feels so strange to see him standing here, taking in his surroundings like a guest would. So I play the host and say, "This way, please."

He chuckles inwardly but follows along as I lead him into our bedroom. Yet as I twist the handle and open the door, I can sense his uneasiness growing, so I turn and say, "It's just to help me undress." And I hope my words have managed to ease him, because it seems like he's already regretting to have come so far.

"Sure," he mumbles politely, despite keeping a straight posture. To my disappointment though, I read nothing in his gaze that states otherwise.

After we get inside the room, I go and close the door behind us. Since he gives me a skeptical look for me doing so, I say, "I don't want Maria to wake up."

He nods at my explanation, and as I look at him, it's clear to me that he's only here to help; the warm connection we felt in the car disappeared and I can only imagine he's regretting to have tried kissing me. Despite being in our bedroom, an uncomfortable energy settles between us, but I try to ease the mood and sit on my bedside, my feet on the floor, and looking him with batting eyes, I extend one leg and say, "Do you mind taking off my shoes?"

The sound of his laughter makes my heart bounce harder inside my chest, Alex takes a few steps in my direction, squats down in front of me, and starts removing my first sandal, before doing the same with the left one. Suddenly though, a kick hits me from the inside.

"Ah!" A gasp rolls off my lips and I put a hand on my bump to steady myself, but then I realize... "They are moving!"

"Are you sure?" Alex asks, standing up just as fast.

"I swear." Then tapping on the spot beside me, I say, "Sit here."

Alex sits beside me and taking in the moment, I turn my back on him, and pull my hair in front of me to show him the zipper of my dress. "Undress me, I'll show you," I tell him, excited. He considers my request for a few instants and my heart starts racing, apprehensive at his reaction. Fortunately, I hear the zip unfastening and he pulls it all the way down. Then I stand before him so that I can take it off. To my surprise, Alex immediately averts his gaze and his attitude hurts more than I'd like to admit.

"I'm sorry, I shouldn't be staring like this."

"It's okay," I say in a whisper, despite him looking away, clearly embarrassed. "You have seen me countless times."

"It's different now."

I want to cry at those three words because I don't want this to be any different. We are married, expecting two babies, and no matter how much we went through, nothing makes it feel any different to me. Pushing away my thoughts, I sit again beside him and take his hand to my bump. I try to locate the first baby and it doesn't take long to feel him kicking again. "Can you feel it?" I squeak, my smile growing up to my ears.

"Jeez, yeah!" The excitement in his voice is alluring. And I'm not sure if it's because of the energy that radiates from his hand, but one of the babies keeps responding to it like he's trying to communicate with his dad. "This is insane!" I can't stop laughing at him, Alex looks totally marveled as he scratches his index finger softly to say hello. "Do you think they know it's me?"

"Maybe, they do. They have never been so active before." While Alex keeps rubbing his fingers on my bump to play with them, I keep my eyes on him just as smitten. Being this close to him and sharing such an intimate moment with him causes my heart to patter against my ribs. I fucking love this man to a point that nothing feels bad enough to not forgive him. Does he still love me like I do though? And can he also forgive me? I guess there's only one way to find out.

"Can I ask you something?" My voice, low and soft, makes his attention fall back on me.

"Sure," he breathes as he straightens himself again.

Eye to eye, I find myself lost for words. So I just lean in, and slowly enough close the small gap between us. My heart explodes recognizing the warmth of his lips pressed on mine. Oh gosh, I missed them so damn much. Lust awakes my every sense giving me free rein to deepen our kiss and cup his jawline as I do so. Alex doesn't halt me, instead, he opens his mouth slightly, letting my tongue inside to stroke his. My fluids coat my panties at the sensual touch of our tongues entwining and dancing together like they used to. And I moan with pleasure, wanting to feel so much more of him. His hands go around my waist, and my body melts as he keeps devouring me with such devotion that I truly feel how much he missed me. He pulls softly on my bottom lip before nibbling my chin and going down to my neck where he pulls softly on my flesh to suckle on it.

"Ahhh…" Then he keeps tracing wet kisses around my neck with a hunger I haven't seen before. A grunt rolls off his throat as I tilt my head back, giving him free access to my chest. His hands go up to my bra, and in a quick move, he finally opens the clasps, and takes it off. His mouth leaves my skin for a moment, only to look more closely at my boobs. A smirk grows on my face as I see the lust in his gaze. "Yes, they are bigger and yes, they are also more sensitive."

Alex wets his lips before pressing them again on mine for a quick peck. Then he softly starts circling my right nipple with his thumb as he contemplates my breast like it's some sort of masterpiece. "You are so damn beautiful." The compliment comes off totally unexpected and with my swollen feet, back pain, and huge bump, I never expected he would say something like that. "Me or my boobs?" I ask, humoring him.

His lips spread wide in a grin, his white teeth in full display. "Everything about you is beautiful," he breathes.

And in the heat of the moment, I lean in to slam my mouth on his, forgetting everything but us and then say, "I love you." He creases his brows slightly, unsure how to react. Maybe those words aren't meant to be said when a couple is on a break, but I have never wanted to be on a break in the first place. With parted lips and loud breaths, he keeps looking at me, mesmerized and speechless. "And you?" My voice is barely audible, maybe because I'm too afraid of his answer.

Something in his gaze switches and his face softens with a tender smile. "I have never stopped loving you."

My pussy tingles in excitement and his declaration drenches me even more than I'd like to admit. His fingers start threading sensually across my chest; an invitation for what is yet to come. My hands go up to his jacket and I help him take it off. Biting my lower lip, I start unbuttoning his shirt, my fingers quite giddy, eager to see him naked again. Alex senses my impatience growing so he takes the matter in hand, stands up, and removes his shirt giving me a full view of his sculptured abs. Oh gosh... I heave a sigh, my body heat rising at every second. Then he starts unbuckling his pants, and the simple sound of his belt makes my heart race in anticipation for his touch, his body hovering on top of mine and the heady sensation of having him inside me. We haven't made love since that day in the dining room and since then, my bump has grown quite a bit, which makes me wonder what making love at twenty-seven weeks pregnant feels like. My lips part in fury and I skip a breath at the sight of his boner. I drag myself a bit back onto the bed, never leaving my eyes off of it. Then I lay myself on the sheets, yet I wince at how painful it is for my back.

"Are you okay?" he asks immediately. And I crack a smile at his serious tone. "How is your back?"

"Maybe adding some pillows wouldn't be too bad."

And instantly, Alex takes the fluffier pillows to put under me. "And now? Is it better?"

With one pillow under my back and two under my head, I ease myself, and nod at him. I angle myself so that I can look at him as he stands in front of me and reaches for the waistband of my panties, slowly pushing them all the way down to my feet. My breath becomes ragged, and I nearly pant from being naked with him here in our bedroom. He then wraps my legs around him and leans in just enough to reach my mouth, kissing me hard. "If you don't feel comfortable at any moment you tell me immediately, okay?" he asks, between kisses.

"Okay," I whisper, wanting both to hold him closer to taste his mouth and to have him immediately inside me. Alex naked is like a buffet, and I am starving. I nip his bottom lip briefly before he pulls back, casting me in the shadow of his tall form.

Alex's pupils dilate, growing dark and wide as he takes my naked form in. I try to memorize everything in this moment, just in case it's the last time for the foreseeable future. The soft down pillows cradling me, the bronze velvet of his skin, the strained expression pulling at the corner of his mouth, all of it. Every second seems to slip through my fingers, and at the same time, I am sure I will never forget any of it.

"Alex, please touch me," I plead.

He nods sharply, exhaling as if he was holding his breath. I know the feeling. It seems like any sudden wrong move could ruin the moment, and if my heated skin and wet pussy are any indications, I need him desperately.

He starts by running his long fingertips down my body, starting from the hollow of my neck down my collar bone, barely grazing my overly sensitive nipples without stopping. He reverently strokes my belly bump before moving his roaming hands to my full hips, squeezing gently, and continuing down my legs, to the back of my knees, and finally the curve of my ankles before starting back at the top. My skin is raising in goosebumps as he seems to light a fire with each pass of his fingers.

On the third pass, he stops at my breasts, plucking my nipples and rolling them between the pads of his fingers carefully. My breasts are so heavy and sensitive that even this slight sensation has me arching my back off the bed, pushing the mounds of my tits further into his hands. Alex and I both are new to pregnant sex, and he seems surprised at my intense reactions.

"If I didn't know better," he starts, before lowering his head and pulling one of my nipples into his hot, wet mouth before releasing it, "I might think that you missed me a little."

"God, yes," I pant, burying my fingers in his tussle of hair as he gives all of his attention to my chest. The scratch of his beard combined with the slippery perfection of his tongue has me alight from within. It's as if everything is cranked to maximum, the sensations, the empty feeling where I long to have him inside me, everything.

Alex moves lower to pepper kisses across my swollen belly, melting my heart in the process. I have been waiting for this for what seems like forever.

"You're so beautiful," he says softly, "glowing, and radiant…"

"You really think so?" I hadn't thought to be self-conscious, but here naked with Alex and his perfect, gorgeous body, I would be lying if I said I hadn't considered he might not find me as attractive as before. I'm softer and bigger, not to mention how big my boobs have gotten. He should like that, at least.

"I'm positive that there has never been a hotter sight than seeing you like this," he says between kisses. "And knowing I did it to you…" he continues before he kisses my lips hard, his tongue darting into my mouth quickly. "You're mine, and this proves it," he finishes as he skims his hands over my stomach before he plants a longer, sweeter kiss on it.

My lips curve up at his words, but apparently, the heartwarming interlude is over, because his mouth is back on my breasts and nipples. The chilly air has hardened them to stiff peaks and his warm mouth is a relief. I feel his fingers parting my nether lips as he moves his mouth from my nipples, kissing up my neck until he can whisper in my ear. "You're so hot and wet for me, baby."

"Only you," I reply, voice quavering.

He starts with one finger, slipping it inside of me. It feels amazing to finally have him touching me again and to let him make me feel good. He crooks his finger upward, brushing the secret spot on the upper wall of my pussy. I nearly jump out of my skin, and he slowly pulls the finger out, inserting two. Alex repeats the come hither motion with his fingers, and the delicious pressure of him pressing against my g-spot causes me to get even wetter, soaking his searching digits.

He fingers me like this for a few minutes, and if it wasn't for my huge belly, I would have pulled him against me already. He's driving me mad, and I think he knows it. My clit is all but screaming to be touched, but Alex keeps his hands away from it, only stimulating my g-spot.

"You're killing me, Alex," I say softly.

"Hush, Petra," he scolds, holding my legs in place around his waist as they begin to shake with hard tremors. I'm tossing my head from side to side, turned on and frustrated at the same time. His fingers inside me feel so good, and I can come if he would just touch my clit, even for a second, but Alex seems to be in no hurry.

Well, that makes one of us.

I think I'm going to scream as he removes his fingers, and the obsessive desire to be filled comes rushing back. I bite my tongue, knowing Alex will drag it out even more if I complain. He can play my body like a harp. He knows which touches will drive me the craziest, and he is pulling out all the stops tonight. To make up for lost time, I guess.

Alex looks breathtaking in the warm, honey tinted light of the room. The light pours over his broad shoulders and rests in the shadows of his rippling abdomen. My hands itch with the need to touch him, and I raise myself to my elbows, preparing to reach out to him when he suddenly plants both of his hands on either side of my head. I fall back onto the fluffy pillows, looking up into his laughing eyes as he kisses me again.

"It's my time right now, baby, just lay back and let me love you," Alex says.

"But—" I begin to protest,

"There will be plenty of time for your turn later," he murmurs before locking his lips on mine. His tongue teases me, our teeth bumping gently as we share breaths. I'm awash in his presence, the feeling of his heartbeat where my hands are pressed into his chest, and the smell of his cologne that I have missed so much.

I'm about to completely lose myself in the make-out session when he pulls away. He shifts his hips slightly and I can feel the steel rod of his erection. My anticipation is climbing higher and higher, knowing Alex is about to fuck me.

Alex makes a few passes over my swollen clit with his thumb, before I see him grasp his cock with his free hand. His manhood is rock hard and straining, a drop of pre-cum glistening on the tip.

"If it hurts, you tell me, okay?" Alex asks.

I nod, transfixed as I watch him position himself at my entrance. He grasps my thighs, holding me in place as he slowly feeds himself into me, inch by inch. It's torturous and electrifying all at the same time, as I feel my walls stretch around him for the first time in so long. My body remembers, though, and opens for him willingly.

I tear my gaze from where we are connected to glance at his face. His eyebrows are drawn together in concentration, the veins in his neck visible from his effort to take this slow and give me the gentle lovemaking I need. I know that if I wasn't pregnant that he would have bent me over and slammed deep into me by now. Instead, he's pacing himself for me and I can see how tightly wound it has made him.

After what seems like an eternity of us re-familiarizing ourselves with one other, he starts to move. Feeling Alex pull out of me and push back in is driving me insane with need. His speed is agonizingly slow, and it allows me to feel every inch of him moving within me.

"I'm not that fragile," I say, gasping between thrusts. "You can go faster. Please, Alex."

"Need to take it easy," he bites out. I can see the tension in his body as he bottoms out inside of me again and again, the head of his cock kissing the end of my channel each time. I'm making desperate noises in my throat with each stroke. Alex is stoking the flames running across my nerves higher and higher.

"Just...just a little more..." I beg.

Alex curses, digging his fingers harder into the flesh of my hips, and thank goodness, he finally picks up the pace, just a small degree, but it's enough. Seeing him here in our bedroom after so long working himself in and out of me over and over fills me with a fierce satisfaction. Alex pulls me forward, angling my pelvis up and causing his member to push against my g-spot. Shamelessly, I let out a long moan, and I'm rewarded by a flash of Alex's white teeth in a triumphant grin.

"Are you gonna come for me?" Alex demands.

"Yes, yes," I moan.

Alex's slow and steady tactics have worked their magic, and I can feel my orgasm preparing to roll over me, stemming straight from the places deep inside me that Alex is hitting. It isn't an electrifying shock striking me like when he fucks me hard, instead, it's a swelling wave, rising and rising, and when it finally breaks over me I feel for a moment like I am drowning.

My toes are curling and I'm wrapping my legs even tighter around Alex when he bends over to catch my mouth in a savage kiss, drinking in my moans as I spasm around him. My climax triggers his own, and on the tail end of my pleasure, I feel him spurting deep inside my channel. The feeling sparks a few last orgasmic aftershocks until I am well and fully wrung out.

Alex stands straight again as he moves inside of me for a few more seconds, his head lowered and his sweat-drenched hair curling over his forehead. I don't think I've ever seen anything as beautiful as him in this moment—buried in me to the hilt, his skin glistening with effort and satisfaction written all over his face.

As I slowly regain my breath, Alex leans down to reach my lips, giving me a few pecks, then he kisses the tip of my nose, playing with it.

"You feel so good," he whispers to me. And I can't help but smile at his words, knowing he's still inside me. "It's so damn hard to leave."

"Then stay," I tell him, my tone low and inviting. Then wetting my lips, I add, "We can spend all night long trying a few more positions, you know…"

He chuckles at my humor, before smashing me with reality. "I'd love to, but Lily told us you need eight hours of sleep per night, and it's already getting late for you."

What? I heave a sigh in annoyance, rolling my eyes at him. Why does he have to be like that? "Alex, I'm fine, when I'm tired I'll sleep."

"I have an idea…" He gives me a quick peck on the forehead and then slowly pulls himself out of me. Then he goes to the other side of the bed—his side of the bed—and slides inside the sheets, before helping me out to do the same. He rearranges the pillows and I switch positions lying on my side, a pillow under my bump. A quick smile settles on my lips, feeling his cum dripping down my swollen lips, and the sensation of feeling him nestled against me makes me want to have him inside me all over again.

"This feels right," I murmur before yawning. I can feel Alex burying his face in my hair and inhaling, and a smile plays across my lips. Domestic bliss, with a side of kinky. My favorite.

"What's on your mind, love?" Alex asks, kissing my shoulder.

"Just thinking of how nice this is. It figures that we wouldn't make up without sex, huh?" I reply.

"Well it is us." He laughs. "Plus, I'd be crazy to pass up the chance to get such a goddess between the sheets," Alex says, sounding amused.

I giggle, turning my head so we can kiss. It's slow and languorous, and Alex rubs my belly as he kisses me deeply, running his tongue over my top lip before delving back into my mouth. I can hear the small breathy noises coming from my throat, but I'm too content to worry about how desperate I sound.

The moment is still sleepy and calm until Alex grinds his pelvis against my ass, and I feel how hard he is. Any tiredness that has been hanging over me dissipates, replaced by lust. Jeez, pregnancy libidos are really confusing!

I push back against him, and he growls deep in his chest, pulling away from our kiss to bite the skin of my shoulder gently.

"You've woken the beast, Petra, when you really should be resting," he rumbles against my skin.

"Says the man who just had his tongue in my mouth," I quip back.

Alex pushes hard against me again and I inhale sharply.

"I'd like to have my tongue in other places too, woman, but not until you've gotten some sleep," he says, and his words make me shiver in anticipation.

The mental image of his dark head between my legs washes me in a wave of heat and desire. I have to figure out how to convince him to fuck me again, and fast, or this entire bed is going to go up in flames.

"Where exactly," I pant, "would you want to have your tongue?"

Alex nips the shell of my ear before he replies, "I can think of a few places. I already had the opportunity to taste those sweet little nipples of yours. Maybe you'd like me to lick deep into your pussy. Would you like that, Petra?"

I shiver at his words, "Yes, God, yes I would."

"Say it," he demands.

"I...I would like you to lick my pussy," I stammer, face heating at the words coming out of my mouth. It's simultaneously embarrassing and hot as hell.

He laughs, low and seductive, and grinds his hips into me again. The length of his member slides between my nude ass cheeks and stops right before slipping into my drenched core. I try to reposition myself, so he slides into me, but Alex holds me still.

"Quit that. You know you have to wait," he says, his voice both strong and soothing.

I try to shake his hands off, but he just pulls me closer, brushing my hair away from the back of my neck to kiss it, laughing at my struggles.

"Petra, Petra, I want to give you what you need just as much as you want to have it, but the doctor said you need to take it easy, baby," he says.

"Then stop teasing me!" I whine, wiggling against him.

"Maybe there is something we can do," Alex says, seeming to consider his options. He can't see my face, so I scowl, horny and annoyed. Why does he think he knows what's best for me, better than I do? I feel him repositioning us again, my butt tilted higher, so he's pressing firmly against my entrance.

"I'm going to make love to you, but only if you promise to go right to sleep afterward. No getting up, you understand?"

Alex says firmly. I can tell there is no room for negotiation from his tone.

I nod swiftly, and I hear Alex hiss between his teeth as he pushes inside of me. My pussy is still swollen from before, and it's a tight fit from the spooning position, but after a few long seconds, he is in. Laying here, with my legs pressed together and Alex buried in me makes everything feel so intense, but my body welcomes him.

"So tight," he grits out, pulling out slowly before pushing back into me as far as he will go. I want to ask him to slam himself deep, to push my limits, but I have to think about the babies. We still have to be gentle.

Alex pumps himself into me while I push back, meeting his thrusts. It's intoxicating, and my channel is still so sensitive from the previous orgasm that pleasure pours over me with each little movement.

I am losing track of time, wrapped in Alex's warm arms, the silken sheets whispering over our moving bodies and the fluffy mattress and pillows underneath me. It's all so good, so wonderful, that I don't want it to end. Earlier I wanted to rush Alex, to come as fast as possible, but now I just want to soak in the moment.

My sex drive has other ideas, and I whimper. Alex, knowing my body better than even I do, reaches around me to trace small circles around my aching clit. It's like a burst of lightning when his fingers connect, and what had been slow and warm turns hot and heavy.

Alex's clever fingers, and his hard manhood moving within me, has my climax rushing forward at breakneck speed, but before I can hit that glorious point one of the babies tumble in my belly, kicking out, and Alex freezes in place.

"Petra," he whispers as if the babies might hear him, "They're moving!" His tone is bordering on panicked.

I turn to look at him, and the expression on his face is a mix of worry and alarm. I grin, trying not to laugh outright.

"Yes. They do that. It's fine, Alex, please don't stop," I tell him reassuringly.

He inhales deeply, considering my words before replying, "I have to if they're moving...I don't want to hurt any of you three."

"You won't, I promise, but I might burst into flames if you don't help me come," I plead, all of my energy pent up and ready to blow at any moment.

He hesitates for a second, and I'm about to give up when he gently places his hands on my thighs, pulling me back against him fully again, his cock still seated firmly inside of me.

"Fine," he says quietly. "You know I can't deny you."

Alex seems to touch me more reverently now, driving me higher and higher, his fingers moving between my legs as he fills me again and again. With his free hand, he strokes my breasts, then my bump, and the tops of my thighs while he whispers promises into my ear.

"Beautiful girl, I've missed this," he tells me, his voice strained.

God, I love this man.

"I want to cum together," I breathe between his thrusts. "Cum inside me, Alex."

"If you keep talking like that, I'm going to," he growls, the movements of his hips stuttering before finding their rhythm again. He continues to play with my clit, and I cover his hand with mine, refusing to let him pull away.

"Please don't stop," I all but sob, overcome with need.

Thankfully, he doesn't, and with his fingers sending sharp pleasure to join the deep sensations of him fucking me, I am suddenly on the precipice of climax.

"Gonna cum," I gasp, right before my orgasm overtakes me. All of my inner muscles clamp around Alex, and with a strangled noise he empties himself inside of me at the same time, his warm seed bathing the inside of my pussy. We are both shaky and breathing hard, our simultaneous orgasms leaving us both exhausted. He remains inside me cherishing this moment as we can. After a few moments, Alex pulls himself out of me, rearranging our blankets and my pillows before wrapping himself around me again. Usually, I wouldn't want to go to bed still sweaty and drained from sex, but I'd make an exception for tonight. The idea of leaving this bed seems impossible.

He cups my bump with his hand, touching me softly. My eyes are growing heavy, and I sigh, resting fully limp on the pillows now.

"I think tonight I'm gonna finally sleep peacefully," I admit as he keeps softly stroking the lower part of my bump while placing soft kisses on the crest of my neck.

"You don't sleep well at night?" he asks, his tone low and surprised.

"Without you here, no…" And as I say those words, I instantly freeze at the idea he could leave in the middle of the night. "Please, don't leave the bed without waking me up first," I tell him. "I don't want to wake up and see you gone. It hurts me more than you probably know."

"I promise." And he pins one more kiss before whispering, "Good night, little Petra."

CHAPTER 30

Manhattan, May 16, 2021
Petra Van Gatt

There's nothing better than waking up and feeling Alex spooning me from behind. Jeez, this must be a dream. After so many months sleeping without him by my side, it can only be one and nothing else. I start rubbing my butt against his crotch, and I hear him responding to my movements with a sleepy, "Mmm."

Damn... Is it really him? Turning around, my lips spread into a smile as I see Alex peacefully asleep, his eyes still shut. I softly stroke his stubble, watching him sleeping as if it was the very first time he was here beside me. Wow. He usually wakes up so early that is very rare I can enjoy his presence in bed. Discreetly enough, I take my iPhone from the nightstand and take a shot of him. Now, no matter what happens in life, I will always have a photo of my husband sleeping on a Sunday morning with me. I can't stop looking at him. To me, he's getting more handsome and charming with every passing day.

I just love everything about him—his medium stubble, his thick dark-brown hair, the locks falling on his forehead, and the cute fine lines under his eyes. Alex would freak out if he knew I noticed them, but I think it gives him a certain charm, and I don't mind.

Words can't describe how blissful I am, feeling his warmth and looking at his perfect face. I lean in just enough and kiss his forehead. Oh! I should paint an oil portrait of Alex sleeping. As I come to think of it, I should do two different paintings; one of Alex and one of us two as a couple. This would be such a nice gift to offer him upon the birth of our twins. Maybe Emma can give me a hand and take some pictures.

"Good morning," I hear him saying. The warmth in his voice makes my heart go wild and I can't help but smile like an idiot in love at him.

"Good morning," I reply as our eyes keep contemplating each other. "Did you sleep well?"

"Jeez, like a baby," he answers, stretching himself out.

Putting on my most innocent voice, I ask, "Does it mean you are coming back home?" I'm scared of his answer, but I need to know.

Alex just smiles in return. In silence, his hand goes to the back of my head and starts stroking my hair. "Do you want me to?"

"Of course, what a silly question," I answer, pinching him playfully.

Alex pulls me down to his lips and instantly a wave of electrifying energy spreads trough me. I could literally fly from that kiss. Jeez, what a blessing to have him back, especially the

Alex I fell in love with—the caring, attentive and affectionate Alex.

"Then, yes, I will."

Now it's my turn to press my lips on his and show him how happy I am, but as soon as I want to deepen our kiss, his iPhone starts ringing and I can't help but sigh in annoyance.

Alex turns to his bedside to take his phone and check who's calling him. Surprisingly, I notice how his brows furrow in confusion. "Um, it's my dad." He accepts the call and puts the phone against his ear. "Yes?" A short silence ensues while Alex is listening to him. Then he lets out a long breath and runs the other hand through his hair. "Dad, you didn't have to…" he tells him, rolling his eyes. "No, we don't even have a nursery yet."

A nursery? "What's going on?" I ask.

Alex turns away from his phone and says, "My dad bought a few plush toys for the babies." A quick chuckle escapes me at his kindness. Oh gosh, we had totally forgotten to tell him our no-gifts policy until they are born. "I guess he couldn't help himself before coming for lunch."

"Wait—we are having lunch with your dad?" Now that's something I didn't know.

Alex stands a finger up, letting me know to wait a bit. "Dad, that's okay but please we don't need pajamas or shower lotions or whatever the lady is offering you." Alex starts laughing and shaking his head at the same time. "I understand the seller is pretty, but no, you aren't buying more stuff to please her."

Oh my gosh! I can't imagine Hendrik being left alone to do some shopping here in New York. He's gonna be eaten alive by those sales reps.

"Alright, see you in a few minutes. No more gifts, okay?" And Alex hangs up.

Looking at him with amusement, I ask, "So that's why you slept here?"

He laughs, but doesn't deny it. "That might have been a contributing factor."

I gasp in shock at his blunt answer, but I give him a quick punch to the chest, and continue teasing him. "What an opportunist you are."

"Guilty," he says, his tone so delicious I can almost taste it.

I remain observing him attentively while a new question arises and is now on the tip of my tongue. "Can I ask you something?"

He cocks his head to the side, slightly surprised. "Sure."

"Are you still pretending that everything is fine between us or is it real now?"

The corners of his lips spread across his face, and I can even see the glitter in his eyes. "It has been real since the moment I kissed you yesterday." Then I shut my eyes and let him close the small space between us, reveling in the blissful kisses he's giving me. No matter how many times he has kissed me I'll never get tired of it. "I'm willing to give our marriage a second chance, are you?"

"Of course I am," I reply, and I wet my lips as if I could still taste his lips on mine. "Thank you for doing this," I whisper. "I won't let you down again."

He cups my jawline and gives me a quick peck on my forehead. Before I can even reopen my eyes, Alex jumps out of bed and seems to be filled with a morning energy that I can only dream of. "Alright, let's go and take a shower. My dad is gonna be here soon."

"Does Maria know we are having lunch here?" I ask, dragging myself sleepily out of bed.

"Of course she does."

"Of course," I repeat in sarcasm. So everyone knew but me. Fantastic!

* * *

As Maria opens the door wide to welcome Hendrik, my jaw literally drops at the amount of gift bags he's carrying.

"Dad! Is this a joke or what?" Alex snaps as he helps him out with the bags.

"Those are just the plush toys I told you about," he doesn't sound very convincing though, "and maybe a shower set or two. But it was a promo," he adds.

While Alex doesn't look very pleased, I can't help but shake my head in amusement. It warms my heart to see Hendrik so excited for the birth of his grandchildren. Even if my mom were still alive, I doubt she'd have been as excited.

I greet Hendrik with a hug and invite him to the living room where some appetizers and cold-pressed juice is waiting for us. Maria made my favorite flavor, which is a combo of mint and pineapple. Alex finally comes in, looking slightly untidy from stowing all those bags. God knows where he put them. Not surprisingly we raise a toast to the babies and as soon as we finish to take our first sip, Hendrik shoots his first question. "Do you have a delivery date already?"

While Hendrik sits on the armchair, ready to listen carefully to my answer. Alex and I take a seat on the sofa and exchange a quick look. "Well, so far not really," I disclose, before giving another drink of my juice. "My obstetrician wants me to go to the hospital at twenty-eight weeks. But that's because she's convinced that something bad is gonna happen to Jasmine."

"I'm sure everything is gonna be fine," Alex steps in, his positivity lightening my mood. "Those are just preventive measures doctors like to take in high-risk pregnancies."

Hendrik seems confused. "But is it high risk because of the Turner's Syndrome?"

"It's mostly because of another condition called Twin-to-Twin-Transfusion Syndrome," I tell him. "Jasmine is less developed and, therefore, smaller than her brother, and according to the doctors, she'll need at least one month in intensive prenatal car after her birth." Jeez, I'm already talking as if I had some kind of guarantee that Jasmine is gonna make it. Maybe it was a mistake to call her by a name instead of *Baby B* like Mariana does. We are talking as if we knew her fate, as if her life would depend only on us. What a big mistake that was. The sooner I get used to the idea I might have to grieve her loss, the better. Despite the joyful smiles and applause of yesterday evening, nothing when it comes to my babies are guaranteed. Believing otherwise is just fooling myself.

"Once both of them are healthy and back home, we need to have a celebration." Hendrik's excitement pulls me back from my dark thoughts and I look at him, a smile settling on my lips.

"That's a great idea," I reply. Despite knowing the likelihood of Jasmine surviving is not high, I can't help but picture a family party for her and her brother. Oh God, how much I'd love this to become my reality in a not-so-distant future.

"Maybe a baptism, what do you think?" Hendrik asks us.

I blink twice, a bit troubled that he is still thinking about the celebration. "A baptism?" I repeat.

"Yes, my son got baptized when he was around three months old. That's maybe a good way to celebrate."

"You were also baptized around the same age," Alex tells me. And I don't know why, but the fact he reminds me of such a special moment makes me chuckle a bit.

"It just seems so far away," I tell them, trying to manage expectations. "We don't even know when they will be born, and how long they will need to stay in the hospital for…"

"I understand," Hendrik says, noticing I'm not interested in planning any baby-related stuff for now. He might be on cloud nine with the news, but he doesn't know how hard it is to be told over and over again that the chances of Jasmine making it to this world is near to none. Then as he tries to change the subject, he looks at his son and asks, "Do your mom and sisters know already?"

"Not yet," Alex answers. "I will call them afterwards."

"I think they already know," I disclose. "Emma told Yara yesterday. So I suppose your sister already shared the news with your entire family."

"Oh God," Alex breathes out, leaning back on the sofa. "I just hope they're not gonna show up here uninvited."

"Do they know I was at the dinner?" Hendrik asks me, and I'm not sure if he wants a positive or negative answer to that question.

"It's hard to say," I answer as honestly as I can. "Emma didn't tell me."

"Alex," Hendrik says, leaning forward as if he wants to draw further attention to himself. "I want to be present in my grandchildren's lives. I'm perfectly comfortable attending their baptism, birthdays, school plays, etcetera, even if your mother is there too."

"Well, I don't see why Margaret would have a problem with that," I tell Hendrik. Despite my comment, they don't seem as relaxed as I am. "After all, New York is supposed to be a neutral ground for both of you."

"Yes, *supposed* is the key word here," Alex says, before drawing out a breath.

"What?" I ask Alex, seeing his face filled with concern. "She isn't gonna do here what she did at the castle. You have nothing to worry about." Despite the confidence in my tone, Alex and his dad don't seem much convinced.

"Let's hope so," he just says in return.

* * *

After spending the whole afternoon with Hendrik, the poor man was having a hard time saying goodbye. I can't blame him; the last time he had seen his son was at his wedding, five months ago. But before he leaves the condo, I insist for him to come and visit us at least once a month. Alex looks slightly shocked at my decision, but I genuinely like Hendrik and it's always a pleasure to spend time in his company.

Once Alex finally closes the door behind us, I can't help but say, "Your dad is really on cloud nine knowing he's gonna be a grandfather." The simple thought of it actually brings me joy, but my gloomy thoughts come back to haunt me, erasing any brightness. "Jeez, if something happens before then—"

"Hey," Alex interposes, trying to soothe me. He takes me in his arms, removes some loose strands of hair out of my face, and presses his lips on my forehead. "Don't worry about it; stay positive. Even Mariana is starting to bite her tongue at how strong Jasmine is."

"I know…" I try to shut down my concerns and fears, but when your obstetrician, Auntie Louise, and your own mom told you your life will be filled with death and misery, it's hard to ignore such warnings. "By the way," I begin, wanting nothing more than to change the subject. "Emma told me about the affair." Despite the revelation, Alex doesn't seem surprised. I imagine he was already anticipating it since our conversation back in Venice. "Do you know if Elliot knows about it?"

"I have no idea," he says. "Why?"

"Well, I don't think Yara is a good influence on Emma and, um, I think she's trying to coerce her to do things she doesn't want to."

"I'll have a word with my sister." His plan sounds actually much better than the one I had in mind. "I've already tried to dissuade her once when I caught them at our wedding reception, but I'll talk to her more seriously now."

"Wait—they were doing it at the castle?" I ask, my jaw dropping at his statement. "Seriously?"

"Yep," he answers, a smile pulling at his lips. "I think their little affair started way before the wedding though."

"Wow," I utter, still under a wave of shock. "It sucks knowing Emma kept such a secret from me for so long. I thought I was her best friend."

"Well, even best friends can keep secrets from each other." I nod at him in understanding, and a few moments of silence ensue while Alex seems to be engrossed in his own thoughts. "Look, I know you don't want to think about celebrations, baptisms, and so on, but don't you think we should at least start thinking about... the nursery?"

That's what he was thinking about? "No!" I snap right away, suppressing a laugh. "Stop it," and I playfully hit his chest. "I don't want anything baby-related until they are born."

"Fine, fine," he answers, before bringing me into his arms. "But we're gonna have to call my mom and let her know the news."

I heave a long sigh, unable to hide my displeasure of having to talk to Margaret again. "Do you think she's mad at us?"

"That would be a very poor move from her side." He takes me by the hand and we go to the living room again.

Before he makes the phone call though, I look him straight in the eye and say, "Promise me you are not gonna invite them here until the babies are born."

"What are you afraid of?" he asks, his voice laced with concern. "They will most likely want to see us before that."

481

"I know, but their energies…" It's hard to explain what my intuition is telling me, so I pause for a moment, searching for the best words to put on. "It's not good. I can't explain why, but I feel it's not healthy for me to be around them while I'm still pregnant."

"Alright," he says in return. "I will tell my mom to come only after they are born."

CHAPTER 31

Manhattan, May 21, 2021
Petra Van Gatt

"I'm staying at the hospital because my obstetrician thinks Jasmine is going to go into reverse cord flow, in which case that would mean she has to be delivered immediately or it can become fatal," I explain to my dad over the phone who has been extremely worried at the idea I'm spending some time at the hospital.

"But what are they planning to do to you over there?" Dad keeps asking, still visibly confused.

"They plan to hook me up to monitors twenty-four seven that are wrapped around my belly, keeping track of heart rates and umbilical flows."

"Oh gosh…"

"Dad, everything is gonna be fine," I interpose before he can get even more anxious than he already is.

After finishing our call, I put my phone back into my purse, and try to decompress, taking some deep breaths in and out while Alex and I step into the lift at Mt. Sinai.

Jeez, I can only hope everything is gonna be okay as I just said.

Alex and I had gotten up bright and early, finished packing my bags, and had breakfast at one of our favorite places before heading over. Now he's beside me in the elevator that climbs floor after floor, holding all my copious luggage and trying to chat with me, but my mind is elsewhere.

"I was thinking convertible cribs, so when they get older—hey, Petra, are you even listening?" he interjects, snapping me out of my daze.

"What? Oh, sorry. I've just got a lot on my mind," I admit.

"Understandable, but I promise you I'll make you listen to my diatribe about cribs sooner or later," he states firmly, teasing me to try to lighten my mood.

I rise to my tiptoes and brush my lips over his cheek. "I can't think of anything I'd love more."

The elevator dings and we exit, Alex rolling both of my suitcases behind him. We stop and check with the nurses' station, and the woman there directs us to our hospital room. I say a silent prayer for Mariana when we find room 451, because it's more like a beautiful hotel suite rather than a birthing room.

The floors are a lovely light-colored wood, reflective with the sealant that would keep errant stains away, the walls painted a soothing sage. Most noticeably, is the back wall, which isn't really a wall at all. Instead, floor-to-ceiling windows dominate the space, looking over an emerald-green

Central Park. Attached to my room is a private bathroom, and next to my bed is a plush fold-out sofa bed, currently in its sofa form. The only thing giving this place away as a hospital room is my bed. It's a bit larger than other hospital beds I have seen, but it still has the railings and adjustable frames, along with the machines and wirings tucked neatly behind it.

I don't love it here, but at least I'll be comfortable enough. It's just a little past 9 a.m., and the sunshine we had earlier is now broken up by an early rain shower. It makes the city hazy, and the minuscule droplets hung on the vast windows of my room, darkening it, and giving the whole place a sleepy vibe.

Alex nods in approval as he follows me in, tucking my luggage next to my bed before walking around the suite. "Mariana did well. This is an acceptable place for you to stay for as long as you need."

I join him where he is standing in front of the window overlooking the city, a pensive look on his face. When I sidle up next to him, he slips his arm around my waist and I lean my head on his shoulder, both of us gazing outside.

"We're in the home stretch now, love," he rumbles, kissing the top of my head. "Almost to the finish line."

I close my eyes, soaking in his quiet nearness while we are still alone. "I feel like it's too soon and we aren't ready," I disclose, letting him know my concerns. "But I also feel like this week is going to take forever."

"Don't count the days, Petra. You're going to obsess over each hour until the babies are here and it's going to drive you insane. Just let your body decide when it's time."

I huff, "Easy for you to say."

We stay like this for some time, slowly adjusting to our new normal for the time being. My feet are aching after a bit, so I take a seat on my bed, slipping off my sandals and tucking them neatly under the bed before donning the non-slip hospital socks that are hanging over the railing for me.

Alex settles himself next to me, giving the socks an amused glance. "You've never looked sexier."

"I'm sure they can get you a pair if you really want," I reply, wiggling my now warm toes.

After spending the next thirty minutes unpacking some of my stuff, including a soft down comforter and feather pillows, to make my bed more comfortable, Mariana arrives with a nurse in tow.

"Well, how do you like the new digs?" she queries.

"It's nice, and I like that it's so bright," I tell her, pushing down any sadness I have about not being able to spend my days and nights at home with Alex.

"Yes, I hate for my expectant mothers to feel like they're in a dungeon. The happier you all are, the healthier the babies will be," Mariana agrees.

She and her nurse power on the machines and untangle the wires. Then she has me sit on the bed, pulling my shirt up to attach the sensors to my skin. The largest of them wraps completely around my belly, and I can tell it's going to take some time getting used to. It's awkward and uncomfortable, but a necessary evil, I suppose.

Once I'm completely hooked up to the machines, Mariana checks my vitals and investigates the readouts from the sensors. She nods thoughtfully, seeming pleased with the setup.

"Everything looks just as I thought. Are you comfortable Petra?"

I shift around, standing up and sitting a few times to test the range of the wires. "It's weird, but not too bad. I definitely feel like a science experiment though."

Mariana chuckles as she does a few other minor adjustments before standing back and dusting her hands off.

"Now that you're hooked up, we have one other thing to discuss today." And by her tone, it sounds quite serious. "My colleagues and I are confident that you'll need a c-section in the next few days," she announces, and it makes my heart fall to my knees; twenty-eight weeks is so early. "We recommend a steroid shot, called glucocorticoids, that mimics natural cortisol and speeds up lung development for the fetuses. Underdeveloped lungs are one of the more dangerous complications associated with premature growth."

"And you think my babies will need this shot?" I ask. I'm reluctant to add any extra medications that aren't necessary, so I need to be sure before I agree to anything.

"In my opinion, it'd be beneficial. I recommend it to any mother at risk for premature growth. It's a tried-and-true treatment with few side effects," Mariana explains.

I frown at the words *side effects*. "And those few side effects are…?"

Mariana sighs, pulling up a chair and sitting down. She knows me well enough by now that she must realize she's going to have to explain everything to me. "There are the usual non problematic side effects that come with all steroids; flushing of the face, increased urination, trouble sleeping, and water retention, meaning you might swell up a little. Nothing of any long-term consequence." Mariana pauses for a beat, and then proceeds. "The only side effects of note are that rarely, birth weight for the baby may be lower, there is a chance for decreased fetal movement, and recent studies seem to suggest that children of mothers who receive these shots have a higher chance of mental health and behavioral problems in childhood and young adulthood."

The two that really catch my attention are the reduced fetal weight at birth and the mental health problems. I roll the options over in my mind, torn. I look to Alex for his opinion.

"I say do it if the serious side effects are as uncommon as Mariana says, but it's your choice. I'll support whatever you decide."

Thankful for his support, I know what my answer will be. "I'm going to decline. Jasmine is already going to be so small, and she'll also be dealing with Turner's Syndrome as she grows up. I can't risk her being even smaller at birth and I don't want to add any mental health issues on top of the Turner's Syndrome."

Mariana rubs her temples. I know I'm a pain in her ass, but my instincts haven't steered me wrong yet. "Okay, no shot then," she says, resigned. "You can change your mind at any time, but knowing you as I do, I imagine you won't."

"Thank you, I really appreciate that." I hope flattery will make her a little less annoyed with me, but she just gives me the side eye while she gathers her things.

With a long-suffering exhale, she explains nurses will be in and out to check my vitals during the day, and if the monitors detect anything strange, an alarm will go off. I guess Lily will be in to see me periodically as well, to make sure I'm still eating enough and being mindful of my delicate condition.

"I've heard the chef makes wonderful vegan meals here for the patients, so you don't have to worry about it, but if Alex wants to bring you some snacks or meals from outside, that's perfectly acceptable. Are there any other questions you have for me before I go to finish the rest of my rounds?"

I shake my head. "No, I'm good."

"Help is right at your fingertips if you need it, Petra. Get some rest and settle in and I will see you later." With that, Mariana leaves, and Alex and I are alone in the room.

He helps me get comfortable on the bed, and I raise the top portion up with the remote control until it sits upright like a chair. I have brought a plethora of books to read for my exams, but right now I honestly feel like having a nap.

"You can go to the office for now," I tell Alex. "I'm going to be here all day and night, so don't worry about me. I know you have work things to take care of."

Alex looks hesitant. "It isn't fair to leave you here alone."

"You don't have to babysit me twenty-four seven, Alex. I'll be fine, promise."

He frowns, but nods. "I do need to get some things done, but I'll be back tonight, okay? Decide what you want for dinner and text me. I'll bring you anything you want."

"You really know the way to a pregnant woman's heart," I murmur as he leans over to kiss me soundly on the mouth.

"If I'm lucky, you'll always be this easy to please. I'll see you tonight, love." He gives me a quick wave before heading out, and then finally the room is quiet—aside from the pitter patter of the raindrops on the window.

I power down the overhead lights and yawn hugely. Trying my best to be mindful of my many wires, I burrow down into the bed and close my eyes for a quick snooze.

***

It's 3 p.m. and I'm munching on a cucumber salad, watching a few pre-recorded classes on my laptop, when there is a knock on the door to my suite.

"Come in!" I yell, assuming it's another nurse here for my vitals.

To my surprise, my dad walks in, whistling low as he looks around the suite.

"This is quite the place, for a hospital at least," he comments.

"You know Alex, no expense is spared." I hug him when he walks to the bed, aware of my monitors.

Dad attentively inspects the room, and sits on the couch, absentmindedly flipping through one magazine on the end table next to it as he gathers his thoughts. Then he stands and walking back in my direction, he says, "Doctors think you're gonna need an emergency c-section in the next few days, is it true?"

I grimace. "Ugh…don't remind me." So much for the *everything is gonna be alright* speech I told him over the phone this morning.

"I have to say, I'm relieved you're under constant observation," he discloses, walking toward me. "I know you don't want to talk nitty-gritty details about complications, but twins can be rough even in the best of circumstances."

"These circumstances are anything but typical," I retort. "I just don't want to get into it right now Dad."

"No worries, Petra. I won't ask."

We chat about Columbia, the book about objectivism he offered me, and other light subjects. It's nice to have a break from the constant baby-centric conversations. It can't last, though, and Dad eventually asks a more serious question that has been on his mind.

"Have you heard from Margaret or any of your other in-laws? I sent her a message but never heard back. I'd think they'd want to be here, too."

The subject sends a needle of remorse through me. "Alex and I spoke to her a few days ago to let her know about the pregnancy," I disclose. "And, um, we told her only to come once the twins are born." I pause for a beat, letting out a sigh. "I get the feeling Margaret hates me because I rejected her invitation to come sooner."

Dad scowls. "After everything she did to your mom, hating you would be a big mistake." His comment brings a smile to my lips, but as I keep looking at him, Dad seems to be hesitant whether to ask another question or not. "Do you think it was her who gave the order to…you know?"

His question doesn't shock me; I have asked myself that very same question over and over again. Who activated those nano-particles in my mom's body? Eric failed to prove that Alex knew about them, but I'm sure Margaret and the rest of my in-laws knew. "I think it was all of them—Margaret, Julia, Yara, Maud…" Before letting those gloomy memories settle in, I force myself to smile and say, "But it belongs to the past now. All I want is to keep my distance from them." I sink back down into the bed, trying not to dwell on the dark past of my in-laws.

"Hey," Dad says softly. "Fuck them, am I right?"

I gasp at his language, and then laugh. "I guess you're right."

"One more thing," Dad says, becoming more nervous at every passing second. "I'm not sure if you and Alex have already thought about the surname for the kids, but…" He glances down for a second, searching for his next set of words carefully. "Just in case you want to be a bit more, um, you know, modern, Gatt-Dieren is a fine option too."

I can't help but laugh at his suggestion. Oh gosh, my dad will never change. I look at him tenderly as I finally understand his concern. After all, he's an only child just like me and I know he's afraid his family name will fall into oblivion after he passes away.

I don't know what to tell him, but I love my dad too much to at least not have a thought about it. "I'll talk to Alex about it," I say to appease him.

"Oh, I already gave him a word before coming here." Another laugh rolls off my lips as I see how tenacious he is about such a small detail.

"So just have a little talk between the two of you," he presses on and before I can close the subject once and for all, he adds, "But Jasmine Gatt-Dieren sounds very nice to me."

"I get it," I step in, shaking my head at his behavior. He can be really persistent sometimes.

"Alright, alright…" He leans down and gives me a quick kiss on the head. "If you need anything, and I mean anything, just call me. Even if it's a bagel at midnight or a book you forgot at home. I'm here for you. And I love you, very much."

Touched, I hold my hand over my heart. "I love you too, Dad." His smile is warm and reassuring, and before it gets too awkward, I say, "Now, let's talk about grandparent nicknames. I'm thinking about Grandpa, or Pop Pop. What's your opinion?"

* * *

Manhattan, May 29, 2021
Petra Van Gatt

The first night wasn't too terrible, especially with Alex on the sofa beside my bed. I had trouble getting comfortable, but it wasn't the end of the world. Now, the next morning, after Alex has already left, one of my nurses is checking my vitals when an aid knocks on the door.

"If you're about done, she has a visitor," the aid tells the nurse. I'm a bit curious to know who is visiting, but I wait patiently for the nurse to finish up her duties.

The nurse scratches down a few more notes before clicking her pen shut. "All done! Send the visitor in."

I'm shocked when Emma walks in. She's given me no heads up, and since we are still a bit at odds because of our last discussion about Yara, I hadn't been expecting her.

"Emma!" I gasp, sitting up straighter on my bed.

"Hey," she says shyly with a little wave. "Is this a bad time?"

"No! Never! Come in." I motion her forward, excited to see her despite any lingering animosity there may be between us. After all, she's still my best friend.

She walks in, a bit apprehensively at first and stops at my bedside. "Um, here. I got you something," she says as she hands me a small burlap bag. My eyes widen in surprise at the unexpected gift.

"Oh, thank you," I say, shaking out the contents into my hand. I take from there a small box and after opening it, I find inside a bracelet made with smooth red stones shot through with darker scarlet and brown veins.

It's a strange gift, but if I know Emma, there's a meaning behind it. "It's gorgeous, thank you," I tell her, slipping it over my wrist.

Emma smiles slowly, ruffling her short obsidian hair nervously, before taking a seat on the side of the hospital bed. "It's made of jasper crystals, which block negative energy toward you and help you heal. I heard from… I heard that you're being admitted and thought it might help."

I turn my wrist back and forth, so the stones catch the light. "What a beautiful stone. What's the name again?"

"Um, jasper." She picks up the discarded burlap bag and pulls out a tiny booklet, handing it to me. "Here."

I take the small pamphlet in my hands and start reading out loud the description of the stone. "Jasper brings vitality and a surge of life force energy. It inspires a positive attitude, giving you the motivation to chase your dreams." I chuckle. "Seems like exactly what I need, especially the positive attitude. I feel like I have a nurse poking and prodding all over me every five minutes."

Emma winces. "That sucks. How long are you going to stay here for?"

"I don't know. The doctors seem to be as clueless as I am. I might be the first of my kind when it comes to this pregnancy." I groan with exasperation. "Mariana, my obstetrician, is certain Jasmine is going to go into reverse cord flow and will need to be delivered this week. Yet, so far, she seems all good."

"Jasmine? Oh, so you already have a name for the girl?" Emma sits up a little straighter at the news, interested.

"Yep," I say, a small smile playing on my lips. "We are still trying to figure out a name for the boy, though."

"I always thought boys' names were harder, too," she tells me. "I'm sure everything is gonna be alright, though."

For a moment neither of us speak, but then Emma blurts out, "Yara told me Alex spoke to her."

Oh-oh… I bite my lip, carefully choosing my next set of words. "And, um, are you still seeing her?" I ask.

"I am." She sounds defensive. "And I want you to stop interfering with us."

"Emma—!" I try to interject, but she keeps talking, on a roll now.

"You are behaving like your mom right now," she rants, "And frankly, that's ridiculous."

Her words hit me like a ton of bricks, cutting me right to the core. "I just don't want her to abuse you or break your heart," I tell her sincerely. "You are my best friend and if she does anything to you…"

"I'll be fine," she hisses. "I'm an adult, you know." Her mouth is pinched, expression serious. "I don't want you or your husband mingling between us. Plus, we just see each other from time to time, so it's not like we are a couple." She heaves a loud breath in annoyance, and then says, "Let me deal with my own life, okay?"

I ponder her question for a moment. "Okay. You're right, I need to do a better job at trusting you." I lay my hand on top of hers and, looking her in the eye, I say, "I'm sorry for not loving you as you do."

"Don't be silly," she answers, slightly uncomfortable. "You love me exactly the way a best friend should."

"I know, but I hope one day you'll find someone you can be with openly." I wrinkle my nose. "Not someone like Yara though."

Emma laughs, relief plain in her tone. "She's not so bad. Plus, I'm good, don't worry about me."

"Are you spending the summer here?" I ask, trying to change the subject a bit.

She tilts her head one way and then the other. "Well, I have a plane booked for Nice but with you pregnant, I don't know if I should go or not…"

"Of course you should!" I insist. "God knows when they are gonna come out. At this point it could be in the next five minutes or the next five weeks. Please enjoy your life, Emma. Be careful with Yara though. You're not going to convince me to like her."

"I'll be cautious, I promise." She embraces me tightly and I return the hug, thankful that we are back on good terms. "If you need anything, you call me, alright?"

Teary-eyed, I nod. "I will."

We cut the tender moment short when Alex saunters in, still in a suit and tie from work. He raises his eyebrows. "Hello, Emma."

She stands abruptly, grabbing her purse. "Uh, hi Alex. I'm just leaving."

Emma gives me a last quick hug and hurries out. My head is spinning at her hasty departure, and Alex shrugs. "Guess she still hates me for speaking to my sister," he comments, taking Emma's place on my bed.

"Give her some time," I tell him.

"So any news regarding their little affair?" he asks.

"Yep, Yara and Emma are still together," I confess. "And she came here to let me know I should mind my own business—actually, that *we* should mind our own business."

Alex looks contemplative for a moment. "I told my sister to leave Emma alone, or else I'd call Elliott. If you want, I can still go ahead and call him."

I consider it for a second before shaking my head. "No, Emma would hate me. I just told her I trusted her and wouldn't let Yara come between us."

"I personally think that's the right choice too."

Alex, still fully dressed, lays back against the raised bed with me, threading his fingers through mine and holding my hand up to eye level. "What's this bracelet?"

"Oh! Yeah, Emma brought it for me. It's jasper, a healing gem full of positive energy." I shake my wrist so the stones jingle together. "Alex... I was just thinking... What about the name Jasper for Baby A? It starts with the same three letters as Jasmine."

Alex hums as he thinks about it, before bringing my hand that he's holding to his lips for a kiss. "I love it."

"Really?" I ask, beaming at the news.

"Absolutely. Our little Jasmine and Jasper. It sounds perfect."

I snuggle into him, inhaling his scent deeply, feeling content and comforted. "It really does."

CHAPTER 32

Manhattan, May 28, 2021
Petra Van Gatt

"So," Mariana begins, typing away on her laptop she has on top of a rolling trolley. She looks a mix of embarrassed and happy at the same time. Embarrassed because, despite her and her colleagues telling me otherwise, it has been a week, and so far, no emergency c-section has been needed; happy because obviously this is great news for everyone. "I've never had a pregnancy as unpredictable as yours before," she finally admits. And I definitely believe her on that. "By the scans we did, it was clear by now a lot could have happened and an emergency c-section was very likely to happen."

"But it didn't," I interpose.

"Exactly, so I think it's safe to assume that we can deliver later on, maybe around thirty-six weeks."

Wow! Now this is excellent news! I look instantly at Alex who's standing beside me, beaming with joy as much as I am, and he gives me a quick squeeze on my arm.

"I wanted to confirm with the two of you if it would be okay to schedule the c-section."

I knew talking about delivery schedules was coming but confirming that I'd have to have a cesarean is still a little disappointing. "Are you positive we can't have a natural birth?"

"Since the babies share the same placenta, the second baby would be at a substantial risk directly after the first is born. With a c-section, both can come out within seconds of each other. It's the only way my team and I deliver any set of twins sharing a placenta, not just yours."

Resigned to my fate, I sigh. "I get it. Okay, let's schedule it, then."

"Perfect," Mariana says, handing me a stack of papers for the birthing plan. "I'm going to give you two some time to fill this out, and we will try to make it as close to what you're wanting as possible."

"And, um, do I need to stay at the hospital until then?" I ask.

"We can discharge you after doing a last growth scan. But I want to check on you again in three weeks time."

Alex thanks Mariana as she leaves while I flip through the packet. Once Mariana is gone, Alex sits on the bed with me, carefully avoiding the monitor cords. We look through everything, and Alex runs a hand through his hair.

"This is… a lot more than I expected."

"Me too." I moan, grabbing my pen and getting to work. "I'm not going to be able to finish this all today. I have studying to do."

Alex frowns. "It's insane to me you didn't take time off to give birth."

"I did," I counter. "But I have no excuse to not take the exams since they are online."

Alex waves my excuse off. "Never mind, I know I'm not going to talk any sense into you." He pauses, reflecting on his next words. "Speaking of exams, have you talked again to that boy?"

The question takes me off guard and I sit the pen down. "Matt? No. Why do you ask?" I say hesitantly.

"Because I've spoken to him. He wanted to know how you were doing and he told me he understands why you're ducking his calls and texts, but he wishes you well."

I'm shocked to hear that Alex spoke to Matt. So shocked that I open and close my mouth a few times, trying to find the right words. "You.... what? You talked to Matt? Why?"

Alex looks serious as he continues on. "When you were lonely and suffering, and I wasn't there for you, he was. That's reason enough for me to set aside any animosity I had toward him. I still think he's a chronic boundary-pusher, but I took his call." Alex takes the pen and paper from me and sets them aside, wanting to have my full attention. I look up at him expectantly. "I just want you to know that if you want to continue to be friends with Matt, I won't oppose it."

"Alex," I whisper. "Thank you. I'm so surprised, but still... thank you."

It seems silly, but even though Alex is older than me, his accepting Matt really shows me how much he's grown as a person these last few months. I know he's right, and that I should call Matt, but the thought just makes me incredibly uncomfortable.

I shudder, thinking about the gala, when Alex had exposed to me Sarah and Matt hooking up.

Had Matt messed up by not telling me about Sarah? Yes. But he's still someone who cares for me, and I need to stop avoiding him.

"You alright in there?" Alex asks gently, tapping my temple with one finger. I blow out a breath before nodding.

"Yeah. Let's finish this baby homework," I say, reaching to grab the packet again. "So I can get back to doing my real homework."

*** * ***

After doing a last growth scan and checking my vitals one last time, I'm finally discharged and good to go. Jeez, one entire week spent at the hospital for nothing.

Reaching back home, I isolate myself in our study and settle in with my laptop and books to give one last review for the exam in macroeconomics that will happen online tomorrow morning. With the books spread all over the desk, I try to focus as much as I can, but the talk with Alex about Matt hasn't left my mind. I heave a sigh, trying to shove it off, but it simply doesn't go away. The thought makes me nostalgic for the afternoons I spent in the library with Matt, struggling to read beneath the old lights as we worked through everything as a pair. It also makes me think of our chess games, and how many hours had passed as we played away, two competitors almost evenly matched.

Damn. I should really give him a call, at least to let him know the babies and I are fine. I go over my MacBook to the launchpad and see the FaceTime app. I tap my fingers nervously for a moment. I'm reluctant to take the step, but I gather the nerve and go ahead.

A part of me hopes he doesn't answer, so I can at least feel like I've made the effort, and the other part is terrified that if he doesn't answer, it means that he's given up on our friendship, but I don't have to wonder long.

"Petra?" Matt says, surprised, when he pops up onto my screen.

"Uh, hi," I start lamely.

Matt exhales, gathering his thoughts. "It's been a while."

"Yeah... I'm sorry about that. I shouldn't have ignored you," I say, unable to meet his gaze on the screen.

"Hey..." Matt soothes, "Don't worry about it. Things are weird. I get it."

I sniffle a little at hearing his voice and seeing his face, but I make an effort to keep my composure. "How are you doing?"

"Studying hard," Matt says, his voice pleasant. "Look, um, I want to apologize for not telling you about Sarah. We spent so much time together, and I never told you that she and I were more than just friends. This is all my fault."

"I'd have been a little weirded out, but I just want you to be happy," I say with a touch of sadness in my voice. "I want you to trust that we can share anything with each other."

"Same goes for you," Matt says seriously. "How long did we hang out before you told me all the complications with your pregnancy? That wasn't right either."

"I know," I reply miserably. "It just hurt to talk about."

Matt sighs and rubs his eyes. "You're right. It's a much more sensitive subject."

"I probably wouldn't have been so sick if I had just talked to you or another friend about it, though. My midwife told me that holding all of that poisonous stuff inside can make you physically ill."

"At least now you know," he says awkwardly.

"Hey, so Alex said you two talked. Why in the world would you call him?" I ask, wanting to get all the uncomfortable things out of the way.

"Um, I wasn't exactly looking to be his friend, but I hadn't heard from you in so long and I was worried sick. So I called him, and shockingly, it was cordial." Matt takes a deep breath. "Petra, can we just let bygones be bygones?"

What a relief. I'm so glad that he suggested just moving forward, because I had not been looking forward to hashing everything out. "Yes, please."

"Awesome." I can see his brilliant smile across the screen. "Now that that's over, how are you? What are you up to?"

I roll my eyes, holding the laptop a little higher and waving it around the desk and the study room so he can see where I am. "Only the most miserable thing in existence: studying Macro."

"Ouch," Matt comments with a chuckle. "Why don't you fill me in on the last few weeks before I help you with it?"

We FaceTime for over forty-five minutes, discussing everything from my birthing plan to what I thought about our online professors. Matt is always quick to laugh, and his goofy mood lightens mine significantly. Matt is just explaining a few concepts in Macro I was having trouble with when I hear his dad bellow his name in the background of the call. I grimace.

"Uh-oh," I comment while Matt's shoulders fall in dejection.

"I've got to go," he tells me reluctantly.

"It's okay, I—" I stop as the door opens, seeing Alex come in with another man behind him. "Oops, me too. It was nice to see you."

"Nice to see you too, P. Talk to you soon. Bye!"

"Bye!" I echo, clicking the laptop off with a happy sigh. It feels so good to let the negativity of my strained relationships go, one by one.

Setting my homework aside, I turn to Alex and his guest. "Hey baby, what's up?"

"Petra, this is Leonardo, the interior designer I hired for the nursery. Leo, my wife, Petra."

"A pleasure to meet you," Leonardo drawls. He's a shorter man, fashionably dressed with an eccentric jacket and matching glasses frames, and holding a briefcase overflowing with papers.

"We've got a few ideas for how to start the nursery, but I wanted your input before we make a final decision," Alex says excitedly, hustling over with a ton of printouts, pulling them on the desk and spreading the papers out in front of me. It's a cacophony of colors and pictures, some bright, but most of them muted neutrals.

"What is all this?" I ask slowly, my mind struggling to switch from Macro to baby room design.

"It's all the designs Mr. Van Dieren has resonated with," Leonardo says sagely, "We believe with one boy and one girl that the nursery will need to be twice as big as normal and done in neutral tones that have no association with gender." Leo walks closer and plucks one page off the desk. It has ivory-colored cribs with diaphanous netting flowing around them from the ceiling, everything ranging in hue from dark khaki to stark white, with hints of a natural green here and there. "Of course," Leo continues, showing me another page where instead of green accents, there are blush pink and powder blue hints in the room, "We could also incorporate the traditional blues and pinks in small amounts if that's something that is important to you."

I shake my head, my brain feeling like a spinning top. "Slow down, please."

"I didn't want you to have to worry about it, but I also wanted you to have a big part in picking everything out," Alex explains excitedly, practically buzzing as he speaks.

I frown at him and wonder if he has been working on the nursery with Leo while I was at the hospital, but he doesn't notice, and instead, he pulls out around a dozen Pantone color swatches and spreads them out in a fan for me. "Pick your three favorite," Alex cajoles.

"No," I say bluntly.

This time it's Alex with a sour look on his face. "Petra, Leo and his team have been working on this all week."

"I understand that, but you can't just spring this on me out of nowhere," I yelp, getting more hot-headed by the second.

Leonardo flinches. Alex clenches his teeth before telling the other man, "I'm sorry, Leo, can we try this again tomorrow?"

"Absolutely, sir," he gushes, gathering his errant papers, suddenly in a rush to get away from my crazy pregnant self.

"I'm sorry, Leo. It was lovely to meet you," I assure him as he prances out quickly and shuts the door of the office behind him.

"Petra," Alex grits out. "Please explain why I just had to send away one of the best interior designers of the city when you might give birth at any moment?"

Ugh. Here we go. "Alex, the pregnancy is so high risk. I don't want to make any plans until we are sure everything is going to be okay. What if we make a nursery for two and only one makes it? It'd kill me inside." I try not to have any hitch in my voice as I speak, but it still catches, much to my embarrassment.

He continues to scowl. "Stop being so fatalistic. You can't avoid making some decisions forever."

"Even after both babies are born, they'd still be in the NICU for weeks!" I insist. "You're getting too far ahead of yourself!"

He shakes his head in displeasure, and snaps, "And you not enough." He tries to hand me the paint swatches. "At least pick out a color for the walls."

I cross my arms. "I said I'm not talking about this."

"Fine," Alex hisses, tossing the swatches in the nearby garbage can. "They can just have bare drywall. Is that what you want?"

"No!" I groan, rubbing my temples. "I just...I don't want a reminder of what I've lost if something goes wrong."

Alex's expression softens, and without a word he fishes the swatches from the trash can and stacks them with the nursery room example pictures. "Okay. I'll lay off for now. But only if you promise that after the next growth scan you'll go over the nursery decor with me and buy some baby clothes."

Relieved that he wouldn't push the issue, I remove my backpack resting on the chair beside me and pat the empty seat for him. My grumpy husband sits down with a huff and I wrap my arms around him. He's stiff at first, but as I pillow my cheek on the crest of his neck, he gradually relaxes.

"Thank you for understanding," I tell him, kissing him swiftly. "I promise."

CHAPTER 33

Manhattan, June 18, 2021
Petra Van Gatt

"I know we've been over this, but can you explain it one more time, Mariana?"

The obstetrician smiles patiently. She's been easier to talk to the further along I get, and secretly I think it's because she's becoming more and more sure Jasmine and Jasper are going to make it. After all, I'm already at thirty-two weeks, and in four more we have the c-section scheduled. Mariana may rival me for stubbornness, though, so I bet she won't confirm my suspicions until she's one hundred percent sure.

"No problem. We're going to put a blood pressure monitor on you and a fetal heart rate monitor on your stomach to chart the babies' movements, oxygen levels, and heart rates," she explains, slower this time. "We'll probably have you sit here for around twenty minutes so we can get the best idea possible of how the babies are doing, but if anything abnormal is detected, then we'll extend the test to forty minutes." She works on attaching the sensors, as she continues. "What we're looking for is their heart rates to raise above a certain level for fifteen-seconds twice in a twenty-minute window."

I blow out a breath, my hair feathering away from my face as I do so. "This sounds way better than the amniocentesis."

"Almost anything is better than an amniocentesis," Mariana commiserates. "I still hate that you had to go through that."

"Not as much as I hated it, I assure you."

Mariana shrugs after attaching the last monitor. "You're probably right. Are you comfortable?"

I nod. I'm actually quite cozy this time around. Instead of a stiff hospital bed, I'm getting to chill in a cushy recliner and read one of my books while the test goes on. Mariana checks a few more things on the attached machines before placing her hands on her hips.

"We're all set," she says. "I'll be back in twenty minutes to read the results."

"See you then," I tell her, settling in to read.

I'm fully absorbed in my story when Alex comes in, after finishing a call with one of his clients. "All good?" he asks, before leaning down to give me a kiss on the forehead.

"Mmm," I utter, still engrossed in my reading. Then I turn the page, and add, "Just waiting for the test to be over."

A few minutes later, one machine beeps and Mariana comes back. "Let's see what we've got here," she murmurs, tapping on her always-present laptop to see the results. Her expression is pleasant at first, but after a few minutes, she furrows her brow.

"Nothing to be concerned about yet, but we aren't seeing the right results for Baby B that we'd like. I want to go another twenty minutes."

Of course it hadn't gone right. Would anything ever be easy? "Alright, then."

She resets everything, checking the sensors for accuracy. "Sometimes the babies will be sleeping, so we're going to give them a little surprise to get them up." She holds up a small device that's smaller than her hand. "This will feel like a buzz on your belly, but it's like an alarm clock for fetuses."

"Hear that?" I ask my belly with a little pat. "Time to get up!"

She presses the buzzer to my belly and presses the button. It feels like my cell phone vibrating from a text, turned up to ten. I actually jump before laughing nervously. One baby was equally taken aback, jerking in my stomach as if someone had shaken them awake.

"That was really weird," I comment, rubbing the sensitive spot where she had zapped me.

Mariana sets the timer again and leaves, and this time I find it hard to concentrate on the book. I try to squint and read the computer screen on my monitors, but it's no use, so I eventually sit back and close my eyes. I've almost dozed off when the machine beeps again and Mariana returns.

She looks over the readouts and sighs heavily this time. I feel the blood drain from my face.

"What's wrong?" I demand.

"It's nothing huge. We're still reading two heartbeats, but the test was considered nonreactive. Neither heart rate elevated for the full fifteen-seconds."

I start to breathe heavily, a million questions racing through my mind, but Mariana kneels in front of the recliner and lays her hands on my shoulders. "It's going to be fine. We can try the test again later and remember both heartbeats are still there. Let's go get your growth scan and try to unravel this mystery, hm? Just breathe."

"Okay…. okay…" I breathe slowly in for three counts and out for three counts until I get control of myself again. "I'm good," I say, giving her a shaky thumbs up.

Next, it's time for the growth scan, which is a longer detailed ultrasound that includes specific measurements. I've been getting those every three weeks, so I'm already pretty used to them by now. Alex is now holding my hand, running his thumb over my knuckles as we watch the ultrasound screen.

Mariana's face is drawn and tight when she finally says, voice full of trepidation, "Baby B hasn't grown since your last scan."

WHAT? My heart sinks at her words. My *last* scan? That was three weeks ago! I can't breathe. I can't think. All I can say is, "Okay, reschedule my surgery for sooner please." I can hear my own voice, and it sounds thready and frightened. "Like tomorrow or something."

"Are you sure?" Alex asks, with shock in his eyes. "Isn't it too early?"

"Absolutely," I say, not actually feeling certain at all. But if Jasmine hasn't been growing for the last three weeks, and if her heartbeat is being considered nonreactive, something is off.

"I agree. This is the safest option, not that either of you cares much for my opinion," Mariana says sarcastically, in a vain attempt at humor. Neither of us respond, and she pulls out her calendar to check her schedule. "Is Monday at ten a.m., okay for you?"

"Absolutely," I say again, at a loss for other words.

"We've gone over all of this in the birth plan, so it's going to be okay. You're on the back end of premature, so you're hopefully past the worst of the complications and survival rates are pretty high. Don't eat any solids twelve hours before surgery, alright?"

Alex looks between the two of us, having gone pale under the tan of his skin. "Holy shit," he mutters.

Oh my gosh, this is really happening. And all I have is the weekend to gather myself, my feelings, my thoughts, and to get ready to do this.

***

Arriving home after such bad news is bittersweet. My mind is frantically thinking about every little detail of the birth and afterwards, and I'm wringing my hands as we walk into the front door, not even seeing my home through the haze of panic.

Alex takes my hands gently and pulls them apart, encapsulating them in his own. "Hey, you. Earth to Petra. Come on, like Mariana said, deep breaths."

Once again, I follow directions, three in and three out, until my galloping heart grows quiet in my chest.

"I'm so scared," I force out, my throat feeling as narrow as a straw, making my words sound thin.

"I'm scared too," Alex tells me, squeezing my hands, "But we're facing this together. So let's prepare for battle. What do you say?"

"O-okay," I agree, and Alex kisses me on the forehead.

I can do this. I have to do this!

Later, I sit on my bed, surrounded by my maternity clothes and post-maternity outfits I had chosen for comfort. I'm folding them neatly in my newly emptied suitcase while Alex handles the non-clothing essentials. He brings me a duffle bag full of toiletries and drops it on the floor by the bed.

"I just realized we don't have a single outfit to bring the babies home in," he says, throwing his hands in the air in exasperation. "How are we so far behind?"

"Well, we don't even know for how long they are gonna stay in the NICU, anyway," I answer.

"And they won't wear anything there?" Alex asks, crossing his arms.

"Fine, pick out whatever you want," I reply smugly, not even bothering to look up from my folding. Mariana told me they will have everything they need at the NICU for the preemies, but it's pointless arguing about such a tiny detail like clothes with Alex. He reminds me of his dad when he came here full of gifts despite telling him it was unnecessary.

Alex sits next to me on the clothing covered bed and pulls out his phone, showing me the screen. On it is a cart filled with over fifty items in it, with the "next day delivery" option checked.

"Ninety dollars in shipping!?" I guffaw.

"It's next day!" Alex retorts. "Do you even want to look at them?"

I groan. "No. Just order them and I'll pick out some more later when you're not breathing down my neck about it."

Alex complains under his breath, but I see him hit the "buy" button. He's seemed almost incapable of containing his excitement since we arrived home, getting distracted from every task I assign him to shop online or paint test stripes on the nursery wall with the eleven cans of sample paint he had acquired.

"You promised you'd look at this kind of stuff after the scan," Alex reminds me, a trace of frustration in his voice.

"Alex... things have changed! I had no idea I'd be giving birth on Monday! I've got things I have to do to prepare."

"Yes, and that includes getting the babies' nursery ready," he responds.

"Look—" I sigh, setting the clothes I'm folding aside. "When I found out I was pregnant, I always imagined I'd have a normal delivery—water breaking, contractions, pushing, and so on," I tell him. "And then I thought I'd go home the next day and take my babies with me. But this is not the case here. This pregnancy is everything but the one I imagined."

"I know." His tone is low and serious. "Sometimes life doesn't go according to plan," Alex says, reaching out to lay a hand on my belly. "But the most important thing is that they come to this world alive and healthy."

"That's what I'm so worried about." I gulp, not even wanting to give voice to the terrible thing on my mind. "I keep thinking about what Auntie Louise said... about death and misery. I'm terrified at the idea that Jasmine—" I choke back a sob. "That Jasmine will be stillborn."

I can see Alex wince at the word, pain evident in his features. "You can't think about that. We've come so far and defied too many odds. We're going to defy this one too, and be a perfect, strong, healthy family of four in just a few days."

I wipe the tears streaming down my cheeks, looking at Alex from under my wet lashes. "You really think so? You're not just telling me what I want to hear? You really believe we will all be okay?"

"I do. I have to." I'm surprised to hear the genuine emotion in his tone, his voice thick with it when he speaks. He brushes the last of my tears away and kisses my lips gently, lingering for a long moment before whispering, "I've been waiting for all of you my whole life."

***

"Alex, I'm so freaking tired. I don't want to have brunch!" I tell him when he ushers me to the bedroom to get ready.

It's 11 a.m. on Sunday morning and the last thing I want is to go out to a crowded restaurant for an avocado toast. Yet, Alex hasn't stopped insisting until I put on the adorable gauzy bandana-hem maternity dress he had bought and let Maria curl my hair. She pats some concealer on my dark under eyes and brightens my skin with some highlighter until I almost look like a catalog maternity model. I blink at my reflection a few times, turning back and forth in the mirror as the pastel yellow skirt swings around my legs. For a second, I'm feeling lightheaded and even excited to go out.

Except, when I exit the bedroom, we aren't leaving at all. "The brunch is here," Alex says, a Cheshire cat grin on his face.

"What the heck are you talking about?" I demand, looking around.

"Hush, you." Alex takes my hand and leads me to the outdoor terrace.

"What's going on?" I ask Alex, my instincts tingling. What is he up to?

"Come on," he insists, ignoring my question.

We head up to the terrace, which is half shaded and half open, and I'm dying to know what Alex has up his sleeve. As the doors open, a cacophony of voices yell, "SURPRISE!!!"

Before I can get my bearings, I'm being pulled into one set of arms after the other, receiving cheek kisses and gentle belly rubs along the way. Alex is laughing as I'm caught in the whirlwind of well-wishers until I come out the other side dazed and laughing.

The faces of Dad, Janine, Emma, and Matt look back at me with brilliant smiles, and it's all I can do not to cry seeing all the people I love. I turn on my heel to Alex.

"You did this!" I marvel, hardly believing he had planned this thing on such short notice.

Someone had set the table with all sorts of fresh fruits, muffins, and scones. To drink there is an enormous variety of fruit juices, sparkling waters, and decaffeinated iced tea. But the food matters very little to me. I'm completely absorbed in the guests my husband had managed to get here the morning before my surgery.

Emma tells me she had literally just landed in Teterboro not even an hour ago and came straight here. While Dad explains he had to pick Matt up himself as he was too shy to come over on his own. It's a bit awkward between us at first, but it all melts away as the minutes pass and we all enjoy the food and conversation.

I can't stop looking at my husband, the early afternoon sun making his eyes as deep as the ocean. He had given me the greatest gift he could give me to ease my soul before tomorrow: my family.

"How's the nursery coming along?" Emma asks, glancing at Alex.

"Don't bring it up," I groan, but Alex is already talking over me.

"It's coming along great. I've actually bought two sets of everything in case once they're born, their personalities don't match up with the way the room looks," he explains. "Do you guys want to see the designs Leonardo and I came up with?"

Dad, Matt, and I all say, "No," but Emma nods enthusiastically. I lay my head on the table remorsefully as Alex runs back inside to get his swatches and printouts.

"Look what you've done," I whine to Emma.

Alex, like he's giving a business presentation, goes over the room designs for forty-five minutes. At one point, I think I see Dad take a swig from a flask and pass it to Matt, but I pretend not to notice, even when Matt starts to cough. Finally, to lukewarm applause from the four of us, Alex sits back down, positively glowing from having gone over his nursery plans again.

"What's the plan when you finally get rid of all of us party people?" Dad asks.

"Alex is probably going to call poor Leonardo for the eighteenth time today to discuss the difference between eggshell and semi-gloss paint, and I might pass out in the jacuzzi tub because all I do is eat and sleep," I tease.

"So how is that any different from before you were pregnant?" Matt asks with a smirk. I toss a grape at him, hitting him squarely in the nose.

"Smart ass," I mumble while everyone laughs.

Drawn in by everyone else's joy, I laugh, too. A deep belly laugh that sets the twins to turning in my belly, kicking excitedly. I clamp my mouth shut, holding my stomach with my eyes wide, and Emma, sitting next to me, leans close.

"Are they moving?" she breathes in awe. I nod, taking my best friend's hand and laying it gently over my bump. Under her fingers a baby tumbles and Emma gasps, tears pooling suddenly in the corner of her kohl-lined eyes.

Everyone else at the table looks a little misty eyed actually, myself included. My dad clears his throat before holding up his glass of pineapple juice high into the air.

"To Jasmine and Jasper!" he calls out.

"To Jasmine and Jasper!" everyone echoes, their voices loud enough to bounce off the walls of the nearby buildings.

All of my worries leave me like a bundle of helium balloons. They'd pop and come down soon, but for right now, I'm as light as air.

CHAPTER 34

Manhattan, June 21, 2021
Petra Van Gatt

"I think you're breaking my hand," Alex says quietly as we walk into Mt. Sinai together.

"Sorry," I say with a grimace, easing up on the death grip I have on his hand. To say I'm feeling anxious is an understatement. It's almost identical to when we came here the first time; Alex with my luggage, arriving in the morning, and the misty weather, except for one thing—Our observation is over, and I'm headed straight for surgery.

"Come here." Alex stops before we walk into the door, holding me close. "It's going to be alright. It's almost over."

"That's what I'm afraid of," I sob. "I'm afraid it's going to be over and something's going to go wrong and there's no taking it back."

"Positive thoughts only," Alex reminds me for the millionth time this morning.

"I'm really trying. It just isn't working."

We take a few minutes there in front of the hospital breezeway, not talking, just basking in each other before we go through the hardest thing either of us have ever experienced. Unfortunately, the clock keeps ticking, and finally we have to go inside and check in.

Mariana and Lily both come to retrieve me and lead me to pre-op, discussing exactly how everything would go from here on out.

"We're going to get you on a saline drip before we apply the local anesthetic, but first we're going to do a quick check on the little ones. The entire time during the c-section we will monitor all three of your vitals, and they should both be out within fifteen minutes of opening you up. If it all goes well, we will be done within an hour," Mariana explains as the nurse places my intravenous line. I nod, at a loss for words as we barrel down the path of this birth.

"I'll take each twin as they are born and clear their noses before cleaning them up," Lily assures me, holding the hand of the arm without the intravenous while she speaks. "I won't give them a proper bath before you hold them, though. We've talked about the importance of skin-to-skin contact. That includes you too, Alex."

"Got it," Alex says curtly, almost as silent as me.

"You're both nervous, and understandably so," Lily says, her voice low and soothing. "Mariana and I are here to guide you every step of the way, so if you have questions, don't be afraid to ask."

Mariana picks up where Lily left off. "Afterwards, it's likely they will have a hopefully brief stay in the NICU since they are premature. But if all goes well, you can be with them once we confirm they are stable."

The nurses in the room and Mariana hook up the monitors for the babies' heartbeats and they spring to life over the speakers, fluttering and quick. The sound gives me a bit of comfort and I'm able to take a full breath.

"Petra, the plan is for you to just have the local anesthetic. We've opted for the spinal block instead of the epidural, so you will be more aware, and it will fade quicker. It provides the same level of pain relief, so no worries there, but since this is a high-risk birth, we want you conscious to make any decisions along the way," Mariana continues.

"Decisions like what?" I ask immediately.

Mariana doesn't answer right away, so I turn to Lily.

A look of apprehension passes over her lovely face before it clears. "Birth is beautiful, but also unpredictable, Petra. We will cross any bridges after we face them."

"Alright, my girl," Mariana says. "We're almost there. Let's sit you up so we can give you the spinal block."

I do as I'm told, sitting up with some difficulty with the IV in, assuming the position. My back is arched and I'm leaning forward over the side of the bed while they find the right place. Alex crouches in front of me as they part my gown in the back, and I feel the cold kiss of the alcohol prep pad on my skin. He cups my face in his hands, touching his forehead with mine. "Breath with me," he murmurs softly.

I try my best to only pay attention to Alex as Mariana counts down from three behind me, but I tense and scrunch my eyes, crying out as the needle slips neatly into my back, stopping right before the bones of my spine. Pain wracks me, but I stay as still as I can while Alex talks to me the whole time, doing all he can to distract me.

It's finally over, and almost immediately, I can feel my upper legs tingling. Alex and Lily help me back into the hospital bed as my body from my ribcage to my knees quickly loses all feeling. It's all happening so fast!

Alex continues to comfort me, stroking my hair. Lily and Mariana chat with me about lighter topics while a nurse inserts the catheter into my bladder. We talk about the clothes the babies will go home in after the NICU, whether I plan on breastfeeding, and what I'm most excited about. I answer woodenly, my mind miles away.

Twenty minutes pass, and Mariana checks her watch, all the monitors, and finally nods. "It's time."

Her words are like a bucket of ice water thrown over me, and I start to shiver as my obstetrician and midwife kick the brakes off my bed and wheel me down the hall. Alex sticks with me, keeping pace with the rolling bed as we move down the empty hallway, the only sound the hiss of the bed wheels on the linoleum floors.

Two steel doors herald the entrance to the surgery, and two nurses in complete surgery dress take my bed from Mariana and Lily while they and Alex go get scrubbed in.

The operating room is so cold. So sterile. So bright. So full of people. I can see Mariana, Lily, and three other doctors I don't recognize, all now masked in green surgery scrubs. This is really happening.

"Alex," I cry desperately. "Please don't leave."

"I'm right here," he swears, his voice steady and firm. I hold on to the sound of him speaking on our future, our babies, and the happiness we have to come while the nurses wash my numb abdomen and drape the sterile sheet over it. They then haul the dividing sheet in front of my chest so I can't see below. Mariana's team introduce themselves, but they are just masked talking heads to me, and I hold Alex's gaze the whole time, even when Mariana goes to stand with her team lower down my body and Lily at the other side of my head.

"We're about to get started," Lily tells me in her gentle voice. I spare her a glance, and her brown eyes are soft as she stands with me. "Both babies' hearts are still steady. Are you ready?"

I gulp, mouth dry from the drugs coming down my IV. "No… Yes."

Lily huffs a tiny laugh before nodding at Mariana, who gives the team the thumbs up, and they get started.

I can't feel the incision, thank God, but I see Alex glance behind the dividing curtain briefly and all the blood drains from his face before he locks eyes with me again.

"The incision is made," Lily intones.

"Oh fuck," Alex whispers, voice shaking.

"Alex, if you're going to faint you need to leave," Lily tells him. And I'm not sure if she is joking or not.

"Fine… I'm fine," Alex says, shaking his head to try and clear it. If my organs weren't on display, I might even find his reaction funny.

"Heart rates are still strong. Mom and babies are good," a nurse calls.

"You're going to feel some pressure now," Lily tells me, her face serene. "They're piercing the amniotic sac and getting ready to remove the first baby."

"Oh my God," I whimper, clenching my eyes shut. If I could feel my stomach, I'd probably be on the verge of puking. It's the most terrifying moment of my whole life, but as the minutes both race and drag past, a thread of exhilaration starts to pulse through me. It's all going right so far. We might just do this!

Lily makes a small, happy sound at the same minute I feel a bizarre pressure inside of my numb belly. Alex takes a huge breath and releases it slowly, right as Lily claps her gloved hands together. "I can see the first baby. He's out. Petra, he's out!"

Before she can even finish talking, a cry pierces the air, more holy to me than an angel's trumpet. There are some quick movements of the doctors below me and to my amazement, someone hands a shrieking, blanket wrapped package to Lily. She whisks him away for a second and I nearly scream at her, but I hear the telltale suck of the nose bulb and she's back. Jasper is howling louder, indignant over being taken from his warm home and having something shoved up his nose.

I raise my shaking arms and the world stops turning as she places my son in my arms. I see his pinched, scarlet face as he continues to scream, his tiny fists clenched in anger. He's covered in the white film Lily had called "vernix caseosa," but I'm oblivious, holding him snugly against me so our skin connects, and almost as if he somehow knows it's me, his cries taper off and he opens eyes the color of the sea to look at me.

I don't even have thirty-seconds to marvel at him before I hear Mariana exclaim, and I feel that familiar pressure again. I hold Jasper like he's my own connection to this Earth as I wait the longest seconds of my life.

Jasmine. Jasmine. Jasmine. Jasmine. I repeat her name like a mantra, like a prayer, in my mind. It isn't until I hear Alex, his eyes shooting from Jasper to behind the curtain and back constantly, saying her name with me, that I realize I'm praying for her out loud.

"She's out!" someone yells, sounding like a triumphant fighter after a hard-won victory.

Lily clenches her hands in front of her, and I watch her brown eyes as if they are a mirror, waiting for her reaction. Suddenly, she sucks in a loud, shaky breath. It's only when she lets out a single, joyous laugh do I feel hope blossom in me anew.

Jasmine's cry is a crystal shattering the fear in my heart, high and pure and clear.

* * *

Alexander Van Dieren

My chest shakes, and I try not to sob like an idiot, but they are finally here, and while Petra is holding Jasper in her arms, I hear the cries of my daughter as Lily finishes to clear up her nose and mouth and wraps a towel around her. Jeez, she is so tiny. The smallest person I have ever met in my whole entire life. And the strongest willed, greatest fighter I've ever known. My hands are shaky, but I take a few deep breaths to calm myself before Lily passes her to me.

Her tiny head is covered with a dried white substance, and her eyes are closed, but her mouth wide open to test her vocal cords. And I can testify that they are working pretty well. "Here is our little warrior who defied all odds," I say, the tears resting on my eyelids as I walk with her and stand in front of her mom.

"She's so beautiful," Petra says airily, clearly exhausted. Jasper blinks owlishly at his sister, and Jasmine, sensing him near, quiets as well, opening her eyes to stare at him. He dwarfs her, a giant compared to the tiny girl in my arms.

Mariana appears at our sides. "Congratulations, you two. Petra, you're all put back together so I'm going to release you back to your suite."

Petra laughs a bit, but her attention is focused on the babies. She reaches out and strokes Jasmine's cheek, a look of tired bliss on her face.

"I hate to interrupt but I'm going to put matching ID bands on those two, so we don't lose anyone," Lily interjects. I notice there's our room number—541—written on both bands as she places them on each of our babies' wrists. "Now we'll take these two little fighters to get checked by the pediatricians," Lily adds. Petra reluctantly gives Jasper up, and with a final devoted look, I hand Jasmine over as well.

Mariana takes Petra, who looks to be falling asleep already, back to her suite to get settled in and I follow Lily as she takes the babies to the NICU. I take a video for Petra as the pediatricians reverently do the routine checks and take their weights and measurements. Then I go back to the suite to find my wife.

Petra is surprisingly awake, sipping water from a large plastic cup with a straw while Mariana checks her over one last time.

"How are they?" Petra inquires. I show her the video and she smiles indulgently as the babies complain the only way they know how, by crying.

"They're shockingly loud," Mariana says with a laugh. "Nice, healthy lungs."

Then she explains that both of the twins would need some time in the NICU, at least one month for Jasmine, and just a week or two for Jasper.

One of the pediatricians comes in, greets us, and flips a page on his chart. "You two are the proud parents of one four pound and fifteen ounce baby boy and beautiful, tiny girl weighing two pounds and nine ounces," he says with a grin, coming over to shake my hand before he continues. "We are going to start them both off on the feeding tube, but barring any complications, Jasper should come off of his pretty quickly. We'll play it by ear for Jasmine. Her heartbeat is not quite where we would like it, so we are gonna put her on nasal oxygen through a tube. Her slower heartbeat is called bradycardia, and it isn't unheard of in preemies this small. All in all, folks, they look well. We've still got a long way to go before Jasmine goes home, but we know the road from here on out."

Lily goes over the basics of pumping milk for the babies while they are still on the feeding tubes with Petra, and the pediatrician shows me the ins-and-outs of the small heart monitor that would be sent home with Jasmine after her stay. It's all a little blurry to me, and I think Petra too, because we are desperate to see our babies again. Once the pediatrician leaves, Lily smiles at us knowingly.

"Before you ask, yes. Let's go see them."

She pushes Petra in a wheelchair, and I walk beside them, holding Petra's hand in mine. The NICU is close by, and we have to wash our hands and get sanitized before they let us in, but finally we make it into the darkened suite with two clear bassinets, both with tubes running from them.

All cleaned up and resting, we can really get a good look at the twins, even with the tubes. To me, they are flawless little humans that have crawled into my heart already, stealing it away.

While Petra has to go back to bed to rest, I decide to stay a bit longer here with them. I notice the NICU floor has a few chairs spread around, so I move one close to the bassinets after Lily takes Petra back to her room, and I sit—keeping an eye over the precious beings that we have waited so long for.

* * *

I'm jolted awake in my chair when the door opens. Sitting up, I drag my hand over my eyes to see emerging figures entering the room and walking in my direction. At first I think it's two nurses, but the tattoos, piercing, short black hair, and winged eyeliner around the eyes of one of them don't match.

"Hey," I say quietly, standing from my seat when I finally realize it's Emma and Matt coming in. I had texted the group—which included Roy—after the babies were born and had invited them to visit.

"We aren't interrupting, are we?" Emma asks, before giving me a hug.

"Not at all!" I insist. "Come see them."

Emma is vibrating with excitement, wringing her hands as she gazes at Jasmine and Jasper in their beds. "They're so tiny!" she whispers in awe.

"No joke," Matt says, amazement in his voice. "And they're okay?"

I nod, a knowing smile on my face. "They're even better now that their godparents have come to visit."

"That's great," Matt responds absentmindedly, until it clicks. "Wait… what?"

Emma lets out a tiny squeal, not taking her eyes from the sleeping newborns. "You mean it? I never expected this!"

"You're family," I say quietly. "And you two will be the best godparents they could ever wish for."

"Yes. Of course. Yes," Emma gushes, tearing her eyes from the twins to embrace me gently.

Matt is still in a daze when I come to shake his hand firmly, pulling him in for what looks like a hug but actually telling him under my breath, "You can say no, if it's too much. But I think you'll be a good fit."

He shakes his head. "No, it's just… Well. I'm honored. Of course I accept," he babbles, and I see him shutting his eyes tight trying to contain the tears from falling. Something tells me the boy is gonna take his duty very seriously and I shake his hand harder. After all, he decided to give Sarah a shot and the two have been dating ever since the gala dinner. A move I had recommended him to make, and Matt followed it throughly and dutifully.

"Good to have you then, man. Welcome to the family."

I release him and we both gaze around the room at the sleeping infants. I look at Matt from the corner of my eyes, and I can tell how much the invitation has impacted him. A quick smile settles on my lips as my heart, that I had often assumed was damaged beyond repair, is incredibly full.

CHAPTER 35

Manhattan, September 21, 2021
Petra Van Gatt

"Are you nervous?" I ask as I watch my husband finishing to put the new cufflinks I offered him on his shirt.

Today's not only the three-month anniversary of Jasmine and Jasper's birth but also their baptism at St. Patrick's Cathedral, located in midtown, not too far from here. Which means it'll be the first time since our wedding that Hendrik and Margaret will be reunited.

"Me?" he asks, looking at my reflection in the mirror. "Of course not." A quick chuckle rolls off my lips at his palpable sarcasm. "It's the first time our babies are gonna step outside the house and see so many people, so I'm just a bit apprehensive."

"Lily will come with us don't worry." When our little Jasmine finally came home after a month and a half in the newborn intensive care unit, Lily—the midwife Mariana had recommended—became full-time help and moved in with us.

Jasmine still needs to be fed through a tube though as she's slowly learning how to suck in order to eat without one. And due to her bradycardia, we are still constantly monitoring her heartbeat with the portable machine. Jasper, on the other hand, is the chillest baby I could have ever wanted. Heck, he barely cries! I even called the pediatrician once wondering if it was normal for a baby to cry so little. I thought a baby would cry every two to three hours or so, but little Jasper just make grimaces and pouting lips when he is hungry. He loves being immersed in water, that's something Alex and I have noticed. Each time we give him a bath, he's over the moon and giggles as if he recognizes his first home.

I remain standing in the doorway, observing the most handsome man as he finishes adjusting his tie in front of the mirror of our dressing room. "You look perfect."

His lips twist into a smile at my words and he takes his time to check me out. "You too. This white fit-and-flare dress reminds me of some good old memories."

Before I can dwell on those good old memories, a few knocks on the door of the bedroom startle me, and I can tell by the rhythm they are being delivered that they are from Maria, so I go and open the door.

"Emma is here, ma'am," she announces upon seeing me.

I frown at her words, glancing at my watch. "Okay…" That's weird. All guests were requested to go directly to the cathedral. I didn't invite her to come here before. "Where is she?"

"In the living room, ma'am."

I leave the bedroom and Maria escorts me to the living room.

"Hey!" Emma greets, elegantly dressed in a black dress and a pair of stilettos. "Wow, you look stunning."

"Oh, thanks, you too." We hug each other very tightly as always and I can't help but say, "I thought we'd meet at the Cathedral?"

"Yeah, I know, I know," she says, brushing that off. "But I came earlier to take a few pictures of the kids." And to make her point, she shows me the DSLR camera she brought with her.

"Oh, that's a great idea, actually." Taking a few pictures pre-reception when they are freshly dressed is something I had totally forgotten about. "Let's go to the nursery then."

Emma takes her camera bag and we leave the living room. "Are they ready?"

"Yep," I say as we finish to cross the hallway. Then I twist the handle of the nursery door and we quietly step into the room.

"Oh my God!" Emma says in a whisper, silently clapping her hands out of excitement, as her gaze catches Jasmine wearing a white dress with a silk ribbon sash and a white headband to complete her look. "What a princess!"

Jasmine is perched on Lily's lap, who is sitting on a rocking chair. That lady must have some soothing powers, because each time she starts singing, Jasmine either stops crying or falls asleep. I must say she also has the voice of an angel. Emma delicately starts stroking Jasmine's pinkish cheek and the little girl stretches herself in response, a big smile spreading across her face. "Such a cutie. I feel she's gonna be even more spoiled than me."

"With a dad like Alex, that's for sure," I reply, chuckling. "He already opened a trust fund for them."

"Don't worry, girl, I'm gonna put them in line," she replies, before heading to Jasper's crib. "Hello, Mr. Jasper," she greets, putting on a childish tone. Jasper is lying on his bed and replies burbling happily. His eyes are already wide open, and he throws his arms in the air inviting Emma to take him. Without even thinking twice, she reaches for the back of his head with one hand and holds his back with the other to take him out. She snuggles him close to her chest and gives him a quick smooch on his head. "Damn, he's already so tall and big. And his eyes are so blue."

"Yeah," I say as Jasper grips one of my fingers in his little hand. "He's growing like crazy and he's such a quiet baby. All he wants to do is play in the water. The only time he cries is when I take him out of his bathtub."

"And he's so expressive already, look at his smile. Hellooo, hellooo…" Jasper giggles with glee at the weird sounds coming from Emma. "I love their outfits, they look so great."

Jasper is wearing a three piece suit—jacket, pants, and onesie. His jacket and pants are made of ivory quilted cotton, a super soft and plush material, edges trimmed with silk in a lovely shade of champagne. I love how the jacket is thoughtfully designed to bring an elegant look to this cotton outfit. I stroke his little head and give him a kiss, catching a mix of his little baby scent and mine.

Then looking at Emma, I lower my voice and say, "I'm so happy you're their godmother. Thank you so much for accepting."

"Of course," she answers, her lips twisting into a smile. "By the way," she starts. "Did you manage to fix that issue we spoke about?"

"No, unfortunately, I stopped after five weeks." I try to conceal my sadness, but Emma sees right through it.

"You know, it's not the end of the world. Like, if your body is not producing, maybe it means they don't need it."

My lips curve up at her answer; she always knows how to cheer me up no matter what. "Well, all the doctors told me not to worry about it, so we switched to formula, and so far we have been good." After the twins were born, I started pumping the next day. And at first I was producing very well. Enough for both babies as well as some for storage. But when Jasper was released and came home, production slowed big time. I was afraid to even try and latch him because I didn't want to "waste" Jasmine's supply if there wasn't enough. So between feedings with Jasper, pumping (and cleaning parts), and spending time at the hospital with Jasmine, the first month after their birth was very stressful and exhausting. Fortunately, Alex has taken a paternity leave for an undetermined period, so at least we have been going through all of this together. Once Jasmine was released, I had storage for a few days and managed to pump for a few more but after about a week I truly just gave up because there just wasn't enough. According to Mariana, it was already a miracle in itself that I had managed to produce milk for so many weeks. After all the challenges we went through with the pregnancy, I must say I didn't have high hopes I would be able to breastfeed, but at least I managed to feed them for a little while, even if only via pumping for a few weeks.

We all go to the living room and start doing a mini-shoot of Jasper and Jasmine in their matching white outfits. We set them against a few pillows on the couch and Emma starts pointing her lens and capturing their best smiles and pose.

Click, click, click...

She then shows me the first images on the screen of her camera and I can't help but say, "Those pictures are so beautiful! Damn, you are really good at that."

"Yeah, I have been practicing around, especially portrait," she says, before continuing the shooting.

A few moments later, Alex walks in and Emma decides to take some family pictures of us four. It was definitely not part of our plan to turn the future godmother of our kids into our photographer, but she seems to be truly enjoying it.

"Emma, we should at least pay you for those," Alex tells her as she shows us the pictures she took of us. "Those are really great shots."

"Nah, I'm gonna print them and then send you an album with all the pictures taken during the baptism. It's actually my gift."

"Oh," I utter, unaware that this was for an album. "That's wonderful! Thank you!"

Once the shoot is over, two cars take us to the cathedral. I can already see Matt, standing at the entrance from my window, all dressed up in a suit and a tie, holding hands with Sarah. I'm actually glad they are together, He truly needed someone in his life to bring him some emotional stability. I find that standing not too far from them are my in-laws who just came all the way from the Netherlands. I see Margaret, Julia, Maud, Yara, and their respective husbands—but not Hendrik.

After dropping us off at the curb, we go and head to the entrance where everyone is gathered. Alex is holding Jasper in his arms while I'm holding Jasmine. Lily carries their diaper pack and Emma her camera. As we greet our guests, everyone starts looking at the babies like they are some sort of new toys to play with. Jasmine starts feeling overwhelmed by so many faces surrounding her and giving her so much unwanted attention that she breaks in tears. Fortunately, Alex asks everyone to give them some space and time to adjust to this new environment and noise. I start moving away with Jasmine in my arms and trying to soothe her the best I can. Yet, she doesn't stop screaming and whining, like she is in pain. And despite trying all the techniques Lily taught me, I have never managed to make her stop crying. For some reason, Alex and Lily have no problem in calming her down, but me? I don't know why, but when she starts crying in my arms, she simply doesn't stop. It's as if her goal is precisely to drive me crazy.

"May I?"

I look up at the voice and find Hendrik standing in front of me, his arms wide open.

"Oh, sure," I say, carefully handing him Jasmine. "She isn't used to having so many people around her. I think she's just very stressed."

My jaw nearly drops; as soon as Hendrik starts snuggling her and singing a lullaby with his deep baritone voice, she immediately calms herself like she wants to impress him.

At this point, I'm starting to believe she's really doing it on purpose to drive her mom to the edge.

"Well, here we go," I say in a whisper. "You are now in charge of carrying Jasmine into the cathedral."

Despite this little girl being a piece of work, she still manages to make me smile when I see her tucked in against Hendrik and peacefully asleep.

"Are you ready?" Emma asks.

"Yes, let's go." I lead everyone into the cathedral and I'm welcomed by a man in his thirties who seems to be one of the deacons. We shake hands and I look briefly around, trying to find Alex, but all I can see is Hendrik coming in with Jasmine on my left side, and Margaret with Jasper on my right. What the heck? I can't believe Alex gave Jasper to his mom!

"Here's our little Jasper," Margaret says, introducing him to the deacon. Her voice is bubblier and sweeter than usual, and it's a weird thing to witness. I wonder if she took Jasper with her because she wanted to, or because she saw Hendrik with Jasmine. A question I might never have an answer to.

"Gosh, the difference, he's already so big," Hendrik points out.

"I imagine these are the twins, Jasper and Jasmine Gatt-Dieren, correct?" the deacon asks me.

"Uh, I think there's a mistake in the surname," Margaret says in confusion.

"There is not," I tell her. "That's the correct surname." And I can already anticipate her rebuke.

"What?" Margaret snaps in clear disapprobation.

"Really?" Hendrik asks, his tone simply surprised, but not loud.

"Yes," I reply, focused on Hendrik. "Since they are the heirs of the Gatt-Dieren Capital, and given the fact it's a well-known brand in Wall Street, we have decided to make it their surname."

"That's ridiculous!" Margaret ripostes, and before she can add her two cents, Emma steps in.

"I think it's a brilliant idea." She puts a hand on my back, showing me some support. "Jasmine and Jasper Gatt-Dieren is genius! Well done." I give her a smile in gratitude for her kindness.

My gaze drifts to Hendrik who has been quiet the whole time, but I realize he's just too busy snuggling Jasmine in his arms and playing with her to participate in the conversation. He notices I was looking at him and then he simply says, "Oh, I'm good, whatever makes you guys happy." Then he looks at Emma and her camera, and asks, "Can you take a picture of my granddaughter and I, please?"

"Argh," Margaret rolls her eyes and shakes her head in disapproval, before turning around like she's either trying to avoid me or looking for someone.

I knew she'd hate the idea, which is why I didn't include their surname on the invitation cards.

"And you agreed to it?" she asks as she sees Alex walking in with my dad.

Alex is caught completely off guard by her obnoxious tone. "Agreed to what?"

"Never mind," she grits between her teeth, most likely realizing how it would be so tone-deaf to keep her outraged attitude in front of my dad and everyone else.

The deacon shows us the way and we follow him across the beautiful neo-Gothic cathedral. While everyone is still taking in their surroundings, I sit in the first row of pews facing the chancel, and smile internally at my little victory against Margaret.

A few moments later though, she comes and sits right beside me, and despite not paying any attention to her, I notice she is no longer holding Jasper. Quietly enough, Margaret leans slightly toward my ear, and in a very discreet manner, she says, "I know what you are trying to do." Her tone is not aggressive or high, but rather steady and firm. "You declined my help both during and after your pregnancy; you declined my help for the baptism; you declined using the christening gowns that have been passed on for generations within our family; and now this new family name…" I can hear her inhaling deeply from her nostrils and then exhaling as she tries to keep her irritation under control. "This is your way to punish me for what happened to your mother, isn't it?"

And this is just the beginning. The question twists my lips into a smile. After all, I could see it coming from miles away. Looking her in the eye, I revel in her displeasure. "Every choice we make has consequences, remember?" I ask rhetorically, quoting the exact words she said to me at my mom's funeral. "Every. Single. One." And before she can snap something at me, I add, "You'll never have any other say in my family, Margaret. So it's better you start getting used to it early on."

She sniggers like I'm telling her some sort of joke. "Or else what?"

I lean closer to her ear, and then whisper, "Or else, I'll make sure to send Elliott a picture of Yara's naked painting that I was commissioned to make for her mistress." Margaret freezes at my words and her body stiffens immediately. She bats her eyelashes a few times, her lips pressed in a straight line. It seems like I rendered her totally speechless. "What? You didn't know your precious daughter was having an affair with my best friend?"

Then my attention returns to the deacon who is now asking everyone to stand up, and the ceremony finally starts. A smile plays across my face for both the day itself and for yet another win against Margaret.

THE END

WANT TO READ MORE ABOUT THEIR HAPPILY EVER AFTER?

A collection of 4 novellas following Alex & Petra as they face parenthood and everything that it entails will be out very soon! Go to blossominwinter.com to get your bundle.

ACKNOWLEDGMENTS

A big thank you to all of you for reading my debut series. I'm so grateful for the amazing support, positivity, and excitement you've shown throughout this entire journey. Thank you so much!

A special thank you to Jami Marie from Ohio to have shared her story with me about her twin pregnancy and the struggles she faced along the way. You were a big inspiration for Petra's pregnancy and I truly admire you for holding your ground no matter the adversities you faced.

A big thank you to all the editors who've worked on this series and made it what it is today, from Ann Leslie to Tiffany, Jessica, Haley, Susan, and Caroline. I'm blessed to have met you all.

To all the influencers and bloggers who have spent their free time reading, reviewing, and sharing the story online and offline. I love you guys!

Last but not least, to my life partner, best friend, and *compagnon de route*, Diogo, thank you for always standing by my side and trusting my craziness. Ten years with you have only felt like ten minutes.